A piercing v   everything.
Jill and Georgio   ound. She fully
expected to see th   olice. Instead a tall
figure had appeared with muscles rippling
through a thin black silk shirt, feet apart,
arms folded, blue eyes like flint, his
expression was one to wilt the hardest foe.
And if he'd spun round transforming his
clothes to tight trousers, blue cloak and
shirt with a large red 'S' on it, she doubted
she could have been more surprised!

With their full attention Ben Fletcher
demanded, "What is going on here?"

In relief Jill gasped, "I never thought I'd
be so pleased to see you."

Ben, his eyes appraising the situation,
nodded, and giving her a brief smile said,
"In that case I'm glad I came!"

RUTH JOHNSON

JILL

The Heart's Desire Series

BOOK 2

EMANUEL PUBLISHING

ISBN: 978-0-9554898-1-5

A catalogue for this book is available in the British Library

Biblical quotes are taken from 'The Living Bible'
Published by Coverdale House Publishers Ltd.

Printed and bound in Great Britain by:
Cox & Wyman Ltd, Reading, Berks

Published by Emanuel Publishing Ltd
36 Kenmore Crescent
Bristol BS7 0TL

www.HeartsDesireSeries.com

Trust in the Lord and do good;
Dwell in the land and enjoy safe pasture;
Delight yourself in the Lord and he will give you
the desires of your heart.
Commit your way to the Lord and
Trust in him and he will do it..
Psalm 37: 3-5

ACKNOWLEDGEMENTS

Thank you my dear friends for your
advice, input and proof reading:

Louise Adams
Janet Beaty
Naomi Johnson
Graham Weakley

&

All the readers of 'Jane'
who encouraged me to write and
publish this second novel.

Please note:
Biblical quotes are taken from 'The Living Bible'
This Bible wasn't published until 1971, but is used
because it's text is easy to read, and simple to understand.

DEDICATION

To my beloved husband, Brian
who has encouraged and inspired me
with his continual support and patience.

Without his technical knowledge
of computer programmes and website formation
none of this would have been possible.

Thank you so much.
I love you.

Ruth
xx

LONDON, 1968

CHAPTER 1

Chris County, head of the Press Department issued Jill an approving smile as he remarked, "You've really changed. That move from Receptionist to Personnel and Social Liaison Officer has given you confidence - you seem more fulfilled. What's it been – two months?" He lifted his hand, waved her draft article and headed towards his desk by the French windows. "That's not long, but you have proved you have the capability and talents needed for the job."

Flattered, Jill smiled, but to his back she retorted, "Typical press guy - you exaggerate." Until today Chris, early thirties, tall, lean, a ready smile and quick wit, had never shown any interest in her. Rumour had it that two weeks ago Chris and his long-term girlfriend Patsy had split up, if he was ready for a new romance she was happy to step into her place.

Chris nodded toward the window where David Reinhardt's car was turning on to the semi-circular drive in front of the mansion that housed the offices of ITP (International Trade Promotions). "I still find it hard to believe you're his sister. I suppose there are similarities, the jet black hair and eyes, but your chiselled features are less harsh, and he has muscle where you are, let's say, more rounded." He gave her a wink and settled in his chair. Jill drew herself up, and in, as Chris continued, "Business wise I suspect his formidable features are quite an asset, just as I suspect he thinks you are these days."

"I hope so, but if I take up your idea of profiling each Company Director, and for David, dig out and print personal photographs, any appreciation he may have will be wiped from his memory!" Chris chuckled. Was his laughter, along with the previous flattery, an indication of his interest in her?

"If you'll do it, I'll take full responsibility as Editor. Now make me a coffee while I read your latest magazine offering."

Jill stared down at Chris' bent head. Even as a Receptionist her job hadn't included doubling as a tea lady! Chris glanced up, and then grinned at her expression. "Sorry! Please! Be a dear, I'm desperate for a drink." She raised her eyebrows, but decided to comply because being a 'dear' was a start! If she followed Jane, her sister-in-law's thinking, friendship was the basis for love. She moved through the desks to the kettle and on to the Ladies toilet to fill it.

At twenty-one she'd come out of College with a variety of skills, but with no mind to carve a career because she'd found Stephen, who she'd believed to be her 'Mr Right'. Her only desire was to care for him, their home and future family. A frown darkened her features remembering her shattered dreams. Afterwards she'd come to London, taken the first clerical job offered and buried her loneliness and hurt under bravado. Three years ago she'd changed that dull, boring job to be a Receptionist at ITP. Unbeknown to David who already worked there, she'd applied shortening her surname from Reinhardt to Hart, had been interviewed, offered the job and started work before he found out. How surprised he'd been that first morning!

Judy, the current receptionist who was leaving to have a baby had pointed to the window, "In that big white car is Mr Reinhardt. He'll park at the side of the house and come through here. He's sometimes brusque, but can be charming. When he looks at you and smiles - well it's enough to make you go quite weak at the knees."

At that she'd asked Judy as seriously as she could muster, "Is that just you, or would you say other women react like that?"

"Oh - it's a general thing. Of course I'm married... But if ITP were to vote on the Company heartthrob it would be Mr Reinhardt. Have you read 'Pride and Prejudice'?" Donna in the Press Department compares him to Mr Darcy, handsome, aloof and mysterious. Here he comes, you'll see for yourself." Judy had pasted on a sweet smile, and probably unconsciously, batted her eyelids in preparation. Earlier having been introduced to the contents of the tall cupboard behind the Reception Desk Jill took that moment to investigate them further! The speed in which Judy said, 'Good morning Mr Reinhardt' it was apparent she expected him to walk briskly by, and that he hadn't because she offered, "Can I help you Sir?"

Out of the corner of her eye she saw Judy look in her direction before a familiar voice boomed, "Yes. Good morning Judy. I see you have someone new with you, perhaps you could introduce us?"

"Oh yes, yes, of course, Mr Reinhardt. This is Jill."

With a pleasant smile, that barely contained her mirth, she turned to face David.

The cold stare with which she was met went undetected by Judy, who, in a slightly breathless voice, explained, "Jill started today so she could learn the job before I leave at the end of the week."

Determined not to be put off, Jill stepped into her role and put out her hand to shake his. "Good morning Mr Reinhardt, pleased to meet you. As Judy said my name is Jill, Jill Hart. I am just getting acquainted to my new role, but if, in any way, I can help you I would be pleased to do so."

From the quizzical expression of raised eyebrows, there was a slight pause before he grasped her outstretched hand. From their childish rivalry there was no doubt she was one up on him, however, there was no denying he recovered well. "Well yes, thank you, Jill Hart, I'll bear that in mind." He had then bestowed a stunning smile on Judy and said, "And Judy, we shall be sorry to lose you. All the best with the baby."

Judy astonished, and seemingly weak-kneed by her bobbed curtsy, stuttered her thanks at his receding figure.

The moment he'd disappeared Judy turned to her. "It's obvious Jill you haven't done Reception work before. You see although we are here to welcome people, we don't usually shake the hands of visitors, or those it would be considered to be above our position. Still no harm done, he didn't seem put out, in fact quite the opposite, perhaps he fancied you. He's not married. And you see what I mean about that gorgeous smile."

Hours later when David had turned up at her bed sit he hadn't been wearing the gorgeous smile, and certainly was put out by her working on the Reception Desk. But as she informed him then, no-one but he and the finance people need know, and what better than a spy in the camp. This had proved to be the case on several occasions including the part she'd played in getting him a wife. But she still hadn't found a husband.

Her return to the Press Office with the kettle was met with "here comes the new tea girl." Marcus received her tight smile with a grin. Viciously she shoved the plug into the bottom of the kettle. Men were like kettles, they plugged in, came to the boil, but once they'd finished steaming they had no further interest until they wanted to boil again! Her mind went to the variety of men she'd known. From wealthy business men who frequented clubs, to poor salesmen who went to dance halls and pubs. It wasn't that she was ever short of a man, some exciting, others simply boring, and it wasn't always obvious which would be which. But it had become it obvious that men were eager to practice baby making skills, but the making of a baby was not something they desired to achieve.

However at ITP she'd achieved far beyond her hopes or dreams. Three months ago Jane, her friend and David's wife had bluntly told her that at 26 it was time to stop wasting her life. She should use her education and talents to find a suitable job, stop indulging in casual sexual relationships and leave God to find her a mate! Irritated at Jane's attitude and assumptions she'd become angry and the conversation heated, and one from which she was still smarting.

A few weeks later ITP had a company reshuffle. From that emerged a new post encompassing staff recruitment, welfare and organising the social club which included writing and editing the company magazine with Chris. In knowing her qualifications David suggested she apply and was the first to congratulate her on being appointed. She may not have a 'Mr Right' to go home to, but she did feel in the right job, and as she placed the mug of coffee on Chris' desk and received a rewarding smile she wondered if she was on the right track for the right man.

"Thanks Jill. This article's great. Next month how about a comparison of the midsummer ball against your idea this year of a dinner and boat trip? Chris handed back her foolscap sheets. "How are the plans going for that?"

Her hand played nervously with a piece of hair that had escaped from her French pleat. "I must have been mad to think of such a complicated evening with so many opportunities for things to go wrong. Still, if it means people like Sam Bennett come when they felt the Midsummer Ball was for 'toffs', it's worth it. I might need extra help on the night…so if you're free…"

"Oh you'll be fine. You are right about ITP. When they sponsor an event it should be something for all staff to enjoy. Now, that article profiling the Company Directors - if you did one a month from September that would take us up to Christmas."

Was Chris' change of subject deliberate? She pushed that thought down and took up his conversation. "I suppose with David being the youngest, and my dear brother, it would seem sensible to start there - I certainly know more about him than the other Directors!"

Chris put down his coffee. "He's the one who has said in the past he wants to blur what he calls, those hierarchical staff lines, so an article to expose the real David Reinhardt would give people an opportunity to understand the man behind the business mask. The advent of his and Jane's romance, the wedding here and inviting all the staff, did make that work for a while, but I doubt new staff would think of him as approachable. Even I, who call him David, find it difficult"

"Oh surely not! You're of similar ages and background." And she thought, yet another qualification as a candidate for 'Mr Right'.

"Age and background have nothing to do with it. That brother of yours has an authoritative air. I know part of it is the sheer hard work of knowing his subject, but his confidence, clarity of thought, ability to pinpoint the spot, ask questions, win an argument makes me feel inadequate and half-baked. He's pleasant enough, but he's not a man I'd want to tangle with, or could imagine having as a friend. I can see the potential in working as one with a common aim and purpose, it's a good managerial concept and one I'd like to see promoted, but he needs to appear more human and less awesome."

Would David act as a deterrent to Chris considering a relationship with her? In a lowered voice she countered, "When you know him as I do you'd realise he's not awesome? In the context of family you'd see him in quite a different light!"

Chris looked at his watch, downed the remainder of his coffee, and leapt up. "Gosh – is that the time, must dash."

In following him from the office she considered perhaps it was too soon after Patsy for him to feel anything for her. It was in this entrance hall she'd witnessed Jane's confrontational encounter with David. How fascinating it had been to watch her big brother taken on by what her father later referred to as 'a mere slip of a girl'.

The lift gate clanged from several floors up. Across the entrance hall a middle-aged man was demanding of Penny, the Receptionist "I need to see Mr Reinhardt now!" Eighteen months earlier a burly policeman had demanded much the same of her. Then, anxious, her mind vacillating between the different aspects of that unfolding drama, she'd been even more troubled when Dr Paul Stemmings arrived announcing he'd been summoned by the police to see David, and apologised for his delay.

Worried, and with a babble of nervous talk, she'd accompanied the doctor, of similar age to David, in the lift to the second floor. Her mind recalled as she travelled upward those golden flecked, warm brown eyes looking into hers with compassionate amusement before briefly resting on her mouth. To stop her flow he'd reached out, put his forefinger across her lips and in a soft, gentle voice said, "Shush now, it will be alright." Had the tension of the moment been the cause of a connection that locked them in some kind of thrall so when the lift stopped neither of them moved to open the gate? And ridiculously, when he had leant forward, she'd anticipated the moulding of his lips on hers and the soft brush of his beard against her cheek. Instead he'd opened the lift gate and said softly, "One thing at a time."

Today, as she opened the lift gate on the third floor where her office was situated she remembered how nonplussed she'd felt at that uncanny sense of being drawn to him as if by some unseen force.

On that day David's door had whipped open the moment she'd knocked, his voice booming with impatience "Ah, the doctor, at last, you're here. Come in, come in." And barring her entry he'd shut the door, but not before she'd glimpsed Jane, her head swathed in a blood soaked towel, lying on the settee. It was David's involvement in that incident which revealed to her his more than a passing interest in Jane.

Jill frowned. Paul Stemmings' interest in her hadn't been more than passing! After courteously murmuring his thanks he'd added, "I'll see you on my way out" but nothing had come of that. Would he have stopped to chat, maybe ask her out, if David hadn't accompanied him off the premises? Later when telling Jane, she'd put the odd 'connection' down to something supernatural, but then Jane had a thing about God and the supernatural!

Jill entered her office. Time to stop the maudlin thoughts and do some work before lunch!

An hour later as she pushed open the swing door that separated the main hall from the old servants' quarters a smell of curry assailed her nostrils. The noisy queue was already along the corridor and down the stairs that lead to the basement canteen. There were many new faces at ITP. Jill remembered Jane's comment on those she once worked with. "Like Grace, I've married and moved, like Pam I've changed my job, but unlike Nikki I'm not getting pregnant!" Her dear brother had subtly manipulated most of those things in Jane's life, but the latter he wasn't finding so easy.

Nor was she finding it easy to put up with the forty-nine year old staid and matronly Miriam, who had replaced Grace, David's secretary. Each lunch time she was stuck with her and constantly irritated by her superior attitude to other members of staff especially Sam who headed up the Printing Department. Today was no exception for as he sauntered over with his coffee, Miriam gave a sour look in his direction, picked up her bag and left. With a nod towards her retreating figure Sam winked and said with glee, "See how she runs. She's a funny one, ain't she?"

Jill gave a short hum. In her new role in ITP she no longer received, or could be the carrier of office gossip, but she missed airing her views and passing on comments.

"So how's Jane? Me Missus is still getting over being invited to the wedding, what a do that was, amazing it was nearly a year ago. Jane is coming on this Thames trip ain't she? It's not as though we 'ave to dress posh or nothing so me Missus says she'll come. And as that Rolf Harris says, we'll get some good tucker!"

Not having told Sam that over the past couple of months she'd barely been on speaking terms with Jane she fudged her answer. "David says he'll just attend the meal and speeches."

"But Jane'll come for all of it?"

"I expect so, especially as it will be her opportunity to say 'goodbye' to Ian. Are you sure there's nothing we can do to persuade him to stay working in the Print Department?"

"No, 'fraid not – 'e's made up 'is mind. The money's the same, but working locally 'e'll save the fares, but it's not just that." Sam's hand smoothed down the lock of hair covering his bald head. "'E liked Jane, 'e didn't just want to win the table tennis championship cup, 'e'd also 'oped to win 'er 'eart. With Jane no longer 'ere, he won the cup back, but there ain't no other girl 'ere for 'im. Best 'e moves on."

"What is it that draws people to Jane?"

"I know what she'd say, her religion." Sam chortled, "But I don't fink that's what drew Mr Reinhardt to her? I chuckles to meself every time I fink about 'er and 'im. Ooh I don't mean that nasty, but I do wonder sometimes, does she still rattle 'im?" He grinned, "You know what I mean. I was doubtful she'd last working in 'is office with Grace, but as 'is wife. Sam's eyes looked heavenward, "...still they say love conquers all. And I still can't get over you're 'is sister. When I fink of some of the fings I said..."

"Dear Sam don't worry about it, I found it most amusing. Now I must go, but before I do, I'm interviewing someone this afternoon for Ian's job. If he's suitable I'll bring him down to you

17

about four o'clock, is that alright?"

"Right you are luv, see you then."

It was a relief to have diverted Sam's conversation. It was difficult living under the same roof not to divulge that Jane and David did indeed still rattle each other. Despite her rudeness about Jane's opinions and her Christianity, Jane had still congratulated her when she'd got this job. And over the past three months Jane had made several friendly overtures, but she felt to talk to her would be tantamount to acknowledging Jane's being right, and she wrong. She wasn't ready to do that.

Sat before her was Ben Fletcher age twenty-seven, whose blond hair was cut so short it stood on end. His round shaped face had large observant bright blue eyes that seemed full of mischief and a cheeky smile which continually popped up. On seeing his tall, well built appearance in Reception she'd been taken aback by his heavy lidded appraisal of her. In other circumstances she might have entertained his interest, but here she had a part to play, a job to do, and a position to uphold. His lively manner could be seen as endearing, but as this was an interview she found it irritating. Nor was she happy at his apparent fixation on her rather full breasts when she leant over the desk to clear up a few discrepancies on his application form. Was her scooped neck blouse more revealing than she had thought?

"I see you've worked at Wilson Printers on and off over ten years, and it seems you have an excellent reference. However I notice there have been a couple of gaps in your career, perhaps you would like to explain these?"

With a crooked grin, Ben tipped his chair and swung on the back legs. His nonchalance was such she was hard put not to say, 'sit up straight' instead she gave him a hard look and pointedly stared at the chair legs.

He dropped the chair back on four legs. "Sorry." Her response was a tight smile, and a questioningly look. As if to recall her question Ben hesitated, then answered, "I didn't leave school until 18. I wanted to get my 'A' levels so worked part-time at Wilsons for two years." He voice tailed off as if he hadn't meant to tell her that.

Jill glanced at the form and commented, "But you didn't put them down here."

"No, because I thought I would seem over qualified for the job." There was no answer to that and she waited for him to

18

continue. "When I finished them I went travelling, I wanted to see the world before....." he paused in thought, and finished quickly, "Before I settled down."

"Where did you go?" Her question was more from awareness that he was covering something up, rather than interest, but as he described his journey he held her attention, caused her to ask questions and made her realise his stories would make a wonderful series for the company magazine. Enrapt it took several seconds before she realised he'd stopped talking and his intense study of her felt unnervingly intimate.

Straightening up in her chair she sought to ignore it. "Right, err Ben. Thank you. You certainly have had some adventures. She treated him to a tight business-like smile, but when his expression remained unchanged, she asked sharply, "Then you went back to Wilsons – was that full or part-time? At his preoccupied reply of 'part-time' she presumed, "And then you couldn't settle down because I see you had more time out several years later.

Into those unusually bright blue eyes it seemed a dark cloud formed on what had been a sunny day. Ben nodded his words brief, "A difficult time".

Patiently she waited for him to expand his answer. When he didn't she gathered the papers on her desk and wondered whether to give him the benefit of the doubt. In talking of his travels he'd seemed guileless enough. Disturbed she glanced up to catch his sad, despairing look.

"Have I have blown this interview?"

"Not necessarily." Troubled, her eyes went back to his application form. Despite taking a brief course on interviewing techniques she'd little experience and wondered if she should risk going further with such a glaring question mark over his life. On paper he had more than the experience needed - it wasn't exactly a high powered job, and with 'O' and 'A' levels he could surely have done better. But then hadn't she done much the same after her heartbreak? In a few years when Sam retired, he would be more than qualified to take over the Print Shop, or perhaps something more challenging. So should Ben's reticence at explaining aspects of his life affect his getting a fairly menial job?

"With your qualifications why do you prefer to work in a print shop?"

As though to appear nonchalant he smiled, tipped the chair back on two legs and quipped, "I'd prefer to be a brain surgeon!"

19

That was it! That was enough! She jumped up and with pursed lips stated coldly, "Thank you for coming Mr Fletcher. I was about to take you to the Print Department to meet the person who heads it up, but to quote you, 'you've blown it'!"

Ben jumped up too. "I'm sorry! I could have put that better, but it is the truth. I spent every spare minute working for Wilsons to help pay my way through med. school. Three years in, I had to take two years out, and after I returned to Wilsons full-time."

"But what about your career?"

Those eyes filled with a deep sadness. "Like now, I'd blown it. I'm no longer a suitable candidate."

What had happened to so change his life? Despite the mischievous cheekiness she instinctively felt he would have made a good doctor. Was his bravado a façade for hidden pain? She knew all about that! Pain that it seemed he'd faced and forced into submission with a determination that events in his life were not going to break him.

Flustered by their now close proximity she waved him to sit again, "You have made me curious. Why, as Wilsons have been so good to you over the years are you now leaving them?" Comfortable with the desk once more between them, she sent him an encouraging smile.

With a small, brief, rueful smile he explained, "My father had a heart attack two years ago which left him in a wheelchair." Puzzled she frowned. What had that got to do with his employment at Wilsons? As if realizing her problem Ben said, "It is, it was, our family business. Dad's Dad was called Will, and as both sons worked for him he called it Wilsons. Dad's brother sold out to him and emigrated to Australia. It was obvious after Dad's heart attack he could no longer run the Company, so Fred and I tried to keep the business going. Fred knew the machines, so he ran the print shop while I went out on the road. Unfortunately, I didn't know Dad's contacts. With his being so ill, I didn't want to burden him, but within a year I'd offered so many deals to get business that we barely covered the bills let alone made a profit and, to cut a long story short, in the second year we went bankrupt, and then that…"

Emotion seemed to catch in Ben's throat bringing her to wish she hadn't pushed for an explanation for this was obviously a sensitive and personal issue he was sharing with her. "I'm sorry please don't feel you have to continue."

"I'd like to. You see I felt I'd failed my father when he hadn't failed me. It seemed fortunate that Dad had, some years before, privately invested in some stocks and shares, but I had to lay off six men. Fred had to go into retirement at 60 instead of 65, less pension, but there wasn't a choice. And Dad…" Ben paused, at what were obviously painful memories, and gave a deep sigh, then continued, "Poor ole Fred he thinks it was his fault and no matter how I assure him it was mine, he won't have it!"

"And would this job be of interest to Fred?"

Ben brightened, "You mean you might offer it to him?"

What had made her say that? This was only a preliminary interview. Cross with herself her reply was sharp, "How could I? I haven't any knowledge of the man."

Ben stood and proffered his hand across the desk, "Thank you for the interview. I've really enjoyed meeting you." He hesitated, his cheeky grin appeared as he added, "Maybe one day we could meet again in less formal circumstances?"

In spite of her earlier misgivings, and knowing he was the only applicant, she made a snap decision. "I think Mr Fletcher if the Department Head decides to employ you there is every possibility of seeing me in less formal circumstances. Now if you would like to follow me to our Printing Department…"

His hand dropped to his side as he said ecstatically, "Oh yes, yes please."

"If you are as enthusiastic in doing the job as you are in accepting it you may find a whole new career open up for you within the company. ITP are always keen to reward and promote staff."

On the way to the basement he chatted away. Somehow she'd have to make it clear to him the less formal circumstances only meant during office hours. Thankful to hand Ben over to Ian to talk about the machines she moved on to speak to Sam. Through the huge machines that provided ITP with high quality printing she could see the door of Sam's cubby hole office open, with him scratching his head over paperwork. Sam's forte was machinery and he much preferred working with them, or under them doing maintenance or repairs than sitting at a desk. Her appearance in his doorway had him standing to attention. "It's only me – you don't have to stand."

"A gentleman always stands when a lady enters!"

"Thank you, kind Sir - full marks for manners." With a nod in the direction of Ben, deep in discussion with Ian over the machinery, she added, "If you take on this applicant you could teach him a few."

Sam glared in Ben's direction. "'e weren't rude to you was 'e?"

"A bit cheeky, rather over confident in manner, but if you and Ian think he knows his stuff, that's fine by me." Even as she was talking to Sam, well out of earshot of Ben, she was aware of his glances in her direction. He obviously admired women with a fuller figure, and this was one she strove each morning to encase in tight girdle before putting on her suit which had a skirt a little longer than the current trend in order to hide her rather plump thighs.

Sam rubbed his chin, "Seems to me the lad can't take his eyes off you."

Jill cringed. "Tell me about it."

"Don't worry, if he fits our bill I'll soon tell him he don't fit yours. You're way out of his league."

It struck her as she left Ben with Ian and Sam that appearances were often deceptive.

Later both Ian and Sam told her they had no doubt Ben could do the job, the latter reiterated her thoughts that Ben would be an ideal candidate to take over his job in the future. Ian, blushing drew her to one side, "I think you ought to know he was very interested in you, but of course its up to you whether you give him a go."

Startled she exclaimed, "Ian, really!" Then, seeing his puzzled expression, she clapped her hand over her mouth. "Oh God! You mean the job!"

Ian's blush deepened, but although embarrassed he admitted, "Ben, like me, has good taste, but as Sam has told me many a time, 'you're out of our league.'.

It was doubtful Sam's words would act as deterrent to Ben Fletcher if he'd set his sights on her. David in the wings could be useful, but often he was criticising her moral standards, rather than upholding her virtue. "Ian, Sam's got it wrong, there is no league, but I've found it's unwise to date other staff. It can cause too many problems. But employment wise, with you leaving on Friday I think its best we 'give Ben a go'!"

"Can Ben come on the boat trip? It would be a shame for him to miss out."

Quickly she thought of an excuse, "Well strictly he's not an employee."

Ian looked sheepish "He could come as my guest. To be honest I felt rather sorry for him. I don't know why I just had the feeling he'd had a few hard knocks in his life and a riotous evening would do him good." Ian chuckled, "And also a chance for him to meet people, especially the lovely young ladies who could take his mind off you."

"Now that is good thinking, but I hope you aren't intending to have too riotous an evening?"

"Riotous or drunk enough to steal a 'goodbye' kiss from you and Jane! I doubt I'll see either of you again after Friday unless… well… unless you would …"

Jill smiled, patted his arm and walking away said, "See you Friday." She had no wish to encourage Ian, 23, tall, lanky bordering on skinny, and probably inexperienced with women. However, he had been astute enough to see under Ben's cheeky, confident façade. It did seem that Ben Fletcher had a chameleon-like ability to gain what he wanted, but she determined she definitely wouldn't be giving him a go!

CHAPTER 2

The clock on the bell tower of the church struck seven as Jill crossed Kensington High Street. Tired, damp and hurrying through the drizzling rain she focused her thoughts on a hot bath, then lying on her bed and watching TV. If this weather didn't change the disco boat trip on the Thames on Friday would be a disaster. Her mind wandered to the interview with Ben. There plenty of single women at ITP, he was sure to find someone else to pursue.

Her work had become a balm to her home life. Her row with Jane in April still festered in her mind which was awkward when she and David lived in the flat upstairs. The problem originated from the family dinner on Jane's birthday when David had spoken out against the contraceptive pill, and Jane in her own inimitable way had retorted, "What do you think I've been taking every morning, vitamin pills?" Two days later giggling over the scenario she'd confessed she took that pill too, and puzzled, Jane had stated, "But you're not married."

With a little laugh she'd pointed out, "You're so naïve. Anyone who is sexually active can take it. It gives me freedom with little fear of pregnancy."

As enlightenment dawned on Jane's face the words spilled out, "You mean...you...sleep...around." Basically her reply had been variety was the spice of life, men had their enjoyment, so why shouldn't she? To her annoyance Jane began to lecture her to which she, in no uncertain terms, told her what she could do with her opinions and her religion before stomping off and slamming the door behind her.

It was only a few days later she heard her flatmates Tania and Helen criticising David being interviewed on News at Ten. Admittedly, in hindsight, she'd over-reacted by turning off the TV, standing in front of it to declare that David owned this house, it was to him they paid their rent, and if they couldn't show some respect perhaps they'd better find somewhere else to live. But since then their conversation stopped whenever she appeared making her feel banished from her own flat. A month ago she'd consulted David, but he'd been dismissive saying, "You women make mountains out of molehills – you need to sort yourselves out." Cross she'd have told him the tension started after she'd stuck up for him, but Jane arrived, so she was left to fume.

Unexpectedly, David had gone to Edinburgh so she just hoped Jane wouldn't attempt another reconciliation tonight. She opened the inner door to the hall and jumped as a loud crash echoed through the house followed by the sound of breaking glass. Immediately Jane appeared at the top of the stairs to exclaim, "What was that?"

"How the hell should I know, I've just this minute walked in."

At her rudeness Jane winced, but still bounded down the stairs advising, "It sounded as if it came from the back of the house. They listened, and in the distance could hear shouting. "That's Tania! You know Jill, you need to speak to that girl. Earlier I asked her to ensure her rubbish went in the dustbin and got a mouthful of abuse. And Mrs P has apologised twice for not giving us a fair share of her cleaning time due to the state of your flat."

Confrontation now unavoidable she scowled at Jane "I'm not responsible for Tania. But as you are so concerned, come, two are better than one."

Not giving Jane time to refuse she stalked through the flat door, past her bedroom and down the stairs. Tania's belligerent voice taunted as they came into view of the lounge. "Well if it ain't Miss Hoity-Toity coming to pay us a visit, along with dear little Mrs Goody Goody, or perhaps Goody-Gody is better! Upset your puritan niceties, did I? Complained to your bosom pal did you? Come to tell me off have you?"

Across the room Tania, hands on her beautifully slender hips stood defiant, as if ready for a fight. Helen looked white-faced and dishevelled and judging by the mess of Tania's expensive and usually immaculate clothes, the two up tipped dining room chairs, and the ransacked appearance of the lounge, she and Helen had already been doing that. A deep anger at their treatment of her flat caused her to demand loudly, "What the hell is going on here?"

Helen looked scared and glanced at Tania. Tania with the sneering curl of her lips answered, "I'd say that… "

"Oh - the window!" Jane's exclamation drew them to look where she was pointing wide-eyed at one of the large picture windows now sporting a gaping hole surrounded by fragments of triangular shaped glass.

Arms akimbo and tight-lipped Jill snapped, "Tania, Helen, an explanation if you please?" Jane moved nearer the window to investigate as she warned, "Careful, that remaining glass could fall out." And as if to prove her right one of the upper pieces slipped to crash down adding further mess on the patio where amongst the shards of glass were the remains of a big, heavy vase, the evidence of what did it, but who threw it?

Tania mimicking her stance said belligerently, "Ask Helen."

From Helen came a sobbed, "I'm sorry. "I didn't know what to do. Tania said I had …" Tania advanced menacingly towards Helen expelling a volume of vindictive abuse. If it was meant to be an explanation the profuse swearing garbled it beyond comprehension. Was the woman, drunk, drugged or demented? The shiver that went down Jill's spine wasn't entirely due to the damp chill from the misty rain coming in through the broken window. Jane appeared to be in thought.

Ready to defend Helen, Jill moved forward to command, "Let Helen speak."

Eyes blazing Tania rounded on her, her fists balled. Jill, determined not to step back as Tania, almost spitting in her face, shouted, "You keep out of this. I'm not having you tell me what I can and can't do, what I can and can't say. Haven't you got that message yet, you stupid fat cow?" Tania's raving went on in a similar vein while, despite her anger, Jill remained remarkably calm. With a lack of response Tania ran out of steam giving Jill opportunity to state, "Tania you really aren't being rational. In fact, to be honest, you seem totally off your head. I think the wisest thing would be for you to leave…"

"Leave!" Tania, shrieked the word, cursing as she proclaimed, "You can't make me leave. It's you who's off her head. Think again! I'm here, and I am here to stay! You can't get rid of me. I've paid my rent. I have a contract. You should know that, Miss Hoity Toity, that Mr High and Mighty brother of yours arranged it. I know my rights. I'm not going anywhere."

Jane who had been quietly observing spoke up. "Tania, I typed the contract written by my husband. Your use of abusive language would be enough, but drug taking, excessive drinking, all come under the heading of unruly behaviour. This would evoke a clause of instant dismissal from the premises, and any damage done to property would mean a forfeit of deposit and rent already paid. Will you pack and go quietly, or would you like me to call the police to remove you?"

Helen, stared at Jane, opened and closed her mouth. Jill equally surprised tried not to look puzzled. She was sure that the contract both Helen and Tania had signed was only an acknowledgement of their having paid a deposit and agreement to pay the rent on the first day of each month. Tania who had looked ready to brazen it out suddenly seemed less confident. Jane headed towards the stairs.

To reinforce Jane's statement, but still trying to be reasonable, she suggested, "Look Tania take what you need for tonight. Helen can pack up the rest of your things, and you can collect them tomorrow."

Tania glared at her, and then with words peppered with invective turned to Helen, "...it's your fault, you silly little bitch. You did it on purpose, didn't you? This was a set-up to get me out. I'll get even though, you see if I don't. No-one crosses me and gets away with it. And as for you, Miss Hoity Toity, you should be renamed Miss Jilly, the Filly who's probably had more men..."

"Leave me and my life out of this."

"Why should I – you're..."

Tania's taunts and accusations finally got to her. Angry she shouted over her. "What I indulge in is my business, what you indulge in is yours, but this is my flat and …"

Helen moving from cringing to courage butted in, "Indulge, Tania does that all right. It's her business in every sense of the word, she charges for what she calls her sexual favours."

Tania rounded on Helen. With a tight voice filled with deadly sarcasm she said. "So sweet innocent Helen, will you cross your heart and hope to die if you tell a lie? So deny you've been paid for your sexual favours too?"

White-faced, Helen's voice and bottom lip trembled as she begged, "Believe me Jill. Please. Tania kept drawing me in so they thought I was part of her set-up."

In a cold and emotionless voice Tania began to reel out how she'd partaken willingly, while Helen continued to cry out over her, "I didn't want to do it. They said it would be fun. It wasn't. It was horrible. I hated it. I wanted to throw the money back in his face."

Tania sneered, "But you didn't, did you? Oh! And look - Mrs Goody Gody is looking shocked!"

Aghast Jane stated, "You've been using our house for prostitution?"

In mock delight Tania clapped her hands. "Oh well done. I wouldn't have put it quite so baldly, more high class sexual favours for the gentry."

Helen injected. "They may have money, but they certainly

27

weren't gentlemen."

Tania's lip curled into a snarl. "But you think Freddy is a gentleman? Did you really think he likes you? He's using you, he said your face was pale, insipid and uninspiring, but when it came to nude photos who would notice that."

Helen let out a sob, slid to her knees, covered her face and began to cry.

The obvious contempt for Helen on Tania's face brought Jill a desire to slap it off. Instead with hands firmly on her hips she decided to hit her with words. "You Tania are a hard-hearted, mean bitch, you've got the mouth of a sewer, the mind of a rat and eyes that see beauty at face value. And I doubt you've ever had that fresh, clean and wholesome appearance that Helen's freckly face, red hair and big green eyes, portray."

"Oh, and what would you know you fat frump who …"

Now embattled she stormed over the top, "And you've got a skinny body, bleached hair and I don't think first thing in the morning I've ever seen a face more blotchy, haggard and uglier than yours."

Tania came closer, her eyes full of hate, yelling words interweaved with profanities. Infuriated she yelled back with as good as she got. Helen put her head in her hands. Jane seemed in a different world. As if noticing Jill's glance at Jane, Tania raved spitefully "…believe me that husband of hers, that brother of yours, doesn't exist on the sexual favours given by prim and proper Mrs Goody Gody."

Incensed Jill lifted her hand to slap Tania, but a very loud whistle took them both by surprise and turning, Jane several stairs up was removing two forefingers from her mouth. With a small grin she informed them, "I learnt to do that when I was at school. Now let's have an end to this. Helen stop crying and bring me Tania's handbag from over there. Jill, there's a good-sized cardboard box in the boiler room, please get it. Tania if you've got a suitcase I suggest you start packing your clothes."

Jane backed up a few stairs as Tania strode threateningly towards her, a beautifully manicured forefinger poking the air as she mocked, "Oh my dear little Mrs Goody-Gody don't start suggesting to me what I should do. You just get out - before I kick you out. I live …"

Tania broke off, seeing Helen about to hand her bag up to Jane. Mayhem broke out as Tania made a grab for it. Helen tossed it high over Tania's head. Tania attempted to intercept it. Her hand caught the bag's clasp. The bag spun back, opened and spilt its contents in a trail across the carpet. And from her elevated position Jane called, "Jill, get Tania's house keys - over there."

Helen retrieved several small white packages from the floor and holding them aloft squealed, "Look what I've got?"

Tania, a nasty expression on her face demanded in a voice laced with menace, "You play funny with me I'll play funny with you. And believe me you'll come off worse. Now give me those!" She made a dive for them, but Helen moved out of her reach. "Okay, how about I tell Freddy to sell those nude photos of you?"

"He wouldn't, he's my friend."

"That's what you think. I don't expect your parents buy 'Playboy' magazine, but if you don't give me those I will personally ensure they receive their very own souvenir copy."

Helen looked at Tania in disbelief, her voice a whisper, "Playboy magazine – my photos in Playboy magazine?" Jill intercepted Tania as she stepped forward to grab the packets from a stunned Helen. Tania shrugged, "Don't worry she'll give them to me. It's her look of innocence that makes those photos so sellable."

Jill frowned. Helen wasn't 'innocent', but Tania's influence it seemed had taken her into unfamiliar and dangerous territory.

From halfway up the stairs Jane put out her arm and said gently, "Helen, come here." With a sob Helen almost ran into her arms. "Now Tania you either start packing or I call the police. I rather think the evidence of a fight, a broken window, prostitution, drugs, threats and blackmail, will interest them, don't you?"

Tania's hostility returned to Jane. "You won't do that. Think what that would do for Mr High & Mighty's reputation if it got about that he lived in a house of ill repute!" With a nasty laugh and a triumphant smile she added, "And of course there's the illegal drug dealing!"

Briefly Jill considered Tania had a point and looked at Jane for her response. Jane unflinching commanded, "Do it Jill". And she realizing that they could easily repel Tania if she did physical attack them slipped across the room to the telephone. Why did the emergency services use 999? It was the furthest number, and the dial's return was so slow. At the third revolution a hand with long red painted finger nails snaked past pressing the button cutting off the call. Jill turned as Tania, her voice light and friendly suggested, "Let's not be hasty. I'm sure we don't want to involve the police." And having pasted on a parody of a smile she looked around the room to declare, "After all, this is nothing more than a row between friends."

Jill followed Tania's gaze at her so called 'friends'. Helen was as white as a sheet, with one eye beginning to look bruised and Jane's hard stare reflected her contempt. As if Tania had just read her mind she said, "If you will just give me my 'stuff' then we'll say no more. I've got a suitcase, so if someone will get me a large box."

It occurred to Jill it was time to bargain. "I'll get the box, but first there are conditions and failure on any of these means we involve the police. One, you pack everything up and go this evening. Two, you ring your friend Freddy now, tell him you have a friend who wants to buy all Helen's photos, and to bring those and the negatives with him as it's an exclusive deal. That exclusive deal is Helen is given those, and they'll be no further retaliation from you. For my part I'll not call the police to investigate your 'modelling' activities and involvement with drugs. Three, you write a signed note agreeing to forfeit the rest of this month's rent, and your deposit, to pay for the broken window. Now I'll get that box while you think about it."

She moved across to join Helen and Jane on the stairs, "Oh, and Tania, if you were thinking of getting your 'stuff' from Helen, it's too late, I've taken it, as insurance."

Jane followed her into the boiler room under the staircase on the ground floor and closed the door. "Phew! That was scary! Do you think she'll go for it? Are we doing the right thing not calling the police? Oh I wish David was here. He would be horrified to know what's been going on."

"It's a good thing he doesn't, and best he never knows. If we can retrieve those photos and get Tania out as quickly and quietly as possible, then it can all be over tonight. I didn't intend she leave, but it was odd the way she pounced on that word. That was a stunner you pulled about the rent contract, and goes to prove that when needs must even you will lie."

"I didn't. I merely stated what a contract could contain. If Tania assumed the one she signed contained that, so be it. But maybe we should include those things next time?"

"Well, Tania's definitely frightened of the police. We need to play on that because I reckon there is more to this than meets the eye. By the way what made you mention drugs?"

"I don't know. I was praying for help and wisdom when the words popped out of my mouth." She grinned, "They certainly hit the spot! Tania certainly wanted to hit me! But thanks to the Lord, He answered and has done more than I asked. Now we'd better get that box, help Tania pack and keep Helen company, we don't want any more eruptions."

"I tell you, if we pull this off, I'll be thanking God. Don't look at me like that. This incident is a blessing in disguise. Tania and Helen haven't been speaking to me for weeks. I've felt banished from my own flat."

Two hours later a taxi carrying Freddy, Tania and her possessions drove away. Jill sighed with relief. In her hand were the house keys and Jane had the note of forfeiture of rent and deposit. And a very subdued Helen with a large envelope of photos and negatives, was tidying up the flat for Mrs Perkins to clean.

Jane reflected, "I think Freddy was embarrassed by Tania using his photos to threaten Helen, and it was kind of him to help cover the window and offer Tania a bed for the night. How easily Tania isolated Helen from us, it just shows how easily things escalate when people don't talk to one another. I'll go and see if Helen's okay, perhaps you'd both like to come up for coffee?"

For the first time in weeks Jill felt free of tension and smiled at Jane's invitation. "I need to change, but if you don't mind, and after what we've been through tonight, I'd like a drop of David's brandy in, and with a coffee. I was going to watch a TV drama tonight, but now I rather feel I've been in one!"

A short while later Jill, heeding Jane's call to help herself, opened their sideboard, took out the brandy and poured herself a glass. By the time Jane brought in a plate of homemade scones with the coffee the brandy had induced in Jill a comfortable euphoria. Jane put down the tray and informed her, "Helen's not coming up. She'll be better after a good night's sleep. I'll call the glazier in the morning. You know I often think TV dramas seem unreal, but you were right, tonight it was here, we were in it, in our house, invading our lives – sex, drugs, and prostitution. Do you remember you described David and I being like dogs on heat? I laughed, but this… It's as if people searching for love have reverted to a primeval instinct to mate with whoever, whenever."

Determined not to take Jane's words personally she concentrated on adding cream to her scone, but the need, the desire to be loved, stirred within. Different partners only brought a short-lived satisfaction. Tonight had shown her that her life was only a step away from the degradation of Tania's world.

"Do you think we'll have Tania's clientele turning up?"

"It's unlikely. I'd say she got her men via an escort agency, although companies can sometimes provide dinner companions, both of which turn a blind eye when it extends into an upmarket form of prostitution."

Disgust was written on Jane's face. "That's horrible! What kinds of men do that?"

With a rueful grimace she replied, "I'm afraid, the David's of this world - business men, lonely in big cities, away from home, away from wives. Don't look so shocked. Men usually use their hotel rooms, but if the girl has a decent place to 'entertain' them the charge is much more."

"Did David…you know?"

"Oh come on, he'd hardly tell me." With a long chuckle she added, "Don't look so worried. What I do know from my observations, is married to you he doesn't need to!" Jane blushed, grinned and then more serious asked, "So how come you know so much about this escort business?"

"I don't think you'd like the answer to that."

Jane's eyes widened. "You haven't – have you?"

Her answer was a non-committal shrug. "I worked on ITP's Reception Desk. It's an obvious place for a man to ask. I've accompanied men if I've liked the look of them, if not I know of several escort agencies. Now, don't look like that! I make it clear it's just an evening out, but sometimes it becomes more, although never for payment." In seeing Jane's eyes fill with tears she wondered if she should have been quite so honest because she'd just reinforced Jane's perception of her, and the cause of their row in April. Then, in denial and anger, she'd accused Jane of being a prude and a religious fanatic. After tonight she'd seen a different perspective. She changed the subject.

"Poor David, having to go to Edinburgh at such short notice. I really can't see why we should be blamed for a company's defective goods because we in all good faith promoted them. I bet he's mad though - he hates his, or the company's integrity challenged."

"Oh he's mad alright! He gets very terse when his mind is working through a problem and I interrupt his thought patterns. And heaven help me if I have a problem when he's engaged his mind to another! Men just can't do two things at once can they? There are times when he's very hard to live with!"

Jane's frankness was always refreshing, and at times

disturbing! Did all sisters hold their elder brothers in such esteem and model their future husbands on them? Was there any hope she might find Mr Right and be happy ever after? Her thoughts congealed into one word which she uttered in sympathy, "Men!"

"But I guess with any marriage you have to adjust to each other." Jane gave a wry smile.

Amused Jill poured brandy into her coffee. "Adjustment, that's a good word for it? You certainly expressed that about a month before your wedding? Remember I was in the kitchen when David announced in a voice that would have frozen the Caribbean that he didn't appreciate you discussing yours and his problems with others. Anyone else would have be cowed by that, not you, you stood your ground with eyes blazing!"

"Well what did he expect when I'd stepped into Grace's role for six weeks before Miriam was appointed, then with no further ado, he'd discarded me? On reflection I could see his point about how as his fiancé, soon to be wife, my familiarity could undermine his authority, but he wasn't going to get away with making decisions about my life or work without discussing them with me first."

"I thought that might be the end of what Sam and Ian call the great romance, but nearly one year on, despite being somewhat stormy, you both seem to be surviving."

"David doesn't mean to run roughshod over me, I keep telling him he's supposed to talk to me, share his thoughts and plans. I was a bit down the other day, and Mrs P. our beloved cleaning lady said, 'that ducks is what love is all about – ups and downs.' But I'm determined to communicate my feelings for it's so easy for a relationship to be eroded away by blame, unforgiveness, frustration, resentment, anger, hurt and bitterness."

Jane offered her a scone. Before biting into it she commented, "After years of only thinking of himself, David may take a while to adjust to considering you, but I'm sure he loves, appreciates, and has your best interests at heart."

"I know. And he was pleased, and encouraged me, when just at the right time that job came up in our church. I've said before Jill, if you have the right attitude God will bless you."

With a smile and words reminiscent of her brother she uttered, "Um. Is that so? At Jane's stare she diverted the conversation to tell her of Chris County's suggestion for an article on the Directors. Even as she was speaking Jane was rummaging in the sideboard for the photo albums. As the phone rang she dumped what she had retrieved into Jill's lap instructing, "Take a look through these."

Five minutes later she returned to report, "David's only just arrived at the hotel. I told him all was well, and we are looking at photos of him for an article you are doing. He wasn't too tired to demand sight of the article and photos before publication! Oh you're looking at my family album, that's my Mum and Dad's wedding."

"It was a shame your Dad died so young, but who is this? She pointed to the best man, "He looks like your Dad".

Jane peered over to see where she was pointing. "Oh, that's Uncle Bob I've never met him, he was Dad's twin brother. Mum said one day, after a row, he upped and left with his wife for Australia. Dad said as boys he felt they were like chalk and cheese. Gran once referred to Bob as the black sheep of the family."

"Has anyone ever heard from them since?"

"When Dad died Mum didn't know where to contact him. But if he came back I suppose he could trace us."

"Life's funny like that - people can play a major part in your life, then they're gone and you know nothing more of their existence." Sadness must have reflected in her voice for Jane gave her a quizzical look.

A few days after their row in April when Jane had apologised for being so blunt, she'd added 'I only said what I did because I care about you." At the time, she'd ignored her, but maybe this was the time to tell her the truth. Mellow and relaxed now from two glasses of brandy that thought was followed with a strong need to spill out her darkest secret. If Jane knew why she behaved the way she did perhaps she'd judge her differently? With Jane reaching out to take her cup and plate it seemed symbolic of an invitation to unburden herself. While she was considering this a tangible peace began pervading the room, inviting, encouraging and drawing up the pain that she'd carried deep within for years. Jane hugging her knees, nestled back in the corner of the settee.

Awkward, and not knowing where to start, her voice came out a croaky whisper. "I'm sorry Jane about...well, that row we had in April..." She cleared her throat. "You touched a raw nerve. I was upset. But I'd like to explain why I do what I do."

"I'm sorry too Jill, spouting all that religious stuff and judging you. I had no right, so forgive me. I've so missed being friends."

At least Jane was honest and ready to admit her mistakes, and

34

it pleased her to think Jane had missed her friendship. Nodding she agreed, "Friends." There was a pause as she thought about that, and then she burst out, "I went out with Stephen for three years, and then he was gone!" Jane's interested and questioning look encouraged her to go on. "It was at the beginning of my three years at College. Stephen was thoughtful, kind and attentive. We started dating and as our relationship progressed I felt he was my Mr Right. But as he pointed out, we were in the midst of furthering our careers, not a time to think of anything permanent. I'd always thought I'd wait for marriage, but my desire for him outweighed that and we drifted into bed together. In the second and third year we rented a flat and Mum and Dad presumed I shared with another girl. On the two occasions they visited Stephen stayed away, just as I did the same when his parents came in the belief that they would disapprove of us living together. We didn't go home the second summer we kept the flat on and worked in the local area.

"Stephen was always reticent to introduce me to his family and not keen to be involved with mine. Of course afterwards I realised why! When I visited home I spoke of Stephen, but kept it low key. I didn't tell him that my parents were coming to my 21st party, which I celebrated in the college at the beginning of my third year. Mum was so pleased to meet him." She chuckled at the memory.

"They asked him to join us at lunch the next day, and so liked him they invited him to come and stay during the Christmas holidays. At the time he agreed, but later backed out. After that, things began to go down hill. When I mentioned settling down, he, being six years older than me, commented I was too young and I needed to experience living in the real world first. When I pressed it, or got upset, it became, 'we'll see what happens when we finish college'.

"The time came to take our exams and Stephen insisted we get those out of the way before we made any decisions. The moment we finished he announced he wanted to spend the summer travelling and applying for jobs. He just didn't understand that in the suddenness of that decision, and without his rent coming in I'd have to give up the flat, which left me feeling homeless and abandoned. Upset I went home. Mum was sympathetic and inveigled Dad to organise a summer job for me at his place until I knew where and what I wanted to do. At my suggestion we'd planned to spend the weekend together after our results. My thinking was that he'd know by then where he'd be working, and with my qualifications I could easily get a job in the same area, we'd be together and that would lead to marriage.

"It was only six weeks, but I missed him terribly. I found out his parents' telephone number and rang them for news of him and his travels. They seemed surprised to hear from me, and afterwards I realised they'd been friendly, but rather evasive. On several occasions he was there and spoke to me, but seemed uncomfortable and each time cooler towards me. I guessed that was because his parents were probably in earshot, and believed things would change when we were together.

"We'd all had good results and a large group of us went to the pub to celebrate. As people drifted off Stephen suggested we take a walk. It was a lovely day in August and we wandered by the river for a while, then he told me." She couldn't stop the catch in her voice – it still hurt after all these years. "He said he'd really enjoyed being with me and I'd got him through a difficult patch in his life. But he'd been offered a job in Canada with wonderful career prospects which he couldn't refuse. Immediately I said I'd go with him, he said that wasn't feasible. I said I could follow him at that he looked really guilty, sat me down and explained that the 'difficult patch' in his life had been a separation from his wife."

"His wife! Oh no! Jill - how terrible!" Jane's hand covered her mouth, her eyes widened in dismay.

"Yes it was. But six years dulls the pain."

"But Jill its still affected your life."

Not wanting Jane to dwell on past emotions she continued in a matter-of-fact tone. "I asked why he hadn't told me. His excuse: he thought his marriage was over. He said they married young, had a council flat and by staying on the housing list knew they'd be transferred to a house once they started a family. His wife was content, but bored at his mundane job he looked into further education. He found a course he liked, and the college he wanted, but it meant relocation. His wife didn't want to move from her nearby family, or lose their chance of a house, so she issued an ultimatum that if he went their marriage was over. In those interim months he said he spent many heart searching hours trying to make her understand, and couldn't believe that her love was so shallow, or her commitment to him so weak. In the end he felt so much resentment towards her attitude he took the college place, and hoped she'd change her mind. Furious, she packed his clothes, told him to get out and that was the end of their marriage. In the month he'd stayed at his parents she wouldn't respond to any contact so once at College he'd given up hope.

"But in our final year she'd been in touch with Stephen's· parents." Jill's voice filled with bitter sarcasm. "Apparently realizing how foolish she'd been! Anyway his parents suggested that as they hadn't divorced, they use the summer to see if they could patch things up. He didn't tell me because he wasn't sure if it would work out. Great, isn't it, his keeping his options open? Anyway, they realised they still loved each other, and with the prospect of money to buy a house and have the family she wanted, guess what, she was willing to move to Canada that October!"

Throughout, Jane's face expressed her sympathy, now her eyes filled with tears. "Oh Jill, how awful, you must have felt betrayed. How did you cope?"

"Well you can imagine how much I hated the woman who in selfishness had given him up, then taken him back when it suited her. I was devastated because I believed we'd have married and gone to Canada. Later I was more rational. Stephen had never promised to marry me, only said he loved me and time would tell if it was right for any commitment. It was my foolish fantasy that made me think one day it would happen."

With a grimace she added, ""But at the time… Well it didn't end there. Only Mum knew I'd had a broken romance and I've never told anyone this before. You see I did everything in my power to hurt and ruin Stephen's life. I found out who he would be working for in Canada and wrote to tell them of what I saw to be his infidelity or untrustworthiness. I sent a letter to his wife telling her how much Stephen loved me, and not her. I didn't have a reply from the company, but she replied saying she and Stephen did love one another, but she could understand my hurt and hoped in the future I'd put it behind me and allow myself to love again. My, I was mad at that!

"Throughout September I kept ringing his Mum, until one day his father answered and said, 'Look we're sorry our son hurt and upset you. There's nothing we can do about that, but he has a wife, they are making a go of their marriage, Caroline's pregnant and they will shortly be off to Canada. So I'm afraid I have to be blunt, there's no point in you keeping in touch, please don't ring again. Goodbye Jill.' Before I could say anything he put the phone down. I did respect his wishes…there was no point…" Her voice trailed off as the hurt brought tears pricking at the back of her eyes. Embarrassed she looked down at her hands in her lap and admitted, "That's my sorry tale."

"Oh Jill, I should have realised you were living out of a deep hurt, it makes me feel even worse about the way I spoke to you in April."

In seeing Jane uncurling to come close, maybe even to hug her, she drew back and waved an assuring hand. "It's okay. Just telling it has brought back the emotion, but I'm alright."

Back in her corner, Jane sent her a sad smile. "Thank you for trusting me enough to tell me. You know the way I see it, Stephen did love you for you lived together happily for two years. What a dilemma to find himself in, but we have to credit him in sticking to his marriage vows. Not that that helped you. You had a double whammy, betrayal as well as heartbreak to cope with. I imagine you told your Mum, but of course she wouldn't have known the extent of your involvement. Would I be right in thinking after consoling you she said, 'you'll get over it, there are plenty more fish in the sea'?"

Surprised Jill questioned, "How did you know?"

"I know your Mum. She means well, but your Dad is very gruff and she's learnt to be stoic so guessed that would be her way of comforting you. The way I see it you've taken that on board and are continually out fishing in the hope of finding love, but not letting anyone get close for fear you'll get hurt again. If you are able to forgive those who wound you, it does help to let go of the memories and move on." Jill grunted for forgiveness was always part of Jane's philosophy, it being the basis of her Christian faith. Warm affection filled Jane's face as she acknowledged, "I know you want to find Mr Right, but you can see how your current strategy isn't working. No-one is perfect, and as you found with Stephen everyone has the potential to hurt us. We all want to love and be loved, and that may seem impossible to you now, but believe me it's up to you because there is a man who knows, loves and wants the best for you."

Eagerly Jill sat forward her mind racing through their mutual acquaintances, but unable to come up with anyone she asked with scepticism, "Oh, and who is that?"

"You don't know him, but he knows of you, and is keen to form a relationship with you."

Puzzled she frowned and waited for a grinning Jane to reveal his name. Suddenly she knew and burst out laughing, "Honestly Jane, I might have known you would find a way to bring Jesus into this!"

38

"But it was my faith and belief that Jesus loved me, despite the scrapes I got into, that set David thinking about God. And after he asked to taste and see that love working in his life the Lord began to answer in extraordinary ways, and his faith grew ..."

"Yes. Yes. We'd all agree David has changed, but I'd put it down to you putting that spring in his step."

With a coquettish expression Jane stretched her limbs. "Um that's as maybe. But David also searched and found out that real love is born out of a deep desire to live to please the Lord first. He would say it felt as if he'd been given a new heart to understand what real love was. It made him want to open up, care, share and be part of something bigger than himself. Like you he had past relationships, but has said, nothing before could begin to compare to the oneness we feel together, and that's the way God intended it to be." In feeling there was no answer to that Jill watched as Jane stacked the dirty dishes on the tray. Jane looked up to add, "I guess you aren't unusual for in these days a sexual relationship isn't considered special, but something to freely enjoy. But, although unfair, it's still a man's world where men want to sleep with lots of women, but don't want a woman who's slept with lots of men."

Irritated by that perspective Jill bit out, "Well I hope you don't mind me saying, but quite honestly Jane you're just plain old fashioned. After all when I find the right man I don't have to tell him I've slept with dozens of men."

"But if it was going to be a serious relationship then you'd have to base it on truth, otherwise it would fail at the first hurdle. And it strikes me that sexually experienced men probably recognise sexually active women."

There was truth in that for the men she attracted did expect her to sleep with them and weren't interested in a relationship. Ben's interest today had obviously been sexual. Jill sighed, "Okay then so how am I to find a man who wants me for who I am, rather than what I am willing to give?"

"You could start by not sleeping with anyone who shows up. Even better would be to just say simply, 'Jesus come into my life and show me your truth' He'd then sort it out for you. Don't pull that face, you did ask! Think about it. There's David and I, my Mum and Ted, and then what about Grace? Bless her. She waited, admittedly a long time for the right man, but look how deliriously happy she is now, and looks ten years younger."

"Oh great Jane! I'm nearly twenty-seven I don't want to wait to fifty-seven thank you very much! And I've just seen the time it's fifty-seven minutes to midnight and if this Cinderella doesn't get her beauty sleep she'll never attract a Prince Charming."

"Don't worry about it, you'll probably be married and have kids long before me?"

"Not if David has anything to do with it and you can't keep him waiting too long, he isn't getting any younger!" She moved from the settee, stretched and said cheerfully . "In a way I'm glad we had that ruckus this evening, Tania and Helen are sorted out, we've cleared the air between us, and as you would say, 'confession is good for the soul'. I do feel lighter and brighter, more at peace with myself, but I put it down to the brandy!

Jane lifting the tray turned to grin, "And as my dear husband and sister-in-law say when faced with something they don't want to acknowledge, "Um, is that so!"

CHAPTER 3

The brandy had certainly given her a good night's sleep, but all day she'd been fighting both a physical and mental headache juggling the magazine articles, Ben's contract and the final details of the river trip. It hadn't helped her equilibrium when her stiletto heel caught in a crack between paving stones on her way to work and had broken off. She hadn't suffered injury, but had suffered the indignity of wearing the only shoes available - a pair of men's black plimsolls. To add to that it hadn't stopped raining and in waiting for the bus the plimsolls proved non-conducive to wet weather! If only she'd been able to evoke sympathy for a sprained ankle, it might have saved her from the risk of trench foot!

Finally on the bus she vied with others for a seat, a polite term for pushing, and won. The victory was short lived when coldness seeped to her bottom bringing the realisation the seat was soaking wet. She could only hope it came from an umbrella rather than someone's incontinence! The twenty minute ride turned into forty because of traffic congestion, so by the time she arrived home she felt like something nasty the cat might drag in!

It didn't help when Jane appeared and said cheerily, "Hi Jill, did you have a good day?" And then giggled at her expression and added, "Oh, maybe not. You should see yourself. And what's with the plimsolls?" Jill, afraid she might say something very rude pulled the offending shoe from her bag and waved it at her. "You should have rung me I'd have come and picked you up."

Now why hadn't she thought of that? David was away in his car, but the faithful Morris Minor was in the integral garage, accessible by the door from the hall. Jane wouldn't have even got damp by fetching her!

"Oh poor Jill. How about you have a hot bath then come up for supper? I've some wine."

The thought of that did cheer her, and smiling she answered, "Now there is an offer I shan't refuse. Give me half an hour."

"Take as long as you like it'll be ready when you are. I've a couple of things I need to talk to you about."

As Jane returned upstairs to prepare one of her culinary delights, she realised how good it was to be welcomed home, and recalled some of the fun they'd had sharing her flat. Jane could say, or do, the most outrageous things, at times making her wonder if you could die of laughing. It would be good to spent the evening with her and would save her getting embroiled again in Helen's troubles. She entered her bedroom on the ground floor with its en-suite bathroom and started the water running for a bath. Striping off her clothes she considered the bright room with its floor to ceiling windows, and the cream walls and carpet. Her armchair in terracotta and matching candlewick bedspread on her double bed brought a sunny warmth even on a miserable day.

At the window she could see the rain had finally stopped. The trees at the end of their garden, now full of leaves, broke her view into the gardens backing onto theirs, bringing privacy to her room. Their patio garden on a level with the basement could do with a weed. Her eyes took in the other gardens which had so matured over the years, they now made a long oblong of a quiet, pleasant oasis of natural beauty from the major roads of Notting Hill Gate and High Street Kensington only minutes away.

The bath filled, she luxuriated in the deliciously hot scented water with the accompaniment of Jane playing haunting melodies on the baby grand piano upstairs in her lounge.

Jane's first floor kitchen was over her bedroom, and as she followed Jane into it the evening sun began streaming in. "I hope it stays like this for Friday. I've hung my clothes up to dry in the boiler room, but I think the plimsolls have had it."

Jane handed her a glass of wine, "Try this. It's Australian, but David thought it was quite good. Take the bottle. I'll bring the tray through."

Once in the lounge they used little plastic fold away lap tables and started eating their salad and quiche. "Jane, this is delicious. So what did you want to talk to me about?"

"Umm and I want you to be honest. Did David have anything to do with me getting my job at the church?"

A wide impish grin melded with her chewing, but she wasn't going to confess to her brother's sins. "Come on Jane, it would be more than my life's worth to answer that - you draw your own conclusions, but don't involve me in them."

"Do you know I thought I'd recognise David's ploys and manipulations, but I didn't? I suppose I should be thankful the job is everything I enjoy. And they are taking up my ideas, the services are livelier and new people are joining. David might have my best interests at heart, but he does have this problem of wanting to help God out!"

Glass in hand Jill raised it and said with wicked amusement, "To you and your little ones!"

In a determined voice Jane stated, "And in that he's not going to help God out. I'm not going to stop taking the contraceptive pill. I think in April he was more upset at my announcing that to him in front of the whole family than my actually taking it. As I said to him then and since, "David, get real, it was a family gathering, not a wretched board meeting!" She arose from the chair. "That's enough about me. I'll make you a cup of coffee. I had a few scones left over from the church tea do you want one?"

"How could I resist?" Jill put aside the tray and flicked through the photo albums still out from the night before.

Jane returning leant over with plate in hand, "I found a good one for you." She turned pages of a family album, pointed to a photo and then giggled for written underneath it read, 'David, Bournemouth, August 1934'. "Would a nude photo aged eighteen months be a challenge to David's circumspection?"

It was impossible not to grin, or resist the comment, "Maybe the word here is circumcision. And being well hung this photo could be his pride and joy."

It took a moment before Jane laughed and in her own imitable way said, "Jill you are awful, but I like you."

Jill turned the pages of the album. "So how about a baby photo with 'born at a young age'; naturist at 18 months; bedraggled at 4; school at 6; swimming at 10; tennis at 15; rugby at 18; car at 19; joint honours degree at 21; accountant at 24; barrister at 30; director at 32 and we could end up with married at 34 and, Jane providing kids at 36! That gives you about 14 months to produce!! Oh, and if you're pregnant before the article comes out I'll promise to leave out the stream of young ladies that appear with David from about the age of 15 onwards."

"Jill Reinhardt! That sounds suspiciously like blackmail to me. You just feel free to add as many young ladies as you like because I'll be proud to know he picked me from a bevy of beauty!"

"Oh well – it was worth a try!"

"Whose side are you on? I have to say this new job really is you! Your creativity and writing talents are coming out. In using your training and abilities you've gained confidence, you've even lost weight and maybe fulfilment in your job will take your mind off the man hunt."

Jill frowned. "Let's not go there again. Anyway I don't have to be on a man hunt for yesterday three men took an interest me – without me so much as trying. Chris County said much the same as you about my new role. Now I'll confess I'm interested in him – did you hear his Patsy has left the scene?"

"How would I, David isn't one to gossip, and you and I, well I've missed you. Who are the other two?" Jane listened carefully as she gave her the run down on Ben and Ian's comment. "It'll be interesting on Friday if they all vie for your attention. Don't worry I'll occupy Ian, I never fancied him, but I like him, we've had some fun together."

"You won't, because David will be there to keep you in order."

Her face cringing Jane said, "Actually Jill he rang just before you came in to say he'd asked Arthur Tyler to fill in, because he doesn't think he will make it."

Cross she retaliated, "He'd better! Arthur's speech will bore us to death."

"That's one of the annoying things about David's job, his need to up and go if there's a problem. It puts our plans awry, yet when he gets home he expects me to drop everything to accommodate him."

To suppress her laughter she blew her nose, but Jane recognising that ploy knew where her thoughts had gone. "Jill Hart you've got a one track mind!"

"Well you must admit one minute, either he, or you, are barking up the wrong tree, barking mad at each other, or embarking on making love on the carpet. Isn't that why David put a door at the top of the stairs so you and he could have more privacy?"

Embarrassment had Jane blushing and then giggling, "Oh well you know what they say about making up, so in that department there's no limit of supply on demand! We're still in our honeymoon period!"

That brought Jill to draw Jane's wedding album from the pile. "Now which one of these shall I use? You - looking like a princess stepping out of the Rolls Royce outside ITP House. David - the 'Prince Charming' waiting at the top of the stairs. It's amazing how many family, friends and colleagues were packed into the hall, the stairs and the first floor balcony overlooking the stairs. This is a nice one of you and David making your vows standing on the landing where the main stairs split left and right. It was a good idea to face outward, and these taken by the photographer from the balcony looking down on you putting your rings on is good despite the back of Keith's head as he bent over to bless them.

"And look at this picture of the food your church provided! I heard one of Dad's friends ask if he could have the name of the caterers! And Joanne who did the flowers was very creative in the decoration of the ground floor, stairs and conference rooms. Even the weather was perfect for photos on the lawn and drive."

With a faraway look Jane agreed. "You know there were times that day I wondered if I should pinch myself to see if it were a dream.

"Well, three hundred people witnessed it so you've got him - for better or worse."

A small secret smile flickered across Jane's face, "Definitely for the better." It was odd to be married the day before in that thirty minute ceremony in the Registry. It felt as if we'd just been to the solicitors to sign a few legal documents, which I suppose we had! Your brother may be tough to live with, but he can also be very romantic. What about those real rose petals for the guests to throw, the horse and carriage drive from ITP through Hyde Park to the hotel, the honeymoon on a Caribbean island and...." Jane blushed and went into silent revelry.

Jill voiced her thoughts. "I just wish there was someone out there for me."

"Oh - there will be. Doesn't catching the bride's bouquet mean you're next?

"Some hope of that – it's been a year and not a suitable man in sight."

"That's what you think, you may have already met the man but not know it."

"Oh like a 27 year old printer, who seemed fascinated with my cleavage?

Jane chuckled, "Well he might make a good partner for me if David doesn't make Friday! Mind he tells me I'm to remember I'm his wife, and I need to be more circumspect! What, I ask, could I possible do that wouldn't come under that heading?"

A wry smile twisted Jill's mouth. "Try an over-the-top rock and roll jive with Ian at the Christmas party! You should have seen David's face. I said in his ear, 'no-one knows about your feelings David, but make a fuss and they will, especially after your lunch time performance'."

"You've never mentioned that before."

She shrugged, "It's never come up. You weren't aware of my brother's lovesick state, but now you're married to him you need to know jiving with Ian is dodgy territory."

Unperturbed Jane grinned, "Not if he's not there."

"That sounds similar to my not telling the man of my dreams I've slept with dozens of men before him." At seeing Jane's raised eyebrows she added, "Take it as exaggeration, but you get my point."

"I do. But my point is, if he wants to appear more approachable, people seeing that his wife is friendly and fun, they will believe he is too!"

At the risk of sounding like her brother she murmured, "Is that so."

Jane smiled. "On another subject Helen is subdued, but she'll survive and she suggested we choose her next flatmate.

"What are you thinking? Resurrecting that awful questionnaire David sent out to our prospective flat-mates?" Tempted she took another delicious scone.

"No, that was a bit much, and we didn't pick up on Helen's lack of cooking skills, or that she'd dislike David! But there are no guarantees, are there? I do have an idea. I ran it past Helen. I wondered…well…rather than advertising err… would you consider Rosemary?"

"What! The impassioned exclamation shot crumbs of scone from her mouth. In an attempt to swallow, the rest went down the wrong way. She grabbed her wine, attempted to drink and ended up choking and coughing. Was Jane out of her mind? With difficulty, her voice hoarse she gasped, "You must be joking" as Jane rushed out to get a glass of water. Jane couldn't be serious? Rosemary with her malicious gossip had nearly driven Jane from ITP?

"I'm sorry. Drink this. I didn't know you'd have such an adverse reaction."

A careful sip, followed by a long drink eased the irritation in her throat, but not the irritation of having to consider Rosemary's unfriendly, snobbish attitude and snooty manner. Her throat cleared, she asked, "Why? At work she made your life hell." Even as she spoke she saw there were positives. Rosemary didn't swear, didn't drink, didn't do drugs and as far as she knew didn't do men!

"Okay I can understand your cynicism. Perhaps you'll understand if I say, like you, she's been through a difficult experience. In self-hatred, she cursed herself by being churlish and nasty so people disliked her. Imagine then sharing an office with someone who was perpetually happy? I got on her nerves, so she did her best to get rid of me."

"You've never told me what happened to change that. Or why you asked her to be a bridesmaid."

"It's not my place to go into details, but it came out of you informing David she was gossiping about his engagement, and his challenging her. You know how scathing he can be? I intervened, that small crumb of sympathy was enough for her to break down and tell me her story. I cried with her, but like I said to you…"

"Yes, yes she needed to forgive whoever or whatever, and if she thanked Jesus for dying for her on the cross she could ask Him to come and live within her, and He'd help and bring her healing."

Jane sighed. "Okay, that's it in a nutshell, but she responded to the truth in that, and you'll admit she has changed. But for God to restore her she needs friendship and people around her." There was silence as she pondered on Jane's suggestion. How would Rosemary get on with her and Helen? They spoke at Jane's wedding, but her words were few. It was the same at work, but she'd lost her nasty edge and did occasionally smile. The only thing she knew about her was she went to the same church as Jane and David. "I told David that Tania had left suddenly and mentioned Rosemary might take her place. He didn't make any comment, and although Rosemary is intimidated by him she's unlikely to see him any more than Tania did."

Jill gave a resigned grunt. "Where's she living now?"

"On her own in a mews cottage, off the Brompton Road."

"Nice. How does she manage the rent of that on her own?

"I've never asked. I assume its one of those places where there is some kind of tenure agreement which keeps the rent reasonable. But I'm sure she could manage to live here, her salary is more than mine when I worked as Grace's assistant to David."

"Would she want to give up her independence to share with us?

"I don't know. I was asking your opinion first."

"Well I can't say I'm convinced, but okay, you can ask her?"

After that they discussed the merits of flat mates and sharing until tired from the previous late night she went to bed.

By Friday, Jane had organised Rosemary's visit to the flat for that afternoon, persuaded her to go on the boat trip that evening and suggested Jill take the Morris Minor to work so she could give Rosemary a lift back.

Despite all the planning the morning proved hectic and she would have forgotten Rosemary if she hadn't been in the hall waiting for her. The usual enigmatic smile and toss of long, dark shiny hair was the only response to her excuses. In a desire to know more about Rosemary, part of her busyness had been to read her personal file, which David wouldn't have sanctioned had he known. On the way to the car park Rosemary commented in her plumy accent, "This is awfully kind of you. I mean … we don't know each other."

This time it was she who gave the enigmatic smile. Rosemary Elizabeth Dawes, born 8th January 1940, present address in SW7. Education: private boarding school, with 'O' and 'A' levels followed by secretarial skills gained at a Swiss finishing school no less! Unusually the file had no record of past employment, but contained a letter of personal recommendation from a senior MP Rosemary had worked with during his election campaign. She'd been at ITP five years and Mike who she now worked for knew little about her except she was a gem in helping him keep the Publicity Department running smoothly.

When Rosemary hadn't said anything further she commented, "I do know from the way you work you're a tidy person so I'd better tell you I'm not." Rosemary gave a cool smile but didn't comment. She continued, "Helen is fairly tidy. I rarely use the kitchen to do more than tea and toast, but we do have Mrs Perkins who 'does' for us. In the lounge in the evenings we mainly sit and stare at the TV." Silence! Oh this was ridiculous she decided to ask outright. "What do you do in the evenings?"

"Much the same."

After several more questions and short answers she began to wonder if Rosemary ever initiated a conversation that wasn't work related. Well she was doing her best to be encouraging. "You know Helen from the wedding, you'll like her, but she's no cook. Do you cook?"

"I manage."

For the next few minutes she concentrated negotiating the car around Sloane Square and through the back roads. She picked up the conversation, "If you manage, you'll be better than me. I keep telling myself I must go to cookery classes, but never get round to it. Mum designed the kitchen its fantastic, but you have to know how to cook to enjoy it! What's the place like you've got now?"

"Quite pleasant."

Compelled to know more she continued, "But not big enough to share?"

"Not convenient."

Frustrated she said pointedly, "After living alone you might find sharing difficult."

She glanced across at Rosemary who gave a small, rather sad smile. If only Rosemary would allow herself to really smile with her rosebud mouth, beautifully sculptured cheekbones, and large brown eyes, she would be stunning. They were of similar height, but she'd always envied Rosemary's willowy frame, her high full breasts carried with such a straight back she guessed she'd been taught to walk balancing a book on her head. Someone had once said, 'Oh Rosemary walks the walk, and talks the talk of the aristocracy. We are all beneath her - a nod of her head is a bestowal of favour'. Two words strung together, or even a monosyllabic reply could then be a sign of friendship!

The moment she backed up on the hard standing space by the garage door Jane was opening the front door, no doubt watching for them from her lounge window. To her surprise Jane's welcome hug and chatter didn't faze Rosemary as she led her upstairs.

Jill found the irritation of the day melting away once at the hairdressers. It was fascinating to see her hair transformed from a straggly French pleat into beautifully sculptured curls on the top of her head. Once lacquered she was assured no gale hitting the Thames that night would blow them away, but it did feel as though she wore a wooden crown. And it put three inches on her height, but with low heels because of safety on the boat she'd not be taller than Chris.

Back at the flat, dressed and applying the final strokes of mascara, she heard Jane talking to Rosemary as they entered the flat. When she descended into lounge Jane looked up. "Wow! Jill, you look fantastic, doesn't she Rosemary?" Half expecting a sneered sarcastic comment she was astonished when Rosemary gave her an approving smile. Jane continued, "David rang to say he was on his way home, but doubted he'd be back before midnight. He's spoken to Arthur about the speech. And said I was to have a good time, and this time didn't remind me I'm his wife and should…" Jill chorused with her, "be circumspect." Jane grinned. "Actually he laughed and said, 'I'll get my spy, Jill to give me a report."

"He can think again, those days are long gone."

Jane chortled, "But the days aren't long gone for me to enjoy myself, and I rather think he knows I'll blow the circumspect."

From Rosemary's expression, Jill guessed she was surprised to hear Jane being so frank about David. Hopefully she understood they trusted her not to repeat it. "So Rosemary what do you think of the flat so far?"

"Lovely."

Frustrated at so short a reply she was pleased to see Helen skipping down the stairs, and was relieved she seemed so chirpy. "Hello Rosemary nice to see you again. I managed to slip out of work earlier to show you around. Hey Jill - you look fabulous in that trouser suit. And love that hairstyle, it makes you look tall and slim."

"Good, money well spent then, because I want to be belle of the boat tonight."

Helen dumping her jacket and handbag over the back of the settee said happily, "Ooh, a special fellah, then." And turning to Rosemary suggested, "Let me show you around, we'll start with your bedroom – it was once Jane's." As they moved through the door as Helen explained, "My room is an oblong which makes your room an 'L' shape, you've got your own wash-basin…"

In a whisper she commented to Jane, "Helen's more herself, but Rosemary's very quiet, do you think it will work out?"

Jane shrugged as Helen emerged still talking. "That brother of Jill's used to spend a lot of time down here, I couldn't believe I went away for a weekend and came back to find Jane engaged to him."

"And she still feels I've lost my sanity by marrying him." Jane joked.

Helen quickly reassured Rosemary, "He doesn't come down here any more, well not if I can help it. He's no reason to. He knows I don't enjoy his company." Bewildered Rosemary looked between them as they laughed at Helen's honesty.

Jill looked at her watch. "Sorry folks, got to go. I'll leave you and Rosemary to make the decision. Miriam and Chris are waiting for me at Westminster Pier. See you later." At her grin, Jane gave her a knowing look.

CHAPTER 4

The taxi sped along the Thames embankment. Outwardly confident, she was inwardly nervous of getting nearly two hundred people on and off a boat, on and off coaches, in and out of a country house restaurant and transported back in reverse order. In her handbag she had a check list to ensure everyone was aboard, but it would only take people arriving late, or getting left behind, to put the whole schedule and evening in jeopardy.

This was it. She paid the driver, took a deep breath and made her way through the gap in the wall, down the stone steps toward the wooden jetty on the river. Moored and waiting on the deck of the festooned boat were Chris and Miriam their backs to her as they watched the middle span of Tower Bridge lift to allow a large vessel out towards the sea. Her heart soared as Chris turned, gave her a beaming smile and always the gentleman rushed over to offer his hand to aid her final step from the gang plank on to the boat. His head bent to kiss her hand as he said, "Welcome aboard, lovely lady."

She laughed, "Thank you. And hello sailor! My you look the part with that cable knit jumper tied by it's sleeves around your neck, even white trousers and deck shoes!" She tucked her arm possessively into his and headed toward Miriam leaning on the rail at the back of the boat.

Across the river a pleasant breeze twisted and played with the hem of Miriam's very outdated, full skirted, calf length dress which she had to hold down to stop her stocking tops showing. The nod of approval at her outfit from Miriam disappeared at seeing her arm tucked into Chris'. "Right now you are here Jill, Chris you can tell them to cast off."

As he obeyed Jill pointedly called after him, "And as I am in charge I appoint you Captain of this ship." Chris turned and gave a salute, Miriam frowned. Seconds later the engine putted and choked into life and above it Miriam shouted, "It's a bit noisy isn't it? I hope that smell of diesel isn't going to make me sick." Chris gave a wry smile as he took Miriam's elbow and drew her forward, "Come, it'll be better at the front."

Irritated she offered, "If you don't feel well Miriam, you could always get off when we get to Westminster Pier."

"Oh no dear, I couldn't do that. I'm David's representative he would expect me to stay with you to settle the bills. And it would be most unwise to leave you on the boat with four brutish men."

Riled by her assumed authority Jill retorted, "And if they decided to be brutish what would you do hit them with your enormous handbag? I'm sure Chris you'll stay and keep me company later?"

A current of air tossed up Miriam's skirt she struggled to keep it down, but her pursed lips told Jill she wasn't intending for Chris to usurp her.

Five minutes later as Jill discussed the music with the DJ Miriam's voice floated up the stairs lecturing Chris on its disturbance to others, its derogatory effect on the ear drums, and older people not liking rock and roll. Jill cringed for Chris, having assured her the DJ would have sedate music for the occasional waltz, Miriam replied, "In that case Chris dear, I shall look forward to you partnering me."

Jill moved to the stairs and called down," I could do with a strong drink, anyone else want one?

Disdain etched Miriam's face. "Oh dear me, it's far too early for that."

"Coffee Miriam, nothing else"

Chris' sympathetic expression warmed her heart. She admired his patience with Miriam who seemed to be perpetually complaining. Miriam may call herself a Christian, but she didn't reflect David and Jane's attitudes and behaviour toward people. In the salon she quickly drank her coffee and to get away from fawning Miriam she went on to the deck. Westminster Pier was still some way off, but she could see the landing stage crowded with people, and across the water cheers and whistles reached her – ITP staff were ready to party!

They docked to the song, 'Rolling down the River'. Miriam, bristling with assumed authority demanded, "I'll take the check list. You and Chris welcome and direct people." At her hard stare Miriam went on blithely, "It's an opportunity for me to put names to faces." A rebuff was on Jill's lips, but seeing Chris' wink she squashed it.

The funnel effect of the gang plank slowed up boarding. Miriam's chatting caused another bottle-neck and on chivvying her she received a sour look. Positioned further down the deck they had a good view of the hub of excited people waiting to clamber aboard. Chris became distracted, and then exclaimed, "Oh my god, it is! I thought I was seeing things, it's Patsy, she's here." The obvious joy in his voice and the speed at which he'd left her side to push past those getting on, in order to get off, told her that Patsy was still very much in his heart.

The bubble of happiness which had been steadily growing instantly deflated. She'd pinned so much on a romantic evening with Chris. Disappointed, but with a fixed smile, she continued welcoming guests, while catching glimpses of Chris swinging Patsy around as he kept shouting, "She's said 'yes'. Tears filled her eyes, this was not the time to cry, but at least Chris hadn't known she had designs on him. The DJ having picked up on the excitement was playing 'Congratulations' Cliff Richard's latest hit and people were laughing and singing along while joining hands to make an arch for Chris and Patsy to go through before reaching the gang plank. Once aboard Miriam met them all fawn and smiles. With the attention on the happy couple she took the opportunity to search her bag for a hanky for her wet eyes, it wouldn't do to have her mascara run.

"It's funny how love and romance does that. Here, have mine." A large white handkerchief fluttered before her.

Jill took a deep breath…of all people. "I'm fine Ben, thank you." She dabbed her eyes with her own hanky, plastered on an excited smile, and agreed, "Isn't it wonderful. Right, let me tell you, there are two bars, one inside, one on the upper deck, toilets off the Salon or bar area. Oh hello Arthur, I hope you've prepared a riveting speech?" A covert glance revealed Ben had gone. In seeing Chris and Patsy approaching she uplifted her sagging smile. What could Chris possibly see in that tall, painfully thin woman? A straight crop of mousy hair framed a skeletal face from which her eyes protruded, as did her teeth from her mouth. Plain, bordering on ugly! With amusement she certainly didn't feel she commented, "It would appear the Captain of the ship has abandoned his post for love."

"Sorry Jill, in such a moment all else was swept from my mind. Let me introduce Patsy, the love of my life." Chris smiled down into Patsy's eyes and drew her to him. "I can hardly believe it, darling, you are here." No, she thought, neither could she! And, as if she wanted to know, Chris informed her, "When Patsy four weeks ago turned down my marriage proposal I was devastated, so you can imagine my joy tonight, and what a romantic night to celebrate our engagement. Miriam says Patsy can stay because David isn't coming."

There arose within her a desire to throttle Miriam, and it seemed she wouldn't have to wait long for she was heading toward her blooming with enthusiasm and pleasure. If that was due to her problem solving, it would soon be extinguished! Jane's arrival with her usual bounce and verve diverted Miriam with a need to kowtow to the boss' wife! And Rosemary in a cardinal red sheath dress with long slits up the side looked stunning, but tense. As they joined her Miriam was saying, "To think, Chris and Patsy engaged, it's enough to send my heart in a whirl." The wretched woman sounded as if she knew them both well, and behind her Jill opened her mouth and made a sick gesture not caring who saw. Jane pursued her lips in an attempt not to laugh, but her eyes questioned to ask if she was okay before interrupting Miriam's raving to point out, "Shouldn't you be checking on those boarding?" All of a dither Miriam rushed away to pounce on people innocently strolling the deck. With a rueful smile Jane suggested, "Rosemary and I'll go and get a drink, I expect you'd like a brandy?

A crewman approached, "That it then, Miss? I can't see no others. We need to get going to keep the schedule." On giving the 'go ahead' Jill glanced around, seeing Miriam she made her way through the crowd to ask, "Is everyone accounted for?"

Clip board in hand she confessed, "I've done my best. I don't know everyone yet."

Cross Jill grabbed it from her. "You haven't ticked off Jane, or Rosemary. She's taking David's place."

Miriam paled, "Oh no! You didn't tell me that. I've given his place to Patsy."

Nonchalantly she retorted, "I wasn't expecting you to take over, but now you have I'm sure you can sort it out. I'm sure they'll appreciate your giving up your place for the sake of love. The sight of Miriam's face made her lips twitch with laughter, and spotting Ian she excused herself to jostle through the people to ask him, "Hi Ian, just checking, did you bring a partner?"

Ian blushed. "You did say if I hadn't anyone I could ask Ben. He's over there."

Automatically she glanced in the direction he indicated and wished she hadn't for Ben noticing her separated himself from Pippa and Jackie to head towards her, while they cooed after him, "Come back soon."

Bright blue eyes smiled into hers. "Thank you for allowing me to come. I'm glad of the opportunity to meet you in a less formal setting." Inwardly she sighed, it would be best to put him in his place before he got any ideas. "TTP has quite a bevy of beauty among the staff, you'll have plenty to choose from. Now if you'll excuse me I have a few things needing my attention." Through the crowds she could sense Ben's eyes following her as she headed off to find Jane and her brandy. Ben coming as Ian's guest meant a spare place, but she'd let Miriam stew a little longer!

The last of the guests straggled down the road from the coaches returning them from the country house restaurant to the river bank. Despite her personal tensions and undercurrents the evening had run extraordinarily smoothly and they were only a quarter of a hour behind schedule on this, the final leg.

Throughout the dinner she'd been bored by Arthur Tyler, and his speech, nauseated with Chris and Patsy's devotion to each other, irritated by Ben being in her line of sight and his continual glances in her direction, irked by Miriam's cold fish eyes displaying their dislike of her and peeved that she was so obviously the subject of her conversation with Phyllis. It had been gratifying to see Ben finding conversation difficult. Rosemary was seated one side, and Joe's girlfriend with a fixed interest on Joe, on the other. But she noted how he stood and held Rosemary's chair when she left and returned to the table, and caught his frown at Rosemary's cringe when he touched her shoulder. Later he leant over to speak to her, and was obviously taken-aback when she swiftly drew away. Bet that dented his ego!

An outbreak of laughter and screams drew her attention to the river bank. Wrong! Ben's ego had every reason to blossom, he now had a lady on each arm and four others hanging on to his every word. Jill watched his progress along the tow path while chivvying people back to the boat. Jane, in her own inimitable way had managed to avoid Arthur, and the Directors table, to sit with the Print Department, and was now hanging on Ian's arm and chatting to Sam & Mrs B.

As they came near Jane broke away to say to her, "I think Ben's very nice. And he can't take his eyes off you."

Cross she grunted, "Tell me about it."

"Don't fret about what you can't have, enjoy what you can." Jane laughed, "Oh, well to a point!" On that she skipped back to link arms again with Ian.

A resounding cheer drew her attention to the river where Ben had obviously jumped from bank to boat rather than use the gang plank. Arms outstretched he was enticing several girls to do the same on the promise of catching them. Donna, dressed in an unlined white crocheted trouser suit, ran past her down the tow path calling out, "Hey gorgeous! What's your name? Catch me, and you've got the catch of the night." Those already on board moved to see what the commotion was about, while those on the bank stopped to see what might happen.

To give Ben his due, his cheeky smile didn't waver, and his arms outstretched further to welcome Donna, blonde with a vague similarity to Marilyn Monroe, leaping across the gap into his arms. His reward, as he placed her feet on the deck, was a very smoochy kiss which had the men cheering, and the girls somewhat piqued. From her viewpoint higher up the bank, Ben was playing to the captive audience, but when he'd finished he seemed to know exactly where she was standing to issue a challenging stare.

Well she wasn't Donna! Any favours she might bestow would be quiet, not public and Ben certainly wouldn't be a recipient. Her mouth tightened as she stared back at him in the hope of communicating that she wasn't amused. Neither it appeared was the swarthy man who emerged from the wheel house of the boat to shout and gesture wildly, "No jumping, Stop! Stop! We don't want no accidents. Use the gang plank. Hurry up. Hurry up." The sound of the boat's whistle had those lingering hurrying forward, and within a few minutes they were underway.

Most of the crowd headed for the upper open deck, a long queue formed in the bar. The DJ turned up the music for the dancing. Dusk was beginning to turn into darkness, and at the guard rail, she looked at the reflection of the coloured lights on the water. Near to tears at being alone on such a romantic evening she jumped at the light touch on her arm. "Sorry I didn't mean to startle you. I wonder Miss Hart may I get you a drink?"

It would be rather terse to refuse Ben's offer, but his cheeky smiling face did little to cheer her mood.

"Thank you. I'll have a brandy." Even on the way to the bar, girls accosted Ben eager to talk to him. The man obviously had charisma, so why did he so annoy her?"

"Now girl we must have a dance?" Jill groaned, oh no, trust Arthur Tyler to accost her. She couldn't be rude, but he was such a bore. And without his wife he seemed to have rather over done his drinking.

"Ben's just getting me a drink."

"Boyfriend eh? No matter, let's have this waltz, you can have him and the drink later."

With no choice she moved into his arms, tried to avoid the smell of his alcohol laced breath, and pushed back against the hand that rested heavily on her back. His hope she felt to draw her large bosom into his chest, which, no doubt, would be Arthur's thrill of the evening.

The moment Ben reappeared with her drink she greeted him with enthusiasm, excused herself from Arthur and tucking her arm in Ben's led him away. Ben squeezed her arm in his. "This is a nice surprise. You gave me the impression I'm not your type, how delightful to find I've been mistaken."

Exasperated she retorted, "Don't get too delighted, I wanted to escape from Arthur's drunken clutches."

Ben undeterred by her honesty drew her closer with his arm and smiled saying, "That restaurant was superb, an idyllic setting and their prices aren't extortionate. How did you find it, tucked away up that long drive?"

Not about to tell Ben she'd been there with one of her business men 'friends' her reply was vague. "Oh, someone I know had been there and recommended it."

"I hope you don't mind me saying that you look incredible. I love your hair up like that, it shows off the delightful sculpture of your face, your eyes look darker, bigger, pools I'd like to drown in."

Crossly she countered, "That sounds more like a 'come-on' than a compliment. You haven't started working for ITP, yet I'd bet you know more people after one evening than others do in months."

Ben gave his cheeky grin, "That sounds like your way of saying I've been putting myself about a bit?"

"Well, you aren't slow in coming forward." They sipped their drinks while she looked around hoping someone would join them. Her eyes rested on Chris and Patsy dancing cheek to cheek - there was Mr Right, and she was stuck with Mr Wrong!

"I'm afraid you've missed out there." Stunned Jill turned to stare at him. "He would never have been man enough for you."

Infuriated she bit out, "What! And I suppose you think you are?" And then wished she'd bitten her tongue.

Ben gave a nonchalant grin, "I think first we need to get over the hurdle of my being able to call you Jill?"

The man was beyond belief! She snapped back into formal mode. "Generally in ITP we call each other by our Christian names, it is a fairly informal company, even the directors are coming around to feeling that management and staff boundaries should be less tangible."

Ben nodded thoughtfully then pursued, "So would that less tangible boundary include me and you?"

Warily she replied, "Everyone at ITP calls me Jill."

"Then Jill I'll take it we have moved a step forward." Ben looked around the deck where people were dancing to the "Hippy, hippy, shake. Everyone seems to be enjoying themselves, all credit to you for making it a success."

"I'd say so far so good. I'm amazed I didn't lose anybody, nothing has gone wrong, and despite your dare-devil prank no-one fell into the brink." Unexpected laughter burst forth from her remembering Donna, "And with that I rather think you got more than you bargained for!"

Ben's eyes twinkled in the reflected light from the bulbs over his head. "You're right there. Some girl that. Would I get more than I bargained for if I asked to have the pleasure of this dance?"

"Thank you for the drink Ben, now if you'll excuse me."

"Hey I'm sorry. Oh dear, I don't seem to be able to say the right thing with you. But before you go, thank you, that despite that rather fraught interview, you gave me the job, it means a lot to me." His bright blue eyes stared into hers.

"I didn't. It was only the preliminary interview, the decision was made by Sam, with Ian's recommendation, thank them."

"In that case I'll do that. Before I go, please, may I ask more seriously, Jill would you do me the honour of partnering me on the dance floor?"

To break the eye contact she glanced toward the deck now filled with couples parodying a quick-step. Without answering she put her drink on a little circular shelf riveted to one of the columns of the deck, and stated, "Come on then, what are you waiting for?"

Ben's response reminded her of a small boy being given a toy, he leapt forward with such delight she felt guilty that her acceptance was only to get this over and done with so she could rid herself of him for the rest of the evening. His warm breath fanned her cheek as, drawing her into his arms, he said quietly, "I feel I've been in waiting a long time for this." Nonplussed she stumbled slightly. His hold tightened and moving her with the music he commented, "It's quite easy. Relax into me. You will get used to it."

Was there an edge, a double meaning to his words? She

certainly had no intention of being drawn into whatever he thought she would get used to. Her irritation surfaced. "I'll have you know I have a bronze medal for ballroom dancing,"

Ben chuckled, "Guess what? I've got a gold one." Before she could retort, he pulled her tightly against him and the force of his lead made the steps come naturally. His mastery was quite heady, as they whirled around the deck, but she resolved not to be drawn in.

The music ended. Ben didn't let go, his eyes gazed into hers. Annoyed she pulled away. "Thanks for the dance. Now I must circulate." Before she could step aside his hand at her waist drew her closer to murmur in her ear, "Do you have to leave so soon."

What was the matter with this man? Did he think he was Rudolph Valentino? She masked her response in politeness. "Ben I feel I should dance with anyone who asks. Now please excuse me I need to mingle."

Even as she spoke, she blinked in surprise. Ben genuinely did seem rather dazed, his response somewhat confused, "Yes! Oh yes, yes, of course, I'm sorry. Thank you."

Was the man drunk? Drunk or not, she recognised that heavy eyed look and determined Ben Fletcher was going to be the first victory in her new order of sexual abstention!

After that Ben's eyes seemed to follow her. What was wrong with the man, for he had no shortage of willing partners? Bill Hailey's "Rock Around the Clock" brought her to wonder the whereabouts of Jane and Ian. This was their song and their last opportunity to do their dance routine, Jane wasn't likely to miss it. Within seconds the deck was clearing to watch Jane's small, light, flexible body matching Ian's complicated moves. What started with the traditional ballroom jive quickly changed as Ian swung Jane through his legs and up and over his back before catching her at the waist, twisting her into the air before righting her on her feet. The action brought first a stunned gasp, then cheers and clapping from their audience. After more sensible steps, her hands held by Ian, he swung her off her feet and round until her body was at full stretch horizontal to the floor.

While everyone enjoyed their dancing display Miriam's expression was one of shocked disgust. Afraid she'd tell David Jill moved to warn her against that. Miriam, unaware of her presence was commenting to Phyllis, "David's got a handful in that wife of his. I would have thought in his position he could have found someone more suitable. Fancy her behaving like that in front of his employees. Of course she's been flirting with that Ian all evening. Disgraceful, that's what it is. And this - it's not a dance - it's ...well...!" Miriam grunted in disbelief. "And she calls herself a Christian..."

To resist the temptation to thump the bigoted old bat, Jill took a deep breath. And while she couldn't deny David wouldn't be pleased to see his wife's abandonment, she wasn't going to let Miriam say such things. She stepped forward. "I heard that Miriam. And as a professed Christian you'll know better than me, but doesn't the Bible say something about if you judge, you'll be judged?" Miriam's mouth opened, but she didn't give her the chance to speak. "You need to know Jane is having a bit of harmless fun with an old friend in front of people who know and love her. I consider your remarks out of order, and would suggest David wouldn't appreciate them either. I won't tell, if you don't." Jill widened her eyes questioningly and she waited for Miriam to process her words. Flushed in anger Miriam looked at Phyllis for support, but she, obviously embarrassed, turned looking as though to escape. Sam appearing thwarted Miriam's response. "Hey, ain't that something. Me & the Mrs weren't too old to go and see that Cliff Richard film. Their dancing is as good as that. ITP ain't been the same since Jane left - we all loved 'er and woe betide anyone who speaks against her." Mrs Bennett next to him was making loud oohing sounds, along with most of the audience as they watched Ian and Jane's antics in their finale, which ended on loud clapping and shouts of 'encore'.

When she turned back, Miriam and her faithful friend Phyllis were gone.

Sam winked. "I hope she's now well warned off, that one's got the sensitivity of a fly, often felt like swatting her myself! And that Ben's a right one ain't he, getting an invite before he's employed? He's chatting up all the women - was even interested in our Jane." Sam guffawed, "He asked me as we left the restaurant, 'Is that girl with Ian his wife?' I said 'no' and he said, 'Thought not, I'd say those rocks on her finger would cost at least two years of Ian's wage. I guess she's hitched to some rich old man, who isn't here tonight?' I just grunted. Don't look at me like that Jill after all it wasn't up to me to enlighten 'im!"

"And what's he going to think when he finds out?"

Sam nodded sagely, "I had my reasons. He thinks he's God's gift to women, look at the way he was with you. And he said, 'Bet that Jane wouldn't mind a good night out with someone young, and she might just be the bait to make the woman I really like jealous!"

"What! Just wait until I tell Jane!"

"I think she'd probably laugh, he's such a cheeky bugger - oops 'scuse the language."

"Do you think he was talking about me?"

"He hasn't been able to take his eyes off you all evening. Do you want me to give him a message?" The wry smile and twinkle in Sam's eye made her laugh.

"Oh yes, Sam you can give him a message alright, using your 'oops word and add the 'off'."

Sam guffawed loudly as Ian said by her ear, "Jill Hart I'm surprised at you! And I can guess who you were talking about, but what's he done to deserve that?"

Jane flushed from her exercise, her reddish brown hair sticking to the sweat on her face laughed. "I have to say Jill what I've seen of Ben tonight I've rather liked. He has a strength about him, yet seems quite endearing - could be Mr Right."

Aggravated she felt like throwing something, but instead threw the remains of her drink down her throat. "I need another one. Go on Sam, tell Jane the whole story. Anyone else want a drink while I'm there?"

"Yes please, a big glass of cold lemonade!" Jane used her arm to wipe the sweat from her brow. The rocks of her engagement ring caught the light and sparkled. Ben it appeared knew about diamonds, for the diadem of seven marquee cut diamonds set half way around a two carat pear-shaped one was indeed worth more than two years of Ian's salary. She joined the queue at the bar. In an unusual gesture their father had insisted David borrow the money from him to 'get that slip of a girl something of value, she's worth her weight in diamonds and gold.' Then he'd added, 'don't worry about the loan my boy, you mark my words, that house of yours will be worth a million pounds in twenty years!" She smiled to herself, If her Dad was right even her small investment in it, would reap dividends!

The moment she appeared Jane grabbed her lemonade and gulped it down. "Whew I could do with another one of those - dancing makes you thirsty."

Jill grimaced and said pointedly, "Dancing like that could give you more than a thirst."

Jane shrugged, and grinned at Sam, "Like Ben said, if you're married to an old man there are times when you need to let your hair down!!"

"Oh come on, David's not that old."

Sam and Mrs Bennett discreetly moved away as Jane commented, "No, he's not. And there are times when he surprises me and does something romantic that defies convention or circumspection, usually after I've challenged him not to be quite so staid, or like a bear with a sore head! I told him I was going to enjoy myself, he's not here, this after all is a party, a farewell and the last opportunity to dance like that with Ian, so what's a girl meant to do?"

Jill couldn't help, but laugh at Jane's innocent expression. "Put like that you have me convinced."

"Maybe then I can convince you that Chris wouldn't have been right for you, but Ben might well be."

"Why is it you lose the ones you like and win the ones you don't? Ben is definitely a non-starter, far too cheeky for his own good."

"Who's too cheeky for his own good?"

Jill felt her face reddening. Jane grinned inanely over Jill's shoulder at Ben.

It was obvious Ben knew for he didn't wait for an answer but said to Jane, "That dance with Ian was truly amazing - did you and he practice long?"

"A couple of years ago when I worked at ITP it took us a few lunch hours - Ian, like me, had the basics, and we just improvised until we knew each others moves, but we haven't danced since I got married last year."

His expression was mischievous as he suggested, "Well I'd certainly like to make moves like that with you."

Wide-eyed Jill couldn't believe the gall of the man!

Unfazed Jane laughed. "With remarks like that you'll get yourself into trouble."

Ben gave a wry grimace, "Believe me I already have. But I am a bit of an expert with the cha cha cha, and wondered if we could dance and see what we can do to liven it up?"

"Then I hope livening up the cha cha is better than your chat up lines!"

Ben's cheeky grin appeared, "That bad eh! I must get more practice. But my cha cha moves - classic and style!

"Well Jill, do you think I should risk dancing with Ben?"

"Only you know, but you might as well be dead as damned!"

"What she means Ben is that my old man isn't that thrilled

when I, and others, enjoy my dancing expertise."

"It's more than that. Roused, David has been known to knock a man out with one punch."

Jane exclaimed, "The man was attacking me at the time."

"Ben needs to know the risks, and you weren't David's wife then."

Their banter appeared to amuse Ben rather than bring fear. "Ladies, I assure you, the only moves I am going to make will be on the dance floor. I can't believe Jane's husband will object that strongly, but don't worry I'll fix it. Let's get the music put on and believe me, all will be well."

Ben left to speak to the DJ. Jane giggled. "I like him. He's charming and funny, and I sense behind that is a strong character. He's the committed type - good husband material."

"Jane, I don't even like the man so there is no...."

"Ladies and Gentleman, if you haven't already met me I'm Ben and will be starting work shortly at ITP. I have asked our amazing dancer Jane to partner me in the cha cha cha. We may make a spectacle of ourselves, and therefore, in order that she may consent, I'd be grateful of your assurance that if any of you should meet her husband you wouldn't mention it to him"

Jane's hand shot across her mouth, her eyes rounded. Jill buried her face in her hands. Laughter and words mingled as across the floor people responded: "No chance of that mate. You must be joking. Not likely. Wouldn't dare. Bravo Ben - great way to start a new job. You may not have one by Monday!"

Ben's cheeky grin showed he hadn't comprehended that their words were more warning than jest. Fortunately their cha cha cha wasn't as outrageous as Jane's jiving with Ian. David wouldn't have been amused at Jane's first dance performance, but to be fair, he'd have probably admired the consummate skill and expression that made the cha cha cha flow making it a stunning presentation worthy of 'Come Dancing'.

However David would not have appreciated the conversation between them afterwards, "So Jane what made such a lively person as you get tied down so young?"

"I'm 24 - not so young - but the answer is friendship and love?"

"Well, if you ever want a fun night out when the old man's away, just say the word, and I'll be round."

Jane wagged her finger at Ben, and grinned, "You may wish you'd not said that."

Mystified Ben turned towards her, "What do you say Jill, will I regret those words?"

It wasn't difficult to place a sweet smile on her face, and point out, "I've said all I'm going to say on the subject. I'm off to get another drink before last orders." One day it was going to be very amusing when the over confident Ben found out just whose wife he'd been chatting up.

"Ah there you are Jill." At Chris' smile her stomach churned, along with the hope that as the ugly Patsy woman wasn't with him he was going to ask her to dance. "Would you mind awfully if, in the circumstances, I didn't come back with you to Tower Bridge? You'll have Miriam with you." He chuckled, "Although the men don't seem too brutish to me."

She forced a smile, but it was more difficult to say cheerfully, "That's fine."

.   Chris smiled down at her. "Thank you. You've organised this so well. It's been a truly wonderful evening." Maybe for him! Disappointment gagged in her throat, but she determined not to dwell on it. The party was now in its final throes. Balloons were released from their net, people began popping them, blowing paper whistles and throwing streamers. Over the screams and laughter of a well inebriated crowd the DJ announced, "Last dance folks, so in tradition take your partners for the last waltz."

Miriam drew up beside her and was about to say something when Ben arrived. "Hello ladies, its Miriam isn't it, we've not met before." In delight Miriam became all of a twitter as she clasped his outstretched hand. Obviously no-one had told her Ben was taking a lowly job in the Print Department. Jill grinned as Miriam turned to retrieve her handbag from a nearby chair, then realised Ben thought she was smiling at him. In response he asked, "May I have the honour of the last dance?"

Before she could reply Miriam, in a fluster, turned to answer, "Oh how lovely. That is so kind of you. I don't dance much, but I do like a waltz. I'd love to."

At Ben's ill disguised despair Jill's smile broadened. But to his credit, he went along with it.

In an attempt at comradeship with Rosemary she sidled up to her at the rail and watched Westminster Pier draw closer. "Rosemary, do you see what I see? Is that who I think it is?" In the distance, under the pier lights a lone figure stood watching the boat's progress with a bouquet of flowers in his arms. Rosemary followed her gaze, and gave an enigmatic smile. "That brother of mine always seems larger than life, even when you can't hear him. I'd better find Jane."

Jill's eyes scoured the dancing bodies pressed together in the semi-darkness. The intricate steps of the waltz had been abandoned for lack of space, and Ian, looking moonstruck with Jane, the girl of his dreams in his arms looked sad, knowing it was unlikely they'd meet again. In deciding not to spoil their last moments together she slid back into the shadows ready to grab Jane the moment the music ended.

The boat bumping slightly against the quay signalled their arrival, and with perfect timing the waltz music ended with the DJ announcing, "The party's over" and playing the record of the same name. Jill moved forward to where Jane remained in Ian's arms. "Sorry to interrupt, but I think you need to know David is waiting for you on the dock." With that she slipped away ready to waylay David if he decided to board, and discovered Sam too had spotted and recognised the waiting figure. His call to Mrs Bennett resting her feet in the salon, "'ere luv you gotta come out 'ere and see this me ole duck, our Jane's man's here and looks as if it could be a romantic moment" had brought everyone out on deck to take a look. Seconds later Jane appeared laughing as those who had known her at ITP issued forth drunken, cheery taunts and jeers as they made way for her to be first down the gang plank. By the time they'd safely tied up the majority of the party watched as she left the boat and ran towards David. Quickly he laid down the flowers so he could receive his wife with open arms. At her arrival he hugged and swung her around as his audience cooed at the romance of it. Over which, loud enough for Miriam to hear, Sam commented, "Well ain't that just grand, no doubt where 'er love lies."

And Jill, knowing in all probability her brother had guessed Jane would behave in a less than circumspect manner was using this moment to show, 'this woman belongs to me and I love and accept her'. It wasn't then a surprise to see him in best romantic fashion, tip Jane's face up toward him while staring into her eyes, before slowly, oh so slowly bringing his head down to take her mouth with his. The thorough kiss, brought cheers, laughter and catcalls from the drunken rabble. Behind her Jill heard Miriam's astonished gasp, and at Sam's wolf whistle Miriam's hands shot over her ears. What was Ben making of this? She looked around, but couldn't see him. David having made his point, picked up the bouquet, placed it in Jane's arms, and with a royal wave to his audience, he put an arm around the waist of his now besotted wife and led her away.

That was the cue for the noisy crowd to disperse down the gang plank while she moved against the flow towards the salon. Ben caught her arm, and for once his face was minus the cheeky grin, his voice one of challenge. "So why did you lead me to believe Jane's husband was old, disapproving and unattractive?"

"I did not! You made assumptions which I couldn't be bothered to contradict."

Confused Ben considered out loud, "Sam didn't either. I've talked to several people no-one is keen to speak of Jane's husband. Why the conspiracy of silence? After that performance he has to be an actor, so what's he in - plays, films, television?"

Another assumption! With only a second of hesitation she answered, "Television!" And as a wicked grin threatened to appear she averted her face and ducked into the drunken humanity still channelling down the deck towards the gang plank. It wasn't a lie! David had represented ITP three times, for three minutes on News At Ten. A hand caught her arm, and thinking it was Ben she turned and scowled. Rosemary took a step back, her face full of trepidation. "Oh sorry Rosemary, I thought you were someone else. What can I do for you?"

The dulcet tones had a forlorn edge. "Jane was giving me a lift home. I can't go on the tube looking like this."

Rosemary was right. The low cut dress, which clung to every curve of her marvellous figure was very provocative to the male eye, and an astounding contrast to Rosemary's dour demeanour and quiet personality. It would take a very special man to have the patience to get beyond what troubled Rosemary. She looked up to see the one she'd hoped to be her special man rushing towards the boat without his Patsy. Her heart lifted, perhaps he was coming to Tower Pier after all. Slightly breathless he arrived to state, "David asked me to give you these. He says the car is parked just along the embankment. Got to dash Patsy's waiting for me with the engine running."

He turned to head back as she put on a brave face to say cheerfully to Rosemary. "Well problem solved. With these you can drive the car to Tower Bridge and wait for Miriam and I to arrive." Rosemary's expression told her she'd said the wrong thing. "What's the matter? You do drive, don't you?"

"Not that car. And not in this dress."

Jill shrugged, "That's your choice."

"But what if I couldn't open the door? Or the engine wouldn't start?

In the office Rosemary exuded a quiet, slightly superior confidence, and, until Jane had befriended her, she would have been quick to criticize the frailties of others. Had that been a façade against fear? As if believing she'd make a negative response Rosemary murmured apologetically, "I, I, don't like being on my own. Or out in a strange place at night!"

Despite the unexpected rush of compassion, she thought quickly, her voice abrupt. "Okay, forget that. You'd better stay on board with me. But you'll have to walk if there isn't a taxi to take us to the car." Rosemary nodded. "Wait for me in the salon, I'll join you there."

A few people were still milling about causing the crew to scowl as they swept up around them, counted the glasses and removed the bottles from the bar. Ian, now at a lose end was helping Ben to carry the DJ's dismantled equipment on to the pier.

"Ah there you are." Jill turned as Miriam continued, "I gather Jane's abandoned Rosemary and she's staying on board with you, in which case you don't need me. Phyllis has offered me a lift home so I'll say goodnight."

Before she could respond Miriam had trotted off to Phyllis waiting on the pier. What a great evening this had turned out to be! Abandoned by Chris for Patsy, Jane for David, Miriam for Phyllis and now landed with Rosemary!

CHAPTER 5

Ian headed towards her. "That's the last of the DJ stuff unloaded. So I'll say 'goodbye'. Thanks for a great evening. A wonderful way to end what has been a good life at ITP, I'll miss everybody."

"We need to move off Missus, time's getting on." The crew man began untying the gang plank.

Ian glanced between her and the captain. "I'd better go."

Jill kissed his cheek, and as his face flushed in surprise she encouraged, "All the best with the new job, and this time when you find a nice girl, sweep her off her feet before someone else does." The boat engines chugged into life, she moved up the gang plank to allow the crew to pull it up. At the top she called, "Bye Ian" and waved as they began to move.

On the empty wooden pier Ian gave a small smile, returned her wave and she watched as he walked away almost colliding with a man running past him towards the boat. Without a care for the ever-increasing gap between it and the shore the man jumped, his short, rotund body landing heavily on the deck as one of the crew men laughed, "You're getting too old and fat for those antics, we didn't think you were going to make it."

In seeing her, he covered the short distance to say in a breathless voice, "I'm Georgio, the owner of this pleasure craft." His eyes flickered to her full breasts as his tongue licked his thick, rubbery lips. "You must be Jill Hart. My cousin's the skipper – Eric. Dom, the barman is my younger brother, my two nephews the crew men. You had a good evening?"

The full-lipped mouth curved open into smile revealing a missing front tooth. A pudgy hand adorned with several cheap rings stretched out to shake hers and held it too long. A feeling of distaste ran through her as she queried, "I assume then I am to settle the bill with you?"

Georgio's podgy arm moved to go around her shoulders, she manoeuvred away. He gave her what could only be termed as a gruesome grin. "Come on inside, have a drink."

In her mind she summed him up: mid-thirties, Greek, greasy and lecherous. If he had any ideas she'd soon put him straight. "I'd prefer you work out the bill, I don't want to be delayed at

Tower Bridge."

"No problemo. Come this way. We've plenty of time to do that and have a drink." She followed him into the salon, and wished Chris or Miriam were with her, but she had Rosemary. Any thought of support or camaraderie from her was short lived for stepping into the salon Rosemary stared helplessly at her because she was virtually pinned behind a table by the tall, thin, swarthy-skinned man seated beside her. "Ah - my cousin, Eric I see has already made acquaintance of... what's your name love?" Rosemary stared, but didn't speak.

Jill frowned. "It's not important. Now, I paid for the boat hire weeks ago, so it's just a matter of the stock take of the bottles consumed." Georgio unperturbed said cordially, "Dom, fetch these ladies a drink?"

Jill glanced at Rosemary, "Orange juice for both of us – thank you."

"Bring us a couple of brandies." Georgio winked at Dom, then leant across the table to Rosemary, "I forget me manners, I'm Georgio." His rubbed his podgy hand against the rib of his widely stretched, rather grubby fisherman's sweater and held it out to Rosemary who shrank back.

Did Rosemary have an aversion to all men or just revolting specimens like these? Sharply she bit out, "Leave her and just get that bar bill?"

Georgio's hand dropped. He slid himself along the bench to sit opposite Rosemary. "No 'arm in being friendly is there?" He patted the bench next to him, "Here Jill, you sit next to me and we'll soon get the business over and done with."

It was hard not to flinch at the gruesome smile, the odorous breath and smell of stale sweat that pervaded her nostrils. As she sank down beside him and reached in her bag for his letter, she said bluntly, "It's Miss Hart to you. Now here is your quote, the price of the boat hire, and cost of any breakages. I've already assessed there were six glasses broken, so your barman just needs to count the empties of beer and spirit from the consignment we agreed would come on board."

"You're a canny miss, without a doubt." Georgio patted her knee,

Her mouth was decidedly tight-lipped, her words curt, "One has to be in business." Her eyes looked down at his hand resting on her knee, as she added, "And Mr Rodriques, this is strictly business!" She waited until he'd moved his hand before continuing, "It may be quicker if you give Dom a hand. The sooner the count is done, the sooner I can write the cheque."

Unexpectedly Georgio's fist hit the table. Both she and Rosemary jumped. "Cheque? I don't want a cheque - I said 'cash'!

Jill gave him a hard look. "I assume you are Mr G. Rodriques?" Before he could do more than nod she produced from her bag another letter attached to their invoice. I wrote confirming our booking and said we would pay with a company cheque, but should this be a problem to let us know. And since that letter I visited the boat, discussed decorations and bar provisions with Eric here, nothing was said so it's a cheque, or nothing."

Georgio glared at Eric. Eric shrugged using that movement to bring his knee into contact with Rosemary who tensed and moved her leg. "What do yer mean, cheque or nothing? You don't think you're getting off without paying. I've paid out good money to stock this boat, I need cash to restock it again for tomorrow."

Jill glanced through the window. Westminster Pier had disappeared, and she could only hope it wouldn't be too long before they reached the mooring at Tower Bridge. "Look, don't blame me if you and Eric didn't read… "

Eric jumped up causing Rosemary to bounce on the bench's air cushion . "Who said I couldn't read, did you tell her, did ya?"

"Oh sit down Eric. I'll sort this." Deflated Eric sat back down almost on top of Rosemary whose expression turned to panic.

"Here's Dom with the drinks, he does the figuring and lettering. Now Jill, I'm sure we can come to some suitable arrangement." Georgio sent her what she presumed he felt was a sexy smile, and a fat hand again rested on her knee.

"Mr Rodriques, the only arrangement will be for you to accept my company's cheque." Seeing his antagonistic expression she thought quickly and said, "Remove your hand from my knee, because my strong, handsome boyfriend would be very angry if he thought you'd been bothering me. I'm sure you get my meaning?"

"You don't expect me to believe that do ya? He'd have been here with you if he existed." Georgio gave one of his grotesque smiles.

Perhaps Georgio wasn't quite as stupid as he appeared. Jill stood, and pointed her finger, "You seem to forget Mr Rodriques that ITP hired this boat and the crew and they have connections with the city's major companies." Georgio slid out from the seat as she continued, "One word of any indiscretion in the way you do business, or hearing of unbecoming behaviour to ITP employees, will, believe me, really reek havoc for your business, and your cash flow."

With eyes wide she watched as her words permeated his brain. Comprehension arrived at the same moment a strangled cry arose behind them. She and Georgio whirled around to see Rosemary, white-faced, her eyes rounded and stunned looking like a rabbit caught in headlights. On Rosemary's face near her mouth was a wet mark, and Eric, as if puzzled at her response was frowning.

Georgio lumbered forward. "Eric leave her be."

"Why should I? What's the matter with the silly bitch anyway? "

Annoyed Jill pointed out, "She's petrified, that's what's wrong with her."

Eric gave a sneering smile, "I ain't done nothing 'cept give her a kiss."

Was the man mad? Was he blind? Coldly Jill stated, "This is sheer stupidity. You can't really believe that Rosemary would want to participate…"

Eric interrupted. "Ooh 'ark at you, darling! I bet you do a lot of participating, not like this one though, right cold fish, she needs the kiss of life." With that he lunged toward Rosemary. In an instant the frightened rabbit eyes filled with a ferocious madness. Long finger nails lashed out in a flash of colour, heading to gouge out Eric's eyes. He yelped and pulled away. They missed his eyes, but scored down his cheeks making three deep strips on each and drawing blood. A string of invective shot from Eric's mouth.

Rosemary in the tiny gap now half stood, half lent over Eric. Her eyes full of crazed fear, her hands drawn up as claws with red talons ready to strike and tear. The long dark hair and red dress added to the portrait of a witch, but more frightening was the banshee wail that went with it. It was horrible, as if something awful trapped inside Rosemary was now breaking out. It frightened the hell out of Eric. He knocked over a glass of orange, cursed, swore and catching Rosemary's hands, thrust her back down into the seat. All the while shouting, "You stupid bitch – you're mad, start, staring mad." Stunned by events she watched Eric slap Rosemary's face. The effect was immediate. The wail stopped, she went limp, her eyes filled with blind terror and hatred.

Eric now able to escape dragged himself out from behind the table, wiped his hands across the front of his grubby jumper, and with his scored, bleeding face he looked like something out of a horror movie. Shaken he leant against the bar.

Dom rushing in demanded. "Hell's teeth, what was that terrible noise?" He took one look at Eric, moping his wounds with a bit of oily rage from his pocket, and went decidedly pale. "Cor blimey! What 'appened 'ere?" Fascinated he looked around as though trying to piece together a puzzle. No-one moved or answered.

In a shocked daze, they looked at Rosemary slumped in the seat, her dress awry and a good amount of breast exposed. One side of her face was red, with a trace of Eric's blood from where his hand had touched his face before hitting her.

They jumped as Georgio bellowed, "Eric, get yourself up them stairs and this boat to the Bridge fast."

Completely out of her depth, she moved to sit next to Rosemary in the hope that meaningless words would bring comfort.

Georgio warily watching finally answered Dom's question. "Eric give her a little kiss and the woman went crazy."

On seeing Dom staring at Rosemary's half naked breasts bouncing with her erratic breathing, she leant to pull Rosemary's dress to cover her up. For one tense moment, despite her reassuring words, Rosemary opened her mouth as though to scream, missed her breath and gasped for air.

The boat's engines revved as Dom observed, "Fresh air might help." Then with nothing more to say, or to see, he ambled off to finish washing the glasses.

Georgio's lip licking wasn't desire now but anxiety about his business if she carried out her previous threat. In trying to help Rosemary she suggested, "Try to breathe more slowly. I'm going to stand over there and no-one will come near you."

With a grab at her bag she moved out of Rosemary's hearing and drew Georgio with her. "Maybe ignoring her for a few minutes might help. Get that bill added up, I'll write the cheque, and then if she's better we needn't hang about on reaching the Pier. Severely rattled Georgio did as he was bid, while she wondered if Rosemary's gasping for breath was as frightening to her as it sounded to them.

A few minutes later the boat juddered, the engines died. In the quiet lapping of water the frightened gasping sounded twice as loud. "It's okay Rosemary, I've paid the bill. We can get off the boat now." Rosemary seemed incapable of movement. After

72

several tries of being either brisk or cajoling she decreed, "Mr Rodriques you're going to have to find a telephone and call an ambulance?" Georgio's language was even more profound than it had been earlier, the result being he wasn't calling no ambulance for any stupid girl. "You know what comes with ambulances... police and you know what they'd have to say."

"Well how else are we going to get her off this boat? I can't carry her, she won't let any of you near her, and I can't leave her to get assistance. It's your fault, so you'll have to take the consequences."

Scared Georgio bellowed, "Get her off my boat."

Infuriated she yelled back, "And how to you propose I do that?"

At that Georgio marched across to the table, slammed down his fist, and said, "I've had enough. Pull yourself together and get out, or I'll drag you out!"

If Rosemary's face could have gone paler, it did. If her breathing could have got worse, it did. "Right then, you've asked for this. Glad you've come back in Dom, be my witness, I don't want anyone to say I molested her." The boat rocked against the wharf as Georgio dived in behind the table.

Jill in an attempt to stop him grabbed him from behind, shouting, "No, No. Stop you'll make things worse. Leave her. Please. Stop…!"

A piercing whistle stopped everything. Jill and Georgio whirled around. She fully expected to see the police. Instead a tall figure had appeared with muscles rippling through a thin black silk shirt, feet apart, arms folded, blue eyes like flint, his expression was one to wilt the hardest foe. And if he'd spun round transforming his clothes to tight trousers, blue cloak and shirt with a large red 'S' on it, she doubted she could have been more surprised! With their full attention Ben Fletcher demanded, "What is going on here?"

In relief Jill gasped, "I never thought I'd be so pleased to see you."

Ben, his eyes appraising the situation, nodded, and giving her a brief smile said, "In that case I'm glad I came!" With that he removed the slumped rag doll in the red dress with the trailing long hair from Georgio's arms while asking, "What happened?" No-one answered as they watched him carry Rosemary to the long padded bench seat near the open door and lay her gently on it.

In finding his voice Georgio attempted to explain. "Err I, don't know. She got frightened, couldn't breathe, wouldn't let us help, I grabbed her, she passed out."

Fascinated Jill watched as Ben sat on a low coffee table, tipped back Rosemary's head and peered down her throat, "Did she choke on something? Has she been sick?"

When neither of the men answered she volunteered, "No, she was frightened by the skipper. He made a pass at her."

Ben checked Rosemary's vital signs, examined her face and stated, "And he hit her."

Georgio grimly countered, "You haven't seen what she did to him." Ben righted Rosemary into a sitting position and stuck her head between her knees. "Eric didn't mean nothing. But we had to get her out from behind that table and off this boat. She'll be alright, won't she?" Rosemary stirred.

"Get a glass of water, and a clean cloth," Ben demanded. Then crouching in front of Rosemary he gently pulled aside the curtain of hair and spoke quietly, "Hello Rosemary. It's me, Ben, remember me? We sat together at dinner. You'll be alright, you fainted."

As Ben continued to reassure Rosemary Jill sat down beside her and contemplated his unexpected appearance. What was he doing here? Although grateful for the way he'd taken command and his obvious ability to deal with the situation, she wasn't going to pander to delusions of Superman! At Georgio's re-entry she refocused to realise Ben, with a small smile, was taking in her ruffled appearance. With a tut and a sigh she attempted to straighten herself out.

Georgio proffered a glass of brandy, "Look I'm sorry about the girl, give her this."

In helping Rosemary sit up Ben said curtly, "I asked for water."

After a stumbled apology Georgio mumbled, "Shame for it to go to waste" threw it down his own throat before disappearing again.

Still crouched down in front of Rosemary Ben's again looked across at her this time to talk as if she were his patient's relative. She wasn't sure which was more irritating, that, or his lusting after her. "Rosemary's had a panic attack which caused what's known as hyper ventilation. It's as frightening to those around as to the victim. The best cure is to get the person to breathe slowly in and out of a brown paper bag. She passed out through lack of air getting to the lungs, but the body is amazing how quickly it rights itself."

Tight-lipped and on the verge of sarcasm at his superior attitude it was probably fortunate Georgio reappeared with the water.

"Now Rosemary try sipping this? Can you hold it yourself? Still a bit shaky, I'll help you. Once you feel stronger we'll get you safely home."

Jill admitted to herself she too felt a little shaky now that it was all over. And despite the way she felt about Ben, it was a relief to hear him take the responsibility from her, which brought her to ask, "How come you're here?"

"Later, let's get Rosemary home first. When she's able to walk I'll nip off and call a cab?"

"Jane left the car for us on the embankment near Westminster Pier. Originally she and Rosemary were going to drive up here to pick me up, but well…" Ridiculously she could feel the tears she'd been holding back all evening threatening. Quickly she stood up, and moved away to fumble in her bag while muttering, "I must blow my nose. Now where's my handkerchief?"

Concerned Ben came up behind her. "This must have been frightening for you too?"

With a wave of her hand she brushed him off. "I'm fine."

There was a brief silence in which she blew her nose and then Ben said, "It's not too late for me to get the tube to Westminster, I'll bring the car for the two of you." He addressed Georgio, "No more antics, and whilst I'm away get these girls a hot, strong and sweet cup of tea. Now Jill give me the car keys and I'll be back as soon as possible." Without hesitation she dived in her bag, while telling him the make and registration number. It wasn't until he'd gone off at a run she realised just how ridiculously trusting she'd been with a man she'd only met a few days before.

Eric hadn't reappeared, probably in hiding. Around the red mark on Rosemary's cheek, her colour was returning. Georgio having disappeared into the small galley on Ben's instructions returned with two hot mugs of steaming tea, and then went out closing the door behind him. In a forlorn voice Rosemary whispered, "I'm sorry. They scared me."

Jill gave her a rueful smile. "I think in the end it was you who scared them! You certainly had me worried, and thank God for Ben, I didn't think I'd ever hear myself say that about either God or Ben!"

Rosemary responded with a faint smile, and they sat in companionable silence. Ben had gone up in her estimation, but the antagonism he ignited remained.

They drank their tea listening to the gentle sound of water lapping against the mooring. It was so quiet she wondered if they'd been left alone on the boat.

Thirty minutes later she glanced again at her watch. Each time she tried to figure out how long it would take Ben to walk to the station, get the train, find the car and drive back, she drifted off. Rosemary curled up on the seat seemed asleep.

The cabin door opened. From the doorway Georgio announced, "Your boyfriend's back." Jill roused herself. "You know I thought you were having me on earlier, but I recognised him immediately from your description, a special bloke, ain't he?" Georgio's gruesome grin was somewhat rueful, "I wouldn't want 'im giving me a punch on the nose!"

Ben came up behind him. "The car's here, top of the steps." He looked at Georgio, "Who wouldn't you want punching you on the nose?"

Georgio gave a tense laugh, "You, her boyfriend!"

As Ben sent her a seductive smile she had a distinct urge to punch Georgio in the mouth.

Turning to Georgio Ben's face hardened, his voice cold, "If I find someone has touched a girl on which I have staked a claim…" Ben sucked in his breath. Georgio looked suitably apprehensive. At that Ben lightened up, "But I'm sure that won't be necessary here." The relief on Georgio's face was evident, as was the chameleon character of Ben that gave him the ability to rise to every occasion.

Staked his claim – not on her, not likely, but a chivalrous man who stood up for his woman was romantic! With a thinly disguised sarcasm she purred, "Come then my knight in shining armour, take us to our chariot!"

That ever mischievous grin appeared as he challenged with a sultry gaze, "Indeed my lady, and be aware I wield my sword with equal dexterity."

She gave him a sick, humourless smile, her thought, oh spare me that!

Georgio gave a lewd laugh. "Cor blimey mate, you acts and speaks like something out of a film, I can see the woman loves it." No marks out of ten then for Georgio's sensitivity and perception

Rosemary awakened by their voices was sitting up looking dazed. Ben asked, "Do you feel strong enough to walk?" As she attempted to stand he put his hand under her elbow, steadied her then ventured, "Will you trust me to carry you?" Amazed she saw her nod, and realised that despite her height and figure Rosemary was quite frail. Her thought confirmed by Ben. "You're very light, this part won't be a problem, but you'll have to climb the steps to the road they are too narrow for me to carry you. Right Jill, you follow me."

Inside she seethed, but obeyed. First he'd given the impression he'd 'staked his claim' on her, now he was commanding she should follow him. A hand caught her arm breaking into her thoughts and holding her back.

"Miss Hart, look no hard feelings eh – about tonight? You won't 'err, well what you said earlier? This is a family business if I lose the trade, we lose the boat, and we all lose our livelihood."

Tired from the evening's roller coaster ride of emotions, feelings and revelations, she let anger rip through her. "You should have thought of that before. Did you really think we'd be interested in either of you? Oh I can look after myself, but you, or at least Eric, scared my friend half to death? If that's the way you carry on you don't deserve a family, a boat or a business. In fact if that's the way you carry on I'm surprised you still have a boat."

Georgio whined, "It was just a bit of fun. Eric didn't mean no harm. She, that Rosemary didn't say 'no', and he's not very bright." Worried he rubbed his fat hand across his mouth, then winged, "Please don't destroy my business. What can I say? What can I do?"

"Promise me that you'll never even think about, let alone attempt to do anything like that again?"

"Oh I won't – it fair spooked us all, we're changed men after tonight."

"You'd better be, because if I should hear even as much as a whisper that something like this has happened on your boat - you will be finished." She stalked away across the gang plank and to where Ben was helping Rosemary up the last step. Noting her grim expression Ben asked, "Am I to understand you've sorted that problem out?"

She nodded, "I hope so."

"Good. Let's get Rosemary in the back of the car, you sit with her and I'll drive you home." Too tired now to argue, she climbed in next to Rosemary as he settled himself in the driving seat. In a stately, but amused voice she commanded from the rear, "Drive on Benjamin, and careful as you go."

Ben catching her eye in the mirror touched his forelock, "Yes ma'am, but perhaps you'd like to tell me where to go."

Unable to resist she laughed, "Ah yes, Ben, I've been trying to do that all night, but in these unusual circumstances I'll be more amenable."

With his eyes on the road ahead he answered, "I'd like that."

She didn't reply beyond giving directions. Within minutes Rosemary was dozing against her shoulder giving her the opportunity to ask, "Ben, I'm grateful you rescued us, but why were you at Tower Bridge?"

"I stopped Ian when you didn't leave with him. He explained you were going with the boat to Tower Bridge to settle the bills. I asked if he thought that was wise, a woman alone and he said Rosemary was with you." Ben gave a derisive laugh. "I saw that man jump on as the boat slipped its moorings, and didn't like the idea of you both alone on the boat, or making your way home from the embankment." He chuckled, "I considered diving into the Thames and swimming after you but decided that was unwise. Instead I caught the train to Tower Bridge and was at the top of the jetty steps when the boat arrived. It tied up, but you didn't get off so I sauntered down to the pier to find where you were. It was then I heard you shouting and peered through the cabin window as Georgio dived on Rosemary. I jumped on board, the rest, as they say, is history!"

Jill smiled in the darkness. "You and Jane could have a competition, she makes a piercing whistle too. And thank you, I'm not sure what would have happened if you hadn't showed up. You could have a career as a policeman? Although from what I've seen tonight I think you would have made a good doctor."

Ben gave a sad grunt. "Thank you. As to being a policeman, I'm afraid that career is out for me too. But in those circumstances my body building does give me that edge of authority! And tonight was just a case of basic first aid. Everyone should know that. You can go on a short course with St Johns Ambulance, you never know when it could be useful and you might save a life?

"Turn right at those lights, then straight on where the main road bends to the right. I don't know about that, but as you're going to be working at ITP why don't you run a course for the staff?"

"That sounds good to me." With a mischievous chuckle he went on, "As long as you're my partner when it comes to mouth to mouth resuscitation!"

"I may be grateful Ben, but not that grateful. Now after this next turn, you are on the main road and its fairly straight forward then to High Street Ken." Ten minutes later they drove on to the drive when it occurred to Jill to ask, "Where do you live? And how are you going to get home, the trains will have stopped running by now?"

"Let's get Rosemary inside. I'll think about that later. If you've got her keys open the front door and I'll bring her through."

In a quiet voice he spoke to the sleepy Rosemary gently reassuring her as he drew her out of the car before picking her up and ordering, "Jill, tell me where to go, then lock up the car."

"Through the inner door, along the hall, second door on left, it should be open then follow the corridor and down the stairs. Quickly she locked the car, caught up with Ben as he carefully negotiated his way through the flat door towards the stairs.

Once having turned the bend in the stairs Ben exclaimed quietly, "Rosemary you've sure got a posh pad here."

"Oh this isn't Rosemary's flat, it's mine."

Ben placed Rosemary on the settee. "Then why are we here?"

Jill looked down at Rosemary's pale face, accentuated by the redness of her dress. "Rosemary I hope you don't mind I brought you back here because I don't know where you live, nor do I think you are in a fit state to be alone. As you are thinking about living here you might as well stay and try your bed out before you move in."

A door opened to a sleepy, hair-tussled Helen. "What's going on? I was just falling asleep A beatific smile replaced the somewhat disgruntled features, "Oh hello! Who are you?"

With an amused grin he answered, "I'm Ben, and you are...?"

"Helen. And I am pleased to meet you." Helen put out her hand and giggled when Ben lifted it to his lips and kissed it saying, "Likewise."

Jill made a nauseous expression behind Ben's back and then felt bad as Rosemary on the settee said in a shaky voice, "I don't want to put you out?

"It's fine, that wasn't err... you know for you."

"Crumbs Rosemary what's happened to you! You look washed out." She giggled, "Don't tell me you got river sick?"

"Ben I'll leave you to explain, and perhaps Helen you could make Rosemary a cup of tea while I get sheets and things for the bed."

Helen and Ben were busy flirting in the kitchen when she

returned, which Helen briefly stopped to explain, "Rosemary's in the bathroom, Ben and I are making the tea" before continuing her conversation and ignoring her.

Jill grunted, and headed towards Tania's ex-bedroom as Ben suggested, "Helen you finish off getting that tea, mine's milk with two sugars, and I'll give Jill a hand with the bed, it's so much easier with two."

Ben was right, and very efficient at bed making. Back in the lounge he ordered, "Right Rosemary the bed's ready, you go and get in it and Jill will bring you in a cup of tea. A good night's rest will do you good, and I'm sure there is no need to hurry to get up in the morning."

As Ben disappeared into the toilet Helen followed her into the kitchen to comment, "Now there's a man worth having. He's gorgeous, so wicked and mischievous, yet fancy him being concerned enough to make sure you were both safe. He tells me he's about to start work at ITP. Who is he after do you think, you or Rosemary?

"Why should he be after either of us?"

Helen's eyes had gone dreamy, "Well if he isn't, he's just what I'm after. Cheeky and fun, sultry and sexy, sensitive but firm, I bet he's a good kisser and has plenty of stamina in bed."

Tired, she said somewhat grimly, "If you say so Helen. He's certainly not my type. His turning up tonight was fortuitous, but I'm not sure of his motives. He appeared like Superman - too good to be true. But he's been very kind and caring to Rosemary. And don't forget its only days since you had a lucky escape."

Helen's face reddened with embarrassment. With that Jill poured out the tea and took it into Rosemary. She stayed with her until she drank her tea and hoped when she returned to the lounge Ben would have gone, But he jumped up from talking with Helen as she emerged to ask, "How is she?"

"Ready to fall asleep. She asked me to thank you. And I'd say the same. Now the only problem is you getting home, and as I am too tired to drive you, how about you take the car and bring it back tomorrow morning."

Before Ben could reply Helen chipped, "What's the point in Ben driving home to have to return the car in the morning? He can sleep on the settee, and it's very comfortable it makes into a bed. I'll show you. Jill, why don't you fetch the bedding from the airing cupboard?"

Car keys in hand Jill gave Helen a hard stare. His helping in crisis was one thing, but sleeping over in her flat!

Ben looked between them, "Well if it's no trouble, it would be simpler, it is late, and I am tired, so thanks I'd appreciate that."

What could she say: it was trouble, it wasn't simple, and too bad he was tired! But that would be mean as he'd put himself out for their safety. She pursed her lips as Helen batting her eyelids threw the scatter cushions at him. And with no alternative she went to get the bedding as Ben was already under instruction on how to make the settee into a bed. Cross she was even more irritated hearing Helen's comments as she climbed the stairs. "Your muscles are amazing? You must do a lot of training. I bet you're really strong."

Fiercely Jill pulled the sheets from the airing cupboard. It was bad enough Ben was encroaching on her personal life and flat without Helen making a play for him. On her return to the lounge she dumped the bedding on the other settee and said as calmly as she could muster. "Here you are. I'll leave you to Helen's care. I'm dead on my feet. Goodnight, sleep well." Before either of them could speak she headed back up the stairs and was around the corner before Ben called out 'good night'.

After a restless night she awoke early with her mouth feeling like a sewer and wished last night she'd thought to bring up some milk. Now she'd have to go downstairs to make a cup of tea. For a while she lay contemplating the events of yesterday, then in a fit of exasperation and need she threw back the bedclothes, put on her dressing gown and padded down the stairs.

To get to the kitchen she passed the back of the settee on which Ben was sleeping. Unable to resist the opportunity to study him more closely she paused and looked down on him. Helen was right, even with overnight stubble he was good looking. His face might be boyish, but it certainly wasn't weak. The short blond tufted hair was perhaps a statement to his cheeky spirit. In repose, with his bright, observant, blue eyes no longer assessing, his words no longer irritating, she felt a stir of sexual attraction at the bare muscular chest with its fine hair. And it wasn't hard to imagine those long slim hands and sensitive fingers caressing her body. .

For a moment she allowed herself to ponder on how that very kissable mouth might feel against hers. A rueful smile touched her lips. Why, when his obvious charisma charmed others, did her hackles rise along with a need to put him in his place? In his place…? Was she getting like Miriam, heaven forbid? With a shake of her head she padded on into the kitchen, put on the kettle and considered her new resolution of sexual abstention.

Ben's voice broke into her thoughts, "Tell me, did you like what you saw?"

Already feeling the blush rising, she glared at his half naked body as he leant nonchalantly against the door post and snapped, "Pardon?"

"Come on Jill - you know what I mean."

"The kettle's boiling do you want a cup of tea or coffee? She reached into the cupboard for two mugs.

"I was hard put not to grin when you smiled down at me. Truth is I'd have liked to grab and kiss you, but decided with your flatmates around it might not be wise to be seen making love to you in the middle of …"

Inflamed at his effrontery she spun round. "Just what is it with you?" He'd moved nearer. Annoyed she pushed past him, "Will you move out of my way?" From the fridge she pulled out, and opened a bottle of milk. "Here take this and put it in the cups." With his back to her she took a deep breath and said in a tight voice, "What I saw on my settee was a man I hardly know, and hadn't invited, sleeping in my flat. If I smiled, it was because I was wondering how he had managed to worm his way into a job, a boat trip, my flat and my life in so short a time!"

Ben held up his hands as though to ward off her words. "Whoa, whoa hold on lady! I haven't wormed my way in anywhere! The only place I've been where I wasn't directly invited was your rendezvous with the captain and crew, but I'd say there I had a warm welcome."

Those bright blue eyes held hers, he was right of course, but she determined not to feel bad about it. Why had he been waiting for her anyway? Those men had been harmless enough. It wasn't her fault that Rosemary was foisted on her then had a panic attack. And if Helen hadn't invited him to stay she wouldn't have to be putting up with him now. Annoyed she broke from his gaze and rummaging in the cupboard offered, "Cornflakes or Weetabix"?

"I'll have cornflakes, Ben what do you want?"

Jill whirled round in amazement. What was Helen doing up at this unearthly hour on a Saturday, it was a miracle if she rose before ten, but seven and..... hair brushed? Was that a whisper of make-up? There was certainly a waft of perfume and the sexist nightdress she'd ever seen her in. Well she was welcome to him, she'd invited him, she could entertain him.

While Helen chatted she made herself a breakfast tray and without interrupting their conversation moved passed them into the lounge. She didn't need to turn to know Ben's eyes were on her, and as she rounded the corner of the stairs Helen's comment drifted up, "Oh ignore Jill, she can be tetchy in the morning!" Although untrue, on this particular one she agreed, she felt decidedly tetchy! Through Helen her territory had once more been invaded. Again she'd had to retreat to her bedroom. That man was a challenge, and one she determined she would be rid of.

Back in bed, she looked with pleasure at her room dappled in the early morning sun and told herself it was going to be a good day. Ben couldn't stay for ever, and she was going to have a leisurely breakfast and bath. Even after a long soak she was amazed to find that her crown of curls was still hard and feeling glued in place! Dressed, feeling far more in control of her life, she decided, after two hours Ben must have got the message he'd outstayed his welcome and left.

The instant she headed down the stairs she realised by the voices in the lounge her mistake. Oh this was ridiculous it was her flat, she wasn't going to be shut in, he was going to be shut out! Determined she would smile, be polite, but firm she took a deep breath and rounded the corner.

Ben stood as she appeared, "Hello Jill, I was waiting to see you to say thank you for letting me stay." He looked toward Helen, "I must be going, things to do, places to go, you know."

Her manner and smile as she replied, "Oh must you, and so soon." was so full of sarcasm, he couldn't miss it.

He hadn't. He gave her a long look, and then bestowed Helen a wry grin, "Thank you Helen for your hospitality, for breakfast, I appreciated your efforts."

Helen – breakfast? Then she realised Ben had thanked Helen for her efforts, not the food she produced, hardly surprising, she was no cook. Helen's animated laugh grated on her nerves. Across the room she frowned as Helen, still clad in her sexy nightdress, asked Ben. "Don't you want to wait until Rosemary's up, she'll want to thank you for rescuing her." Ben may not have been welcomed by her, but Helen had done her best.

Jill's eyes rested on Ben, her smile wintry. "I'm sure Rosemary will seek you out at ITP to thank you." Helen scowled, and she felt like scowling back, although Helen wasn't to know how much this man annoyed her. "I'll see you out Ben, have you got everything?" Quickly her eyes assessed the room she didn't want him to have any excuses for coming back. She noted the neatly folded pile of bedding on the settee. Not Helen's way, so full marks to Ben for that.

Those bright eyes twinkled as he looked between them, "I came with little, I go with little, I only leave my heart behind!"

Jill pursed her lips and looked at the ceiling. Helen giggled, "Oh dear, you'd better take this with you, and come back soon." With that Helen moved in to capture his mouth with hers. For a second Ben seemed taken aback, but quickly recovered to clasp Helen against him. In a loud voice, as though kissing Helen would make him deaf, she announced, "When you have finished Ben I'll be upstairs." With that she marched up the stairs into the main hall and gave a silent scream. The last thing she needed was Helen to make Ben her latest man for then he'd have reason to frequent the flat.

The upstairs flat door opened Jane came down with a flight bag, stopping when she spotted her. "Hey Jill, you'll never guess where we're going?"

Aggravation rose up and caught in her throat, she just knew what was going to happen next.

"David's making up for being away. We're off to Paris for a romantic..." Jane's eyes widened and looked beyond her.

Without turning she knew why.

Above her head David called down, "Jane, I'll take the large case to the car, but have you got the flight..." David bounding down stopped a stair up from Jane, "Oh hello Jill" and then followed Jane's gaze.

Now they'd both get the wrong impression! She made a disgruntled face at Jane then turned, "Jane, you met Ben didn't you last night, Ben this is David, Jane's husband." On turning she saw Ben had that ruffled, just had a good toss in the sack look, his lips still reddened by Helen's kiss. Oh great now what would they think?

David slid past Jane to put the case at the foot of the stairs. Ben stepped forward his hand outstretched to shake David's hand. "Ah Ben, yes, pleased to meet you." A brief frown crossed David's face, as if something had triggered in his mind before he gave a wry smile. "I heard you had a good time last night especially dancing the cha cha cha!"

She and Jane exchanged a glance. Ben flashed Jane with a cheeky grin before commenting to David, "You wife is a very accomplished dancer."

Jane giggled. David gave her a brief questioning look before once again addressing Ben. "Well, we must be going. It's good to meet you." He glanced at Jill, and then continued, "I expect we shall be seeing more of you?"

Incensed she began to babble wildly, "Oh no! It's not like that. After you left last night ..." she continued until finally running down, "...so Ben was tired and Helen suggested he sleep…"

David interrupted. "I think Jill we've got the message, and the picture." In his own inimitable way he slapped his thigh and gave one of his roars of laughter.

Jane grimaced and asked, "Is Rosemary alright? I should go and see her."

David cautioned, "No time Jane, we have to go. Jill will look after her." He turned to pump Ben's hand again. "Well done. Good start. I've no doubt my sister will have given those men short shrift." David shot her a bemused look before continuing, "But I'm sure she's very thankful for your help with Rosemary. Now you'll have to excuse us we must go, we've a flight to catch."

"Here let me." Ben, helpful as ever picked up the case. David took the flight bag from Jane, and as they went out the front door Jane said, "I've left the flat door open, there's some food in the fridge that needs eating and take the flowers and enjoy them, we'll be away a week." With eyes twinkling with mischief she quietly added, "Give him a chance." Before she could retaliate Jane was gone. Seething at events she watched as David rolled down the car window to ask, "Ben do you need a lift?"

Ben shook his head. "Thanks anyway, but the airport's the wrong direction and I don't want to hold you up. It was nice to meet you. I'll look out for you on the television."

David gave him a small smile and shot her an odd look before gunning the engine and reversing out into the street, leaving her and Ben on the doorstep to wave them off. Furious at his intruding into her personal life, and now that of her family, she considered jumping back inside and slamming the door in his face.

Had Ben read her thoughts for he stepped back, and in so doing blocked her entry into the house? "How strange, I was waiting to say 'goodbye' to you, and it seems we've said 'goodbye' to them. Why didn't you tell me that Jane's husband is your brother?" The word 'impudent' sprung to mind. "Close to, I can see the family likeness in the face shape, black hair and dark eyes." Ben's eyes crinkled with his cheeky grin, "Same build, except where he's muscle you're curves!"

The coldness of her voice matched her exasperation. "Ben I'm not interested in your observations, and it isn't my practice to explain my family connections with employees."

Ben shrugged, "Sorry – you're right. Your brother must be doing well to have such a beautiful house in such a nice neighbourhood. I can't remember seeing him on television, or the name David Hart in any credits".

"So you watch a lot television, do you?"

Ben's finger caught in the end of a long curly tendril of hair by her ear, and playing with it he murmured, "You don't like me very much do you?"

"It's not for me to like or dislike anyone."

"What an evasive reply."

She pulled her hair out of his hand. "Look, I was very grateful for your help last night. Thank you, I appreciated it. But I didn't ask you to stay the night. And I want that to be an end of it. From now on between you and I its strictly business. Am I making myself clear?"

Bright blue eyes stared into hers as a slow sultry smile endorsed his words. "Has anyone ever told you how beautiful you are first thing in the morning?"

With her finger she pointed down the road to state coldly, "Go before I find reason to abort your employment."

"Or how your face lights up when you're angry, like now."

Every fibre of her being wanted to wipe that look off his face, her hands balled into fists at her side.

He gave a gentle laugh. "I know you'd like to hit me, but I've got a better idea and I'll risk my employment for it." She'd no time to consider what he meant. With speed and agility he moved her around to inside the front door locking her body between his and the wall. His mouth covered hers and powerless to move her mind went into overdrive. How dare he! Just wait Ben Fletcher…

It was impossible to fight and her body was already responding to the cool, gentle, yet firm kiss which was as persuasive as erotic. On her Richter scale of kisses this was one that would rate highly for its earth shaking quality, helped by his instinctive ability to set off her erogenous zones. The promise of the seismic scale of sexual encounter Ben was offering it would be all too easy to throw caution to the wind.

The hands, which had first cupped her face slid to her neck, shivers spiralled through her, a prelude to her body firing up on all cylinders in expectancy of fulfilment. Helen's observations were right this man would be good in bed. But this was Ben, and she didn't like him, or his attitude. Despite that her body cried for satisfaction, she stiffened against it. Anywhere more private, with anyone but him would have probably had them tearing each others clothes off, but she forced herself to cry against his mouth, "Let me go." To her surprise he complied and the sudden release had her almost sliding down the wall. To disguise the weakness she felt in her limbs, and not trusting her voice, she pulled open the door to indicate her wishes.

His eyes gazed into hers, heavy, sultry. With a hand raised as though in surrender, he stepped out, and with a wry smile declared, "I've got the message, rest assured it was very loud, and very clear!" With that he winked, turned and walked jauntily off down the street whistling as he went.

CHAPTER 6

Impatiently Jill tapped the wheel of the car. It being nice weather, the beginning of August, and the Bank Holiday weekend she should have expected this nose to tail traffic hold-up. But with Gemma's husband on a golfing weekend in Scotland they'd still have all day tomorrow together.

A smile touched her lips. Dear Gemma, the fun they'd had, as they called it, 'playing the field'. New to London, too embarrassed by Stephen's defection to contact friends, she'd been stuck in a typing pool of bitchy girls who bullied her when the supervisor wasn't around. It was an all time low. Then Gemma arrived, and to her surprise stuck up for her, only to say later, "I don't know what your problem is, and don't want to, but stop stuffing your face, lose some weight, come out with me and get a life. This is London, the swinging sixties, enjoy the freedom it brings. She'd taken her advice, and 'played the field' of pubs, dance halls and nightclubs from which came subsequent dates, and there had been times when she'd dated three men in one week. She chortled remembering how they'd invented 'star' charts giving points for dress sense, personality, character, fun, fitness and sexual prowess. Shy at first it had taken a while to get into sexual freedom. Boys younger than her often bored her, those older had more finesse, but any that could be Mr Right had no desire for a long term relationship. So their motto had become, 'love 'em and leave 'em, then no-one gets hurt.'

When she moved to ITP they'd upped their stakes by escorting business men, often on business accounts to some very exclusive and expensive places. Some were middle-aged, obviously married, they rarely slept with them, others had potential and they'd added to the motto, '…so if you can't be good, be careful.' They often laughed about that until Gemma became pregnant! With no steady boyfriend to fall back on she hadn't forgotten how distraught Gemma had been and how they had discussed into the night abortion, single parenthood, or finding a man to marry her. Gemma's Catholic upbringing ruled out the former, so the unexpected proposal from an older friend whom she looked on as a brother was fortuitous, except it had come with the proviso that she have a quiet family wedding, drop her London friends and move away. Henry had to be a good man to take on someone else's child, but from Gemma's letters he did sound rather stuffy and boring. The last time they had been together was the housewarming party she and David gave at New Year over eighteen months ago. By then Gemma who had been going to be her first flat mate had accepted her fate and was married three weeks later.

In those days it would have been unthinkable that Rosemary would become her flatmate, but it was now six weeks since she'd arrived and it was working out amazingly well. Rosemary, spooked from the boat incident, had been eager to move in and an accommodating landlady had released her from the mews cottage with only a week's notice. And that brought her to Ben!

In the five weeks he'd been working in the Print Department, she'd heard nothing but praise for his work, attitude and charm. Sam, pleased with his knowledge of the machinery and printing techniques was also delighted to find that he was both brawn and brains and been quick to turn the paperwork over to him while he spent time caring for his beloved machines. To Ben's credit he'd heeded her words. At work he kept his distance, any acknowledgement of her had been a cheeky grin and a touch of his forelock.

She let the clutch in and put the car in first gear to move a car length further up the road and giving a heavy sigh she thought unfortunately, that wasn't true at home!

On the Monday after the boat trip pleased and happy so many people had thanked her she'd arrived home, kicked off her shoes, dropped her coat on her bed and run down the stairs calling, "Helen, fancy a cuppa?" Her glance into the lounge was met with three pairs of eyes. Admittedly, Ben sitting on the settee facing the stairs did look slightly sheepish as Helen jumped up to announce brightly, as if she couldn't see, "Jill, Ben's here. He came to see how Rosemary was."

Rosemary gave an enigmatic smile.

Annoyed, and in a voice laced in sarcasm, she commented, "How lucky for him then that she was here. Rosemary, have you arranged a date to move in?"

Helen, perched on the arm of the settee by Ben's arm, answered for her. "Oh, it's all set for next week. And I told Ben that you wouldn't mind if he borrowed the car to collect Rosemary's things." Then as if noticing her disapproval asked, "Oh, that was alright wasn't it? I mean Jane's away, it's not in use, and Ben drove you home the other night. You once said, if I could drive I could borrow it." Rosemary slipped away to the toilet as Helen now ill at ease babbled on, "I haven't seen you since Ben rang last night to ask after Rosemary. I told him she would be at work today. I didn't realise he hadn't started yet. I told him Rosemary was bringing a suitcase around tonight and he kindly met her at ITP to help her with it." Helen threw Ben a winning smile, and finished, "I thought you might all arrive together. Anyway we were just about to have a coffee, do you want one?"

Her sharp refusal of coffee and the hard look she'd given to Ben had been enough for him to stand and say, "Helen forget the coffee, how about you and me go for a drink down your local pub?"

At that prospect Helen's eyes lit up, "I'll get my bag."

The moment Helen disappeared into her bedroom she'd stepped toward Ben and seethed through clenched teeth, "I thought I told you I didn't want you involved in my life."

Those bright blue eyes laughed into hers. "I can't see how helping Rosemary and taking Helen out for a drink is being involved in your life."

"You're here aren't you? This is my flat. And how do you know the telephone number, it's ex-directory?"

That cheeky smile appeared. "The number is on the dial, I noted it down when I stayed the night." She was about to ask 'why' when Helen emerged from her room on a waft of perfume. Instead she had to make do with glaring at him. That one telephone call had escalated into borrowing the car and being around to help Rosemary move in!

The tooting of a horn brought her back to the present. There were several car lengths between her and the one in front. Her annoyance at Ben refuelled by her thoughts caused her to slam the car into gear, jerk forward and stall the engine. She cursed Ben, and the man behind blasting his horn again. The Morris Minor took several false starts before it chugged sluggishly forward and she noticed the temperature gauge was into the red. What she needed was an open road to cool it down. With time to study the map she saw there was a village off to the left and minor roads would bring her out further up and maybe past the traffic. Pleased with her quick thinking she hummed tunelessly as she waited to indicate and turn. Within minutes she was back in fourth gear, window open on clear air and passing through a very pretty country village with a view of undulating green fields, trees and hedges.

Several miles on through windy, narrow roads she began to wonder if she were lost. These 'B' roads didn't seem very clearly signposted. A triangle of green gave her the option of two roads. This would be a good time to stop and consult the map. The good news was finding a name on the map which was also on the signpost, but the bad news was she'd gone several miles too far. Oh well, it wouldn't take long to go back. She reversed the car, put her foot down and accelerated up the road, but instead of the power increasing it was decreasing. She pumped the accelerator with her foot and exclaimed, "Oh for goodness sake, what's the matter with you, you were only serviced last week?" But neither the car nor the accelerator responded. A glance at the temperature gauge showed it was back to normal, but the petrol gauge showed it was empty! He heart sank and if that wasn't stupid enough, the petrol can David always kept in the back was empty because short of money last week she'd used it and not yet refilled it. There was nothing for it but to steer the dying car in as close to the hedge as possible.

If she hadn't been thinking of Ben's intrusion in her life she'd have remembered she needed fuel, it was all his fault! She doubted that the village two miles away had a petrol station and with such a quiet road it could be a while before she could flag down a passing vehicle to either get petrol for her, or call the AA to her aid. At least it wasn't cold, dark or raining! She rummaged in the back of the car for the travel rug. The grass triangle between roads would provide three directions for help to come. Seated on the rug in the late afternoon sun she realised the hedges around wouldn't allow her to see an oncoming vehicle, but at least she'd hear it. Ben again infiltrated her thoughts.

Hardly a day went by when either he, or his name cropped up. She couldn't complain or warn him off, because to all intents and purposes he showed no further interest in her. But both Helen and Rosemary thought the 'sun shone out of his backside' for different reasons. Helen had what she termed 'the hots' for him and took every opportunity to be near him, while Rosemary seemed to enjoy listening to his chatter and even smiled at his jokes! Her lip curled - they were so pathetic in their hero worship.

Rosemary, delighted with the kitchen had quickly proved herself an adept cook, and they resurrected the old routine from Jane's time. She and Helen prepared the vegetables and took it in turns to make a sweet while Rosemary put the meat and potatoes in the oven before going to church, and did the final touches on her return. Helen had disliked David coming for Sunday lunch despite his paying for all the food, now she was forced to endure Ben in the same way. Helen said he was poor, lived alone and needed a decent meal! Her comment that he ate every day in the ITP canteen didn't seem to register. However, seeing Rosemary visibly relaxing in Ben's careful nurturing and encouragements it would be mean minded to complain. And although it was still rare for Rosemary to initiate a conversation, she would now join in.

How miffed Helen had been last Sunday to discover Ben had driven Rosemary to church in the beat up old car he'd bought a week or so after he'd started work. He said he'd enjoyed the experience, but probably to appease Helen he later expressed a derogatory view of the church always wanting money. To her surprise Rosemary stated in a firm voice, "It's a Biblical principle to give 10% of your earnings towards God's work. Giving is good for you." Then sounding like the old acerbic Rosemary she continued, "But neither God, nor the Vicar, would want your money because the Bible says God only likes a cheerful giver." Their astonished expressions caused a deep blush to fill Rosemary's cheeks, and equally surprising she'd added in a humble and quiet voice, "Sorry I didn't mean to say it like that."

But it had given her a prime opportunity to say something that had been niggling her for weeks. "There Ben, no need then for you to put in your unsanctified sixpence. But we're not averse to receiving your contributions towards Sunday lunch." Ben may irritate her, but he was quick to place two half crowns on the table and ask if five shillings was enough to cover the meals he'd had. Helen glared at her and Rosemary looked even more embarrassed. Undeterred she'd given him a sardonic smile and said, "Just about, and cheaper than a meal in the canteen." Only a few moments later he made her feel guilty by saying Sunday could be very lonely on your own, and how much he appreciated the weekly invitation where he could enjoy the food and their scintillating company!

Had she dropped off to sleep? She shivered, stood and pulled the rug around her shoulders. It was 5.30 pm and the day was fast cooling. In the time here all she'd heard was the sound of crickets in the long grass, birds chirping and bees buzzing. What would she do if no-one came by? Was there a house beyond the tall hedges? Back at the car she stood on the ledge provided by the open door. It gave her just enough lift to see, but her heart sank there wasn't any sign of habitation in amongst the undulating fields. At the drone of an engine she jumped down, and dashed along the road towards the triangle, but the van driver hadn't seen her coming. Damn! If only she'd stayed there a bit longer, but life was becoming full of 'if onlys'! If only she wasn't wearing high heel shoes, if only the flat pair of sandals in her suitcase were suitable for walking. Her head was in the boot rummaging in her suitcase when music wafted on the air. She slammed down the boot and moved to the centre of the road. The vehicle was definitely coming towards her, the music getting louder along with the hum of an engine. Relieved she waited a few feet in front of the Morris for them to arrive. The unmistakable voice of Mick Jagger of the Rolling Stones blared out from the radio, as the Ford Austin with its windows open tore around the bend. Self preservation kicked in, she flung herself into the hedge on her left, as the car veered to the right, narrowly missing the front of the Morris and scraping heavily against the hedge to get by. Undaunted at nearly mowing her down, uncaring as to whether she was hurt, three of the four teenage boys stuck their heads out of the windows to wave, laugh and shout abuse before picking up speed and turning right at the crossroads.

Shocked she looked down at the bleeding scratches on her arm, the tear in her skirt and stared in horror at the dark red staining on her blouse. Was she hurt? She couldn't feel any pain. A glance at the hedge brought relief - blackberry juice! Legs shaking she stumbled back to sit in the car. Anger, frustration and self-pity mixed bringing an onslaught of tears. They soaked the handkerchief she pulled from her bag, all this was the fault of that wretched Ben, she cursed the day she met him, he was the underlying reason for all her problems, she wouldn't be here in this mess if it wasn't for him.

Old and young alike never had a bad word to say about him, until she began to think everyone thought him a saint except her! This had brought insight as to why Rosemary had been spiteful, snappy and always scowling when she shared an office with the ever popular Jane. Now she did those things whenever she heard Ben's name. News of Ben's capabilities had even reached David's ears.

Last Monday she had one of those rare lifts to work with David. They hadn't gone far before he remarked, "This seems an appropriate opportunity to tell you that the Directors are very pleased with the way you're handling your new job. It's always difficult when you make a new position in the company to know if it, and the person chosen for it, will work out, but we couldn't have chosen better." The pleasure she'd felt at those words revived her now flagging spirits. She dried her eyes. David had gone on to say, "We liked your suggestion about having an award for Employee of the Year. And you, of course, are the prime candidate to receive it." Elated she'd thought then her heart would burst and was about to say how much she enjoyed her job when David continued. "But I have to say if your boyfriend keeps up his popularity ratings it'll be a close run thing. He's an asset to the company, and it would certainly benefit his career to earn that accolade!"

Even now she wasn't sure which had upset her most, Ben referred to as her boyfriend; the possibility of the award she'd dreamt up going to him, or that in being the prime candidate he might now usurp her. In her exasperation her one desire was to put David right and her mind re-ran their conversation.

"First David, I would tell you that Ben is not my boyfriend and never will be."

David chuckled, "Um is that so! That old banger of his seems parked outside a lot then!"

"That's because Ben is going out with Helen."

"Helen, well, well, there's a surprise. I rather thought he liked you. Well they say all is fair in love and war. It seems then you missed out there."

"Missed out, missed out on what? That man is like a chameleon, he changes to fit the scene. You must have heard, if not seen, the BBB's – Ben's bevy of beauties as they are known, always swarming around him."

David chuckled, "No I can't say I have, but I've only met him that once at the house, in work there is no reason for our paths to cross."

"Well believe me I think he's too good to be true. I wasn't happy with his attitude when I interviewed him and there were some anomalies on his work records which make me wonder if he is entirely honest."

"Why then is he now employed?" There was hard edge to David's voice which she ignored.

"Because he played the card of being sorry, poor and needy and I took pity on him, so allowed Sam and Ian the final judgement."

"And Sam and Ian made the final judgement and from what I hear he's a tremendous blessing to the Print Department, bringing innovation to the printing, and reorganising the admin to make it easy for Sam to keep job records and printing stock." David pulling up at the lights gave her a challenging look, his mouth grim.

She knew that look, but she cared not a whit, she was entitled to her opinions and she was heartily sick of Ben. "Oh yes, that's about the nub of it. He's constantly pushing forward. Must be seen. Must be there. Must be doing. Must be helping out. Must be pushing. Must be friendly. Must be taking over. It's as though he's trying to prove himself to everyone. I'd say he's covering something up. He puts on an act to fit the bill. And if he is so brilliant why want, and take on, so lowly a job? I'm asking why is he inveigling his way into peoples' lives. What's his purpose?"

The car reverberated as David boomed, "Enough!"

Affronted at his attitude she glared at him and saw he was taking a deep, calming breath. There was silence as she fumed, and was about to retaliate when he continued more gently. "Look Jill speaking as a brother I'll say don't let this man get under your skin. Difficult I know if he is going out with Helen, but I really can't see your problem. Everyone likes him, but you."

What she wanted to say was 'tell me about it. I suspect he's still interested in me, and using Helen, but I can't tell her that, or stop him coming to the flat to see her.' But David had continued in his magisterial tone. "As your employer, for whatever reason you may have, I will not tolerate anyone even you, speaking in that way about someone else in the company, especially when you know so little of them, or their background. That, Jill is called character assassination. I warn you, should I ever hear you have spoken about, or like this to anyone within ITP, you'll be out of a job, taking immediate effect, sister or no sister. Do you understand?"

For David to speak to her with such vehemence she felt slapped in the face and the unfairness of it had brought tears trickling down her face. David had reversed the car into a space with the final comment, "I hope those are the tears of repentance. Here, lock the car when you're over it." With that he got out, dropped the keys in her lap, opened the rear door, picked up his briefcase and left her sitting there.

Even remembering this her exasperation surfaced again. 'Tears of repentance' indeed! Well she'd nothing to repent of, and her dislike of Ben had turned into hatred. She'd find a way to get him out of her life one way or another. It was in desperation this weekend that she'd persuaded Gemma to have her to stay. If she had to tolerate Ben at another Sunday lunch she'd be hard put not to shove the dinner on its plate through his ever smiling mouth!

The emotion of today's calamity spent, she comforted herself by eating the Mars bar she had resisted all week and felt better for it. The now sodden hanky at least could be used to clean up the scratches on her arms. And what of her hair, she pulled down the sun visor and looked in its mirror. What met her eyes was a vision of Aunt Sally, the scarecrow girlfriend of Worzel Gummidge, in the much loved books and radio story. Her face was blotchy and scratched, her eyes red and sore, and her hair mangled with sticks, leaves and... In a scream of horror she leapt out of the car, pulled out the pins to her French pleat and bent over the road to shake her head vigorously before reaching back into the car for her brush.

With the sun getting lower, a chilly breeze getting up, she considered her options. Wait in the car, or walk to the village. She took the petrol can from the boot and her cardigan from the suitcase; she'd need that before the evening was out. At least wearing it covered up her stained blouse which gave the impression of her either having been shot, or in a road traffic accident!

As she strolled along she considered her life. It was ridiculous having to organise weekends away, or sit in her bedroom to avoid Ben. In the past she could have indicated her disinterest by being constantly out with one of her men friends. But since that night with Tania, and talking to Jane, she'd made what she thought was a simple decision. She wouldn't sleep with a man without the commitment of a longer term relationship. It was easier not to be available for those one-off dates, but there were several potential men she thought might become more than bed fellows. Over the past few weeks she met each of them, and explained that she wanted to build a friendship with them, rather than just a sexual relationship. Three had scoffed believing she'd change her mind because of the delights they offered her. Two of them obviously felt cheated because she hadn't told them this before they'd taken her out for an expensive evening. And the worst had been the one she held the highest hope to get to know better. From experience she'd explained at the beginning of the evening her new found chastity, and he didn't seem bothered. They'd enjoyed a romantic dinner, but later at the night club when she re-iterated it, drunk, he'd become verbally abusive and they'd been asked to leave. It had also been humiliating to seek the doorman's help to hold him back as she got in the taxi alone. Only one man had accepted graciously her refusal to sleep with him, and said he'd be in touch, that was five weeks ago, and she'd still not heard from him. Her social life was now dwindling to nothing. Desperate to get out she was ringing around old college friends inviting any in London to meet for drinks on Mondays. Tuesday had become her TV night and last Wednesday when Helen was out with Ben, she and Rosemary had taken to playing Scrabble, just how sad was that!

The soreness of her feet trapped behind the thin leather straps of her sandals drew her attention to the road again. From her now more elevated position she could see the road dipped and rose several times before reaching the sign posted village. Two miles was a long way, but with hills... It was time to turn back and wait in the car where it would be comparatively safe, warm and comfortable. Her eyes scanned the empty road to the horizon. Aloud she challenged, "Okay God of Jane and David, how about you bringing me some help here?" Her eyes widened as the darkening sky briefly lit up. What was that? Lightening? She groaned, that would mean rain, the last and final straw! About to turn, the sky lit again, but there was no following rumble of thunder. Puzzled she waited to see if it would occur again. When it did, the light came over the hill, about quarter of a mile away and remained as it tracked the road. At last, a car!

The driver spotted her and slowed to stop beside her. Quickly she assessed the one occupant in the opened topped car. The wind had tousled his light brown hair, his blue eyes were sharp and cold in their assessment. Under the greenish stubble of a beard was a hard, but good looking man in his late-thirties. When his mouth twisted into a crooked smile an involuntary shiver of fear ran down her back along with the expectation he would speak in the drawl of an American gangster. To her surprise his voice was deep and cultured.

"Oh hello. Don't tell me - you've run out of petrol and had to abandon your car." Taken aback she remembered Jane saying God had used David to be her guardian angel, was this His provision for her - a roughened up one? "My dear woman, there's no need to look quite so astonished. It doesn't take a genius to work that out. One look at your pretty clothes, unsuitable walking shoes, and the petrol can in your hand is evidence enough." His face broke into a wide grin softening the rough, toughness of his face.

With a rueful smile she bantered coyly, "And you, it seems are my handsome knight sent to rescue me in your shining car." After all Jane's guardian angel had become her husband so who knew where this might lead, if she played it right.

"That's me! So dearest lady, do jump in. Unfortunately there's no petrol around here for miles, just small villages of a few houses. The nearest one is on the A404, or back down that way to the A40. Where are you headed?"

"High Wycombe." Her mind worked fast. Should she jump in? He might have a posh accent, seem friendly, but he could be a dangerous criminal. "That's very kind of you, but I belong to the AA. I guessed the village wouldn't have petrol, but it must have a telephone box, could you ring them for me?"

Because she hadn't jumped in, the assumed gangster jumped out. He was taller than she expected, and of similar height to David's 6ft 2 ins. His broad frame was dressed fashionably in light slacks, and over a beige rolled necked jumper he wore an expensively cut tweedy country jacket. What a fat country bumpkin she felt beside this dapper man.

He looked down upon her and frowned. "I can understand your reticence in taking a lift with a stranger, but are you going to be able to walk back to your car? I honestly don't like leaving you out here as it gets darker, its the middle of nowhere. At least let me drop you at your car and then I'll go on to the petrol station for you." Why was she feeling so reticent, the man seemed decent enough? "My dear, I'm sorry. I should have introduced myself, I'm Richard Mallory, Lord Mallory and you are....."

She gave him her name and taking his proffered hand she shook it. He might look like a rogue, but he certainly had all the trappings of a country gentleman, even to the large gold signet ring on his right little finger.

He gave a slight bow. Amused, he commented, "You look like a country lass, but I'm afraid those shoes give you away. You're obviously a city girl. Now are you going to get in the car?"

She still hesitated, after all anyone could say they were a Lord. But what was the alternative? Trust him, or wait by the side of a dark road for either him, or the AA, to come with petrol.

"Look, here's my card." He opened his wallet, full of notes, and produced a very fancy card bearing his name. With a derisive laugh he added, "Perhaps you'd like me to write the number plate of my car on the back as an extra precaution?" Once she would have trusted her character judgements, but just lately... Lord

Mallory took her silence as a 'yes', and began writing on the card.

"Look, I'm sorry, I wasn't…"

"Here, take this and don't worry about it." He gave a deep chuckle, "I may look like a gangster, but I try to rise above it!"

Obviously she wasn't the first to make wrong assumptions! She quickly scanned his card, he was who he said he was, and placed it in her bag. He seemed sincere. It was a risk she'd have to take. "Well, if you don't mind…" At that he was already at the passenger door opening it so she could slide into the low slung leather seat. As he positioned himself beside her she commented, "Calling the AA would cause you less time and bother."

The car throttled into life and sped up the country lane. "Bother, it's no bother I assure you. I've always plenty of time especially when an attractive lady crosses my path, or in this case flags down my car!"

"But I don't want to put you to any trouble."

He slowed down and nodded through the windscreen, "I assume that's your car? If you like I could drop you off here to wait and I'll come back with the petrol, or you can enjoy the ride and we can get to know each other."

The latter option was becoming more favourable by the minute the chance of a friendship with a Lord no less. She gave him a small smile, "Oh I think now I have your name and number I'll come with you for the ride."

"Then enjoy it. And I'd prefer not to leave you stranded. Once we get the petrol, I'll lead you across country and you will be within a few miles of High Wycombe. I have a house just on the outskirts it's a very pleasant place to live. He continued to talk of the area and it didn't seem long before they had drawn into a petrol station on the A404.

"You stay there I'll do this."

It was wonderful to sit back and be pampered. How incredible she should meet a Lord in the middle of a country lane. She grinned into the darkness if this man wasn't married she'd certainly find a way to parade him in front of Ben.

"Right, mission accomplished, petrol stored. I think though I'll put the top up, do you mind waiting while I fix it?"

"No, fine, I must admit I was getting a bit cold."

"Good heavens, you should have said. It's no good me rescuing you and then allowing you to get pneumonia, that would never do!" It wasn't pneumonia she was worried about, more her aching legs and sore feet, she winced as she moved them. He slid back into the seat. "Thank you Richard, this is very good of you."

"My pleasure Jill, but please call me Rich, all my friends do. He grinned across at her, revved the car engine and quipped, "Rich in love, luck and loot."

The return journey seemed over quickly as he told her about his flat in Knightsbridge, his frequent visits to London, and was talking about a good nightclub he'd recently visited when they arrived back at her car. "Well Jill, this has been a very pleasant interlude. Let me have your telephone number. I'll look you up next time I'm in town? We could go to Annabels, or maybe the Savoy for dinner."

It was time to ask the inevitable question. "And what would your wife think about that?"

Rich gave a deep chuckle. "Wife, I don't think so. I've yet to meet a girl who would fit into my lifestyle. But you never know who you might find in the middle of the road with a petrol can in her hand."

"Then, this truly is your lucky night!" Jill gave him a sexy smile.

"What you've no husband, or boyfriend, I don't believe that."

She gave a little laugh, "Let's say I'm between boyfriends, except for a wretched man I don't care for who has become like my shadow. I'm off to visit a friend this weekend to escape him."

From Rich's throat came what she could only describe as a protective growl before he asked, "If you want rid of him, give me his name, I'll have him warned off."

Her previous unease rose up. Why did she think he'd do Ben some harm? Ridiculous really, but suddenly she felt the need to protect him. "Oh don't worry, I'm about to do that myself, I obviously haven't made myself clear enough."

"Right! Should he not get your message, you have my card, feel free to ring me. Now let's get this petrol in your tank and you on your way, your friend will be wondering where you are."

He carefully poured in the petrol as she stood by. "You know Rich you remind me of someone."

"Don't tell me, I hear it all the time. I've nearly been mobbed with people thinking I'm Robert Mitchum"

"Yes, that's it! And driving a sports car I'm not surprised that people mistake you for him."

"Right that's done. Now let's start her up, and we can be on our way." After several attempts the engine gunned into life. Rich gave her a salute from the centre of his forehead, "Now follow me and I'll get you back on to the right road."

She rolled down the window, "You'll have to drive slower than before, as neither I, nor this car will be able to keep up with you, and I've only a gallon of petrol and I don't want to get lost in these lanes again."

"Don't worry, I'll keep an eye out for you"

True to his word he drove at thirty miles an hour, stopped with her at another petrol station so she could fill up, and having pointed her along the main road, he jumped back in his car, calling, "I'll be in touch" and with a handbrake turn and a squeal of wheels he was gone with a roar back up the road from which they'd come.

It only took twenty minutes to get to Gemma's and in that time she considered how charming, debonair, witty, kind and protective he'd been. To go out with a Lord would be interesting.

The weekend at Gemma's proved rather depressing despite her rather sweet baby girl, who smiled and giggled a lot, but it quickly became obvious that Gemma didn't find much to giggle about these days. Henry may have led her surprised parents to believe they'd had an intimate relationship outside of marriage, but his uncommunicative manner was proving a major hindrance to developing that. The reality was Gemma, in saving herself from the stigma of having a child without a husband, and not knowing which of several men could be its father, had given up her freedom to be Henry's maid, cook and bottle washer in a somewhat old-fashioned house in which he was loathe to make changes.

Their conversation mostly hung on their reminiscences, the supposed infallibility of the pill which had let Gemma down, and her celibacy decision which Gemma concluded wouldn't be much fun, but better than being caught in the baby trap. And on Monday it was obvious Gemma was anxious she'd leave before Henry arrived home, as being a London friend and taboo he didn't know they'd even kept in touch. As she drove away she felt thankful she hadn't suffered Gemma's fate. Even if she didn't keep to her resolution of abstinence, she determined to take every precaution to ensure she wasn't caught out as Gemma had been, so being free to fall in love with Mr Right, marry him and have children when they wanted them. With a busy week at work she was late home each evening and, not seeing Ben either at work or home, life was without irritation. She aimed to keep it that way and to escape Sunday lunch she opted on Saturday to go home to

Bath and return Sunday evening. The weekend had been relatively unchallenging except on answering her mother's questions about Gemma, it had led on to her saying, "I'm sure you know lots of nice men, don't judge all men by Stephen. I know he hurt you, but give one of them a chance to win your affections, it's time to start thinking about settling down?" To ensure the conversation didn't continue she nodded and appeared thoughtful. But the subject came up again while she was helping with the Sunday lunch for her Mum reported, "When Jane was here a couple of weeks ago she told me that there's a lovely, friendly man who visits your flat. She seemed to think he had an interest in you, so I wondered why you hadn't mentioned him."

Her first reaction was to kill Jane. Her second was to heed David's advice remembering that her reply would probably be repeated to Jane, if not to David too. Her third was to frown and appear puzzled as she mustered the considerable self-control needed not to scream the words, 'I hate him, I'm sick of hearing about him, I'm here to avoid him, and I never want to set eyes on him again'.

In order to mask her true feelings she put on an air of nonchalance. "Oh I think you must mean Ben. No, Jane's got it wrong. He dates Helen. He's not my type. His only connection to me is he works at ITP, and he was kind enough to help when Rosemary got upset." The diversion of her tale of the boat incident worked beautifully, but she could see her Mum was disappointed that she wasn't interested in the gallant hero who had rescued them. It was natural she supposed she wanted her 'settled down' so she told of her encounter with Lord Richard Mallory. Her father gruffly pointing out he was awaiting his lunch thankfully ended further conversation about her love life.

The only ex-College friend who turned up on Monday evening at the pub was spotty, lanky Peter, who, with promotion to sub-editor on a new satire magazine, was now confident to sport his interest in her. She didn't ever think she'd be that desperate! She'd hoped Rich might ring and in the past she'd have probably rung him! With no man to go out with she was beginning to feel like a fusty, frigid old maid, but how was she to get a man, let alone keep his interest, if she didn't offer him sex? A question she put to Jane on Wednesday after Rosemary having beaten them both at Scrabble went to bed.

Jane, coffee in hand, lent against the kitchen work surface, her voice filled with amusement. "Don't ask me, I'm no expert, my matchmaker resides in heaven. I didn't even know David was in love with me when everyone else did, but I had given Jesus a description of what I felt would be good husband material based on David." She went on to observe, "When Jill I first met you I thought you were happy, chatty and scatty. That maybe the image you want to portray, but this job has proved there's more to you than that. You're attractive, intelligent, friendly and fun, perhaps its time to change the image do something to make you feel different? Your unruly hairstyle where pins constantly fall out fits that first image of you, so how about a new, sleek hairstyle to fit the new, efficient, executive in you?"

Jane was right. On Saturday afternoon with her hair cut to copy the sleek bob Vidal Sassoon had created for Mary Quant she did feel transformed. The result was her black hair was slightly softer and more prone to curl than Mary's, but the style was now neat and tidy. Her second decision was to go to John Urwin's twenty-fifth birthday party. He'd invited the majority of ITP, but especially wanted single women because knew more men than women! With that opportunity, the decision to break her rule of not mixing business with pleasure, was quickly dismissed!

Made-up with thick black eyeliner, mascara and blue eye shadow she swirled in front of her long mirror in her latest purchase of a cream and blue dress in the new high waisted look. She grinned, it wasn't intentional, but her facial features did have a resemblance to Dusty Springfield, however she was probably taller and certainly had a fuller figure than she.

The only blot on the horizon was that Ben too had an invitation. However, it had given her opportunity to talk to Helen and tell her of her dislike of Ben. Helen didn't understand, but agreed it was Jill's home too, and conceded that if Ben could still come for Sunday lunch she'd only bring him back to the flat after 10.30 pm in the evenings when Jill usually would be in bed, and last week it had worked well.

Ready, she stepped out from her bedroom and smiled at Helen coming in, then froze seeing Ben behind her. Immediately Helen apologised, "Oh sorry Jill, I assumed you'd already gone to the party."

Ben undeterred was already exclaiming, "Wow Jill. That hairstyle is so chic. You look a million dollars. I wish I was going to that party tonight."

Helen joked, but there was an edge to her voice, "No you don't. You have me. And let me tell you if you were going to that party, Jill wouldn't be?"

Unperturbed Ben smiled down at her. "And you Helen are adorable, delectable and decidedly different." He kissed the tip of Helen's nose.

God that man was just too smooth! Her instinct was to make a being sick gesture! Instead she gave a stiff smile, and suggested, "Enjoy what you have, rather than that you can't. Now if you'll excuse me."

As she walked away he called, "And you have a wonderful evening too." Was that retaliatory sarcasm for her barb?

Helen giggled, and she heard her say, "Poor Jill. You do wind her up. You are, what's the word, incorrigible. After Ben's amused, "Woman, will you get off me" in the silence that followed she guessed Helen was kissing him.

CHAPTER 7

Predictably as at any party she attended, women quickly outnumbered available men, but with her new image she found herself surrounded. When talking became impossible, she danced, and after warding off several men she wasn't attracted to she teamed up with Richard, an accountant who was new to London. He had a pleasant boyish, smooth skinned face, with a shag of blond hair that fell over his forehead.

The lounge/diner in the terraced house wasn't large so once the room filled with couples there was barely room to move bringing a change of tempo and inevitably Richard began to get amorous which she forestalled by drawing him out to get a drink. The hall was jammed with people, the kitchen awash with booze and the noise level against having a conversation. Once they'd battled their way through, found the paper cups and filled them with wine they headed out through the back door to the paved yard where people were standing around talking.

"I wasn't rejecting you just now, but my brother is a Director of ITP and my job there involved in personnel, so I feel, if I come to an office party, I have to be on my best behaviour." Jill gave a coy smile.

Richard looking shy responded, "I'm happy to just talk out here, or dance in there." At 1.00 am as their fellow dancers drifted into cosy huddles and cuddles, Richard whispered, "Do you want to leave?" At her nod, he offered, "I'll walk you to your car." In an attempt to retrieve her bag she disturbed an entwined couple and noticed Richard looked more embarrassed than she.

With her arm tucked in his they strolled along the street where the front gardens could just about contain a dustbin and push bike. Richard commented, "I brought my bike with me from Nottingham, but I wouldn't want to cycle in the centre of London at rush hour. It is the place to be if I am to further my career, but I'm finding it a big and a lonely city. I have a big brother at work, not a relative like yours who lends you his car, more one who watches what you say and do. If you want to be considered for a partnership in Haylock and Peal its frowned upon, and considered unproductive and unprofessional, if you fraternise with the staff."

"How very Dickensian! Perhaps they should be called Shylock

and Steal, a far more suitable name for a firm of accountants. Richard squeezed her arm, "Oh I must find a way to whisper that in the right ears."

"ITP is forward thinking, David likes to think he has an 'open door' policy, although I'm not sure how many people would go to his office to speak to him, but he did marry his secretary's secretary!"

"No! Really! How interesting. I'd love to hear all about it. Would you like to go out for a drink on Tuesday? It could be straight from work, or a pub nearby your flat."

He wasn't a great catch, but it was a date, and she was bored staying at home. A thought occurred to her and she asked, "Better still why don't you come to the flat for lunch tomorrow, we girls cook together and one more won't make a difference." From the street light she saw happiness fill Richard's face. For a brief moment she felt mean for her motive wasn't entirely altruistic!

When just after twelve o'clock the doorbell rang, despite having assessed her appearance and been satisfied, she had butterflies running in her stomach. This was Mr Nice Guy who hadn't pushed himself on her, just taken a brief kiss 'goodnight' and was gone. He wasn't exactly a country boy, but he wasn't a man of the world either. And she wasn't quite sure how he'd fit in today, or how she'd handle it.

On opening the front door Richard thrust a bunch of flowers in her hand, smiled and said quickly, "Hello Jill. These are for you." The shy gesture of running his hand through his falling locks of blond hair gave her to realise he felt as awkward as she." I biked over, is there anywhere I could leave it where it would be safe?"

"Alongside the dustbins here in the outer hall would be fine." She opened the door wider and to put him at ease as he stowed the bike, she chatted about his journey and explained as she led him into the house, "I live in the basement with my flat-mates, Rosemary and Helen. David my brother lives upstairs with his wife, Jane."

"Ah yes - his secretary!"

"Oh you haven't forgotten." They headed down the stairs.

"This is a very nice area of London, you are lucky to live here. Oh and you have a garden."

"Yes Rosemary particularly likes it. We sit out occasionally. David and Jane rarely use it. It was a bit overgrown before Rosemary came, but she loves digging and planting, it's really coming along now."

To her glee as they reached the last few stairs Ben emerged from the kitchen heading for the bathroom just as Richard commented, "What a beautiful flat." At a man's voice Ben's head jerked round to look at them.

Delighted to see his surprise, she pasted on a friendly smile. "Hi Ben, let me introduce Richard. He's staying for lunch."

Richard with a smile held up the bottle he'd taken earlier from his rucksack. "I've brought some wine." She took it from him, and as he moved towards Ben with outstretched hand she said, "Ben comes for lunch each Sunday too and considered to be pretty wonderful. He rescued Rosemary and I from a difficult situation, he's renowned at work for being both brawn and brains, and is rapidly heading for the award of 'ITP Employee of the Year'."

Ben having nodded at Richard as he shook his hand now looked at her somewhat perplexed. Her smile did nothing to disguise the sarcasm in her voice. "Ben dates Helen who he thinks is delectable and decidedly different, while she thinks he's the best thing since sliced bread!"

Ben's bright blue eyes now fixed on her, filled briefly with pain, but true to form he rose to the occasion to banter. "Please don't take all Jill says to be true, as my number one fan she is rather prone to exaggerate." His smile was one of weighing her up and finding her disappointing.

Irritated she retaliated, "What I didn't say Richard was that unfortunately Ben lives with the constant delusion that he's God's gift to women."

Nervously pushing back his hair Richard glanced between them, then offered, "I think we men sometimes have to believe that otherwise we wouldn't be brave enough to ask out an attractive lady such as yourself."

In a low voice Ben commented, "So Jill you've found a diplomat to join us."

Annoyed she retorted, "Richard is new to London, he needs company just as you do. I have no choice in having to put up with you because you've ingratiated yourself on Rosemary, flirted and whatever else you do with Helen and…"

"Do you dislike me that much?"

The incredulous tone of Ben's voice brought her further frustration. She dropped the flowers and bottle of wine on the settee, stepped up to Ben and stabbing the air with her right hand she proclaimed, "Let this penetrate that thick skull of yours. I have no interest in you. I see through your doing this and being

107

that. You can't charm me to get what you want."

Bright blue eyes stared into hers. She stared back at him and was gratified to see guilt flash through them, and when Ben grasped the top of her shoulders, she realised she'd struck a chord.

Richard intervened, "I don't fully understand what's going on here, but it seems to me that Jill's made her feelings clear. Why don't we just let tempers cool and have a glass of wine?"

Ben's eyes continued to look deeply into hers as though to plumb into the depths of her mind. "I've heard your words Jill, but you and I both know your mind wants to resist, but your body sends me an entirely different message."

"Then believe me, you've got your wires crossed." She tried to wriggle free of his grasp.

Again Richard intervened, "Let it be, Ben."

Again Ben ignored him, his eyes fixed on her. "Right Jill, let's get this clear? You don't mix business with pleasure. In enjoying your flatmates company I've made no advances toward you, despite that occasion of discovering an incredible expectancy of sexual compatibility. Our wires weren't crossed, they were sparking in anticipation. Let me remind you…"

Before she could resist his hands moved into her hair, cupping her face, his mouth caressed hers. Instinctively she tried to push him off, but within seconds her body activated with the throb of desire. When his mouth left hers she was so shaken she could barely comprehend his words, "Now tell me that the earth didn't move for you? And that isn't something special?"

It was special! Way off her Richter scale, but not with him. Oh no, not him! In blind rage she lifted her hand and spat out, "You, self-opinionated, insufferable pig." Quicker than she, he caught her hand before it made contact with his face.

"Me thinks the lady protests too much! But I've proved my point. You can't deny it. There is something amazing that sparks up between us, it certainly lights my fire, and I know it does yours."

She tried to ignore the sensation of Ben's thumb rubbing against the pulse at the base of her hand. With a snarl she asked, "Does nothing penetrate that thick skin? I don't like you!"

Anxiously Richard asked, "Jill, what would you have me do?"

Ben, his eyes not leaving her face, growled, "Just leave?"

Furious at his treatment of her guest she let rip, "Are you insane? Do you think a kiss, however pleasurable…?"

"Aha, so you admit it." Before she could retort, Ben's mouth closed over hers. With her eyes she sent a plea to a bewildered Richard before sinking into the maelstrom of pleasure zinging throughout her body and causing Richard's voice to seem distant.

"Ben I think Jill has made it clear she doesn't like you, and doesn't want you kissing her. I'm not strong enough to fight you off, but I can call the police."

The immediacy of Ben's aroused body left hers. Dazed she swayed, her desire to cling on and meld herself to Ben only broken because he directed her collapse on to the settee. In a thick voice he groaned, "With you, I lose all sense of reason." Then grabbing his car keys from the table, coat from the hook by the garden door, he ran up the stairs, pausing only to call out, "Tell Helen, I'm sorry, I'll be in touch."

In the silence they both jumped as the flat door banged.

"Good grief! "Who did that?" Helen, hair tousled, looking distinctly hung over, was standing in her nightdress in the bedroom doorway. Heavy-eyed she glanced around, "Where's Ben? Is he doing the vegetables?"

Richard stepped forward. "Hi you must be Helen. I'm Richard, I'm with Jill. Ben has had to go, he said sorry, and will be in touch. I'm afraid we had a bit of a run in with him, and it was he who left in a hurry."

Vegetables! Lunch! Ben! Slumped on the settee she looked across at Helen, her mind in turmoil. Had the last eight weeks of starving her body of pleasure caused Ben's kissing her to be as a match to a firework's touch paper? The take-off so immediate it soared towards the expected explosion and magnificent release. Thank goodness Richard had been there, to have challenged Ben when they were alone...she didn't want to think about it.

Helen holding her head sank on the nearest settee to say groggily, "Ben and I got pissed. I've been sick all night. So what did you and Lord Richard here say or do to upset him?"

How could she explain what happened without hurting Helen?

"I'm sorry Helen. You know Ben rubs me up the wrong way, but it got well...heated, and he left when Richard threatened to call the police."

Richard ran his hand through his hair and looking awkward explained, "I didn't know what to do. It worked, but, I didn't expect, well...he scuttled out of here like a frightened rabbit."

In disbelief Helen gently shook her head while holding it in her hands. Then looking up with tear filled eyes said in a puzzled voice. "I know he was always baiting you, and you were always giving him stony looks, but he…"

The flat door opened and shut, they all looked up. Jill half expected to see Ben, but it was Rosemary returning from church.

"I've just seen Ben, he says he can't stay." She looked at the three of them, when they didn't speak, she continued, "I'll finish getting the lunch" and disappeared into the kitchen.

Quietly Richard said to Helen, "Ben said he's going to get in touch, it's probably better you ask him what happened." Helen glanced toward her as Richard recommended, "I think it's best we help your flat-mate get the lunch and forget it. Come on Jill, where's your bottle opener, we'll have some of that wine?"

Helen puzzled, drew herself up, moaned in pain and headed towards the bathroom.

Ben had peeled the carrots, cut the cabbage and made the Yorkshire pudding mix so within half an hour Rosemary had produced a very appetising dinner. In that time Helen had dressed and reappeared to say churlishly, "Ben said he'd do the sweet, no doubt you sent him off before he got that done. I thought he and I…." Tears filled her eyes, she blew her nose into her handkerchief.

Richard suggested. "Have a glass of wine Helen, it'll settle your stomach. And Jill if you've got a tin of fruit, flour, margarine and sugar, I think I can whip something up for sweet." Relieved not to have to say more she produced the goods from the cupboards while Helen, arms folded, watched as though to challenge him. Within five minutes Richard had made a mix, dropped it over tinned peaches and had put it in the oven as the roast potatoes came out. "There you are, fruit crumble just like my Mum makes. If you've got custard powder I'll make that just before we eat it."

Wide-eyed Helen stared at him, "Don't you have a cook and servants to do that."

Richard gave a puzzled smile. "Is that why you don't cook?"

Helen shrugged, "My father is a chef, I've never had to bother, so my only interest in food is to eat it."

The wine was a godsend. Helen recovered, they all relaxed and Richard slipped easily into the space left by Ben. He had opinions, was happy to argue a point, drew out Rosemary, and talked of his ambition to set up his own accountancy firm in the future. Could Richard be the Mr Right she was looking for? The smooth, thick custard to cover Richard's equally crunchy and tasty crumble had Helen inviting him every Sunday!

And he was quick to help with the clearing up, and fascinated by the dishwasher. While he became embroiled in domesticity she went to the toilet to consider Ben's actions. A few men had taken the time to make the earth move for her, but with Ben it was immediate and cataclysmic. Yet she hated his proclaiming he knew her mind better than she in the belief he was some kind of sexual Superman! And what about Helen's feelings if she discovered it was she, not her, Ben had the 'hots' for?

Now adjourned to the settees she joined them as Rosemary poured the coffee, and Richard was saying, "Yes, my Mum is a great lady. She doesn't stand on ceremony and accepts everyone on face value. Sunday is much like this at home. Mum often invites people back for lunch who are lonely, or need a home cooked meal. My parents like you Rosemary go to church, its part of the tradition of their lives."

Rosemary, with a toss of her hair answered abruptly, "I don't go to church as a tradition. Christianity isn't a religion it's a relationship with the creator God, the Father, His Son and Holy Spirit. And being a Lord and Lady, and doing good, doesn't make you a Christian." Richard nodded sagely. Was it the wine causing the vehemence of the old Rosemary? She may not have been a Christian very long, but after Jane's indoctrination she'd be telling them at any minute that the wages of sin was death and they were all sinners in the light of God's glory, but God freely forgave those who believed in His Son.

Helen looking thoughtful piped up, "So tell me Richard, when a Lord marries, does his wife automatically become a Lady?"

Confusion filled Richard's face. Puzzled she tried to follow Helen's thinking when revelation dawned. Immediately she burst out, "Oh no! Is that what you all thought, he's not that Richard."

Helen repeated her last words as though a conundrum. Rosemary wide-eyed said, 'Oh!" And Richard smiled appearing to understand something he so obviously didn't. Fortunately he found her story amusing and at the end he stood to say, "I hope you ladies will you excuse me for not being a Lord, and with only a trusty bicycle for transport and London still something of a mystery I ought to start for home."

Jill gave Richard an encouraging smile as he turned on reaching the front door. His visit had started awkwardly, but in the end had accomplished all she'd hoped. But she did feel disquiet when he confided, "Helen is obviously very keen on Ben. Did you see having produced that second bottle of wine, she drank most of it?" At that he bent down to put on his cycle clips, while she considered that. When he looked up again he asked tentatively, "Will you, would you, still come out with me on Tuesday?" .

This really was Mr Nice Guy so she had no hesitation in accepting. "Of course, I'd love to."

He smiled up at her. "We'd have to go somewhere locally and I'll confess to not being rich, so the pictures maybe? It isn't as grand as the West End, but it would mean I could see you home safely without having to be out late on a work night."

"Richard that's really thoughtful, I'd like that."

"You would? Oh great! May I kiss you, goodbye?" At her inviting smile he moved to nuzzle her mouth with a pleasant, boyish, inexperienced kiss. He drew back and looked into her eyes, "I'm afraid I haven't much experience in this, but I am willing to learn if you'll teach me."

She covered up her reservations about that, and with a laugh commanded, "On your bike. I'll see you Tuesday. I eat at lunch time, but I'll make us a sandwich before we go out."

As she watched Richard cycle off down the road she weighed his pleasantness and lack of sexual experience against Ben who caused within her a disturbing mixture of hostility and physical response, which made her question, what did she want out of life?

Fortunately when she returned to the flat Helen was showing Rosemary an advert in the newspaper offering colour TV's for yearly rental, and all else was forgotten as they discussed their favourite TV programmes and debated whether to club together to get one.

A knock on her office door on Monday afternoon heralded the arrival of Sam. Surprised she jumped up, welcomed him in with an offer of a cup of tea and indicated a chair. "Did you climb the stairs from the basement?" Breathless he grinned. "You should have used the lift?" Sam hummed a reply and watched her thoughtfully as she put on the kettle and got some mugs out. "So what brings you from the bowels of the building up eight flights of stairs? There's nothing wrong is there?"

"'Cause not luv. It's just you weren't in the canteen at lunch and I wanted to see the new 'air style everyone's talking about. Changes you, don't it? I liked the 'omely, scatty-'aired, friendly Jill. And I don't mean that nasty, we're friends, ain't we? But with that black stuff around your eyes you looks aloof and posh like

112

one of 'em in magazine pictures."

Dear Sam, she patted his shoulder and amused answered, "I'll take that as a compliment. But just because I look different, I'm still me on the inside, good ole Jill always open for a chat and a laugh."

He grinned up at her. "That's alright then. With Ben getting on so well down there, I fought I could slip away and have a bit of an adventure. Never been further than the ground floor before. Nice little attic rooms these, cosy. Done alright for yourself, ain't you? I fought the moment I knew you were 'is sister you were wasted as a receptionist. Jane like the 'airstyle?"

Jill handed him a mug. He slurped gratefully as she replied. "She's not seen it yet. They were out yesterday. It's amazing how living in the same house you don't see each other for days. But it was she who suggested I go for a new look."

"Well ducks, I'll no doubt get used to it, fits yer job nows you got your own office and that. Jane ain't changed much though 'as she, despite married to 'im. No offence intended. Enjoyed that dancing didn't she?" He chuckled, "just like that Ben. Now 'e's such a character that boy, cheeky, smiling, teasing, 'e always gives the impression 'e's up for a good time, but I reckon 'e bats one girl against another, and goes out with none. Mind I think 'e might have got 'is fingers burnt over a bird this weekend. Never seen 'im so miserable 'es barely spoken beyond a grunt today, so unlike 'im." Sam looked at her and rubbed his chin thoughtfully.

"From what I've seen he'll soon bounce back."

"I 'ope so ducks, 'cause I've come to like that lad. There's a lot more to 'im than meets the eye. I don't like to see 'im down." Sam put down his mug, stood and chortled, "Well, best be off, or I'll have to sack myself for slacking! I've set Ben on the admin stuff, much better than me, fought it'll take 'is mind off 'is troubles, and free me to give 'em machines an overhaul. I enjoyed our chat. Tell that Jane to come to lunch 'ere one day, we'll all sit together and it'll be like old times. Funny ole life ain't it, 'ows people pair up, some do, you don't expect, and some don't who you do expect. See ya Jill."

When the door closed behind him she resisted the urge to pick up the telephone directory and fling it across the room. Had Sam just come to see her hair, or did he suspect she was the cause of Ben's sombre mood? Well she didn't want to know, and she wasn't going to feel guilty. How else was she, in the words of the musical, 'to get that man out of her hair'? Part of her job was

113

personnel liaison, but hell, what was she supposed to do about Ben 'getting his wires crossed'. Ha! More like unrequited passion! She slammed the cups back on the tray. Determined to forget the existence of Ben she set herself to her work.

On Tuesday evening Richard arrived before her. Helen had made him a cup of tea and she felt faintly annoyed at her sitting happily chatting to him. Was she going to chat up every man she brought in? Or was it, as Richard said later that she was just a cute and friendly person? Quickly she made cheese sandwiches, poured herself a cup of tea and joined them, but was pleased when it was time to go.

As they walked, they talked, of his work and hers. In the cinema she was delighted when he produced from his rucksack a box of chocolates, but more impressive was his thoughtfulness of giving her a packet of tissues, bought as a precaution in case the second-rate romantic film made her weepy. They had time for one drink in the pub on the way home where he explained that his sister often cried during films, particularly ones involving Lassie. That led her to talk of her family and his reminding her to tell Jane's story. On entering her road having put his hand in hers earlier he then asked shyly, "I've heard they have good dances on at the Hammersmith Palais on Saturday nights, I wonder, would you like to go?"

Her first thought was 'not really', having outgrown those days of going to what Gemma called the 'cattle market'. But this would mean she'd progressed to a third date.

On Friday morning in the midst of musing whether the universe contained a man specifically created for her, the internal telephone on her desk rang. On hearing Penny's urgent voice declaring, "Sam's had an accident, I've called an ambulance..." she immediately dropped the receiver and headed down the back stairs. What had happened? How badly was he hurt? Breathless she ran into the Print Room where the machines were clanging away as usual.

Frantic she looked down the long room, where Joe spotting her waved, and called, "Over here." On reaching him he swallowed hard before saying, "I thought Sam was just messing about."

Afraid, she asked, "Where's Jack, with the first aid?"

"Penny said he wasn't in his office, she's ringing around the building." They rounded the machine where Sam's inert body lay beside it. Ben bent over him was working through the steps of resuscitation. Tears rolled down her face. Sam, dear Sam, so loveable, always so friendly, always with a twinkle in his eye, he couldn't, he just couldn't die. Joe put a sympathetic arm round her shoulders. "No-one could do more than Ben is. Thank goodness he's here."

There wasn't room for her to get in beside Sam, but from his feet she urged him back to life. Despite her negative feelings towards Ben, she could see he wasn't about to give up, he stopped depressing Sam's chest, felt for a pulse, gave her a brief cold glance, shook his head, and began again. Quietly she asked, "What happened?"

"I'm not sure. Sam was tending this machine. There was a fizzle sound, and a bang. I came around from the other side laughing and saying, "You're not supposed to blow us up" and found him on the floor. He could play the practical joke, so I said, "Oh stop it Sam and get up, when he didn't, I yelled, 'Help Sam's unconscious.' Ben shot out from the office, took one look at him, said 'electric shock' told me to call an ambulance and has been working on him ever since."

Ben still working on Sam spoke. "How long?"

Joe replied, "Four minutes, twenty seconds."

"Jill get upstairs. Those ambulance men are needed here on the run." This wasn't a time to be offended so she raced down the room to the stairs. At the sound of a cheer she ran back.

Joe delighted stated, "He'd be a gonna if it weren't for you Ben."

Ben grunted before commenting, "He's not out of the woods yet. Get my coat from the peg, we must keep him warm." Then with a face devoid of expression he addressed her to reiterate, "I told you to go and direct the ambulance men down here."

"But he's going to be alright now, isn't he?"

"The quicker he has professional attention and in hospital the better. Now go."

She headed to the stairs as Penny came clattering down with the ambulance men. They rushed past her, she called as she followed them, "It's nearer to the hospital from the back gate." One of the men turned, "We'll stabilise him first, and think about that later."

Together with Ben she watched as they prepared Sam for transfer to the hospital. "You did a good job here mate, if you want to join the ambulance service you'd be welcome. Your quick and effective action brought this man through, we couldn't have done better. In fact I'm not sure we'd have made it in time. John, you get the wagon around the back. Direct him will you love."

By the time Sam was on the stretcher he was semi-conscious, his lips twitched as though to speak. Ben reached out and patted his shoulder. "Hello Sam. Don't try speaking. We're just going to take you to hospital. You'll be okay. You've had a bit of a nasty shock to your system. It's time to take a rest."

"So mate, are you coming with him?"

Ben, his usually bright blue eyes looking dull and pained gave her a questioning look. "Yes, Ben do go, Sam would like that." He nodded and turned away. There was no doubt as Sam had reported to her four days before, Ben wasn't himself. Could it be she who'd upset him?

John, the ambulance man broke into her thoughts, "Miss, Miss, excuse me. I think you should come too. It would be good to have a woman there for his wife when she arrives." She hesitated. Ben although bending over Sam to tuck the blanket around him, shook his head as though he didn't want her there.

"Oh dear yes I wonder if someone has contacted her?" She looked around, "Joe, find out what's happening. I know the Bennetts' aren't on the telephone, and we don't want the police telling Mrs Bennett. Maybe I could go in a taxi and bring her to the hospital?"

"Miss, we really must go. Come with us. The police will already have been notified of the accident from the 999 call, if they have Sam's details she may already be on her way."

"He's going to be alright, isn't he?"

"He's got a good chance of full recovery, thanks to this young man." He patted Ben's shoulder, "But the sooner he's in hospital the better. Let's get going."

"Joe, ask Penny to find out if Mrs Bennett's been told. If not get a taxi and you and Rosemary fetch her, at least she's met you both. Oh and get someone to inform Mr Reinhardt." She ran out across the courtyard, and through the pots ablaze with riotous coloured plants, towards the gates where Sam was being put in the ambulance.

CHAPTER 8

Of all the times, places and people, fate was again throwing her and Ben together. The ambulance journey took only a minute, but they stood waiting in the corridor a lot longer and she felt she ought to say something positive. "You were amazing, the way you worked on Sam. It was your sheer persistence that brought him back to life." He ignored her, but she continued, "It certainly showed me that we must instigate that First Aid training we talked about. I can see now how important it is, how it can save life." The only evidence of his hearing her words was a nod of his head, his eyes fixed on a poster on the opposite wall. Oh well, she'd done her best to be polite if he wanted to ignore her that was his prerogative.

A short while later a nurse arrived and ushered them into a small empty room indicating they should sit on one of the four hard chairs while she took down the little they knew of Sam's personal details. Not wanting to sit side by side, or facing each other, they sat diagonally opposite. When the nurse left, the room without a window seemed to shrink in size and the silence stretched into what felt like an eternity! Eventually she decided to try and address their situation. "Ben I know this is difficult in the light of Sunday. And exactly the kind of situation that I wished to avoid, but we are colleagues and as such we have to work together."

From his hunched position, his elbows on his knees, his head in his hands he looked across to say in a voice devoid of emotion, "This isn't the time, or place, even if I wished to discuss it, which I don't. If Helen wants to see me, I'll keep out of your way to give you your precious privacy. If by fate, or some misjudgement, our paths cross, my response will be, as of now, minimal politeness."

"Oh Ben that's just ridic..." The door opened. Jill leapt to her feet. "Oh Mrs Bennett you're here." She tucked her arm into hers. In drawing her to a seat she could feel her trembling. "This must have been a terrible shock." Rosemary, her eyes big and sad hovered in the doorway as Mrs B said, "Joe, he's a good lad, he and Rosemary came, they told me, about my Sam." Tears filled her pale grey eyes, "They said he was alright. You'll tell me the truth won't you?"

"Of course, it was Ben here who saved his life." Jill smiled at Rosemary, she nodded and slipped away. Mrs B pulled a handkerchief from her bag and dabbing her eyes she stumbled out such a profusion of words in thanks and how much her Sam thought of Ben, that he looked embarrassed and awkward. A characteristic in him she wouldn't have expected to see and it warmed her to him.

That feeling was short-lived for moments later Ben stepped into the role of a doctor talking to a patient's relative. The man was an enigma for again he was displaying an ability to rise to any occasion, but his confidence, the professional way in which he explained what had happened did reassure Mrs Bennett. He then checked that she understood what to expect when she saw Sam and went on to explain how the next few days would pan out as Sam recovered. His calming voice dried up her tears and her shaking ceased.

While Ben was doing his doctor act, she concluded that she had what she had wanted, Ben's presence out of her personal life, but it would have been good to find some common ground for Helen's sake.

It seemed ages, but it was only another half an hour before a rather harassed doctor appeared to announce, "Mrs Bennett. Hello there, I'm Dr Sanderson. Your husband's condition is stable. He's in intensive care because the next few hours are critical, but we have every confidence that he will make a full recovery. He's very drowsy, but you can have five minutes with him, then I suggest you go home and rest yourself. We'll inform you if there is any change." Ben gave Mrs B support and they followed the doctor along the corridor. Mrs B entered leaving her and Ben alone to sit and wait for her. Ben sat forward, his head resting on his hands, a pose she was sure he was using to block her out.

The approach of a very tall, good-looking doctor caused her to more than glance at him, and having attracted his attention she responded with a smile. His eyes went from her, to her companion. Surprised he stopped to exclaim. "Ben, Ben Fletcher. It is you, isn't it?"

With an unreadable expression Ben looked up. "It's me Geoff, Geoff Knight. Oh my goodness it is so good to see you. I heard what happened. To be honest I could scarcely believe it. You were so dedicated and on track. How on earth did you get…" Ben having jumped to attention as the man introduced himself, now had manoeuvred him down the corridor out of earshot.

So what was all that about? She stared in their direction trying to glean information and saw beyond them coming along the corridor a figure that looked oh so very familiar! Oh hell! Her misguiding Ben into thinking David was an actor was about to misfire, and probably backfire on her!

Hand outstretched, David approached, his voice booming "Ben, my good man. I gather you are the hero of the hour." From where she sat she saw Ben's small smile, then recognition before his face registered bewilderment at David's words. Ben's friend Geoff grinned, said something to him, patted his arm and left. David catching sight of her drew Ben back along the corridor toward her while commenting, "It's you we have to thank for saving Sam Bennett's life."

Puzzled Ben echoed, "We. Are you a friend, a relative of the Bennett's?"

David frowned, and as he looked toward her she plastered on a cringing sort of grin. "It would seem that my sister, for whatever reasons best known to her, has never told you who I am?"

Ben who, until now, had avoided looking at her, stared as if knowing instinctively she'd set him up. A blush began to diffuse over her face. At any other time this would have been amusing.

"I know you are David Hart. You are involved in television, but assume, as I've never seen you in anything, or your name on any credits, you must have a stage name."

There was a tinge of amusement in David's voice as he said, "Is that so? And what did Jill say to give you that impression?"

Ben glanced at her again before replying. "When I saw you greet your wife, after the boat trip, I asked Jill if you were an actor and she said you'd been on television."

David's roar of laughter hit the air. Two nurses going by shushed him, he apologised, but blew his nose so noisily they turned to glare at him. Still amused he waved a hand to signal he was sorry.

Baffled, Ben stared as though David had gone mad.

Jill could only hope that as David found Ben's assumptions so amusing, he'd find the rest of it funny.

"Oh dear, that just goes to show how easy it is to jump to a wrong conclusion. The only television I've ever appeared on is News at Ten, and if I have any acting ability they didn't recognise it. However, if Jill was using her full surname you wouldn't have made that mistake. Let me introduce myself, and then I think things will become clear. My name is not Hart, but Reinhardt."

Ben turning a whiter shade of pale echoed in a dazed way, "David Reinhardt. The same David Reinhardt who…"

"Yes Ben, one and the same. And I am a Director of ITP, here because of concern for one of my staff, and with my legal training know the liability we have towards Sam Bennett. I was only a white-wigged barrister for a short while, it wasn't for me. I felt I didn't have the ability to ensure that justice was always served on the right people, so decided to combine my skills and use them in industry."

Seemingly overcome Ben sat down, and David pulled up a chair beside him. She could understand his shock, for it wasn't every day that you found you'd been chasing and trying to ravish the sister of the 'big' boss. And, in pushing yourself on her, had been visiting his home on a regular basis for the past nine weeks!

David patted Ben's arm in a reassuring manner. "I've heard quite a bit about you since you arrived at ITP." He laughed, and to her surprise divulged, "Before I married Jane I had the accolade of being the company heartthrob, and aligned I believe to Jane Austin's Mr Darcy. Now it would seem you are the one to stir the female hearts. And my wife tells me you've been likened to Clark Kent, because there are occasions when you appear as Superman. After today I rather think I'll endorse that opinion." David started his roar of laughter then quickly stifled it with his hand.

Ben turned his bewildered gaze at David on to her. Her response was to send him a wide-eyed grimace, and guessed Ben would rather David didn't know about his antics on Sunday. And seeing his reaction to knowing who David was she realised if she had told him the truth in the beginning he would probably have backed off then, saving her a great deal of frustration and irritation. What was the expression, 'hoisted by ones own petard!' Therefore, she reasoned, she owed it to Ben not to tell David everything, because that might change his opinion and thwart Ben's career at ITP.

David having expected Ben to be encouraged by his remarks pressed on. "I've been hearing about your excellent work in the Print Department. With Sam laid up, you are the obvious choice to do his job until his return. There will, of course, be the monetary reward to go with that."

Ben shook his head as if he couldn't believe what he was hearing, but did inject a somewhat stilted enthusiasm into his voice. "I appreciate your confidence in me. "I, I don't know what to say, but 'thank you'. So when did you …?"

"Here, I am me dears, they let me stay a bit longer. Sam wants to see you both. The doctor says you can have two minutes. He seems okay." Mrs Bennett smiled around, her eyes took in David who had stood at her arrival. "Oooh! Aaah! Err! It's Jane's husband, ain't it?"

Not wanting to be caught missing making introductions Jill stepped forward. "Yes Mrs B. You remember, my brother David, he's come on behalf of ITP to see how Sam is."

David put out his hand and smiled at the woman who was as strikingly tall and thin as her husband was rounded and fat. Mrs Bennett went into a tizzy, "Oh yes. Oh my! You're here to see my Sam. That's kind. I mean, well you being busy with a company to run. Thank you. Is Jane here?"

"I've no doubt she will be. But sit down Mrs Bennett and we'll have a chat while Ben and Jill visit Sam?"

"Oh yes, yes, if you think so. You're a busy man. I don't want to take up your time."

She and Ben walked into the ICU as David was reassuring Mrs Bennett he had all the time in the world and would help her and Sam in any way possible.

Sam, linked up to machines, managed a grin. First in, Jill took his hand, her voice cracked with emotion, "Oh Sam you had us so worried. I'm so glad you are alright. What a terrible thing to happen. Ben here saved your life."

Sam beckoned Ben to come closer. With little space between the bed and the wall, Jill moved back for Ben to come forward. In bending over the bed, Ben spoke quietly and she couldn't hear what he said, but at Sam's thanks he nodded in acknowledgement before brushing past her and leaving the room without a backward glance.

They both watched him go, before she reassured Sam they would take care of Mrs Bennett. He gave a toothless smile, squeezed her hand and closed his eyes. In response she bent and kissed his forehead, with a throaty chuckle Sam murmured, "I could get to like this." With a pat on his hand she retorted, "There's no doubt you're on the mend. Sleep well my friend."

The moment she reappeared David took charge. "Ben, go back to the office, get that investigation started into how this happened. Jill, you and I will see Mrs Bennett safely home."

"It's okay, don't worry about me, I got all afternoon. There's no need. You' ave work to do. I'll get the bus from 'ere to Victoria, and the 185 goes almost outside me door."

David treated Mrs Bennett to what Jill called one of his high 'wattage' smiles. "Now, now, Mrs Bennett none of that, there's every need. Your husband is a respected employee of ITP, he has sustained injury through one of our machines, and I know Jill will have assured him that we will be taking care of you in his absence." Before Mrs B could protest again he'd taken her elbow and was heading out the door insisting, "Now let's get you home, and we'll have a nice cup of tea with you." At that poor Mrs B looked even more phased.

Jill thought quickly, "I'm afraid we can't do that, I've an appointment later."

In seeing Jill's expression David caught her underlying message. "I see. Well another time then."

Engrossed in thought they walked from the hospital, entered ITP offices through the back gate and headed around the house to the car park. As David unlocked the front passenger door Mrs Bennett gave another futile protest, to which David smiled and said surely she wasn't going to deny him the opportunity of getting to know her better. Flattered Mrs B nodded, and on the journey she watched David's charm and friendly manner draw out the details of what support she might need. Mrs Bennett, still smiling at one of David's jokes, pointed out, "My road is next right, after that bus-stop. My house is first left."

David drew into the kerb, and offered her a card, "Ring this number and we'll arrange for a car to collect you."

"I haven't got a phone ducks, but as I said before I'm happy to use the bus, it's no trouble." David nodded as though he was agreeing, but Jill guessed it wouldn't be long before he rectified the Bennett's lack of telephone and provision of payment for taxis back and forth.

On the drive back from Camberwell it was obvious too that David also intended to rectify the 'Ben and Jill' situation. And having determined not to tell him of Ben's invasion into her life, it was even more difficult to explain because David seemed so taken with the wretched man. As the car swung into ITP's drive he grumbled, "I really don't know why you have it in for Ben, he's a popular man, obviously attractive to women." Then he grinned and added, "And I thought your motto was to make love, not war."

Incensed she bit out, "And I thought David these days you were the one who always took the moral high ground. What are you saying? I should take him to my bed to appease him, you and ITP?"

"Now you are being ludicrous! You know what I mean. Ben obviously rubs you up the wrong way, but try and see the good in him." David opened the car door and slid out.

From the passenger side she leapt out and slamming the door exclaimed over the car, "Doesn't it occur to you that the man might have wronged me? But I can't tell you about that because you'll probably say I'm assassinating his character." The wide-eyed look David gave her as she came around the car had her say with scorn, "But then what did you say to Ben earlier, you gave up being a barrister because you felt you didn't have the ability to ensure that justice was always served on the right people."

David, his mouth firmed into a grim line, drew alongside her. "Jill, you are on dangerous ground. Don't let me doubt my wisdom of your suitability for the responsibility you have been given. I'll see you in my office in one hour." With that he spun round and walked swiftly away leaving her staring after him seething in rage.

Penny had stopped David in Reception for news of Sam, but the way she felt it was best she spoke to no-one. With a wave of her hand she sped by to the back stairs, ran up all six flights until breathless she spun out of the door and into her office. Hopefully Penny would realise she was upset because of Sam, and David wouldn't hold that against her too. It wasn't often she gave in to a bout of swearing, but this was just such an occasion. Furious she not only threw the telephone directory at the wall, but did a drum roll on her desk with her fists wishing it was Ben's head. An omission of the truth, the whole truth as David would say, had indeed backfired on her.

Who could she talk to, get advice from? Sam would have been ideal he knew about Ben's attraction to her at his interview. She sighed. Jane could help, but it might look as if she were trying to influence David through her. Had anyone told Jane about Sam? The telephone on her desk rang. She stared at it. The last thing she wanted to do was answer it, but she supposed she'd better. With a deep breath she picked up the receiver.

"Jill hi, it's me Jane. I've tried David, no reply. So thought I'd try you, how terrible about Sam, how is he?"

She gave her a breakdown of the events and thought how strange Jane should ring when she was thinking about her. "We arrived back half an hour ago. David should be in his office. I'm so glad you've rung because I could do with some advice. David's summoned me to his office and I'm in trouble because of Ben.

You know what a pain he was on the boat trip and to me since…" As she reeled off all Ben's crimes including Sunday lunch time she finished, "And frankly, I'm pigging sick at David's attitude, and Ben's ability to invade and mess up my life."

There was a brief silence before Jane answered. "Oh Jill I wish I could help, but you know David was unhappy at me undermining his authority at work, and to advise you now would be considered the same. The only thing I can suggest is I'll pray that you, David and Ben, resolve the issues in a positive way, how's that?"

Jill sighed, "I suppose it will have to do. Mind, if God can manage that I'll believe he's a miracle worker, so there is no harm in asking. And at least talking to you has taken the edge off my anger."

Twenty minutes later she entered David's outer office. Since the boat trip she and Miriam had barely been on speaking terms so she was surprised at Miriam's friendly and sympathetic attitude. "Oh hello Jill. Are you okay? I gather a bit of a difficult day. David's been back from the Print Department about ten minutes, Ben is with him. He said he was expecting you. I'm to send you in, when you arrive."

Dismay surged through her at Ben being with David! Bravely she smiled happily, answered Miriam's question and took a deep breath before entering. Immediately David smiling, arose and welcomed her in. "We're sitting over here, it's far less formal." Ushered by David to sit next to him on one of the two Chesterfield settees she looked diagonally across at Ben and gave him a tight business smile. His acknowledgement was a cold faced nod. David in contrast appeared relaxed as he sat back, crossed his legs and with his arm along the back of the settee stated, "The reason I called you both here was to gather information and resolve a few problems. You will be pleased to know Jill that Ben has made me aware of salient facts about your um…situation so I suggest we shelve that issue."

Jill blinked in surprise, and as he continued speaking she could only conclude that Jane's prayer worked! "I wanted to see you both to thank you for the way you dealt with the incident this morning. There is obviously misunderstanding between you, but you behaved professionally and didn't let it affect the way you supported Sam and Mrs Bennett. Ben, I want to tell you that ITP will recognise and reward your skill today in saving Sam's life. Thank God you were on hand for such an emergency."

Jill jumped in to say, "Ben suggested to me weeks ago that we should run a first aid course. I thought it was a good idea, but we didn't get any further on that. The ambulance men were very impressed with Ben." She looked across at him, "They said, didn't they, that you ought to join them." Ben's bright eyes were unusually dull, unsmiling he nodded. Looking between them she suggested, "Perhaps Ben could teach us?"

David directed one of his high wattage smiles at her as he boomed forth, "Sounds good to me. What do you think Ben?"

"It's possible. You could bring in outside examiners who would sign people's certificates."

"Good, good! Advertise it Jill in the next magazine. Let's do one hour weekly sessions, half in ITP time and half own time. Ben liaise with Jill over it. And as you're going to be busy in the next few weeks, keep a note of the extra hours you work." David turned to fill her in. "Ben has looked at the machine that nearly killed Sam, he says the wiring is old, and feels others might be potentially lethal too. I've told him to check out the latest technology on the market for replacements." David looked across at Ben, "How blessed we are to have your expertise in these two areas." Ben gave a nod, but didn't appear blessed. Maybe David noticed that too because he said, "Now Ben, I'll let you get back to work. I have been interested and appreciated all the information you have given me. Remember I have an open door policy so if you need to keep me up to speed in any area, please get in touch." He stood and put out his hand to shake Ben's. "To save disturbing Miriam you can go out the other door."

At the obvious dismissal a strangely bemused Ben arose shook David's hand, thanked him and walked quickly to the door. As she watched him leave David re-seated himself in Ben's place. Where had the mischievous bright eyes and the cheeky, indomitable smile gone? Surely his lack of emotion wasn't due entirely to her telling him to get lost? He'd bounce back, he'd now two new roles to play, and it occurred to her he was the actor. Had anyone ever seen the real Ben Fletcher?

David sighed. "Well today has had unexpected twists and turns, but it has made things clearer." He nodded introspectively. Quite what had become clearer he didn't elaborate on, but she'd the impression he wasn't displeased. "Now back to the Bennetts. I have Miriam organising taxi's and telephones, and I want you tomorrow liaising and supporting Mrs Bennett. Do all you can for her. I'll leave the finer details to you. Now it's nearly four o'clock, tomorrow looks as though it could be a hectic day, you've often worked unpaid overtime so I suggest you call it a day. You did well today."

Home, in the refuge of her bedroom a reaction to events of the day caught up with her as she picked up the much loved teddy bear she'd had from a child. Bald, battered and tattered from much crying and hugging over the years, he knew all her secrets, fears, and passions. At the sight of Benjy's dear loveable face, she grabbed and drew comfort from his little body, but as she said his name it occurred to her even her beloved bear's name was a derivative of Ben! Tears spilled forth.

The sound of the flat door on the latch banging shut awakened her. A glance at the clock said, seven-thirty. Thirsty, and in need a cup of tea, she got up and glanced in the mirror. As suspected her crying had streaked black eye-liner down her face. Cream removed it, but she now looked washed out and tired.

In the kitchen, Helen gave her a long thoughtful look and at her watery smile she commented, "You're late home. I thought I heard you come in. Bad day eh? The kettle's boiled and I'll put some toast on for both of us, shall I?

She rustled up a 'thank you' as Helen went on, "Rosemary told me about Sam, she said too about Ben saving his life. You know Rosemary, not hot on detail, what happened?"

As Helen cut the bread she described Ben's heroic act, and how he'd so professionally comforted Mrs Bennett and then detuned her ears as Helen regaled the wonders of Ben and was glad of the diversion of the toast popping out of the toaster!

Helen retrieved it and spread on the butter asking, "Marmite?" She nodded and delved in the cupboard as Helen enquired, "What happened between you and Ben? He's not been in touch."

She shrugged. "Basically, his cock-sure attitude annoys me. I tried to discuss it with him today, he refused. But he did say on Sunday when he left he'd be in touch with you." Preoccupied in thought, Helen handed her a plate, then picked up her mug of tea and toast to take into the lounge. To cheer her up Jill offered, "I'm sure Ben would appreciate it if you rang and congratulated him on his performance today?"

Helen sighed as she sat on the settee with her back to the kitchen, "Oh I would if I could, but he hasn't a telephone at home. And at work I've left him several messages, but he hasn't rung back. I don't even know where he lives except it's out Wembley way."

Rosemary's bedroom door opened. "Ah Jill, Penny said you'd left early, are you alright? I asked Ben, he told me Sam's on the mend. It was awful visiting Mrs Bennett. She remembered us, but went white and shaky on hearing about Sam. Joe was worried she'd have a heart attack."

Stunned at Rosemary's voiced concern, Helen was the first to speak. "The kettle's just boiled if you want a drink."

Jill sat down in the corner of the other settee near the stairs and turned towards Rosemary, "Thanks for asking. One way and another it's been an emotional day, but I'll survive. And Helen, it occurs to me, with Ben taking Sam's job, he'll be answering the Print Dept telephone, so will have to speak to you. I don't want to have spoiled it for you, its obvious you like him."

She bit into her toast as Helen grinning said, "Oh he's good fun, enjoys a romp, but he does get uptight about some things. You should have heard him when I said that having an abortion was no big deal, he went mad. I didn't dare tell him I'd had one!"

Rosemary about to enter the kitchen swivelled around with wide-shocked eyes. Tears started to run down her cheeks as she stared at the back of Helen's head as she continued talking. Then Rosemary looked up, caught her gaze, turned and disappeared into the kitchen. Great, Rosemary was up-tight, and Helen...well the light-hearted way in which she was speaking made her wonder how she'd lived with her for eighteen months and not known what she was involved in. "...And oh boy, did he get annoyed when he caught me having a quick joint at a party, he practically dragged me out and then, on the way home I had a long lecture on drug abuse." She guffawed, "it was only a bit of pot, anyone would have thought I was shooting heroin."

Helen was still regaling other things she'd done that Ben had got upset about, when Rosemary with a tightly composed face, cup in hand walked through the lounge into her bedroom.

Jane coming down the stairs stopped the revelations. "The flat door was on the latch so I assumed you wouldn't mind me coming down. Where's Rosemary?"

"Oh Helen here was giving us a rundown of her sins, I think it was too much for her, she's in her bedroom."

Jane grinned. "Oh Helen! You, and your tales! Surely Rosemary doesn't believe them, good job we don't! I've come down because David's gone out to have a drink with some barrister friend I'd never heard of. He seemed keen to go and said he'd be back by ten. I didn't protest because I wanted to chat about what happened today."

Helen excused herself. When the bathroom door closed Jane said quietly, "I told David what happened on the boat trip, I didn't want you in trouble. After all Ben assumed I was married to an old man and did come on to me. David wasn't annoyed, for he chuckled, "Jane you don't have to confess all in order to stick up for Jill. Ben's already done that and told me his interest in Jill is a constant irritant to her. And by David's amused expression, I guess he did tell 'all'! Now I'd say that proves God can work miracles. Now tell me in detail about what happened today?"

It was two hours later before David appeared at the top of the stairs to boom, "I guessed you'd be down here." Jane stood and smiled up at him. "Did you have a good time?"

David descended a few more steps probably fearful the absent flat mates might consider it an intrusion. "It's certainly been an interesting day and fascinating how things come together. By the way Jill, I prefer you without all that black stuff around your eyes. Come on Jane, it's getting late."

Jane retorted as she joined him, "It's not me who stayed out late." David grunted, and Jane called 'goodnight' as hand in hand they rounded the staircase. A few seconds later there was a squeal from Jane, a hearty chuckle from David before the flat door closed behind them. She sighed, how good it must be to have love, sexual compatibility and be married.

Friday passed in a blur of activity. At afternoon visiting Sam was looking much more like his old self and in her relaying the day's activities he asked quickly, "Did Maud give you lunch?" A vision of the lumpy, watery mound of mash potato, dried out baked beans and the sausages burnt on one side and barely cooked on the other brought a smiling grimace, to which he started laughing. On seeing Mrs B approaching he reverted to a slumped, frail figure resting back on his pillows in a pitifully weak state, and at his wink she had difficulty not laughing for it was obvious he was going to make the most of this.

On Saturday she took in the large 'get well soon' card Miriam had circulated around the offices which had gathered a collection as it went. Armed with a large bouquet of flowers and a box of chocolates she put the remainder of the money in the envelope for Sam to spend on whatever he needed. A nurse recognising her explained Mr Bennett was making a rapid recovery and had been moved to the main ward, but it wasn't until she spotted Sam talking to Maud that she realised his other visitor was Ben! What bad timing!

Ben rose from the chair as she drew near and moved out so she could move in.

"Hello Mrs B. My Sam you're looking more perky. These come from the staff of ITP." Tears formed in Sam's eyes as she put the gifts on the tray over the bed.

Mrs B announced, "Jane and her man came just before visiting, they were only allowed a few minutes, just look at the size of this basket of fruit? Everyone's being so kind.

Sam pulling himself up stated, "And 'e, Mr Reinhardt told me, Ben would look after things at work, I was to rest up and not worry. 'e said Ben here, was 'a serious contender' for that 'Employee of the Year' award. There's no doubt 'e deserves it, but you're a bit shy about it, aren't you Ben?"

Forced by Sam's words to look at Ben, Jill could see his discomfort and that he still wasn't his sunny self. With great seriousness he instructed, "Now Sam, you mustn't get excited. You just let that ticker of yours regulate itself. You are only allowed two visitors around your bed, and it is time I was off. If you are still here next week I'll pop in again one evening. Although with the recovery you are making you'll soon be home, and back at work. "

"Well, the Missus and I have yet to discuss that. Now you get off and enjoy yourself, take out that girl Joe says rang you several times yesterday, and stop hankering after the one you can't have."

Ben gave Sam a tight embarrassed smile, and without further ado, he lifted his hand in a wave and walked off down the ward.

Mrs Bennett watching him leave commented, "Now there's a lovely boy and not just because he saved my Sam's life. He's so kind and thoughtful. I thought yesterday the way he was talking he was a doctor, but today he was just telling us that had been his wish, but he hadn't enough brains, that made you chortle, didn't it Sam?"

Sam rested back into the pillows, "I tell you what Maud, he makes me job seem so simple I don't think I'll be missed."

Startled Jill exclaimed, "Of course you'd be missed."

"Now Jill, you sit down love, 'ere by me. See this 'as been a bit of a shock to me and the Missus. I'm a bit too old to be fiddling with them machines, and I'm not into the office bit, so don't go saying I am."

"But Sam I know you need to maintain the machines, but not repair them to the extent you've been doing. Those machines should have been replaced years ago."

"Maybe, but it makes no odds anyway, another shock like that will be the death of me. And would 'ave been if it 'adn't been for young Ben's expertise. And I've seen 'is work, 'e's got the skills, 'e'll make a good boss because 'e cares about people, 'e listens and if 'e feels it's right 'e does it."

If it was true he cared and listened to others why hadn't he listened to her, why had he acted so impulsively on Sunday? If Helen rang him several times yesterday, then obviously he wasn't hankering after her. It seemed everyone liked him, and from what she was hearing of late perhaps she'd misjudged him, and certainly now the cheeky, devil may care façade had slipped it was beginning to reveal a very different man.

Sam's hand touched hers. "You were far away lass, a penny for them?"

"I was just thinking Ben seemed different."

"Oh that confident attitude of his, it's all a front. I told yer on Monday 'e seemed knocked off course, even being 'ero of the 'our don't seem to 'ave righted it." Sam looked thoughtful.

She knew she shouldn't ask, but couldn't help herself. "Has he ever told you about his past?"

"A bit. He worked at 'is Dad's print company. He feels he messed up because it went bust. Can't be true 'cause 'e's a 'ard worker. I fink 'e's 'ad a lot of 'ard knocks." I asked about this bird 'e's been keen on, 'e didn't want to talk about it beyond saying she was far too good for 'im. He seems to have a real down on hisself." Sam gave her a long look and rueful smile. Was that because Sam had put two and two together and realised she was the culprit of Ben's depression?

Maud unexpectedly chipped in. "Men lust, women love. He'll get over it when he finds another woman."

"You maybe right there Maud, for there's been more women visiting the Print Department these past weeks than in all the time I've been there, and it ain't nothing to do with me. And according to Joe, Ben's made a date next week with the girl who kept ringing him yesterday."

With that information she made an inward note to ensure she wasn't about when he arrived, and changed the subject.

CHAPTER 9

On her way back from the hospital she bought a crusty loaf to make a ploughman's supper, along with two fresh cream apple puffs, and told herself that dancing at the Hammersmith Palais was a form of exercise! Richard having cycled over arrived as Helen, dressed in the latest flower power fashion left. Her comment, "I'm off to a party that Ben definitely wouldn't approve of, and I won't be back tonight."

Jill grinned, "Well you know the motto, 'if you can't be good be careful'.

"Yes, but that's not always a lot of fun, is it?" With that Helen was out of the door.

"So Richard that just leaves us, for Rosemary is staying overnight at her parents.

Richard's appreciation of the simple meal, and of her, reminded her of those days with Stephen - comfortable and unchallenging. The Palais had had a face lift, but otherwise was much the same. Joe Loss still had his favourite dances including the outdated, 'March of the Mods'. Richard wasn't a dancer, but he tried, and it was different going with a partner. Back at the empty flat she made hot chocolate, they kissed and cuddled a bit and when he asked if they could spend Sunday together, she suggested he stay the night. At that Mr Nice Guy smiled and admitted, "I've had a few girlfriends, but never, well you know, I hope that's alright." The sad thing was she suspected that however 'right' he might get it, he wasn't going to be a man to make the earth move for her. And she was glad he didn't object when she produced the bedding for the settee.

They ate a leisurely breakfast and decided as the weather was glorious they'd make a picnic of the leftover bread and cheese and go to Kensington Gardens. It was a day for romance as many couples walked hand in hand, sat on picnic rugs, cuddled and laughed, and enjoyed the ducks on the water of the Serpentine. In a simple, quiet way they learned more about each other, and as Richard cooked up a delicious cottage pie and vegetables, with banana custard for pudding she could see with her lack of cooking skills he'd make a great husband, so why didn't domestic bliss with him seem appealing?

On Tuesday evening when the telephone rang Helen obviously thought it was Ben. To give them some privacy she started up the stairs to her bedroom.

"Jill, its for you – Rich."

Taking the handset she smiled into it and said, "Hi Richard, I've been expecting you to ring."

"Well doll, that's good news, so are you ready to be a gangster's moll?"

Jill closed her eyes. Oh how embarrassing! Wrong Richard! Should she pretend she knew it was him and was hoping for him to ring, or confess she knew another Richard? How about a farcical brother, no, one was trouble enough! Without further thought she said flippantly, "I'm yours. Any time, any where?"

Rich chuckled and changed the drawl to his polished tones. "Good heavens! I didn't expect such an enthusiastic response. If that's true then I wish I'd thought to molest you that night when you looked so roughed up and delectable. I hope you weren't disappointed?" Oh dear, she really had given him the wrong impression. And 'roughed up and delectable'? At her hesitation he continued, "I'm in town this week and wondered if I might have the pleasure of your company?"

And what would he now be expecting? It was time to be friendly and flippant again! "My dear Rich, I would be delighted to join you, but despite expecting you to ring I don't have a free evening this week, but I could manage a long lunch hour."

"That sounds good to me, say I pick you up about noon on Thursday then we can aim to return by two. Give me your office address and telephone number in case something crops up and I can't make it." Once she'd given him the information, he said, "See ya then babe" and hung up.

Excited she leapt across the room to bang on Helen's door. The moment it began to open she squealed, "Guess what? That wasn't Richard, but Rich the Lord!" Behind Helen a thin blue haze spiralled. Horrified she declared, "You're smoking."

Helen produced the roll-up cigarette from the ashtray behind her, inhaled deeply and squashed it out. "I don't often. When Tania came, she sometimes did, I joined her, I enjoy it, okay."

"Its not pot is it? You said you smoked it at parties, but here...."

Helen shrugged, "I felt a bit down, needed a bit of a puff that's all, honest."

"Well to be honest with you Helen I'd rather you didn't have the stuff here, or smoke it."

Helen's eyes narrowed, "Look Jill you've already seen off my fellah so he refuses to come in, now you're laying down the law about me smoking. I pay my share of the rent, and I'd say what I do in my bedroom is my business, both smoking and Ben's company."

There wasn't any doubt Helen had a point, but she wasn't happy about it. "I'm sorry Helen, it is your room, and yes, unless it directly affects Rosemary and I you may do as you wish. And Ben as before can come here, but I'd prefer him not joining us for Sunday lunch. Did he tell you what happened?

"He just said you two had a disagreement, and thought it best he leave, but didn't say what it was about."

"Well I don't think it is up to me to tell you, but if I'm away at a weekend it's up to you who you invite around." A sudden vision of hippy's smoking pot in the lounge jumped into her mind. She gave a little laugh, "Well within reason, and you know what I mean."

ITP staff dress code was fairly laid back the only provisos were that clothes were clean, tidy and with rising skirt hems, not indecent. Only the Receptionists wore navy suits and cream blouses. The English saying, 'old habits die hard' could refer to her still wearing an 'office' suit when she didn't need to. But she had few what she would term 'work' clothes and needed to replenish her wardrobe.

Thursday she decided was the day to break out and wear the deep red linen skirt and box jacket she'd recently purchased from Barkers in High Street Kensington. The pencil slim skirt was no more than two inches above her knees with a slit at the back so she could hoist herself up the step on to the bus!. The classy cream blouse she'd had as a Receptionist would be ideal to go with it. But if she was going on any more dates with a Lord she'd better get shopping!

Rich had said noon, so with the intention of pre-empting speculation and gossip she arrived in Reception five minutes before. Penny chatted to her, and commented on her new suit, and they began to discuss the pros and cons of wearing a uniform every day. Her plan was to watch for Rich so when he arrived she could slip out before anyone noticed. Rich though had no such plan, for at exactly noon his bright red E-type Jaguar roared down the drive and came to a noisy halt in front of the door, causing

Penny to exclaim, "Good grief! Some car! And some entrance. Who is this?"

Sunglasses on, Rich jumped out of the car to reveal his beautifully tailored casual cream trousers and hand-knitted V-necked jumper underneath which was brown silk shirt opened at the neck. He took brief stock of his surroundings giving time for Penny to comment before he entered, "A gorgeous hunk in a gorgeous car, I wonder who he's come to see?"

The answer to Penny's question was immediate as Rich entering the hall saw her. With a broad smile and bending to kiss her cheek he stated, "Jill. It's lovely to see you again." Inquisitively his eyes roved around the palatial hall with its expensive décor. "It's unusual to find such a large, charming house in its own grounds in the heart of London. It would make a wonderful hotel. I've always got an eye for property investments." He chuckled and took her elbow, "Shall we go?"

A glance at Penny showed her goggle-eyed and somewhat puzzled, was it because Rich looked like Robert Mitchum?

When deciding what to wear she hadn't considered that tight, short skirts and E-type Jaguar's low slung bodies weren't very compatible. Rich holding the door said laughingly, "Best way is to bend your knees, let your bum fall on the seat, then slide round to get your legs in. And I promise not to look if your skirt rides up to your knickers."

Bewildered at the mixture of posh accent and common synonyms she gave him a sideways glance, but carried out his instructions and, as promised, he looked the other way.

The sheer force of Rich's acceleration out of the drive had her pushed back in her low slung seat and wondering if he'd be safe in the London traffic. However it appeared Rich was very accomplished as he negotiated Hyde Park Corner and the way the car roared up to Piccadilly Circus made her think he was like a professional racing driver, with a speed limit!

He turned into what looked like a builder's yard off a Soho street and explained, "Friend's place. Parking is a problem we'll walk across Shaftesbury Avenue to the restaurant."

Tucked away via a narrow street was a small shop where Chinese girls in oriental dress came forward bowing, welcoming, and eager to please. In leading them to a table for two in the tiny bay window they had a view of the run-down premises opposite and a wet street where an earlier downpour of rain still tried to trickle away into rubbish clogged drains. Not quite the kind of place she imagined a Lord would take her, but the ambience with its red and gold flocked wallpaper and many red paper lanterns gave it a rosy glow. The menu was in English and Chinese, but she'd no idea what to order and had to admit, "Rich I've never seen, or eaten Chinese food before."

"Then you will enjoy it, and bring others, I am sure." Eager to try anything, she let Rich order four dishes accompanied by both egg fried rice and noodles. The only drawback was the constant use of his title, which she found embarrassing, but he seemed nonchalant about it. The wine arrived before she had time to start a conversation. A beautiful girl smiled deferentially at them, placed prawn crackers and peanuts on their table, and then humbly backed away. Rich noticing her interest explained, "Chinese food up until now has been mainly in the Thames dockland area where most Chinese immigrants live. But I am sure you've heard with ships getting bigger the docks are too small and less and less traffic is coming up river. The more enterprising Chinese are moving their businesses elsewhere. The first restaurant in Lisle Street became quickly popular with theatre goers and other punters, so I assisted these people to move to here, they run the business I own the building."

They chatted about that until six dishes were placed on an oblong warming tray in front of them. Rich explained, "The Chinese have a little of each dish separately, but me, I'm English and prefer to have it on the same plate at the same time. You feel free to do it anyway you wish."

She followed his example. It was delicious, but amazingly filling. Throughout the meal he slipped from drawling like a movie gangster, giving a good impression of a cockney spiv and then to being his Lordship. Maybe it was that dichotomy which helped her feel at ease to ask, "Don't you get rather sick of being sucked up to as Lord Mallory this, and Lord Mallory that?

"Not impressed then with lunching with a Lord?"

"Well, you're only another human being like me, but anyone would think you were royalty."

Rich laughed, "So what are you saying, royalty aren't human? I'll mention that to Cousin Elizabeth next time I see her."

She grinned, "You know that wasn't what I meant."

"I hope this doesn't mean you are considering depriving me of your delightful company in future?"

With a coquettish look she murmured, "Umm, that depends..." After his telephone call she'd looked up the meaning of 'moll' in the dictionary. "You see I don't want to be a gangster's moll, or a cockney spiv's doll, and although I'd consider myself a lady, people kowtowing embarrasses me."

Rich sat back and gave her a heavy-eyed look. "But you are a lady. And I like you. The country bumpkin looked like a doll, your response on the telephone sounded like a moll, but today you are just what I am looking for."

Eyebrows raised she questioned, "Am I indeed, and what would that be?"

"I need a woman at my side, host my dinner parties, be my escort at public events and accompany me occasionally on business trips."

"Is that a job offer, or a marriage proposal?"

He chuckled. "Neither! Do you want some fun, enjoy the high life, have adventures? Who knows as we get to know each other what that might culminate in, but I don't expect you to be my concubine, or my servant, I just want you to be my lady, ready and available when I need you."

Rich was certainly forthright, hardly romantic but that probably was his way and she'd nothing to lose and everything to gain, which made her answer glib. "Your wish is my command." At his grin she retracted, "No hold that, I'm not sure about the bit 'ready and available when you have need', give me enough notice and I'll try and be free."

His frown brought her that feeling of disquiet she'd had on the road when first meeting him, but her fears were banished when replaced by his sudden sexy smile, "How about our first outing next Tuesday evening?" She glanced at her watch, "How about we make the arrangements in the car? I've got to get back to work."

The car roaring up the drive to slide to a gravel throwing halt brought faces to the window and eyes watching as Rich leapt out and hurried around to her side to assist her exit. Once she was upright he briefly nuzzled her mouth, then leading her toward the front door he patted her backside, saying, "See ya soon babe." With that he jumped into the car and with a roar, toot and wave he was gone in a cloud of dust.

The man was a combination of rough, tough and she felt some bluff, but who cared, not only was he a Lord, but his kiss was promising. There was barely time to catch these thoughts before she entered the hall to find a small crowd waiting for her.

Chris shot out from the Press Office to ask, "Well, Jill we

couldn't fail to miss the man and his car? Who's your latest beau?"

"Lord Richard Mallory."

"I say, we are moving up the echelons of society."

She grinned, "No more than you are with Patsy."

Chris gave a rueful grimace, touched the knot in his very trendy tie while looking around at those who had gathered around them. "I try and keep that quiet."

Jill looked around at the faces. "I was too, but thanks to you, and Rich, I now feel in the middle of an unexpected press conference."

Chris chuckled, "That's what happens when you fly high Jill, get used to all the questions now, and see the headlines tomorrow! "Who is the dame in Lord Mallory's life? Will she be the next Lady of the Manor? Turn to page three for an expose of Lord Mallory's latest beauty."

"You sound like Marcus with his vivid imagination. And not everyone reads the society column, it was sheer chance I saw that picture of you and Lady Patricia McCline at your engagement party."

They were obviously providing entertainment for the group around them. She'd never fathomed out why, but David's presence always scattered people hanging about the hall chatting, and on this occasion she'd welcome his appearance. David's policy too was give the press a simple statement, he said, 'then they go away'. It worked for five short sentences satisfied Chris, and his returning to his office was the cue for others to depart, although she guessed the story would grow on circulation.

On arrival home Helen was very perky and keen to know how her lunch date had gone. Unkindly she wondered if she was smoking hash again. Rosemary eating her tea, showed an interest and to Helen she joked, "And when he comes here don't try pinching him from under my nose."

Helen grinned. "Well, you can hardly blame me for picking up Ben, and I was only being friendly to Richard. By the way, don't you think he's a bit of a wimp? Wouldn't you expect a man to be angry if the girl you were with was kissed by another man?"

"So Ben's told you what happened. Personally, not knowing the situation I thought he handled it very well, and I told him so. "

Rosemary headed to her bedroom something she seemed to do if she foresaw an argument or confrontation arising.

Helen shrugged, "Personally, I think to go out with Richard to get to Ben stinks."

Jill bristled. "It may have escaped your notice, but I am still going out with Richard. The fact that I invited him for Sunday lunch and Ben got upset was something I didn't engineer. But then Helen, it seems you and I don't see eye to eye on quite a few things."

"And what do you mean by that?"

"Oh I think you know, but unless it directly affects me I'll mind my own business." She walked out and up to her room wondering how had such a simple conversation developed into a row? What would Rich have done if confronted with Ben kissing his girl? Unexpectedly she shivered, probably have thumped him across the room, yet on what basis did she make that assumption?

On Thursday Richard arrived to go to the first of the ballroom dancing classes they'd seen advertised at the cinema. It was then it struck her how the two Richard's lived at different ends of a spectrum. One arrived on a bike, the other in an E-type Jag. One worked to improve his life, the other to enjoy it. One was quiet and homely; the other outlandish and adventurous. One the marrying kind, liking children; the other saw no benefits in marriage and probably hated children! One enjoyed and talked of simple pleasures; the other wanted to be seen at country shoots, house parties and film premieres. One inherently good, the other... she wasn't sure about. Was she two-timing them? It was too soon to make a decision, but when she did have to make a choice which would she choose?

Desperate for a cup of tea on Saturday morning she hurried down to the kitchen to find the milk had gone sour. Was eight-thirty too early to bother David and Jane? Recently David had rewired the front door bell so they now had one each, so the best way to attract their attention was to ring that.

Their flat door opened to reveal Jane looking bleary eyed wrapping her dressing gown around her. She called up, "Sorry Jane, it's only me. My milk's gone off, have you got any to spare?"

"It's okay. I was awake. Come up. I've been dying to hear how it went with Lord Mallory. I've just boiled the kettle." They moved into Jane's kitchen, a bright and sunny room like her bedroom underneath. As Jane chatted she heaved herself on a high stool at the breakfast bar and looked into the rather old-fashioned formal dining room which David so liked. Jane popped a mug of tea in front of her, "So tell me all."

They were just on their second cup with her telling Jane that Rich was taking her to the Savoy Grill on Tuesday night when David appeared in his dressing gown, his grunt not entirely welcoming. "Jill's just telling me about her date with Lord Richard Mallory."

"Bit early for visiting isn't it?"

"Oh David, don't be so mean. Jill hadn't got any milk and I invited her to have a cup of tea with me."

Wearily David ran his hand through his untidy hair. "Um... his arrival at ITP I gather was rather flamboyant."

Jill grinned, "Not what you would call circumspect."

Jane poured David a cup of tea. "No. And to me it speaks of a man who is showing off what he has, to prove what he is."

With his cup in hand David headed towards the dining room door as Jane protested, "David, that's an awful thing to say about someone you don't know."

"Is it? I'd say think about it."

Cross at his obvious disapproval of Rich she said with sarcasm to his retreating figure, "No doubt you think Ben would be a better catch for your sister?"

At that he boomed, "Yes!" And disappeared into the hall and upstairs before she could make a response to provoke him further.

"What's the matter with him?"

Jane shrugged, "Perhaps seeing you unexpectedly here he felt his territory was being invaded! Mind, he used to invade our territory without warning when I lived with you. Anyway take no notice, I feel it's exciting, you could become Lady Jill Mallory, so tell me, how do you feel about Rich?"

When she left half an hour later with a small jug of milk David hadn't reappeared.

After their second Saturday evening at the Palais Richard returned to sleep overnight on the settee, and replaced Ben at Sunday lunch. Rosemary as usual said little, but produced a delicious roast dinner that Richard enthused about. It had been her turn to make sweet, but he'd volunteered to bring it and turned a packet of digestive biscuits, two lemons, two eggs, butter and sugar which he converted into a delicious lemon meringue pie. If he'd a 'star' chart he'd get ten out of ten for cooking, but the score of his other attributes probably would only add up to ten!

Almost concurrent with her arrival in the office on Tuesday Rich rang. "Hi doll. Glad you're back at work, I tried to get you yesterday afternoon, but they said you were out."

"Oh yes, I went to visit Sam who had an accident here last…"

"Sorry can't chat. Just to say as you're uncomfortable when my title is bandied about I thought tonight you might prefer a drive to a country pub where no-one knows me."

For a moment she was disappointed, then realised his thoughtfulness. "It would be nice to be ourselves without having to dress up and perform."

"Going out with me might mean that in the future, but we can discuss that tonight. I'm looking forward to it babe. I'll pick you up from work at five-thirty."

He was gone before she could ask him not to tear up the drive, or suggest she change from her office suit, but guessed they'd go west out of London so five minutes at the flat wouldn't hold them up. No point in having her hair done this lunch time for he'd probably have the top down on his car.

In arriving when everyone was leaving the building Rich had to edge his way through people so couldn't spin his tyres on the gravel, but he and his car got many admiring looks. Despite the power and speed of the E-type the drive to the end of the M4 took almost as long there and back as the time spent at the pub by the Thames at Maidenhead. In endeavouring not to be a Lord, Rich spent most of the evening behaving more like the gangster he looked, but she wasn't complaining for he was good company. Some of his tales reminded her of Helen's more hairy adventures, and she wasn't sure whether to believe him or not. Rich was very much the gentleman when they arrived back. "My dear I have had the most marvellous evening, I hope we can do this again some time. I'm off to Scotland at the weekend to do a bit of shooting," he chortled. "I'll speak to Cousin Liz about you, maybe next time you could come too. Now do you have next Tuesday free?"

She gave him a broad smile "I do indeed, and guess what, it's my birthday."

Rich gave his lopsided gangster grin, "Then doll have I got a birthday treat in store for you. Have you heard of the remake of the film, 'Gone with the Wind'?"

"Of course I have, but we can't go to see it because it hasn't opened yet in the West End."

"I know, because I am inviting you to the Premiere on Tuesday evening."

"You're what!"

His smile broadened at her astonishment. "It's at the Odeon in Leicester Square. Drinks, reception, meet the stars, and first to see the film, what do you think?"

"Aren't Vivien Leigh and Clark Gable dead?"

"I meant the stars invited to the Premiere to aid its publicity."

"That would be an amazing birthday treat, but I've only two evening dresses. I doubt either are quite up to such a fashionable affair?"

"No worries there doll. As a birthday gift I'll buy you a designer gown." At her gasp and refusal, he put up his hand. "Now please don't deny me the pleasure of accompanying the most beautifully dressed woman of the evening. And I'm sure we can make use of the dress on other occasions. I'll get Victor to pick you up tomorrow lunch time to get it organised."

"Oh Rich, how can I thank you?" She moved quickly towards him, the wide area of gear box between them didn't allow for close proximity. Even so as she went to kiss him, the returning tender nuzzle was longer and stronger than before. His hand moving to her neck, his fingers gently massaging sent erotic messages to her body. When he'd pulled back, she opened her eyes and watched fascinated as his mouth and tongue seemed to savour her taste, before returning for more. The whole action wasn't much more than a few seconds, but that act in itself was probably more sensuous than the kiss. In the darkness he'd laughed softly, "You, beautiful lady, have much potential." Then he was out of the car, helping her to her feet, and with a pat on her backside, he left saying, "See you Tuesday." By the time she'd opened the front door he'd roared off down the road."

It was definitely too late to disturb Jane and David, and she could see that the lights were out in the flat. How dare everyone be asleep when she had such amazing news to tell? Sleep was slow coming and fitful, then just before dawn a deep sleep overtook her and she'd only just had time to get up and out for a meeting at ten o'clock. She'd just returned to her office at noon when the telephone rang.

"Jill, at last. I've been trying to get you all morning. Victor is collecting you at twelve forty-five today, he'll take you to chose the dress, and bring you back afterwards. If you need a final fitting he'll repeat the exercise on Monday lunch time."

Irritated at his presumption she was free, she said with sarcasm, "Victor is going to be busy."

Rich snapped, "It's his job?" Then continued more smoothly, "The shop is expecting you. I've chosen a couple of gowns I think suitable, I've guessed your size. They say they can take in, or let out very easily. I shall look forward to Tuesday and seeing you in the dress." Before she could say thank you, or goodbye, the phone went dead in her hand.

Victor's appearance was as quiet as Rich's had been noisy, yet in some ways more ostentatious. Several people were in the hall when she stepped out of the lift and were gazing through the large windows overlooking the drive. There, in full chauffeur uniform, sitting in a beige coloured Rolls Royce was, she presumed, Victor.

Penny was saying to those hanging around the Reception Desk. "Well, he's obviously waiting for someone, and they must know to expect him otherwise he would have come in and made himself known."

Jill smiled. "It's alright he's waiting for me? See you later." Rich's description of her must have been good, for her exit from the building seemed the signal for Victor to jump out, make a slight bow and open the door for her to sit behind him. At the sight of those faces gawping so conspicuously out of the windows she couldn't resist giving a royal wave. What was David going to say when this got back to him?

Victor slid silently to the kerb at a double-fronted designer shop in New Bond Street. And she smiled for, as she waited for Victor to let her out in true ladylike fashion, she'd seen through the window a little flurry of assistants moving into position, and wondered if she was up to playing the lady of the manor.

A tall, thin and chic saleslady stepped forward as one of her assistants opened the door for her to enter. At the sight of her moderately priced suit it seemed her nose uplifted. And probably assuming she was Lord Mallory's courtesan, there was a sense of sneer as she addressed her in a strong French accent.

The dresses selected were beautiful, but Rich had underestimated her size. Was that a tut from Miss French Chic (over 40 and on the shelf) when the second dress couldn't be zipped up, and was that a supercilious smile at her wearing chain store bra and pants?

Having clapped her hands for her assistants attention, and with a wave of authority, she spoke in rapid French sending them scurrying to do her bidding. One assistant produced a silk dressing gown, another led her to a small ante room where she was given coffee. When Miss French Chic reappeared her assistant was carrying a stunning emerald green dress made of taffeta. With her thumb and forefinger in a circle she stated, "This is ze perfect dress for madam. I have chosen it for you. For your colouring. Ze built in brassiere, the boned corset, it will make you look tall, slim and elegant."

Jill allowed the two assistants to dress her, as Miss French Chic watched. On another barrage of French a tall elegant mirror was rolled before her. At her image she gasped inwardly. The woman was right. The neckline sculptured her full bust and the tight fitting panelled bodice dropped to a slimming 'V' below her waist. Green glass bugle beads covered the bodice and shimmied in the light. This dress was in a class of its own, but she wanted to be as aloof, as Miss French Chic was supercilious, so she said nothing.

"You like it, yes?" At a clap of her hands an assistant stepped forward with a long sleeved. matching jacket. "It is September. You will need zis." There was no sign of price, she didn't dare ask. On yet another clap of hands and French instructions, the girls were making a pin tuck here, an adjustment there. Miss French Chic allowed herself a tight smile. Next came a satin pair of pointed toe shoes with small thin heels. "For the hem, please. We will dye these to match." With an eye for business she added, "And a bag I think. But not to detract from ze dress." Somehow it was made impossible for her to refuse. And in truth the entire outfit was so stunning she didn't want to.

By the time she joined Victor patiently waiting in the Rolls, Miss French Chic's attitude had so changed toward her, she could only hope Rich could afford the expenditure, and wouldn't think she'd taken advantage of his generosity.

With her lunch time sortie being bandied about ITP she guessed Jane would greet her on her arrival home. Excited, she burst out, "Oh Jane you don't know the half of it. Come down to the flat, I'm dying for a cup of tea, and I'll tell everyone at once."

How she enjoyed their astonishment on the news of the premiere invite, but even more their incredulous expressions of the gift of a fabulous designer dress.

Helen bounced up and down on the settee. "I'm so jealous. What about all those famous people you'll meet?"

Jane laughed, "What about a wonderful dress for keeps? Jill I'm so pleased for you, perhaps this is Mr Right?"

Before she could answer Rosemary quietly asked, "And what will you tell Richard?"

"He doesn't know it's my birthday. I won't tell him, and would be grateful if you don't either."

So when on Thursday, she and Richard, leaving for their

dancing lessons at the local cinema, met Jane and David in the hall, she hoped David wouldn't speak of it. In introducing them Richard eyed Jane with disbelief, and David eyed him with bemusement. They were about to stroll off down the street when David called, "No Rolls tonight then? Can we offer you a lift?"

At that she cringed inwardly, but Richard believing it to be a joke replied cheerily, "No, left it at home tonight. It's good sometimes to stretch your legs and walk, but thank you for the offer." With that he tucked her arm in his, and as they walked off down the road he commented, "I like your brother, he's got a good sense of humour! And Jane's very ordinary, not a bit how I imagined her. I thought she'd either be a stunner to look at, or the flighty type who'd caught the bosses' eye. That diadem of diamonds on her finger catches the eye, they must have cost a fortune. And your brother obviously has an eye for investments! With those and the house…" Jill let her mind wander, as Richard rambled on with his accountancy brain about different types of investment.

The following night Jane waylaid her in the hall. She giggled. "I must tell you, David was so confused last night. He went on about Richard with his showy entrances and exits, and he not being as he imagined, then went on about him seeming a pleasant, rather unassuming sort of fellow, even preferring to walk rather than take that pretentious car of his. When I explained he hadn't just met Lord Richard he muttered 'just how many boyfriends has Jill got?' Then declared he supposed it was none of his business. A remark I felt sure you'd appreciate."

"Absolutely right." Jill lowered her voice, "And since that incident with Tania, and our chat, I have little desire to sleep with either of them. Isn't that amazing? I haven't stopped taking the pill though, just in case. Have you?"

Jane grinned, "No! But talking of Richard, he didn't seem your type at all. He struck me as the wholesome, homespun, old fashioned kind of boyfriend, a bit like Bruce. Heavens, to think I might have married him. He wasn't a bit adventurous, his conversation was limited to his sphere, and his opinions built on others, not his own. A car pulled up outside, Jane gave a naughty giggle, "Best go. Dinner's in the oven, but there's just time for David to work up an appetite before it needs serving."

"Before you go, can I borrow the Morris tomorrow? Richard and I are planning a day out, and if we had a car we could go further afield."

"I've no plans to use it, so enjoy yourselves, I'll tell David later."

Jill thought on Jane's comments, she was right. Richard enjoyed simple things, was pleasant, but could be boring. She'd see how tomorrow went.

The lovely, bright sunny day was just right for a leisurely drive to Windsor. They held hands, strolled by the river, ate their sandwiches sitting on a grassy bank and threw the remnants to the ducks. In the afternoon they visited the Castle and walked in the town, finally returning to the car about seven o'clock. When Richard suggested they drove back to his local pub for a meal she guessed he wanted to keep down his expenses. Today, with his insisting to pay for the petrol, they'd probably gone over his 'entertainment' budget. Earlier he'd made it obvious any contribution from her was an insult to his ability to pay.

The pub was basic with no ambience, the meal cheap, the food moderate and the place echoed with the noise of many voices making conversation difficult. So she wasn't adverse to Richard's suggestion of coffee at his bed-sit. His room, the biggest overlooking the front of the terraced house was clean, but shabby. However she'd seen a lot worse over the years.

Sensing Richard's nervousness, she made herself at home by sitting in the one rather old, and uncomfortable, leather chair and chattered away. Once the coffee was made, he perched on the edge of the single bed, but seemed distracted. In the end she asked, "Richard is something worrying you?"

In answer he first blushed, then as if picking up courage, he gave a tentative smile and said in a rush, "I've so enjoyed today. I wondered if we could, you know. I'd feel intimidated doing it at your place. It's only a single bed, but after, I could always…?" In seeing the abhorrence on her face his voice lost momentum, but he finished, "...sleep in the chair?"

Her voice reflected her shock. "Richard, you can't be serious!" Then seeing his deflation at her over reaction she was about to reassure him that it wasn't him she was rejecting, when she realised it wasn't just the room and the shared bathroom down the corridor she couldn't contemplate, but of being intimate with him. How could she let him down lightly?

"Look Richard, I'm sorry you caught me unawares. You barely know me, or I you."

"But you realise that I'm serious about you?" The tentative

smile returned, he took her half finished coffee, put it on the table and drew her up from the chair. His mouth took hers, his hands moved up and down her body drawing her closer into his aroused body, but his passion was having the opposite affect on her. To ward him off she put her hands against his chest and said, "Slow down, Richard, slow down."

"I want you, need you, please Jill."

His plea, his voice thickened by desire and his boyish passion brought her to say gently, "Wanting and needing isn't love."

"But I do love you." In a parody of Ben's actions he closed the gap between them to kiss her in a plunging fierceness as if to do so would excite her, and elicit that which he desired. The difference was Ben knew how to kiss, and it wasn't a forcing of his tongue down her throat! But it also showed her that even if she explained that, taught him about a woman's needs, it was doubtful this Mr Nice Guy could become Mr Right, for she felt more turned off, than turned on.

He drew back, his hand ran distraughtly through his hair, "What's the matter? Sadly she wondered how to answer and caught an underlying whine as he said, "Am I not doing it right? Teach me. Show me. I want to know how to make love."

"I'm sure you do, but…well, there's no other way to say this - you just don't turn me on."

Angry, he turned on her. "What is it with you? Is this what you do? Get men so wound up, so in need of you that we make fools of ourselves? Am I another in the line of your misfits, like Ben? So that's it then. The fact I love you isn't to be taken into account?"

At that she sighed deeply. "You can't make, or stop, someone loving you. I like you. It isn't my intention to hurt you. I don't like Ben: his manner, that cocksure attitude, he irritates me, and I've never encouraged him, been friendly, or gone out with him. But, he has kissed me, and when he does it's like the lighting of the touch paper on a firework, he knows it, I know it, but you can't build a relationship on that either, so I need to keep my distance. It's a mess isn't it? One of life's little ironies…"

Richard having winced at her frankness slumped into the chair his eyes fixed on the window in front of him. Not wanting to prolong his agony, and her discomfort she suggested, "I think I'd better go. Look Richard I'm sorry, but it seems best to say 'goodbye' before you are further hurt."

He jumped up to block her exit, and resting his hands on her shoulders said with great seriousness, "Jill, I may come from the country, not had much experience with women, but I do come from a close and loving family where we believe in helping, sharing and caring for each other. I sense, well has it ever occurred to you that you might be frigid?" At her impassioned gasp he went on calmly, "I don't mean sexually, I mean frozen in emotion. No, don't interrupt! I'm sure you cry, laugh and by your face get angry, but I feel you have this protective barrier up against personal vulnerability."

The compassion in his eyes made her groan before wearily stating, "Richard please don't try and psycho-analyse me."

There was no doubt of his sincerity as he offered, "I want to give you the opportunity to be in a steady relationship where you can let down those barriers to see that love has many facets. And in exchange you can teach me about a woman's needs and desires. In that environment I believe you will grow to love me, as I do you." His eyes questioned hers.

Oh God! To have a man declare his love, offer her a genuine friendship with commitment was what she wanted, yet instinctively she knew she'd never be content with the kind of happy families he was offering. A picture came to mind of Gemma's house, filled with overstuffed, old fashioned settees, dark red patterned rugs, on dark floors, with dark red velvet curtains at the windows, an old-fashioned iron bedstead and marble topped dressing table. But added to that came the thought of family members popping in and out on a whim, wanting to help, chat, know your business, involve you in theirs, she saw enough of that on TV, she didn't want to live it.

Her upbringing had been so different from that. Rarely were her parents affectionate in front of them, they didn't discuss their business, wouldn't go anywhere without being invited, and, until Jane came along, didn't hug even their family and certainly not guests, when they came and went.

She said nothing. Richard's arms fell by his side. The droop in his shoulders and glitter in his eyes revealed his raw emotions. They spilled into his voice as he assumed her answer. "Then Jill, it's a great pity, that you either can't, or don't want to hear my heart in this, and therefore we're not in a place to move on from here. You know where I work, I'll be there for at least a year should you wish to contact me. I'll see you to the door."

Good grief, it was no longer her dumping him, but he dumping her, how had that happened?

147

Stunned she walked in silence down the stairs to the front door. Richard's hand combed through his hair as he opened the garden gate for her. "Thank you Jill for befriending me, a stranger to the big city. I'm sorry it turned out this way because I've appreciated your company and will miss you. Goodbye." He kissed her cheek, turned and swiftly walked back to the front door closing it behind him. As she crossed the road to the car, the turn of events, left her feeling strangely disturbed.

The words Richard had spoken last night still continued to go around her mind as she soaked in the bath. Was she frigid in her emotions? Certainly she'd not been upset by ending their friendship, more put out that, in the end, he dumped her. She'd miss their dancing classes, and although somewhat short on cash, he'd been pleasant to be with. Her hope now was her relationship with Rich would expand and fill the void.

She popped on a pair of light slacks and a short sleeved blouse. The sky was cloudy, but when the sun came out it was warm. With an urge for some fresh air she went out the back door into the garden, past the fountain that Rosemary was keen they restore, and along the short curved paved pathway to sit on the bench under the tree.

With two cups of coffee in hand, Helen joined her. "I heard you come down and thought you might like this. You've about half an hour before the vegetables need to go on. Rosemary really enjoys pottering, digging and planting out here, doesn't she? I think she wants to make it a little bit of paradise, but we don't use it much do we? Is Richard coming for lunch?

"No, we've parted company, he wasn't for me, too much of a country boy!"

"As I said before 'a wimp'! I was in Brighton with Ben yesterday. I thought it might cheer him up, fun, food and friendship. He has taken to heart your words about how he tries to be all things to all people because he wants to please them. He says it's true. And he's very down on himself considering what a hero he is. He told me his life never works out as he hopes."

Jill grunted, "Tell me about" Her question entirely rhetorical as she thought of the disappointments of her own life.

"He said it takes a while to forget, but his motto is not to look back on what he can't have, but look forward to what he can." Helen gave a secret little smile, "And he seems to like me. He said providing I am willing to abandon my pot smoking, drug using friends, and only drink in reasonable quantities he'll go out with me so I can make some, what he calls, 'decent' friends. I asked if that meant the things you and Richard do like walk in the park, play board games, do ballroom dancing classes, visit the local flicks? Wide-eyed he asked, 'Is that what they do?' And then he laughed, and agreed, 'yes' that was just the sort of thing that 'decent' people did, and I might enjoy it. Mind, he did add that he wasn't sure that was all you wanted out of life, saying he'd heard rumours that you were moving up the echelons of society. I told him about the dress and the film premiere. I think he was well impressed."

Jill grunted. Then she proferred, "I'll tell you what, I'll be impressed if you can be persuaded to lead what Ben considers a 'decent' life, for Tania's influence seems to have led you astray." Ben might not be coming to Sunday lunch, but through Helen she was still getting a dose of his 'goodness'! And not wanting another dose, she finished her coffee, stood and commented, "Well I'm glad Ben's fond of you. I must go and do those vegetables."

That evening Rosemary surprised her by remarking, "Richard was nice, but not for you. It's good news about Helen and Ben, he's been very kind to me." For once she was glad Rosemary wasn't a person to expand her views.

By Monday evening her mounting excitement made her restless. She was chatting to Helen when Ben arrived to take her out. Rosemary wanted to watch TV, not talk And when she rang the upstairs' doorbell David appeared to explain they were having a rare evening in and hoped she didn't mind not being invited up. He did add, "Enjoy tomorrow evening. This time it might be you who has a minute on 'News at Ten'." Then on a booming laugh he closed the flat door.

After a fitful nights sleep with dreams of tripping over the red carpet, landing in the arms of Rhett Butler, his face a gangster version of Rich Mallory she overslept so it was fortunate she'd taken the day off. Outside her bedroom door were cards and presents from Helen and Rosemary, and more cards on the front doormat.

From her bedroom she heard the telephone ringing and ran down the stairs to pick it up. On the other end Rich was singing 'Happy Birthday'. "I rang you at work they said you'd taken the day off. Victor says the dress is magnificent, and so it should be that woman has robbed me blind."

"Oh Rich, I'm sorry. When Miss 'snooty' French Chic appeared with it, I just loved it. I can't say I was browbeaten, but she made it impossible to say 'no'. I do hope I haven't been too extravagant, but if it's any consolation I'll be the belle of the film premiere!"

Cheerfully Rich replied, "That's the idea, and what's money if you can't spend it. Now Victor will collect the dress and bring it around about three o'clock.. I have arranged for the hairdresser and beautician to be at your house at four, and we'll collect you at six."

The phone went dead in her hand as she considered, a beautician and hairdresser? They might not be stars, but he was doing his best to make a good impression. She'd better cancel her hair appointment up the road.

Punctuality Rich believed was manners, the hairdresser and beautician having done their jobs helped her into her gown and left with twenty minutes to spare for her to gather her thoughts, and admire herself in the mirror. The neckline needed something. She put on a small silver locket and silver ear-rings, and then carefully glided down the stairs to the flat knowing Helen and Rosemary had just come in.

To her surprise cuddled up on the settee were Helen and Ben watching TV. Rosemary curled up on the other, looked up, saw her, and gasped. The other two turned to see what she was staring at. Ben jumped guiltily to his feet, his eyes filling with incredulity.

In a manner as regal as the dress she smiled, "Relax Ben, relax. Don't get up on my account." Excited Helen leapt up and babbled, "Oh my God Jill, that dress, that dress, it's fantastic! You look like a princess, doesn't she? Ben looking dumbstruck nodded. Rosemary came to have a closer look. Rosemary's expression told her she'd a good idea of the cost of the outfit, and was wondering why a man she barely knew had given her such an extravagant birthday gift.

It was something she'd considered, and didn't want to think about right now. Instead she gave a twirl, and said glibly, "Do you think I look like one of the stars?"

"There's no doubt about that." There was no doubt either of the admiration in Ben's voice.

Helen jumped in, "Ben's only here because we knew you wouldn't be. You said it would be okay."

Her gaze returned to Helen, "Its fine, I understand. I came down to thank you for your cards and presents. I was thinking of buying that book Helen, so just what I wanted. And Rosemary it was very generous of you to buy such expensive French perfume, it's just me. I'm wearing it tonight. I feel a bit like Cinderella going to the ball."

Helen grinned, "Looking like that they might mistake you for a star. You could be Dusty Springfield! And with Rich looking like Robert Mitchum..." It occurred to Jill that was probably Rich's idea, now why wouldn't she put that past him?

Finally Rosemary spoke. "Jill you look every bit the lady, go and enjoy your lord."

Helen having given her attention to the design and cut of the dress commented. "I'd never be able to afford anything like that, but I do have the capability to draw the design to copy it, a dress like this might even be able to do something for me!"

Ben moved in behind her and sliding his arms round her waist drew her back against him, "You're all right just the way you are. You don't need some rich man to spend masses of money on you to make you look beautiful."

Jill gave him a hard stare, as Helen responded by leaning her head back into him at which he bent and kissed her forehead. Had Ben meant his positive remark to Helen to be a jibe at her?

Their doorbell ringing stopped further thought, lifting her skirts she carefully ascended the stairs as Helen and Rosemary called out their wishes for her to have a good time. On the way she grabbed the jacket and bag and rushed to open the door, it wouldn't do to keep Rich waiting.

Outside at the kerb awaited the Rolls and at the door Victor looking every bit the chauffeur in his beige uniform and cap. Above she heard Jane's flat door open, she hesitated, had she time to show Jane her dress? But Victor's words had her hurrying away. "Come it doesn't do to keep the boss waiting."

The moment she stepped into the car, Rich said delightedly, "My dear, just as I had hoped - stunning, and a star. But there's one thing missing. He produced from the cupboard in front a small black case. Inside, displayed on black velvet, were an emerald and diamond collar necklace, a matching bracelet, and drop ear-rings consisting of two diamonds and an emerald.

She gasped and asked, "Are they real?"

"Of course. Don't worry they are well insured, on loan and guarded at all times by the indestructible Victor!"

Rich's words probably weren't far from the truth if Victor's harsh, somewhat battered face, was to go by! As she removed her jewellery she commented. "You must have some very rich and trusting friends."

While fastening the necklace in place he murmured naughtily, "What would you say if I said I'd robbed a bank?"

"Oh honestly Rich! I'd say, if that was the case you wouldn't be putting the spoils around my neck for a film premiere!"

Rich gave a long chuckle. "I like you Jill Reinhardt. I think you and I are going to get along just fine."

Crowds had packed Leicester Square in the hope of seeing the stars and famous people arriving. The Rolls pulled up where behind cordons people gathered several deep. Victor jumped out, walked around the car to open her door. And she, followed by Rich, stepped out to cheers and claps. Who the crowd thought they were she'd no idea, but Rich was thoroughly enjoying playing the part of a celebrity. He'd caught her elbow, then waved and bowed from side to side as they regally walked down the long red carpet into the cinema. He said being his lady would be fun and an adventure, she hadn't expected it to be quite so public, but she smiled coyly around and acted the part thrust upon her. Near the door she heard one reporter ask another, "Who are they? A flash bulb went off. "Don't you recognise Robert Mitchum when you see him?" That made her smile, and the comment after. "He looks good for his age, got to be in his late forties by now." Rich drew their invitations from his pocket, as a man behind her queried, "Are you sure she's Dusty Springfield"? At that Rich laughing commented loudly to no-one in particular, "It's great isn't it when the crowd recognises and welcomes you like that?" With another photo taken, and their invitations not even examined, they moved forward as directed to the first floor bar for champagne and canapés.

"Oh Rich honestly, they think we're famous!"

"Then doll we shall act accordingly, come on." If people didn't know Rich before he made sure they did by introducing her "You won't have met Jill, I'm Rhett Butler to her Scarlet O'Hara." That made people laugh and give their names and before long they'd connected to two couples as the room filled with invited guests from all walks of life.

The bell in the bar rang, followed by an announcement. "Ladies and Gentleman please take your seats in the auditorium the film will begin shortly."

"Rich, do our invitations have seat numbers?"

With a grin, he bent to her ear and said quietly, "I don't know doll, let's stay with Karen and Kevin and see what they're doing." He ushered her forward where the seats in the recently refurbished cinema, were wider than normal and tipped back slightly making it more comfortable to sit for several hours in evening dress. Rich kept up the chatter as they sat beside Karen and Kevin. When a couple arrived and claimed they were in their seats, Rich all charm persuaded them to sit elsewhere. Although looking put out, they agreed, and the ushers, not wanting a disturbance as the film was about to start, found them seats just as the lights went down.

And what a film! In the interval, the talk was mostly on how the widescreen version made you feel part of the action. She also spotted faces from TV and film and they linked up again with an older couple Amelia and Barry as they meandered through the crowds to the bar and a drink. And when in the second half Bonnie, Scarlett and Rhett's daughter, fell down the long straight staircase into what seemed their laps she along with others gave a gasp of horror! Rich patted her arm, and a ripple of laughter followed. It was fortunate that the beautician used waterproof mascara because although she'd read the book, on screen the ending was just so much sadder.

As a film premiere of an old film made new, the evening was more a publicity event in which the rich and famous could mingle. She enjoyed the dressing up and the experience, but she did wonder if the expense of it all was worth it. Obviously the rich and famous always lived like this.

After a rather long wait for the toilet, she returned to find just a few people mingling around and Rich leaning against the wall deep in thought. "There is a post-film party we can go to, but to be frank I think I want to call it a day – it was a long film, and I've a busy schedule tomorrow."

"That's fine I've got work in the morning, and it's been a wonderful evening, thank you. "

"No thank you. In that dress you look a million dollars, and I have met people tonight who could make me a million dollars. Don't look so surprised, that's what these kinds of 'do's' are about, making connections."

On the way back, tired, with the film still much on her mind, and Rich obviously in thought, they didn't speak until they drew up outside the house. "Rich, it's been a wonderful evening. Thank you for the dress, the shoes, the bag, oh just everything."

"It's been my pleasure sweetheart to make you into a fairy princess. Now all we have to do is find other occasions where you can wear that dress. And my idea is to make that real soon." He bent forward, she assumed to kiss her, but instead he slid his hands around her neck, "I'll have these back though before you go." Quickly she removed the ear-rings and bracelet, as he pulled out her jewellery in exchange. He chortled, "It'll have to be a quick kiss doll because we don't want to embarrass Victor, do we?"

Victor standing by the car door had his back to her, looking up at the house. The brush of Rich's lips against hers was so quick it was over before it had begun. And his words as he leant over to flick the door open, were, "I'll be in touch. Just look after that gown okay!" Victor turned, helped her out, and before she'd opened the front door the Rolls had rolled quietly away.

CHAPTER 10

She'd hoped to hear from Rich before the weekend, but he knew she was going to be at her parents on Saturday night for her 'ritual' birthday dinner. The drive with David and Jane to Kelston, just outside Bath, took five hours and exhausted she slept most of the way. Her parents had moved during there in her early teens, so she had what was still termed as 'Jill's bedroom' and it retained much of her childhood artefacts, the wooden dolls house, cuddly toys etc. which her Mum said she should save for her children.

After a day with Paula and Jim who seemed unable to contain Philip, six and Richard, eight, she wasn't sure she'd want children. And her parents weren't appreciating the mud on the expensive Wilton carpet, the handprints on the flocked wallpaper, and the screeching up and down the wide staircase! The catching of Richard, closely followed by Philip sliding down the banister it seemed was the final straw for her father. In rage he hoisted the boys off the wooden rail by the scruff of their necks, bellowed Jim's name, which had them all arriving, and demanded, "If you don't give these boys a damn good hiding, I will." Jim shivered ineffectually, Paula at the top of the stairs wanted to know what all the fuss was about. Her Mum tried to placate her father who was determined not to let go of 'these monsters until discipline had been imposed' while Jane and she looked on, their sympathy with her father. David striding forward took the boys' arms, said curtly to Jim, "Do you want me to deal with this?" Jim obviously mortified could only nod. "Okay boys, Jim, come with me. We'll go to the library."

The boys obviously terrified that their Grandfather was going to carry out his threat looked relieved to be going with David, until he said to Paula who had rushed down to join them, "It's time to teach the biblical principle of 'spare the rod, spoil the child' and the right way to administer that." She and Jane looked at each other. No wonder David had chosen the library, the room farthest away from the lounge for the screams from the kids and protests from Paula as they moved in that direction were already deafening.

Her Mum heading toward the kitchen suggested a cup of tea, her father grunted, "We did well with that boy of ours Margaret,

155

that kind of discipline made a man of him."

"Really dear, I always thought you were a bit harsh. Only recently he told me that as a child he wasn't sure you loved him. But those boys know whatever punishment David decides to inflict, he cares for them."

Jill watched as her father grunted, and turned off into the lounge saying, "I'll have coffee, not tea."

When later her nephews came to apologise for their bad behaviour she wasn't privy to what their punishment had been, but it was clear they adored their Uncle David. At his command they went to bed on time, made no fuss about going to church on Sunday morning and came home having clearly enjoyed it. Even Paula and Jim seemed less harrowed. On enquiry Paula had remarked, "It's all about taking authority, making boundaries and sticking to them, and dealing with it together when they overstep them."

Unfortunately that incident prompted a discussion on the return journey about children, and ended up with David looking grim and Jane equally, if not more, determined she didn't want the hassle of children for some time to come. Hardly surprising seeing she'd seen at first hand that negotiating through marriage and children could equate to walking through a minefield.

It wasn't until Thursday she felt regret at the loss of Richard for tonight she wouldn't be learning the intricacies of the quick-step. But as if fate knew that, she answered her office telephone and heard the familiar gangster drawl. "Good afternoon Jill Reinhardt. It's time to get into that dress again. Dinner party my place on Saturday. Come for the weekend."

Not wanting to sound as if she was completely free, she shuffled pages in her diary. "Well... that could be possible… I'm not sure I could do the whole weekend." It was her turn to do the sweet for Sunday lunch.

His voice ordered, "Then clear your diary." Jill frowned she wasn't going to be at his beck and call like some hired hand. Rich's tone softened, "Look, I'd like to spend some quality time with you before the guests come on Saturday. Bring a nice little bikini for I have a deliciously warm pool, and a masseur you won't want to miss. Your ordinary, every day clothes will do for the rest of the time. So come on, I want to pamper you. What do you say?"

In her mind she thought - Oh yes please, to Rich she sounded hesitant, "Well, I suppose it's not impossible."

"Good. My place is at High Wycombe, remember that area?" There was a chuckle. "Victor will collect you tomorrow at seven, we'll have a late supper. I'm golfing on Saturday morning, maybe into the afternoon, but there's plenty for you to do here. Ange will keep you company. Ange and Chris Waverley, he's into property, mainly in the East End. At dinner will be the couple we met the other night, Amelia and Barry Fenshaw, he's with Coutts Bank. I expect you know Gillian and Gerald Mulder, the Managing Director of Mulder Industries and Bryn and Carole Westgate of Westgate and Westgate the investment brokers." She didn't and remained silent. I won't bore you with the details now, but I've got great hopes that the evening will produce a lucrative business deal."

"In that case I hope I can make it. Can I call you back?

"I'll call you in two hours."

The telephone went dead, but she continued speaking into it. "Rich Mallory you take too much for granted." Mind it was an offer she didn't want to refuse, but what did he expect in return? There had been girls who had agreed to act as hostesses at a 'home' party, and found it had been nothing more than a sex orgy. Did Rich see her as his girlfriend? He'd never called her that. And what kind of people were these he'd invited? The Fenshaws' seemed harmless enough. Would David know those Rich seemed to think she would know?

She put down the phone, and on the internal one dialled David's number. "Hi David, have you got five minutes I've got something I want to ask you?"

There was a pause. "I can give you five minutes this afternoon, or walk me out of the building in two?"

"I'll go for the latter, see you on the stairs." The two minutes was just enough time to collect her thoughts, leave her office and clatter down the back stairs to meet David emerging from his. Quickly she repeated Rich's invitation, but didn't add her thoughts.

David, always the wary businessman, or maybe the suspicious lawyer, commented, "It seems the man either wants to impress you, or make an impression on others, maybe both." He shrugged, "Do you know who he is inviting?" On hearing the names he paused in opening the lift gate and gave a long low whistle, "Now that is interesting, Westgate and Mulder are two very influential business men. He strode out across the hall, she was almost running to keep up. "I know nothing of Lord Mallory, but those couples are absolutely bona fide and wouldn't be mixed up in anything untoward." He stopped by the front door to look at her, "But as you are asking did you think they, or you, might be?" Blow David and his astuteness. His face broke into a wide smile, "Lord Mallory isn't expecting you to cook, is he?"

"Oh don't be so silly." Cross she marched through the door on to the drive and then had to wait for him to catch up. His eyes studied her, was he assessing her as a woman, not his younger sister?

Still smiling broadly he asked as he overtook her. "So what's the problem sis, afraid you'll not make the grade? Well don't be." He unlocked his car door, "You need to know you are more of a catch for that man, than he for you, you are a very attractive woman, and you also have a very sharp brain." David lowered himself in behind the wheel, "The trouble is, most of the time you don't use it!"

Several windows overlooked the car park so she curbed her urge to thump him, but eyes narrowed as she retaliated, "I warn you brother dear, remarks like that bring retribution, and you need to know I am exercising great circumspection!" She shut his car door, but it didn't do much to lessen the booming laugh. He rolled down the window, "Seriously Jill, if you feel uncomfortable don't get involved." Already the car was in motion, with a wave he gave one final piece of advice, "Give Jane a ring, I'm sure she'll have plenty to say."

It was true Jane had plenty to say, from excitement to caution and back again, but the consensus was she'd everything to gain and nothing to lose.

Victor smoothly negotiated the Rolls through the evening traffic, and it was just going dark when they reached the countryside. There was no doubt Victor, big muscled, swarthy faced and in his forties wasn't the most personable chauffeur and seemed to wear his peeked cap with silent irritation. He was excruciatingly polite, but rather abrupt when she tried to converse with him. After seeing a large, high wall on their right they slowed and turned right in front of huge wrought iron gates that swung open as they approached. Tall, sparsely planted, trees spanned the drive, at the end of which she could see a very impressive house, the sight making her inwardly quail and wonder if she was really up to this.

Their family home wasn't small with six bedrooms and four bathrooms and equal number of rooms on the ground floor, but they'd never managed to persuade her father to build a conservatory, let alone add an indoor pool.

The Rolls slowly drew to a halt on the gravel at the front of the house, where immediately Rich appeared at the top of a wide, but short flight of steps. He did indeed look like the Lord of the manor in light grey slacks beautifully tailored to show off his slim hips. A dark red silk shirt clung to the broad width of his shoulders making him look all man, and with his lopsided smile very sexy.

"Alright Victor, I'll take care of the young lady." Briefly his lips brushed hers. "Jill, I'm so delighted to see you. Welcome to Mallory Towers." He waved his hand at the tiny rounded turrets at the corners of the building. "Victor, take the luggage up to the peach suite and then garage the car, should I need to go out again I'll take the jag." Rich holding her elbow guided her into the large hallway where several bright flower displays stood on occasional tables in stark contrast to the dark oak panelling of walls and floor. Red carpet with brass stair rods adorned the wooden treads of the wide stairway that went up and around the perimeter of the hall.

"Now Mabel, the cook, has prepared what she calls a light supper for us, but I warn you she gets most offended if food is left. She's a country woman who knows the way to a man's heart is through his stomach! Now I have put you in the peach room because it has a magnificent view of the hills, and," he chuckled, "it's next door to mine." He might exude sexual appeal, but she wanted to keep her resolution, so her response was a wintry smile. "I thought we'd eat fairly shortly, you must be starving. After that we'll go over the arrangements for tomorrow, mainly about the people coming for the evening. Chris and I are playing golf tomorrow morning. Ange will keep you company. Now did you bring your bikini?"

All the while he'd been speaking he'd been leading her up the stairs. Oil paintings at intervals decorated the walls, and from the high vaulted ceiling hung a magnificent chandelier. The top of the stairs opened out on a long landing that went to the right and left and Rich opened the door of a warm and comfortable room while explaining his was the next door to the right. "We have a shared bathroom between us. If you don't want me scrubbing your back in the bath make sure you lock the door on my side, and if you don't want to walk in on me knock before you enter."

Even to her ears her laugh sounded hollow. She stepped inside. Peach and pale green hues adorned the walls, carpets, curtains, chairs and bed covering. The generous sized four-poster bed was already turned down for the night, and on the pillow rested a peach rose. "Oh Rich, this is lovely."

"I'm glad you approve. Victor will be up shortly with your luggage, refresh yourself, and if you need anything now or later, press this bell. Thomas's the butler, Josie the maid." Heavy eyed he smiled at her, "It will of course be Josie who will come to your assistance. Come down when you're ready, the bathroom is all yours. I'll wait for you in the hall."

Unable to resist she bounced on the bed with glee, barely able to believe the size of the room and house. In his own surroundings Rich had become more gorgeous, more delectable, more sexy and definitely a man to be interested in!

Mabel's supper was delicious, light and nutritious in content with several cold cuts of meat, and a variety of salads washed down with a delicious light fruity wine. As Rich broke off a lump of French bread, he stated, "a bit plain tonight, but Mabel's friend will join her for tomorrow evening, she's a cordon bleu cook and between them they would be hard to beat. Now tomorrow afternoon you and Ange will have a massage, Pierre will be here at 6.00 to do hair and Madeline about the same time for nails and make-up!"

"Good heavens that's quite a regime for a dinner party."

Rich didn't miss the note of sarcasm and was quick to reassure her. "Oh don't get me wrong. I thought you'd like a bit of pampering. You are quite, quite beautiful without any of that. I want the men in the party to be bowled over by you both, so much so they'll say 'yes' to anything." He chuckled happily.

Was he naïve enough to believe that two beautiful women would influence people of the calibre he'd invited to dinner? Now would be the time to state how she perceived her role as his hostess. "Well Rich as much as I appreciate your invitation, and am happy to ensure your guests have an enjoyable evening, I think I should make it clear I don't indulge in anything further than friendly banter." She gave him a wide-eyed look

Rich looking offended retorted, "My dear woman I can assure you nothing more will be expected of you."

Abruptly she replied, "Good, I'm glad I've cleared that up." There was silence as Rich refilled their wine glasses, and after several sips, she asked another provoking question. "Why are you out to make an impression on these people?"

Irritation flashed into his eyes, but the tone of voice was amiable. "Aha, not so easily explained, unless you know about high finance. Let's just say I have certain investments I hope they will buy into. And they need to believe that I, the man who is negotiating the deal, is trustworthy and established enough in their ranks to be part of them."

"And are you?"

"Oh I think with a woman on my arm they can respect, opulence of home to see I have the money, a delectable meal and fine wines to show I have taste should overcome any qualms they might have."

After considering that, she felt the need to ask, "Why should they respect me?"

Rich chuckled. Perplexed she watched him throw down his napkin, walk round the table, sit beside her and take her hand in his. She watched as his finger traced the lines on the palm. "My dear, you are not brittle or false, you are a rose that blooms from within." The pad of his finger moved over her wrist as he murmured, "so soft", the words and action causing her pulses to race. Delicately sniffing the air he continued, "Your very scent, fresh as the dawn." His finger moved to tilt her face, his brown eyes looked into hers. The mere grazing of his lips against hers was tantalising, his words like an aphrodisiac, both playing havoc with her senses. "You have been cultured by the society in which you live, untouched by harshness of life from which many stem, so much so you are unaware of your potential and value."

Had he noticed the cynicism in her eyes? For he stopped weaving his romantic spell around her and broke it by pulling her to her feet. "Let me show you round the house."

Hand in hand he toured her from the 'breakfast' room which could easily seat twelve people to the dining room which looked more like a baronial hall with musicians' gallery. Front and back lounges, library, study, office space, conference room and music room with a baby grand piano Jane would have loved, made up the ground floor.

An annexe linked by a corridor off to the left housed a large, modern kitchen overlooking the courtyard, while the other half overlooked the grounds and accommodated the swimming pool. The area had been extended by a modern conservatory with French doors. Wicker basket chairs were placed around a large glass topped wicker table, and scattered around were several thick cushioned sun beds. Beyond a corridor led to a changing room with towel and dressing gown storage, sauna, gym and the masseur's room.

Upstairs on the first floor were 12 bedrooms, smaller than the two master-ones, but of a good size and several made up ready for his guests. Above were more bedrooms that Rich said was the servants and nursery floor, but as he had no need of either he ignored it.

He led her back to the library, the cosiest room with its leather chesterfield settees set around an old marble fireplace and bookshelves and cupboards on three walls. He opened one of the cupboards, took out a bottle and poured two brandies, while she glanced at the books and smiled. She couldn't imagine Rich being interested in reading from the rows of Shakespeare plays and Dickens' novels, or the other classics like Tolstoy's 'War & Peace'.

Handing her a balloon glass he announced, "A night cap and then an early night!"

Surprised at his bluntness, but nevertheless drawn to him, she considered if she'd make an exception of her new rule for Rich. She watched him move across the room to the leather-topped desk under the window, and frowned as he returned to hand her a file saying, "Homework! Read it tonight - you'll find it helpful."

Unable to comprehend why the contents would be helpful she put her glass down, opened the file and read aloud, "Sir John and Margaret Hemingway." A quick glance down the page was enough to ask, "What is this?" Before Rich could answer she flicked the pages over. Each page had the heading of the guest's name attending the dinner the following evening.

Rich leaning back against the desk seemed to be assessing her reaction as he explained, "It's a personal profile containing useful information on their interests, hobbies, etcetera. Memorize it, it aids conversation."

"My dear Rich, I don't need an 'aid' to talk to people. Here…" she pressed the file towards his chest.

The tightening of his features showed annoyance, but he continued as if she hadn't spoken. "For example, Sir John Hemingway owns horses, it will show your interest in him, if you know which year, and which one, won the Derby."

With a nod she flicked the pages again while stating, "ITP does research on companies, we ask for completed applications forms from prospective employees, so I suppose this isn't that different, but it feels odd to do homework on your dinner guests."

"My dear Jill this is a business dinner, but I like my guests to believe I have a personal interest in them too."

"Why is some of the information blocked out?"

"Good grief woman - so many questions! They're business details of which you have no need to know. Now drink your brandy, browse through that file in your room, then tomorrow you and Ange can familiarise and test yourselves."

"My dear Rich, whatever will you come up with next?

Ignoring her cynicism he replied, "You said you enjoyed adventure, wanted fun, that's what I'm offering. Now drink up sweetheart, you'll need your beauty sleep to keep your mind alert for tomorrow."

In dismissal Rich headed toward the door.

With a chilly smile, she deliberately ignored the brandy. and said in a voice etched sarcasm, "I'd better be a good girl then and go and do my homework. Goodnight."

As she stalked past him through the open door he asked, "Doesn't the lovely lady want a kiss?"

"Suit yourself."

"Then I will." His hand slipped into her hair, his thumb circulating on the bone at the top of her spinal column. For about thirty seconds his lips gently teased hers before stepping back to look into her eyes and jest, "I suspect you'd like a little more." In a hypnotic tone he stared into her eyes and continued, "To enjoy a feast, is to partake of it slowly, giving time to savour the flavours, add different courses to the menu, and then in its entirety – it's sumptuous."

Rich may not provide the 'off the Richter scale' passion that Ben ignited, but his words had promise. She moved closer to make contact with his body. He stepped back.

At her frown he issued a wry smile, took her hand and led her towards the stairs. "Remember Jill to enjoy a feast one must first have an understanding of the menu, then with the appetite whetted, a hunger to savour, and not devour, only then can there be the fulfilment and pleasure that dreams are made of. You have barely tasted the first course, there will be many more to try, but for now I bid you 'goodnight and sweet dreams' for I have much work to do." With that he gave her the usual pat on the bottom before he turned went back into the library and shut the door.

Automatically her feet climbed the stairs. This was a new experience. Rich had hardly touched her, yet had a way with words to conjure up actions. The majority of men she'd known had a way with actions, and conjured up few words. It was a pleasant change to be wooed, not used.

The 'sweet dreams' were sullied with unknown men looking her over as if a piece of meat on offer, but despite she awoke at her usual time of seven o'clock. Her first thought a shower, her second to take advantage of the pool. She swapped her nightdress for her rather skimpy, four triangles of blue bikini. From behind the door she pulled down the thick fluffy towelling robe and tying the belt she ran barefoot down the stairs. The house was silent.

The early morning sun filtered in through the large glass doors bringing a warm glow, and the water sparkled enticingly in the kidney shaped pool. Unsure of the depth she jumped in, swam nearly the length underwater, got out, dived in and did two lengths of crawl as another body splashed into the water. Seconds later Rich swam up beside her. "I'm glad you felt at home enough to enjoy an early morning swim. I trust you slept well."

"Yes, thank you. I don't often get to swim. No doubt I'll suffer tomorrow with aching muscles."

"In that case you will benefit from your massage. Perhaps I could give you one now?"

As delightful as that might be she said stiffly, "I'll wait thanks." His, oh damn' caused her to laugh. "I'll just do a couple more lengths if that's okay?"

"Of course I'll race you."

He won easily doing two laps to her one. From the opposite end of the pool to where Rich sat on the shallow steps, she called, "It's not fair, your body is longer than mine!"

His response was to chuckle and declare, "That's a good excuse. I expect all that exercise has given you an appetite, breakfast will be here shortly." She swam to join him. As she came up to him he arose from the water. On a level with her eyes, only inches from her nose, his aroused manhood was on display. Immediately she looked the other way and made to head around him to get out of the pool.

His hand snaked out and caught her arm. "Don't tell me you've never seen a naked man before?"

"Of course I have! It's just you surprised me!"

Rich chortled, his hand caught hers and made as if to draw her closer. "And you surprised me! I didn't expect to find anyone in my pool. I prefer to swim naked, and left my towel over there."

On a derisive laugh she pulled away from him, pushed her

way through the water, ran up the shallow steps, grabbed his towel and threw it at him as he headed towards her. "Good try Rich, but cover yourself up - I'm not interested." She turned to pick up her robe off the chair, but not before she'd seen his scowl, and caught the malicious glint in his eye. Unexpected fear gagged in her throat. With her back to him she wrapped and tied the robe around her. But when he spoke in a matter-of-fact tone she wondered if she had imagined his expression.

"It's so sunny and warm, we'll soon dry, breakfast won't be long." He gave a long low laugh as if something had amused him and with his towel draped around his narrow hips he headed towards the door. Down the middle of his very tanned back was a long red scar, it wasn't new, it wasn't old, and from it's jaggedness it wasn't from a surgical operation. What, or who had inflicted that? Not a question she felt she could ask on so short an acquaintance.

She shivered and helped herself to a warm towel for her dripping hair, and was about to wrap it around her head when Rich returned and started gently rubbing it dry. "Please accept my apologies if I've made you feel uncomfortable or awkward."

"There's no need, after all it is your pool, if you want to go skinny dipping and don't mind being seen…" She shrugged, "Why should I mind?"

He stopped drying her hair, dropped the wet towel to the floor, and headed towards the table. She followed and nearly bumped into him when suddenly he stopped, turned and enquired, "Am I then to assume you won't be skinny dipping?"

"Certainly not!" Why had she been so quick to say that? She wasn't adverse to it - it could be fun.

Rich laughed. "I didn't think you'd be such a prude." Deftly his mouth swung down on hers. Her body quivered in anticipation. "You're cold, let me warm you." On the outside of the robe his hand stroked up and down her back, while the feel of her breasts entrapped by the broad warm chest caused her to tremble further. Her arms wound themselves around his neck, into his hair while her mouth opened to accept his tongues caresses. The towelling robe slipped open, his hands slipped inside, and in seconds her bikini top and bottom bows had been untied and slipped to the floor. He eased the towelling robe off her shoulders while still kissing her. Sexual abstinence forgotten in the romance of the moment she closed her eyes and allowed Rich to lift and carry her naked body towards one of the cushioned sun beds.

It was but a second that her body soared weightlessly in the air, her eyes flew open and she hit the water with a sharp sting before disappearing beneath its surface. The heartless bastard! Was this his way of punishing her for not being interested in his manhood? She came up gasping. Rich, his hands on his hips laughed and taunted her from the side. On her ripping forth with a string of curses he was even more amused, her only consolation was her words proved she wasn't a prude!

"Ah! Now we are seeing the real Jill. And you see skinny dipping feels good doesn't it. Swim around, feel the water moving with you, the freedom brings speed. I can't wait to see you get out, that beautiful body glistening with water. Ah Thomas come on in, put that breakfast on the table over there. I'm just introducing Jill to skinny dipping. She's never done it before."

Dismayed, treading water, she moved against the back wall into the deeper waters. Rich seeing her naked body was one thing, Thomas another. To Thomas' credit he didn't seem amused, didn't comment and when leaving didn't once glance in her direction, which didn't give any further pleasure to Rich in his humiliation of her. The smell of bacon and eggs, and other delicious aromas like hot croissants assailed her nostrils.

"Come on Jill, time to come out." Rich sat down, began pouring the fruit juice and tantalised, "See I knew you would enjoy skinny dipping and wouldn't want to get out." She gritted her teeth, the wretched man, her back still stung from hitting the water. She looked around for her towelling robe and saw it over the radiator. Was that thoughtful of Rich, or to ensure she had to walk passed him naked? He called between mouthfuls, "The bacon is very good, Mabel has cooked it to a crisp, just like I like it. Are you going to be long? It won't stay hot forever?"

Thomas had disappeared, no-one else seemed about to enter, so she moved into the shallow end, then came out as fast as she could. Rich though reached the robe before her, then annoyingly played the matador to the bull at her every attempt to grab it. From her mouth poured more choice words as he kept it from her. "Next time we use the pool, you'll be accustomed to skinny dipping?"

Cross, she jerked her head up and with her nose in the air stated, "I didn't say I hadn't done it before. And I'm sick of your childish pleasures, so you just keep on playing with yourself while I eat my breakfast." Still dripping she sat down, her back to him, helped herself to the food and hoped the water would ruin the chair's cushion. Rich dropped the towelling robe around her shoulders and before he could decide to whip it away again she slipped her arms into the sleeves and pulled it around her. She wasn't going to be caught like that again! Her best policy would be to ignore him.

"Appetite whetted another course to be savoured."

The inference to the sexual feast and his ability to control himself, and her, was becoming irritating. Deliberately she misinterpreted his meaning, and said to her plate, "Yes this breakfast is exactly what I need, far more satisfying than anything else on offer this morning."

There was a brief pause then Rich gave a humourless chuckle. "Well there is much to avail yourself of today so feel free to enjoy anything that gives you pleasure."

She pursed her lips, and looked up at him to say in a snooty tone, "I'm not sure we have the same taste, for what brings you pleasure certainly doesn't do anything for me."

He gave her a sensual look. "Not quite the message you were giving me just now. His face hardened, "But you will learn that I always rise to a challenge. Just because I have a title doesn't mean I can't enjoy what you call childish pleasures." Sitting back he grinned complacently, "And it was one way to cool you off before Thomas arrived."

Incensed she sneered, "I was responding to a man who I thought was intending to give me pleasure, not fright and pain. So you'd do well to learn that just because you have a title you still have to respect the feelings of others, and I, for one, don't appreciate your childishness."

His face lost its humour. "Be careful Jill. For what you call my childishness means I could have deprived you of that robe a lot longer. I am sure Chris would have appreciated your voluptuous nakedness as he and Ange enjoyed their coffee."

Shocked Jill glared at him. Surely he was jesting, but his expression was deadly serious. Almost afraid she watched as he arose from the table, picked up her bikini from the floor and handed it to her. "Now put this in your pocket, pull around that robe, and tighten the belt, because here they come."

Ridiculously, after what he'd just intimated, she heard herself say, "What here, now? With me like this, my hair all messed up, no make-up?" Rich raised his eyebrows, and she'd barely time to stand and adjust the robe before the other couple joined them.

Chris, was an older, tougher, version of Rich, and turned out to be his property dealing brother. Ange petite, pretty with long blonde hair looked half his age and said little, except to smile sweetly and speak when she was spoken to. Hardly surprising she thought for Chris' looks and manner were even more intimidating than Rich had just been. As she ate she tried to ignore his long assessment of her. The inner darkness behind those brown eyes sent a shiver down her spine along with awareness that it would be even less wise to upset him. Like Ange she felt it better to be 'seen and not heard'. But she saw the similarities between them, especially the grim hardness of their mouths when they talked of several problems that needed their attention. Beneath Rich's charming exterior was a tough, hard man with a cruel streak. Chris had that same air, without the charm, and there was a malevolent delight on his face when he reported, "I've got the evidence now that our boy in Bermondsey has been over charging on rents to get an extra cut for himself. If our Charlie Brown persists with his clowning, it might well be time he had a reminder who he's dealing with, shall I, or will you?"

Unexpectedly Rich's eyes caught hers. She took a sudden interest in pouring herself another cup of tea. Had he seen her anxious expression for he suggested, "Jill when you've finished, take your bikini to Josie and she'll spin dry it for you? I suggest once you're dressed you and Ange can sit in the front lounge, or take a walk around the grounds and discuss your files." His attitude and look gave her reason to believe he wanted rid of her, and she was grateful for an excuse to escape.

"Right, if you'll excuse me." Chris gave her a curt nod, Rich a crooked smile. "Ange, I'll see you in about half an hour." Rich rose as she stood, but Chris sat back his cold, calculating eyes sizing her up. Was that for her role of hostess this evening, or her suitability to have a relationship with his brother?

Josie wasn't in the utility room or kitchen so she popped the costume in the spin dryer and considered whether she should leave when Rich had left to play golf. Perhaps she was just over reacting to his less conventional attitude to life. Hands on her shoulders made her jump. Rich said by her ear, "I hope my big brother doesn't frighten you, he can appear rather alarming on first meeting, he works hard and it takes him time to unwind and become a gentleman again?"

Not quite knowing how to answer she fielded the question with something that had occurred to her earlier. "I was wondering why, as he is older than you, you have the title and not he?"

"Umm, good question. I can see I have a lady here who is not just beautiful." He nuzzled at her neck and ears and murmured, "I knew when I met you, you were going to be rather 'special'." He drew her back against him, and turned her to see them in the mirror on the wall. "There don't we look good together?" She stared at their reflection as he buried his face in her still damp, but now curly hair, his teeth gently nuzzling her ear. A warm hand slid down inside her dressing gown and rested against her stomach, sending spiralling sensations to the lower half of her body. He withdrew his hand, stepped back, and as if the last few seconds hadn't happened, strolled away stating, "Should be back about 4.00 pm." Dazed she stopped the dryer, retrieved her bikini and leant against the work surface. This was unknown territory which was becoming both scary and exciting. Should she leave? Or maybe she should have it out with Rich that she didn't appreciate being fondled at his whim?

Back in the bedroom she locked the door. And, despite knowing he was out, locked the bathroom door to prevent Rich's entry. Even as she showered, dried, dressed and went down to meet Ange she still felt disturbed and unsure of what best to do.

Without Chris, Ange was quite entertaining as she could change her accent at a moment's notice. As they strolled around the gardens going through the details of the guests they gradually became at ease with each other, and she drew Ange out to talk about herself.

While continuing to chain smoking Ange took up her different accents. "I'm a cockney. Born under Bow bells me ma said. Come up a bit since then she 'as. Well cos' of Chris really. 'e saw me acting potential and 'e sent me to drama school. I can dance, act or sing. I 'ad a few small walk-ons on tele, but me main role is like tonight, I'm being someone I ain't."

Next came a very believable and cultured accent. "Now this evening I shall be a debutant with whom Mummy is very cross. You see I've married Chris, a man old enough to be my father. That's because he has masses of money, and can give me a good time. While dear second cousin Charles, you know them, don't you, the Windsors'? Well Mummy wanted me to go after him, but really he's only just out of short trousers and so terribly boring. And Mummy has to admit that Chris is very generous and the estate is looking so much better since he's taken charge. As you can imagine when Daddy died the death duties were extortionate." Ange drew on her cigarette and released a thin funnel of blue smoke. "I can also be very silly, and giggle a lot, and say inappropriate things as a diversion if the conversation gets difficult. Chris or Rich lift up their right hand as though thinking, like this." Ange demonstrated with her forefinger tapping her top lip, and I go into a slightly drunken, but beautiful doll mode, diverting all attention, and then they start up a new conversation when my silliness has finished."

As they entered the conservatory from the garden Ange's accent changed again, "So what I shan't say tonight me old duck is that me old man's a drunkard, me Ma's glad to see the back of me, and Chris' dosh makes me 'appy to oblige with whatever 'e needs, turn a blind eye to whatever 'e does, just as long as 'e don't beat me as 'ard as me Da does me Ma."

Ange's wide grin told her she wasn't serious and Thomas interrupting to ask if they would like lunch served by the pool changed the direction of the conversation.

"So Jill, you've not said how come you're in on this 'big' deal Rich says is going down. You're obviously a classy bird, so assume like everything else, he's hired you in?"

"Good heavens no! Rich and I are going out together." At Ange's astonished expression, she added, "It's been several weeks now. We've had a few meals together. On my birthday he, not only took me to the premiere of 'Gone with the Wind', but bought me a beautiful dress to wear, you will see it tonight. He's very sexy. It's a case really of seeing how our relationship pans out." When Ange didn't comment, she continued by telling her how she met Rich, and with her listening so attentively she found herself telling her what had happened that morning.

Ange gave a tinkly laugh, "Oh that's Rich, always up to something. Trust him to fool about. The only thing he's really serious about is business, so trust him to hook a bit of real class."

Before she could comment Thomas reappeared to announce that the lunch was served. Her mind wrestled with all she'd seen and heard as they followed Thomas. If Ange thought Rich was harmless then perhaps she'd nothing to fear, he was just different and a bit wacky. With Ange, holding forth on her favourite topic of shopping, she listened while enjoying the light, nutritious lunch and delicious fruit from the big bowl that Thomas left for them to savour during the afternoon.

When Ange left for her massage she considered Rich. He hadn't actually stated they were going out, but was always assuring her of his desire! She certainly hadn't been hired, but if it came to escort duties she'd experience, and although never taken payment, a very expensive dress could be considered in lieu of that. Well, tonight, she'd use that very sharp brain of hers to figure out exactly where she fitted into his life and plans. For now she'd read again those wretched files while laying by the pool awaiting her massage.

It was nearly four o'clock when Ange skipped back from her massage bubbling with enthusiasm, "This is the life, Jill."

She smiled, "It's certainly very pleasant. I think, with the warmth of the sun through the windows, and the lapping of the water of the pool, I snoozed off for a while. I expect you and Chris pop up here quite often?"

Ange slid on to a nearby chair, lit up a cigarette, and glanced around as if the walls might have ears, "Rich hasn't been here long. This is only our second visit. I'm a bit nervous about tonight, and glad you're here."

The derisive laugh slipped out with the words, "Oh yes, I'm that bit of class Rich has hooked to go with his title."

Horrified Ange's eye's widened, "Shss. I didn't mean anything by that Jill, honestly! If Rich or Chris heard you say that I'd be dead meat. You won't tell on me, will you?" In seeing the genuine fear Ange's eyes she quickly reassured her, "My lips are sealed." Then arose to meet the masseur heading toward her.

Aromatic oils wafted into her nostrils as Jenny gently massaged her back. Quiet music played in the background, but she was finding it hard to relax with her mind trying to assimilate all she'd seen and heard. Under Jenny's expertise the tension gradually faded, the firm strokes moving across and down her back so soothing that she began drifting in and out of consciousness. But when Jenny started massaging her buttocks and upper thighs she decided she'd had enough. Pulling herself up on her elbows she turned to speak. A heavy restraining hand resting neatly on her bottom stopped her leaping off the table while questioning vehemently, "What do you think you are doing?"

"Giving you a massage. I arrived in such perfect timing I couldn't resist taking over."

Flabbergasted, Jill asked, "Where's Jenny?"

"I let her go. My massage will be more thorough." A frisson of anticipation shot through her body, but the indolent satisfaction in Rich's voice had her say sharply, "Forget it."

"I deserve a trial."

From her undignified position, his hands firmly clamping her bottom to the table, there wasn't much she could do, except snarl, "I'm not a doll you can play with just when you feel like it."

"From where I'm standing doll I'd say if I feel like it, I have the upper hand." He chuckled without humour. His words contained just enough threat to tell her she couldn't win, yet she still wriggled to free herself stating, "Not likely."

His voice purred like a cat enjoying the chase before the kill. "As I said before I like a challenge. After I've finished, your body, will glow." Before she could utter another word his hands started slapping across her flesh with an only a bearable sting. It wasn't long before she could feel her body glowing. But his dousing a soothing, beautiful smelling oil over her, and the gentle smoothing of it into her skin, began to make her feel light-headed. Once she began to relax he gently pummelled her flesh to release her remaining muscle tension. When he said turn over she obeyed in a daze allowing him to massage and oil every inch of her body until she couldn't stop the sighs of contentment breaking forth. Throughout he didn't speak as he concentrated on the job in hand, and with her eyes closed she only recognised he'd finished when a sheet wafted over her, and he informed her, "There's a towelling robe by the door, leave when you're ready. Your body is now beautifully toned. Go and rest in your room, the hairdresser and beautician will come to you. Thomas and Josie will show our guests to their rooms, where they will change, then enjoy cocktails by the pool until we make an entrance together. I'll will collect you just before eight o'clock."

CHAPTER 11

Josie arrived with a cup of tea as the final make-up was applied. With a sweet smile she informed her, "The guests are all in their rooms. And you look beautiful miss, and that dress well… you'll stun them all." And viewing her appearance in the mirror she could barely recognize herself, but it brought total confidence in her ability to be the charming hostess Rich desired.

Ten minutes later Rich's wolf whistle drew her to his standing in the bathroom doorway. His looked very typically Lord of the Manor in beautifully tailored white trousers and dinner jacket, with pleated silk white shirt, and bow tie. Admiration filled his eyes as he sauntered forward to inspect her more closely. "I thought you looked stunning in that dress at the premiere, but after my ministrations your body positively glows, just like a woman madly in love with her fiancé."

His ministrations – she shot him a contemptuous look, and frowned at his final remark. Rich's dark eyes gazed at her with equal intensity. Then he chuckled. "Right, remember tonight to call me Richard. If I direct you in some way, you can say coquettishly, "Yes my Lord." The pad of his forefinger touched her bottom lip. "I want you to bloom beautifully, quiet at first and then bring forth conversation and wisdom."

"What am I to be, some sort of mannequin doll?"

"No. But don't question what I say in front of our guests, or give your opinions, unless agreeing with what I've said, otherwise enter freely into the conversation." Good grief what was this? About to challenge him she remembered it wasn't wise. It was as much as she could do not to blanch away as his finger traced around the base of her throat as he commented, "Something is missing from here, and here, he lightly pinched her ear, and here he drew up her left hand kissing her engagement finger." From under his arm, he produced a large flat red case and opened it on the dressing table. Inside were a magnificent set of large perfectly formed creamy pearls, with bracelet and matching ear-rings - they had to be the real thing!

"Rich, they are beautiful."

He indicated for her to turn around, bent his head bestowed a series of butterfly kisses at the nape of her neck before anchoring the five tiered necklace in place. Despite trying to ignore him, the touch of his mouth against her neck, his gentle appreciative murmurs were just tantalizing enough to make her want more. A quiet rumble of laughter near her ear had her flushing in annoyance. "What a delightful blush, my dear, so charming."

Discreetly she eyed him in the mirror while pretending to concentrate on the pearly lustre around her throat. Did he really think he was God's gift to women? He certainly had taste in jewellery because the pearls brought a more refined elegance to her outfit than the emeralds had done. Fixing the five pearl drop ear-rings on to her ears she asked, "Are these family heirlooms?"

"I wish, but one day maybe, I'm working on it. Who knows if this evening goes well I may be able to buy this for you." With that he pulled out a small box from his jacket and turning it opened it with a flourish.

The size of the solitaire diamond inside was enough for her to gasp, "Is it real?" Bemused she watched as he drew up her left hand, planted kisses on the fingers and then placed the perfectly fitting ring on her engagement finger. "Rich, what is this? Your guests will think we are engaged."

Rich shrugged, "Is that a problem?"

"Well, we're not."

"We might be one day, so why not pre-empt that by getting a feel for it. Not only that it will serve as a good ice breaker to announce to our guests."

"Announce to the guests! My family might hear about it?"

"Why should they? They don't deal in foreign commodities or building investments."

"But we hardly know each other."

"Everyone loves a romance, especially love at first sight. You said you wanted fun, excitement, so no buts, and if something unexpected comes up, just look shy and look at me, and I'll do the talking."

Further protests were thwarted as he caught hold of her hand, opened the bedroom door and said to Chris and Ange emerging from their room along the corridor, "Hey you two, here's a good warm-up for the evening, look Jill and I have just got engaged." He lifted up her left hand. The lie spoken aloud, Ange's bewilderment, and the snarl on Chris' face gave rise to even more disquiet about Rich's 'fun' plan.

"She'd never agree knowing ..."

Rich jumped in and said quietly, "Shss bro! It's a ruse!

174

However, the guests won't know that, so with their congratulations and the champagne flowing it'll be a good atmosphere to do business. Just be sure you three only sip at yours, let everyone else get happy and drunk. We don't want any slip ups!"

Chris' grim look had her wondering of the wisdom of this adventure. But there wasn't time to consider for the Fenshaw's appearing on the landing had Chris becoming all charm and smiles as Rich introduced them. Within minutes their news was announced from couple to couple, champagne was served and Rich spent the first course of the meal expounding the romantic circumstances of their meeting when her car ran out of petrol.

He was right, their engagement was the catalyst to relaxation. Several couples told of how they'd met and fallen in love including some very personal anecdotes on the ups and downs of marriage. The details on the profiles came in useful, her only difficulty was in continually steering the conversation away from her to them.

Perhaps a little deceit wasn't a bad thing if it brought such a response from people, but she had a relapse on hearing Rich say to Gerald Mulder, "... Jill's father. I've not been able to speak to him yet, he's away in Germany. Doesn't Jill look beautiful tonight? I couldn't resist popping the question just before we came down to dinner. They say diamonds are a girl's best friend, so I didn't expect she'd refuse when she saw the ring." Jill glanced at him and saw his little grimace before he continued, "I rather think I surprised her, so I just hope she won't change her mind. Of course, we'd prefer it if you didn't take the news of our engagement beyond this room, for it would be better if the family knew before the press did."

Carole Westgate homing in on the conversation turned to ask, "So Jill what does your father do?

"He runs a pharmaceutical company."

Rich laughed, "Professor Franz Reinhardt no less."

Bryn Westgate seated on the other side of her patted her hand. "I don't know your father dear, but I do know of him and how hard he worked to reinstate Inhart Pharmaceuticals after the war. Most drug companies are booming these days, but I am sure that the way the shares have rocketed over the past few years it has been beyond his wildest imaginings. Inhart's certainly have made a good investment for many of our clients and, of course, has made your father into a multi-millionaire." He nodded thoughtfully and added, "He is without doubt a brilliant man, although I should imagine a difficult one!"

Shocked at what Bryn had just revealed she pulled herself together to answer casually, "Oh he's just my Dad." And was glad Carole distracted him from saying anything further for her mind was racing. When had her father become a millionaire let alone multi? Did David know? Bryn probably thought the dress she was wearing was because of her huge clothing allowance, some joke! And what of Rich, was he after marrying her for her money - money she didn't even know her family had?

On hearing her father's name, she tuned back into Rich's conversation with Gerald. "...Franz would agree that the government bringing in the NHS after the war and subsiding drugs, even the expensive ones, has caused the pharmaceutical industry to boom. Of course, he'd also say that profits are ploughed back into research. Rich chuckled knowingly, "He is, of course, reticent to boast, but his company is often the forerunner of new drugs. I've heard rumour he's up for an MBE?"

Startled she stared across the table at Rich. Was this another of Rich's ruses for surely her mother or father would have told her?

"How do you think he will take to his daughter becoming Lady Mallory?"

"In my experience he's not a man to say much. I expect a Lord in the family will be taken in his stride."

Jill pictured her father hearing the news. Like David, he was impressed by the integrity of a man not his title. And Rich's perspective of what was acceptable wouldn't count as that with her father. In fact, she instinctively knew he wouldn't like Rich. He'd be against any romance with him, which made her wonder why she was sitting at his table, flaunting a massive diamond and pretending to be his fiancé. In spite of her father having an overbearing manner he'd little time for pretension, and had summed Jane up in minutes liking her honesty, candour and obvious integrity. David hadn't needed encouragement, but her father's approval had cut across any worries he might have had about marrying his secretary, or, as some might call it, marrying beneath him.

She supposed she ought not to be surprised to find Rich had done his homework on her as well as his other guests, but his apparent familiarity with her family did cause her an indignation which she suppressed for now, but made a mental note to confront him later.

"Jill, Jill? You seem far away. What will your parents think of you and Richard getting together?"

"Sorry Bryn, I was just wondering that myself." She glanced across at Rich feeling his eyes on her. "Frankly I feel a bit swept off my feet, but I expect if I am happy, they will be too." Rich gave what looked to be a tender smile she returned it with a small demure one and wished it was that simple.

"Well, there's no doubt, my dear, you'll be a rich asset for Rich!" He gave a tipsy guffaw, and repeated his joke around the table.

It was time perhaps to put people straight. She laughed, and then said loudly, "I'm afraid the only rich asset I'll bring to Richard is my personality and talents, for despite my father being wealthy, he believes his children should make their own way in life, and we've not seen a penny of it."

There was a stunned silence. Rich stared at her. Chris glared at her. But Rich quickly roused himself, his crooked, and oh so sexy smile directed first at her, and then around the table. "And as I said to Jill, who cares? It's you I adore. What is money? Don't I have enough of my own to make you into the princess you so truly are?" Without exception, those around the table burst into applause. Rich delighted realizing he'd pulled off a hat-trick stood, bowed and suggested, "On that gentleman, shall we depart to the library where cigars and port await. Ladies please excuse us, and if you wish retire to the music room, I'm sure you'll find much to discuss in our absence." He gave a sexy chuckle, and as the other the men rose, he in true gentlemanly fashion moved to her side, lifting the chair back as she stood. His lips brushed hers causing Carole Westgate to coo, "How delicious to be young and in love."

Bryn put his arm round Carole's waist, "But my love remember marriage and love are like the ingredients of fine wine, the longer they blend the more mature and full bodied they become."

Carole giggled, "Full bodied you may be, but I'm not ready to be mature yet!" Bryn guffawed as those around laughed.

If they married, would she and Rich be like that in thirty years? Her parents weren't quite so open, she couldn't imagine her father saying anything romantic, but their love showed in the way they listened and understood each other. She led the ladies from the room and was surprised to see Chris' steely gaze had changed to give her a cool, tight smile. She could only assume she'd gained his approval, not that it mattered in this farce.

"Come on Jill, let's go and compare notes on young and old love." With that Carole slipped her arm into hers,

On opening the door of the music room Amelia Fenshaw squealed with delight over the baby grand piano, asked if she could play, and turned out to be rather good. Josie had left a coffee tray and petit fours on the sideboard by the door, so she poured, while Carole and Gillian handed them around.

The continuing questioning about her wonderful romance, and playing the lovesick fiancé, was becoming difficult. She looked for Ange and hoped she'd recognize that her touching her upper lip was a sign she needed to be rescued. And it appeared Ange was more observant and intelligent than she made out. For she quickly responded by interrupting and insisting they play cards,

In a break between games she excused herself for the toilet where Ange followed to whisper conspiratorially, "Glad I told you about the sign. I nipped upstairs earlier, Chris and Rich were in our room. Chris was saying, "Not such a bad idea after all to get engaged to that bird, we'll have no difficulty now launching our company with Westgate behind us, the share dealing should take off like a rocket." Ange giggled, "Very different to his words earlier about Rich's bringing you into this."

Jill smiled, but was beginning to wonder how wise it was to 'have been brought into this'!

Re-entering the room she refilled her coffee cup and it was obvious Lady Margaret Hemingway and Gillian Mulder seated on the settee hadn't realised she was behind them for Margaret was saying, "Well I can only assume Richard is one of these new peers. He does have some title in land I believe in Scotland, but I gather there is little revenue from that. John tells me he's something of an entrepreneur, with a variety of connections that bring in his wealth. I've also heard that brother of his has made his money putting people out of their homes by raising the rent so high they can't pay, but then you can't believe everything you hear, can you?"

Gillian shrugged, "Gerald told me their company has been buying up those empty, almost derelict tenements in the docklands area, and renting them out to immigrants."

"John says there are plans to redevelop that land. With the houses and I believe disused warehouses Richard has been buying up over several years, I suspect he hopes to make money that way. Do you remember a couple of months back about those high-rise flats, Ronan Point, where one corner collapsed after a gas explosion on the 18th floor? Well, I heard that the land on which they'd been built had been bought and sold by Richard, and his brother had something to do with the building going up. That's not necessarily anything against him, but it will make people wonder if these high rise buildings are a good thing. And problems like that will put people off building upwards making land prices in London go even higher, and those involved even richer!"

Amelia joined her at the sideboard to refill her cup. "I see Jill you're wearing that magnificent dress again. Not something you'd want to keep in the closet."

Out of the corner of her eye, Jill saw Gillian's embarrassment before she covered it up by saying, "Oh there you are Jill. What a wonderful dinner, did you organise it?

"I'm afraid Gillian I can barely boil an egg, but Richard's cook is a gem, isn't she?"

Ange called across, "Come on we're waiting for you to come back to the game."

It was midnight before the men returned in a very jolly mood, well oiled by Rich's malt brandy no doubt, and Chris and Rich broad smiles indicating a deal had been struck. More brandy and port was poured, the ladies imbibing with them and Rich was so attentive, loving and charming she was beginning to believe she was his beloved intended. One by one the couples drifted off to bed, leaving them alone with Chris and Ange. Within seconds of the last guest leaving Chris grabbed Rich and like a pair of kids they patted each other on the back, hugged, laughed, and danced around the room. "We did it bro, we did it! I didn't think he'd sign the papers tonight, but you were right about the engagement, that's what clinched the deal." Rich grinned at her as they broke apart, "And you, doll played your part wonderfully."

Chris grabbed Ange and kissed her, the intimacy of his hands revealing his passion and need. Sickened she turned away and as Rich went to dangle his arm around her she moved out of his reach. That probably caused Rich to drawl, "Come on bro, I know a good deal is enough to incite rabid sex, but not here. We've no inclination to be voyeurs, so please ravage the delightful Ange upstairs in the bedroom provided."

Chris gave a leering laugh and she guessed to bait her he added, peppering his words with expletives, "Oh bro, you know how much more fun it is with an audience!" When the door closed behind them, she turned back to Rich to vent her wrath, but was

179

thwarted by his saying, "Please accept my apologies for that. Chris is a bit of a rough diamond. He's only my half-brother and sometimes he takes perverse delight in trying to shock my friends." Rich picked up her hand and kissed it. "How can I show you my appreciation for your part tonight? I'd like to consider you becoming a more permanent fixture."

Her resentment of earlier bubbled, sarcasm laced her voice. "What, engaged to you, or being part of your deals? I'm not sure I'd see that as appreciation. My father, Professor Franz Heinrich Reinhardt of Inhart Pharmaceuticals doesn't generally approve of people who lie, steal or cheat. Although it would appear you know more about him, his company and his movements than his own daughter."

Rich's eyebrows raised, he looked down his nose, an amused expression on his face, "My dear Jill, you don't seem to have formed a very good opinion of me, what will it take to change that?" His eyes roved over her body in a suggestive manner.

"Look Rich, or is it Richard, I don't know what game you are playing here, but I seem to be becoming embroiled in it, and what I am saying is I don't like it."

"Oh Jill, but I think you do." Jill gritted her teeth, and took a deep breath, ready to bite out a scathing comment when Rich continued, "You can't tell me you didn't enjoy this evening. Not only did you look marvellous, but you carried the whole thing off with an aplomb that only someone of your calibre could do. Westgate was practically eating out of your hand, and he is contacting me next week with a dinner invitation where I can make more valuable contacts."

"Oh yes, contacts, business, what sort of business are you in Rich, the get rich quick kind by the sounds of it?"

His hand snaked out pulling her toward him, "Now Jill let's stop this before you say something you'll regret."

"I am already beginning to regret having taken part in your charade this evening. I feel used, put up as some sort of mascot to enhance your business prospects."

His fingers began to circle her neck line as though to create sexual frisson in a bid to deflect her anger, instead it fuelled it. "Rich, Richard, Lord Mallory... whoever you want to be I don't need you and I have no intention of becoming, or maintaining, tonight's charade of being your fiancé. Your kind of fun isn't mine!" With that she moved from his grasp, marched out the door, up the stairs and resolved that first thing in the morning she'd pack and leave.

In her bedroom she examined closely the ring. If this was a diamond, it was worth at least four times her yearly salary. With the ring and dress, she felt like a fairy tale princess, but this was a strange land with a scary edge. She shivered, snatched the ring from her finger, and then more carefully removed the ear-rings, bracelet and necklace placing them neatly back in their red case still on the dressing table.

"You look so beautiful…" She whipped around. There lounging against the door post between her bedroom and bathroom, his bow tie missing, his shirt open and looking incredibly handsome, debonair and with a sexy smile was Rich. "You did so well being my fiancé, and certainly helped everyone enjoy the evening. I thought you were having fun."

Cross he was now invading her private space she snapped, "It isn't fun when one person deliberately sets out to mislead another. It's serious if deals are struck which might later prove to be detrimental to others. I like Bryn and Gerald they seem honest and genuine men. Our supposed engagement and fantastic ring gave them a false impression."

Rich straightened, but didn't move as he intoned, "She takes the morale high ground!" Was she imagining that those simple words sounded menacing? Her stomach curled in the silence. Well she wasn't going to be intimidated, so she reiterated, "I said it before, and I say it again, I am not going to be a party to lies or cheating."

Like a panther about to pounce, he closed the distance between them. Alarm flared within her as he anchored his hands around the base of her neck, his thumb stroking her Adam's apple causing her to look up into his eyes. Determined to outstare him she held herself stiffly and narrowed her eyes in defiance rather than panic at the hard, menacing look in his eyes. "So Jill Reinhardt you've never lied or cheated. You've never been involved with a married man, or men?" How did he know that, how could he know that? "And you would have me believe that you didn't beg him not to go back to his wife. After that it was love 'em and leave 'em so where was being honest and genuine in that?" The curving of his lips in a deadly smile, not only revealed he'd had her investigated just like the others, but that he was relishing demolishing her stand for morality and enjoying her vulnerability. She wanted to step back from him to establish some kind of control, but he wasn't going to let her move. Her stomach

181

churned, and the words, "Let go of me" sounded feeble and strained.

His hands moved to cup her face. "Was that moral Jill, was that fair?

In an attempt to get free, she pushed her hands into his hard chest, his face hardened, his hands tightened their hold. She compressed her lips and gave him a black look. She wasn't going to answer that. "Was it Jill? Don't make me hurt you to get the answer I need."

Her eyes widened, was he threatening her? His questioning look had her remembering the incidents of the day where she had come off worse in tangles with him. Mesmerized she watched the change in his face, for when he spoke again it was more gently as though the last words had never been said. "We all have skeletons in our cupboards Jill. We all have reasons for what we do. In the world in which we live we have to take many routes, sometimes not always pleasant, but as in the animal world it is the survival of the fittest that lives to see another day." A hard unpleasantness simmered beneath the surface. The subtle play of his fingers around her ears, face and neck didn't distract her from his words, "In meeting you, I feel fate took a hand, and dealt me an ace card, one I wish to keep."

He could think again! She twisted to get away, but he anticipated her move and brought his mouth down on hers willing her to open up to him with light erotic strokes of his tongue. Then still holding her head he murmured huskily by her ear, "To enjoy passion it should be a steady build, not a ravishing from an inward fire. In preparing for the feast it would be a shame to spoil it with a sacrificial burning!" In their altercation they'd moved back several feet, so he was able to stretch beyond her and pull back the bed covers. "Come there's a good girl, let's get this dress off, and you into bed. It's late, we've had a busy day and we're both tired, so let's not do anything hastily. After all an honest and genuine man should wed a woman before he beds her."

To her surprise he unzipped the dress, helped her step out of it and then tucking her up in bed kissed her like a caring brother. "Now don't go rushing off tomorrow in a fit of pique, and I want you to wear the ring until our guests have gone. Goodnight sweetheart, sleep well. Remember tomorrow is another day!" And in true Rhett Butler fashion, he was gone!

A gentle wind flowing over her face and body had her stretch and move like a contented cat, before an alert sounded in her brain. Her eyes flew open to see Rich standing by the bed surveying her with a preoccupied expression. The discovery of the bed covers neatly pulled down to her feet had her demanding "What's going on?"

She sat up and reached to drag them back up. He thwarted her attempt and censured nonchalantly, "It's time, my dear fiancé, for you to rise and shine."

"Give me those bedclothes. I'll get up when I'm ready. And I don't need you watching over me."

"Are you always this tetchy first thing in the morning, sweetheart?"

"I'm not tetchy."

"That's good then because if you were I'd have to take action to overcome it, and our guests will be sitting down to our table for breakfast in about twenty minutes. I'm sure you will want to shower and dress before seeing them."

The arrogant swine, she wouldn't put it past him to carry her from the bed to breakfast, half dressed, tousled and looking sated. "If you'll get out of my bedroom and the bathroom I'll see you down there."

"No sweetheart, I'll wait until you are ready and we'll go down together, with your ring on, looking the fulfilled, blushing and loving fiancé."

Just as the big grandfather clock on the middle landing chimed nine o'clock she and Rich exited from her bedroom toward the 'breakfast room' where they found the party somewhat depleted. The non-appearance of Ange was explained by Chris as her need for a lie in, Bryn Westgate had a hangover and Barry laughed saying Amelia was getting too old for late nights. While she thought how fortunate for those not there, for she didn't want to be there either for Rich took every opportunity to touch and kiss her leaving no doubt in the minds of the remaining guests that they'd had a night of unadulterated passion. And she couldn't help question why they hadn't. Yet, she couldn't imagine friendship with the man, let alone, companionship or marriage.

Uncannily Rich seemed to have read her thoughts, and her desire to depart with the other guests after breakfast. Full of the charm he exuded over breakfast, he said, "I so long to just have one of those old fashioned Sunday's, you know reading the paper, relaxing together. I'd like to have some time alone with you, to get to know you, and for you to know me. You asked me about me being Lord Mallory instead of Chris, so I'd like the opportunity to explain that, and my family history Curiosity, and knowing Ben was at the flat having Sunday lunch, made her hesitate, making Rich more persuasive. "Please stay. It isn't often I get to relax and so hoped we'd have fun together, please don't rush off." The plea, the sadness in his eyes and voice, decided her. She'd nothing better to do and what harm could a few more hours in his company do?

And so they moved into the lounge, ordered coffee, and sharing the Sunday Telegraph chatted amicably about its contents. But determined to take him up on telling her more about himself once they had drunk the coffee, she put her part of the paper down and asked bluntly, "So Rich, why do you have the title and not Chris?" She expected him to avoid the question, change the subject, or distract her as he had to other questions on previous occasions, but to her surprise he put the paper down, stretched out his legs, smiled and answered her.

"Chris is my older half brother, we have a shared mother, but not father. He's never known the identity of his father. My mother, a kitchen maid was raped in the nearby woods of Lord Mallory's estate in Scotland. Lord Mallory allowed her to stay on and have the child, later when his wife died, and probably because my mum was grateful, at twenty-five she climbed into the bed of the sixty-six year old, and then in later years nursed him until he died at 87. Within a year of sleeping with him she was pregnant with his child, me. Chris at five was very jealous, and the easiest way I found to keep him happy was, and still is, is to let him think he's in control. I ignore what I can, and once I was able I made sure he has just enough money to enjoy himself, but not overdo it. Between us we had a difficult time growing up because of being called 'the bastards'. We learnt to bully, fight and win.

"Lord Mallory had two sons well into their thirties when I was born. Then two years before their father died, Greg, the oldest, who would have inherited the Estate died in a boating accident with his best friend, and three years later the younger, Peter, had a car accident which killed him, his wife and two boys. I obviously knew the brothers although they'd never really acknowledged me, as my Mum was never Lord Mallory's wife. We lived in the main house with my father. Greg, his heir, had lived in the west wing. On his father's death Peter then became Lord Mallory, and was within weeks of moving to the main house when his family had the fatal accident. I'd learnt about the Estate under my father's tutelage so just carried on. Greg's wife hadn't want to continue living there, wasn't interested in managing the Estate, nor were her two married girls. On Peter's death I negotiated a reasonable salary with her to look after the place. With no male heir, part of the deal was, as I was Lord Mallory's only living son, I take the title. It was more a legal deed, than inherited. That was sixteen years ago, the estate escalated in value, Valerie died six years ago, and her daughters sold up, leaving me with about 10 acres in Scotland to go with the title."

"So where did Chris fit into all of this?"

"Jill you really don't want to know. Let's just say Chris has never been easy and it's better to find a way to say 'yes' than 'no'. Three years ago when… well let's say I employ Victor as my bodyguard, and to keep an eye on Chris generally. You could say I'm the brains and he's the brawn, but don't repeat that if you value your life." Rich chuckled, "Good grief, this has got far too serious. Anyone would think you were my nearest and dearest, I can't remember the last person I told that to. Come on let's have some fun in the pool, and you don't have to skinny dip if you don't want to."

"Does your Mum still live in Scotland?"

Rich's face clouded over and returned to the gravity in which he'd spoken of the past. "No. I'm not sure what happened. Mum seemed happy with me managing the Estate, and we lived in the main house. I wanted to invest money, I was into stocks and shares and travelled back and forth to London. She got a bit lonely, but that didn't seem to bother her, then one week I came home and she was very troubled, said she'd found out something terrible, but needed to think it through and wasn't ready to tell me. Next time I saw her she was at the undertakers where they reckoned she'd taken a couple of hundred aspirin and drunk a bottle of rum." To Jill's surprise tears welled up in Rich's eyes, "I never got to the bottom of it. It was said to be suicide, but there was no note, and why? Mum was never one for the drink, yet she must have got high on it before she took the pills for it was spilt all over and round her chair in the lounge. Chris was a bit deranged after that, we'd now call it a nervous breakdown, always saying he wanted to do the best for us. I found a way to send him to London, he thought he came to manage my business, but he got on my nerves with his mood swings and I wanted to stay in Scotland to get over Mum's death. I was relieved when for a few years he found a safe environment, but he still has tendencies to go too far, so now Victor keeps an eye on him."

Bolstered by Rich's confidences she agreed, "He gives me the creeps with that cold stare of his."

Rich grabbed her hand. "Oh he won't bother you. You've nothing to worry about, now come on, I've just had a big property contract signed by Mulder, and an opening to invest the money in some very good commodity markets with Westgate, so enjoy the high life with me, and I may be able to make that diamond, a real engagement ring."

On her way upstairs to put on her bikini, she felt pleased Rich had spoken of his early life, yet had a feeling there was much more he wasn't saying. Was the fighting, bullying and winning still intrinsically within him? He'd admitted to rising to challenges, but he hadn't hurt, or humiliated her in public, would he have carried his threats out?

Rich had put in several inflatables in the pool, and any awkwardness died away, as they fell off, climbed on, and played about with them like a pair of kids. Her bikini top fell off in the first five minutes, but they were alone, and she wondered if perhaps deep down he was an old fashioned man who really did believe a woman should be wed before taken to bed. When Victor approached Rich warned her so she could keep under the water, and when he'd gone he produced deliciously large hot towels, wrapped her in one, patted her dry, replaced it with a dry one, and with the customary pat on the bottom commanded she run upstairs and get dressed.

After a late, and deliciously cooked roast dinner, they walked around the garden where Rich surprised her with his knowledge of plants and shrubs. Further from the house a cold breeze caused them to find a spot to shelter and they sat briefly to gaze down at the lake.

"This is a lovely spot Rich, I bet in summer this place would be delightful. I can see it with marquees on the lawn, musicians in the summer house, tables on the patio, and people swimming in the lake."

"Indeed Jill and I'm hoping if I play my cards right I will still have you, my 'ace' in place, to enjoy and experience it with me."

"What you need is a wife and family Rich to really enjoy all the pleasures that such a place as this could afford." She blushed, "Oh and I'm not suggesting me! But you have a whole floor that you don't use, why live in something so big, if you don't mean to fill it with little voices and laughter."

To her surprise, Rich stood abruptly, pointed to the dark clouds which were fast replacing the autumnal sun and suggested they hurry back. Once there he requested, "Go up and pack, we'll have a cup of tea and Victor will take you home. I've an appointment this evening, and I'm off to Scotland in the morning." With that, he walked into the study and shut the door. However when she came down he appeared and joined her for a tea and was again all smiles.

"Thank you, Rich for the weekend. I have had some qualms over our supposed engagement, but it has been good to spend time with you and get to know you better."

Rich gave a small bow, "My pleasure my princess. I'm up in town again next Wednesday we'll go out to dinner somewhere quiet and unobtrusive. We need to get together before the Westgate party, to discuss the guest list and make our plans."

Peeved that this wasn't an invitation to a quiet romantic evening, but to discuss his next business dinner she said somewhat sharply, "Another opportunity to use me as the loving fiancé again?"

"Do you really mind? Enjoy the fun, the pleasure of being rich and influential, you might get to like it."

"By the sound of it I am already heir to a fortune if your facts are right."

"Then here's your opportunity to practice your social skills. If I wasn't so hectically busy with this dockland enterprise we could have more days like today. But I need to rush things through otherwise someone will twig we're on to a good thing and barge into my territory, and there's already rumours of that."

Surprised at another flow of information she said nothing, and Rich seeming to realise perhaps he'd said too much, changed the subject. "Once this is out of the way how about a romantic weekend in Amsterdam? It will be something to look forward to, in a month or so."

That long, before they could spend time together again without all the charades. Rich's finger slid into her hair to do what he knew tormented her, the stroking of the nape of her neck. "You're irresistible do you know that? How I stop myself from making you completely mine I don't know, but its best for both of us that I don't give way to temptation. Now where's Victor, I'll get him to take you home."

Two and a half hours later back in the flat she sat moodily on her bed. She didn't know what to think for as usual Rich had barely said 'goodbye' making it difficult to judge what he felt. Was he afraid to have intercourse with her in case she produced a child he obviously didn't want? Perhaps he had a family already? She opened the lid of the box containing her dress, best to hang and cover it, who knew when she'd get to wear it again. The matching handbag and shoes she popped into a large hat box and climbed up to put them in an upper cupboard out of the way. If nothing else happened between her and Rich there would still be a few tales to tell her grandchildren about having dated a Lord. She grimaced, that was if she was ever going to get married in time to have her own children!

CHAPTER 12

On Monday if it hadn't been for everyone asking if she'd enjoyed her weekend with Lord Mallory it would have seemed a weird dream in which she'd been an actor playing a part.

Jane appearing on her arrival home in the evenings was becoming a habit! Today, she announced, "David went to Birmingham he won't be home until about eight. Come and eat with me, I've a pizza recipe off the radio I want to try out, and I'm also longing to hear about your weekend."

Not knowing how much Jane knew about the Reinhardt family she decided to keep the information she'd discovered to herself until she'd had opportunity to talk to David. But the rest she told her with frequent exclamations and interruptions from Jane! It was amazing how in the midst of that Jane brought her recipe together, and obvious she had concerns about Rich, but was waiting for the right moment to voice them.

"Here's the cutlery, can you lay the table? I'll just stick the pizza under the grill." It smelt delicious and with the cheese bubbling on the top she cut off two good size wedges to place them alongside the salad on the plates. Once seated Jane questioned, "Rich may think being engaged is fun, but what if you bump into those people in a few weeks or months? And would you want this engagement developing into reality? It seems to me he's controlling and manipulating you to do what he wants, if he's not using sexual enticements, he's bullying and even scaring you."

Jill said nothing, it was as if she were hearing her own thoughts voiced. Jane continued as though thinking aloud. "It is good for married women to have the contraceptive pill, but with that freely available and the passing of the Abortion Act last year I think love will gradually be degraded to casual sexual relationships. Those things will erode the need for commitment. Fidelity will go out of fashion and in forty years the word 'bastard' no longer thought of, let alone a stigma, and one-parent families containing children from a variety of fathers could be normal."

Jill put down her knife and fork, "Oh that's ridiculous, it could never happen." Jane took a drink and added, "Believe me if the welfare state extends to help women with babies without men, it is quite possible." They ate in silence contemplating that. The front door opened, closed, and before Jane finished saying, "That must be David" he'd taken his usual two stairs at a time and arrived in the dining room.

He gave a brief, "Oh hello Jill" before hugging Jane and thoroughly kissing her. Jane with shining eyes suggested, "David sit down and talk to Jill while I get you something to eat. Jill can I tempt you to a piece of chocolate cake with a cup of tea?"

"No I better not. I've eaten too many goodies this weekend. I'll let you two be together. But if you don't mind David could I have a few minutes in private with you?" Jane looked puzzled and David having been keen to greet his wife was now in the hall retrieving briefcase and coat from the top of the stairs. "I'll just put my things away. Go into the lounge." It struck her, as David joined her, how tired he looked. "So what is so private Jane can't hear it? If it's to tell me Lord Mallory's title came with a small plot of land in Scotland I already know that." David settled himself on the settee opposite her.

"I expect too that you know he makes his money from property deals and has investments in stocks and shares." David nodded. "Right well that's Rich, but how about you tell me about Dad. I hear he's been put forward for an MBE?"

Concerned David sat up. "Who told you?"

"You checked up on Rich, well guess what, Rich checked up on us! He probably got his information from similar sources. The question is, is that right?"

"Yes, but its not meant to be common knowledge. Mum, being excited, told me in the strictest confidence. Dad would be furious if he knew we knew, it's supposed to be top secret."

"But you can know, but I can't. And then I find out from someone I barely know."

"Don't get upset, you haven't deliberately been left out."

The frustration, lies and deceit from the weekend rose up, and the emotions she'd felt then began to spill over into her conversation with David. "Well that's what it feels like. And that's only the start. How would you feel if people were being told things about your family of which you had no knowledge?"

David sighed heavily his facial expression gave her to believe he thought she was making a fuss about nothing. Cross she sat forward. and said grimly, "You wouldn't appreciate it if you were sitting with guests at the dinner table and heard for the first time that your father not only runs, but owns a multi-million pound company. And his personal fortune is such that your fiancé declares one day you'll be a very rich woman."

The speed at which David leapt to his feet he could have been fired from a cannon. "Fiancé, fiancé! What fiancé? Oh no! Not that wretched Mallory fellow. I tell you there'll be nothing for you if you marry him!"

Jill jumped up to challenge him. "And do I care? Will I miss what I didn't know the family had?"

The door opened. Worried Jane asked, "Is everything alright?" It was obvious from their stance it wasn't so she asked, "What's going on?"

David's boomed reply could probably be heard in the basement flat, "Jill's engaged to that Mallory fellow."

Jane laughed, "Wrong! Jill put him out of his misery."

In bewilderment David glared, first at Jane, then Jill.

"You explain it to him later. For he's got so rattled about that he's not addressed the issue for which I need an answer. Can you give us a few more minutes?"

Curiosity written over her face Jane nodded, and withdrew. David sank wearily back on to the settee and said in a more rational tone, "Sit down Jill. Please, hear me out. I'm sure with the probability of Dad's MBE, and the knowledge there's money in the family, Rich sees the advantages of being with you, and I'd be very wary of what he is up to." David had a valid point, one she had considered. "I know little or nothing about Mallory, but what I have heard makes me think he's a rough diamond, dressed up as a Lord. Little is known about his property investments except that which he allows, and that may not be reliable. It's your life, and it's not up to me to interfere, but a relationship with him could bring you more harm than good."

No longer feeling animosity she agreed, "That's possible, but as you said, I've a sharp brain, and, I am using it. Now tell me about this family money?"

"I hope you haven't mentioned it to Jane."

"No, I wanted to talk to you first."

"Good, because what I tell you must never go beyond these four walls. I don't know how Dad has set up his finances, but you can guarantee it's with integrity and wisdom. He's never been one to discuss money, his business, family finances, or inheritance. His belief is if people have too much money it can ruin their lives. That's why we've never had any massive handouts, and we're not likely to get any. The exception is that trust fund for our education, used also for sensible investments, not money from our grandfather, but set up by Dad. He's never been mean, but he's never spoilt any of us. What about the sports car I fancied? I got a new, but sensible Morris Minor for my eighteen birthday. I was told if I wanted something different I'd have to work and save for it."

Jill grinned, "And he was very reluctant to employ me one summer. He put me in the Orders Department on the average wage, and made it clear I had to leave by the end of September and get a permanent job. And when I said to live in London I'd have to sell my eighteenth birthday present, my beloved mini, Dad pointed out that the London transport system was excellent and to have a car here would be more of a liability than a pleasure." Eyebrows raised she went on, "Last Christmas I thought he was very generous to give us £50 each, which covered my two week holiday in Spain in March!"

"I think Dad is embarrassed by the amount he's made. They could live in a mansion, but Dad says he prefers being cosy, and complains the house they have is too big, but Mum insists she needs six bedrooms when we all go down to stay. I'd no idea he was so rich until Mum confided in me. He ploughs money back into the business. I expect you thought he had the factory in Bristol and the research lab and offices in Slough and that was it, but there's a huge research facility in Ireland and branches of Inharts across the world. This MBE is for his drug donations to charities who serve in undeveloped countries, but he's already begun extending the business to the third world to provide industry and jobs as well. But talking of the Trust Fund Mum says it has more than enough provision for all our children's education and inheritance." David gave a heavy sigh, "But, as yet, there are only Richard and Phillip".

"So what you are saying is your lump sum to buy this house ten years ago, and mine two years ago, was from Dad, not our grandfather?"

David nodded, "And Jane thinks marrying me she 'married into money'! Can you imagine how intimidated she'd be if she knew that Dad's personal fortune is enough to make each of us millionaires."

With eyes wide in shock she murmured, "That much?"

"Dad plays things very close to his chest, and Mallory wouldn't know the half of it, but it doesn't take a genius to work out he's doing well, despite his playing it down with keeping the family house." He slapped his thigh and gave a booming laugh, "And not putting in that swimming pool we always wanted".

"I find the whole thing incredible!"

David gave a broad smile, his eyes glittered with moisture, his voice dropped conspiratorially, "I'll tell you something else that's incredible. When Dad met Jane he took such a shine to her he insisted I have the money to buy her a ring which would be worthy of the diamond he felt she was."

"I thought you'd used the last of your savings."

"That was what you were meant to think. I was amazed at Dad's generosity and overwhelmed at the worth he placed on Jane."

Tears filled Jill's eyes with the emotion of the moment, while David said, "Oh Jill, I hope I haven't upset you telling you this. Dad I am sure will be just as generous when you meet the right man."

"Oh it's not that..."

"Look I've had to tell you this, I'll tell Mum you know, but don't let Dad know that we know! Now you have to forget about it and carry on as normal. Dad wouldn't profess to being a Christian, but he does believe what Keith said at Jane's church that night we all went, 'you can't take your money with you when you die, but you can sure send it on ahead.' He's been doing that for many years, which is where this MBE..."

Jane's head appeared around the door, "Your dinner is getting cold."

"Yes my love and I'm starving for food, and your company." David stood, "So Jill lots to think about, but don't let it rest heavily upon you." He patted her shoulder as he headed her towards their flat door.

On her way down the stairs she smiled. What she didn't have could hardly rest heavily upon her, and barring accidents her Dad had at least another twenty years to live, so if need be, she'd worry about it then. Rich might know about it, but she'd made it quite clear to him, she hadn't any, and wasn't likely to get any.

By Friday with no contact from Rich about the meal they were supposed to have had on Wednesday, or the details of the proposed Westgate dinner party she began to wonder if her outburst of not having any money had turned Rich away. But as he had so succinctly put it, he could be tied up keeping the 'vultures from his ventures'! That morning Helen had announced she wasn't feeling very well and had decided to go home for the weekend, and Rosemary had left with a suitcase probably with a similar intention. She grimaced, with no flat-mates, and no plans for the weekend perhaps she should have kept the other Richard around for company.

After a quick sandwich for lunch, and David's car being available she borrowed it to visit Sam who was now fit to return to work. Mrs Bennett on opening the door looked worried, and then said with relief, "Oh it's only you ducks, fought it might be Jane and her man. Come in, I'll make a cuppa." While Mrs B was making the tea Sam told her of David's visit. "'e's a good man that brother of yours. Told me that machine was lethal, the company was liable and I'd every right to sue. Of course, I told 'im, after all these years enjoying me work at ITP I couldn't do that. 'e went on about insurance, settlements, courts and payment, 'e said whether I returned to ITP or not I'd get compensation, it was all a bit complicated, but I knows 'e'll do me right. Even said if I should decide to leave 'e could, as a friend 'elp and advise me. I was very touched, a toff like 'im wanting to be me friend."

"Believe me Sam, he means it". Conspiratorially she whispered, "And there is another factor you ought to consider, very seriously..." Sam bent his head toward her. "Living without Doreen's hot pot, roast beef dinner, jam roly poly, apricot crumble...? I don't know about machines being lethal, but without that food I'm not sure you'll survive to sixty!" Sam screwed up his face, "Neither do I, but..."

Mrs B entered. She and Sam looked at the wedge of cake on the tray, burnt on the outside, sunk in the middle, its currants lying in doom on the bottom. "Only a small piece of cake Mrs B, I have to watch my weight." One glance at Sam had her stifling her laughter, and Sam snorting into his handkerchief. Bravely she nibbled at it while telling them an entertaining and abbreviated version about 'her Lord' as he called Rich. Mrs B seemed rendered speechless at the wonder of it all.

Sam scratched his bald head, "You could be marrying into money, and it seems I'm about to come into some. This accident brought Maud and I to thinking, and as we'll 'ave enough money for me to stay 'ome, why work? It's been good at ITP, but a brush with death well it changes everything. And I'd not be letting anyone down for Ben knows 'is stuff, 'e'll do well at me job." He chuckled, "So we've decided, like the "Take your Pick" game show, we'll 'take the money'."

194

"Oh Sam, I hoped you'd come back. But I shall certainly arrange a good retirement 'do' you can start by telling me about friends and family you'd like to invite."

Back at work she had to return David's car keys and that seemed a good opportunity to talk to him about Sam's replacement, and leaving party. But before she could access him Miriam delayed her. "Jill, it's so good to see you. We really must have lunch together soon. You have so much to tell me."

Jill gave a small smile, and thought, 'not if I can help it', but said, "I'm so busy these days, but I'll…"

David opened his door, "I thought I heard your voice, come on in." He shut it behind her, pointed to the settees and asked, "Is that Lord of yours behaving himself?"

"No idea. I haven't set eyes on him since we last spoke. Perhaps the MBE and the money didn't have the effect on him that you presumed?"

"Ouch, a bit sensitive there, are we?"

"I'm just fed up of everyone asking after him."

David shrugged, "That's what happens when you go out to lunch in a Rolls Royce." She sent him a sarcastic grimace. He drew his hands together, rested the formed steeple against his mouth and considered her thoughtfully before balancing his chin on his forefingers saying, "In visiting Sam I guess you now know of his decision."

"Yes, and it's a shame to lose him, but I can understand. As I drove back I was thinking about his replacement. Ben has proved himself very competent he could easily take over. I also remembered at Ben's interview he mentioned an older man he'd had to lay off when his father's print works went bankrupt. It occurred to me, Fred is probably about the same age as Sam, and with the difficulty we had recruiting Ben I wondered if that avenue would be worth pursuing?"

Sitting back in his chair David gave her an amused look and said, "Good heavens, I thought, as far as you were concerned, even thinking about Ben was taboo?"

Irritated she snapped back, "This is work! Remember, I have to be unbiased. What do you think?

"My dear Jill, speak to Ben, see what he thinks. I've no problem with him becoming Print Manager."

"I thought the job offer would seem better coming from you."

"So we are still a little bit miffed by the man are we?"

"His attitude annoys me, that's all." David eyed her

thoughtfully causing her to agree. "Alright, I know, it's my job."

"Good, now let's talk about Sam's leaving party. Get Ben involved in that too, let him decide what would suit Sam, and you organize the catering and invitations, I'll consider the speech and presentations."

Although she nodded, and it was her job, she couldn't help think, Oh great! Not only was she left to tell Ben of his promotion, discuss Fred as his replacement, but work with him too! And on leaving David's office, and with a determination to get it over and done with, she marched down to the basement.

Joe grinned as she passed by. "Long time no see, too busy lording it about I suppose."

"With the number of remarks I'm getting like that I'm beginning to wonder if it's worth it."

He winked, "Only you know that!"

"Where's Ben?" He pointed towards the small sectioned off area used as an office. At the sound of the door opening Ben's head rose from the paperwork, the welcoming eyes and smile froze.

"Hi. Have you got a few minutes?"

Ben nodded, and with a voice devoid of expression, stood and said, "Sorry, we're not used to visitors." With that he cleared off a stack of papers from an old kitchen chair in the corner, and put it in front of the desk. "Please sit down."

"Thank you." From behind the desk, his blue eyes looked enquiringly into hers. Uncomfortable she plunged into the reason for her being there. "Sam's decided not to come back. We will need to replace him. I've just spoken to David and it would seem sensible to ...er ask if you'd like to take over the position of Manager?" She paused, expecting a response which didn't come. "Of course, there will be a salary rise for the extra responsibility." Ben's expression didn't alter. "I came straight down here to ask you, so haven't found out yet what that would be."

"What's the hurry? You could have spared yourself the stairs, rung me up, or sent me a memo with the details."

God, the man was so infuriating? Why was she bothering? Well she was here now, and determined to remain cool. "That Ben is true." She shrugged, "I assumed you cared about Sam and would want to be kept informed, and would appreciate knowing how highly he recommended you to take his place."

"In that case, thank you for coming all the way down here to tell me that." He certainly wasn't making this easy for her, but she forged ahead. "It wasn't just that." Ben looked at her with sombre intensity. "You said you had a friend, I think his name was Fred, he'd gone into retirement early because he couldn't get another job at his age. It occurred to me he might be interested in taking over your job?" The blue eyes fixed on hers, flickered with surprise so she queried, "What do you think?"

Irritatingly he asked, "Why would you want to employ Fred?"

Exasperated she bit out, "I've just told you, because we have a vacancy?" She willed herself to stay calm. "You told me that Fred felt he'd failed you, and you felt you'd failed Fred. Here's an opportunity to change that, but if it's a problem, forget it." Annoyed now she'd even considered the idea she leapt up and headed for the door. The discussion about Sam's leaving party would have to wait, she'd had enough of this man for one day.

A hand on her shoulder made her spin round. Ben's face was inches from hers. "You would do that for me?" The cool blue eyes had warmed drawing her as if into a warm sea.

Disconcerted she moved her gaze downward to his mouth and questioned, "Why not?" The proximity of Ben and remembrance of how those lips had felt on hers caused her to step back. Determined not to lose focus she forced her eyes away from his mouth and continued, "We'll save time and money not having to advertise." Realizing her gaze had returned to his mouth, she quickly turned, drew herself up in order to see through the glass at the top of the partition and indicated, "We need someone out there, as soon as possible".

His eyes followed the direction of hers, but the moment she turned, she was trapped by his closeness and saw the amused warmth in his candid gaze.

Surely, he hadn't noticed her momentary preoccupation with his mouth. Flustered she fielded his look with a cool questioning stare and stated, "I'll leave you to consider your job offer. And with your recommendation and willingness to work with Fred, any interview for him would only be a formality. Obviously the sooner you can let me know yours, and his decision the better." Relieved she could now escape she stepped towards the door.

"It would seem his Lordship's kisses don't match up to mine."

Her hand froze on the handle. Wide-eyed she turned to gasp, "I beg your pardon!"

A mocking smile quivered on Ben's lips, "When a woman looks at a man's mouth so longingly it..."

"What utter rubbish. You really are the most maddening man

I have ever met."

His lithe body closed the distance between them, his face stopping within inches of hers.

"Would you like me to prove that to you?"

Jill could feel the telling blush rising up her neck. Ben grunted with satisfaction while she trembling with indignation ground out, "You arrogant pig. I don't know why I bothered ..."

Her words were cut off as Ben twirled her around, placed himself between her and the door, and drawing her out of sight from the Print Room his mouth planted itself across hers. On the one hand she was furious at his audacity, on the other desire welled up as those sensual lips melded against hers. The effect was somewhat similar to tectonic plates rubbing together – so earth shattering that an intense reverberation shot throughout her body. Her token gesture to pull away had her looking directly into bright blue eyes, not heavy with desire, but filled with aching longing. Shocked she closed her eyes, and the obvious invitation brought the return of his mouth, his hands drawing her in as her body shuddered against him. Her head said she had to stop this, but her body already fired for melt down wanted this. This was lust, she'd given lust up. With great strength of will she drew back to whisper huskily, "Please, don't do that." And then unbidden her eyes spilled over with tears.

"Oh Jill, I'm sorry, I'm so sorry. Please, please don't cry. Here, sit down". He drew her to the chair, dazed she obeyed. How ridiculous, why was she crying? And why was she allowing him to crouch before her and gently wipe away the tears slowly trickling down her cheeks.

"I, I don't know what's the matter with me?"

He shook his head. Concern filled his eyes, and didn't leave her face, as he admitted, "I don't know what happens to me either. When your beautiful big brown eyes look into mine, a passion ignites inside me to unleash what's inside of you. I thought it was just attraction, but it's more than that. From that first time I kissed you I knew you were my soul-mate, the 'one' for me."

Jill gave a self-effacing laugh, "You barely know me. So much, for my being cold and rude to you, it obviously had no effect. Soul-mate, I didn't see that coming. Ben believe me it's just sexual attraction, not me as a person. Or perhaps you recognize a wounded soul, you are good at collecting those, with your comfort and empathy."

Ben shook his head. "Oh we've all been knocked by life, but

you are wrong, this is… well I, I just fell in love with you despite it all." He shrugged and gave a rueful smile.

Oh God, what was she supposed to say to that? "Ben I'll admit to a sexual frisson between us and to my changing my first judgment of you, but I couldn't get involved with you."

"Do you want to be involved with Lord what's his name?" She shook her head. "Well then give me a chance. Get to know me. I'm not going to make ten out of ten, but I am sure we could work on it." His smile was one of gentle encouragement.

This was getting ridiculous within three weeks she'd three men suggesting they wanted to consider a future with her! Each had elements of Mr Right, each had a different, but major flaw to becoming that! Maybe Mr Right's were only engineered by heaven! Anxious to escape she pointed out, "Oh Ben what chance could we have? We can't even hold a sensible conversation without my being irritated, frustrated or angry with you."

Regret echoed through Ben's voice, "I'm sorry you feel that way. I do know sexual compatibility isn't enough to build a relationship, but fun and intimacy can break down barriers and bring friendship and love."

Sadly she stated, "Believe me Ben I've tried that way, it doesn't work. I'm now going for fun and friendship first. Rosemary and Helen enjoy your company, but I've found lunch on Sundays so difficult I've had to find somewhere else to go to avoid you. Even our conversation about the job and Fred was a prime example of how you irritate me. Plus you are going out with Helen and I know she cares about you."

The derisory laugh startled her. "Helen! Oh Jill, she knows how I feel about you, has done from almost day one. But Helen, being Helen, wants to get as much from life as she can which includes abortions, drugs, sex. She's a willing partner, giving happily of herself, more than I would ever ask."

"So what you are doing then, using her?"

"I don't see it like that. My hope was to get her away from that lifestyle." He shook his head, "But I don't think my caring, or helping her to see things differently, will be enough, she needs someone permanent to ground…"

The door flew open, a voice boomed, "Joe said you were…" A pair of raven black eyes stared across at them. Ben jumped up from his crouched position, she groaned inwardly, and felt guilty of…she wasn't sure what. "It would seem I've interrupted more than a business discussion."

Now there would be trouble. But to her astonishment, David gave a broad smile, his tone almost jovial as he questioned, "Am I to believe that hostilities between you two have ceased?"

Oh God, her brother could be as annoying as Ben. With a toss of her head, she said, "That's doubtful. Anyway, what did you want? It's unusual for you to appear down here?"

"Nothing that can't wait." He glanced at his watch and drew out his car keys. "There's only an hour until the end of the day, so here Ben, take these, drive Jill home, you can have your discussion there. This is not the place to sort out personal differences." Bewildered, Ben looked questioningly from David to her. David dropped the keys on the desk. "I'll ring Jane. She can come and pick me up later. Leave the keys on the stairs for her."

Stunned neither of them spoke as David ordered, "Don't just stand there, go home." With that he marched out the door and was quickly out of sight.

CHAPTER 13

The only words spoken in the next forty minutes were Ben's who having cleared his throat instructed, "We'd better do as he said. Go and get your things. I'll meet you at the car." With her mind reeling she obeyed while asking herself why was David being so high-handed? Ben was sitting in the driver's seat when she arrived. His expression was blank, but she could feel the tension emanating from him. As they headed to the flat, she considered the way David's mind worked. He may not have manipulated this, but he probably saw it was a prime opportunity to push them together after all, he'd made no secret of the fact he liked Ben, and wasn't impressed with Rich. Did he realise the chemistry between them could spark, ignite and her pent up frustration would act as matchwood, lighting a fire of passion that she alone wouldn't be able to control?

It was rare David had a rash idea, but this seemed like one. Why was she even going along with it? It was unfair on Ben, to give him false hope. What were they to discuss, all the negatives she had against him? Where would that leave him? Why was she worrying about that? Where had the desire not to hurt him come from? Did she care for him, or was this just a mellowing in consideration of the feelings of others?

Ben following David's instructions, left the keys on the stairs. Without speaking they headed downstairs into the flat. Determined to keep in business mode she faced the situation. "Look Ben, you know as well as I do, that I don't think this is a good idea. There's nothing more to say on a personal note, but I suggest I make a cold drink, we enjoy what's left of the afternoon sun, and as David has asked me to work with you to organize Sam's leaving party maybe we can find some common ground in doing that."

The cheeky grin, which had been absent, over the past few weeks, reappeared. "That Jill sounds very sensible."

She stared at him, but determined not to get uptight. The safest way through this was to remain cool and distant. "I'm glad you agree." On her way to the kitchen she informed him, "The key to the garden is just above the door. Deck chairs are under the stairs. Oh I expect you know that already from the time you spend here. I'll get the drinks, paper and pen for notes and be out in a minute." The garden being in full view of the houses around it would be a good deterrent against foolish actions!

From the kitchen doorway a few minutes later she sighed, he'd certainly taken her suggestion of fully enjoying the sun. His shirt was off, his trousers rolled up to the knees and without his socks and shoes he looked like a boy out to play as he bent over the fountain in the centre of the garden. Oh no! Surely, he wasn't tampering with it? They'd had endless men looking at the thing, an original feature of the house, and...

Ben let out a yell as a siphon of water about an inch in diameter shot out and hit him in the face. He leapt back, but not before he was soaked, and his neat pile of clothing on a deck chair had taken a good hit. The sight of his shocked face and dripping body sent her into peals of laughter. He looked at her in surprise through the cascade of water which flowed several feet into the air, splashing over and beyond its intended bowl. After several attempts using his hand he managed to cap the water, and with his free arm wiped the water from his hair as it dripped into his eyes. That left a brown line of dirt across his face making him the perfect picture of a ragamuffin. Not wanting to risk going outside and getting wet she set the tray down on the dining room table and stood in the doorway arms folded to goad, "You should just see yourself. Serves you right, I've warned you before about keeping your hands to yourself." Her laughter like the water rose up and overflowed at his getting his comeuppance.

Not to be put off, or down, Ben struggled against the water pressure to put back the cap over the spigot, each time he took off his hand the cascade shot up and over him. Hand over the hole he said with mild amusement, "Stop that laughing woman, and turn the damn water off."

Without moving she managed to control herself enough to respond. "You will need a dam to stop that flow of water. We don't know how to turn the water off."

Frantically Ben looked around the garden. "There has to be a hose, a pipe, or a tap, somewhere?"

With great nonchalance, she leaned against the door post. "Apparently not! The last person who came to look at it said it was an incredible invention by a mad genius. And the only thing to do was to cap it off otherwise it could be a threat to the environment and a serious drain on the London reservoirs."

The force of the water and exertion was giving Ben a ruddy

glow, but at that news, his face significantly paled. "Well don't just stand there, call the water board, dial 999, do whatever you do when this happens?"

Jill shrugged, "I don't usually do anything when this happens. I've only lived here twenty months and David is the only one who has ever experienced the phenomenon."

Calmly she watched Ben hopping up and down desperate to get the cap back on. Drenched, and probably feeling cold from the light evening breeze, she smiled sweetly as he demanded, "Well don't just stand there, see if David's home yet, ring him, do something, find a way of stopping this thing?"

The underlying panic in Ben's voice she deemed must be a first. "The only man who knows about these ancient fountains retired to Wales and said to David to ensure we wouldn't be flooded it was best to close it down. So you can see our dilemma if it continues, I mean look at the mess already." It was impossible to keep a straight face as she looked at his worried frown.

"I don't know why you think it's so funny. I can't stand here all night in order to stop the flooding of the garden and the draining of the London…" He took his hand from the fountain, the water spouted forth as he strode towards her. She backed inside as he dripped outside. "You little minx, I've a good mind to douse you in the wretched fountain. Come on, you really had me going there, now turn it off."

She grinned, "It is the truth. You can't turn it off, except by capping it, or digging up the patio and probably the entire garden to find the underground pipe."

"Give me that drink, I need it. And tell me what happens next, because I can see you're not too bothered."

"I'm told it lasts until the cistern empties and the pressure goes. There was an idea that the fountain might have been part of Kensington Palace, or a private house with a park. Without the water pressure it is a fairly simple job to replace the cap. David had it capped off because being unable to control it he considered it dangerous, don't worry its not enough to flood the garden, I made that and the rest up."

The sight of his cheeky grin, and the intense brightness of his eyes as he looked at her caused her to say archly, "A lesson I believe in not interfering in anything without asking first." At his drowned state she giggled, "I bet its not often something gets the better of you."

His grin turned wry as he handed back his empty glass. "That's true. And it's a relief to know I've not endangered London's water supply, but I might still be a danger to the local environment if I have to go around stark naked until my clothes dry." His response to her expression of dismay was the emergence of a low rumbling laugh which caused the hilarity of the episode to encompass them both.

From the doorway Ben glanced over at the clock, "Helen and Rosemary will be here any minute."

"Ah 'fraid not they are both away for the weekend, and will therefore miss out on the flaunting of your naked body before them."

"Good grief woman, what do you take me for?"

Not wanting to get into that debate, she looked at the fountain. "I'd say the water pressure is lessening, the water isn't recycling into the bowl so it may not be too long to wait for you to recap it."

Ben shivered, "I hope not because I'm beginning to feel rather cold."

"I'll get you a towel to put round your shoulders and make a cup of tea." While he sat in the deck chair sipping his tea she nipped upstairs. David and Jane's flat door was locked, which indicated they weren't back tonight. Jane had mentioned they were going on the church's weekend away, it must be this weekend! Why was it with Ben everything seemed against her?

On her way back down the stairs with the wash basket, a couple of blankets and towels she could see the spouting water was diminishing. Ben should soon be able to cap it off. From the doorway she announced loudly, "I'll run you a hot bath. Here's a basket for your wet clothes. David's away, so no chance of borrowing his. We'll put yours in the washing machine. Spun and hung up in the boiler room they'll be dry in the morning. Once that's done I'll nip up to Notting Hill to the fish and chip shop."

Five minutes later she returned to find him waiting at the door the job done. "Are you suggesting I stay the night alone in the flat with you?"

"I don't see what else you can do. I'm sure Helen won't object to you sleeping in her bed."

A cheeky grin matched his words. "And I'm not going to object to having my bath run, my washing done, my food provided, and we might even get to be friends."

"Don't push your luck. Remember we're already one man down in the Print Department so we can't afford for you to be ill with pneumonia, in prison for being naked in the street, or dying of hunger in my flat. Now what do you want?"

A long sigh and blissful smile appeared, "Tonight I have all I want Jill."

"Oh shut up. I'm having a steak and mushroom pie. Do you want a pie, or fish and chips?"

Eyes shining with amusement he ordered, "Cod and double chips please. I'm starving, got to build up my strength for the fun and games."

"The only fun and games you'll be getting Mister will be watching TV or playing Scrabble. Dry yourself off. We don't want you dripping on the carpet. Now what do you think you're doing?"

"I'm removing my trousers in accordance with instructions. You don't have to look."

Cross she tutted, started up the stairs announcing, "There are towels in the bathroom, and I've brought down a couple of blankets for you to wrap yourself in once dry – use Helen's room."

"Yes Ma'am. I love it when you're bossy." About to retort, she turned, and clamped her mouth shut as his naked back view ran across the lounge into the bathroom.

Jill shook her head, retrieved the basket with all his clothes and concluded this was going to be an interesting evening.

It all took longer than she expected. When she finally arrived back Coronation Street's theme music was playing on the TV indicating that Ben had made himself at home. He had made a very arresting outfit from a red blanket, slung over him like a roman toga, pinned at the shoulder by a large 'Ban the Bomb' badge. Entirely unnecessary, but very fetching, was the white and blue stripped tea-towel on his head, held on by a string of beads. No guesses needed as to the owner of the accessories! Her frame shook with suppressed laughter. "Oh Ben if only I had a camera, you are a sight to behold. Am I bringing humble offerings of food to a Bedouin Sheik or a Roman Centurion?"

"Whichever you wish, both had their way of bringing a woman satisfaction!"

"The only satisfaction you are going to get Mister is from this food. I hope it's still hot enough. Good, you've laid the table. I hardly think the kind of food we're eating warrants candles – sorry."

He turned off the TV. "Just a thought, I saw them in the

drawer and thought they were a bit decorative. I've made a sweet which I think will warrant candlelight."

"Good heavens, you have been busy. I presume the sweet looks so bad I won't want to eat it if I see it." Ben put on a hurt look. "Trust you to be unkind."

She ignored that and unwrapped the food from the newspaper, dished it up on the plates already on the table stacking his with chips.

"You ought to be grateful I've managed to make a sweet there hardly anything in the cupboards. What do you girls eat all week?"

"I don't know about Helen, usually Rosemary and I have a meal in the canteen and toast in the evening. Saturday we stock up for the week. Now let's eat this before it gets any colder. Today I only had a sandwich before visiting Sam." Sam being a safe subject she continued talking of him and Mrs B. Amicably they laughed, chatted and munched their way through the food and on to a variety of topics. To her surprise she found she was enjoying his company, and the nest of cornflakes held together by a melted Mars bar he'd found in his pocket. With a scoop of ice-cream in the centre and raisins over the top it was quite delicious.

As they stacked the dish-washer Ben asked, "Can we play Scrabble? I want to remember tonight as one when I definitely had fun, and played games."

The sad, almost wistful undertone in his voice touched her heart. And it turned out that Scrabble with Ben was a definite challenge. He was a walking dictionary knowing words she'd never heard of. After she'd demanded he get the dictionary and he was found to be correct for the third time, she commented, "Why when you are so obviously brainy, didn't you choose a new career when becoming a doctor failed? David did. You are wasted as Manager of the Print Department."

"It's not a story for tonight, but if we continue our friendship I promise I will tell you. Now I have just seen the most amazing word, and it fits beautifully here, seven letters using my 'x' on the double letter, over triple word score and let's see, um not a bad score, 153!"

"That's it, I'm not playing with you any more."

The cheeky grin appeared. "Is there any other game you would prefer?"

"No. And I think it's time I went to bed. And you have a choice…"

"Oh good, do I?

"Yes, pull out the settee, or assume Helen won't mind you sleeping in her bed."

"I'd hoped for better, but I'll console myself with a cup of hot chocolate. Do you want one?"

"Yes please." She packed up the Scrabble, put it away and turned on the TV. News at Ten had already started so she sat down to watch as the camera panned from Reginald Bosanquet to Anna Ford. "It was a miracle no-one was hurt when earlier this evening fire ripped through an exclusive designer dress shop in Mayfair causing thousands of pounds of damage. The fire brigade suspected it was caused by a fractured gas main and have cordoned off the area until further notice. There was an unexpected..." Ben handed her a mug of chocolate. And while they sat companionably, watching a discussion programme her mind whirled with thoughts of Miss French Chic. Had it been her shop? Half an hour later feeling a bit sick, perhaps from the direction of her thoughts, or the hot chocolate she announced with a yawn, "I think I need my bed. I'll leave you to choose where you sleep. I will say though it's been an unexpected, but pleasant..." Pain gripped and ran through her, her hand shot to her stomach. "You'll have to excuse me Ben, call of nature I think. I'll see you in the morning." Halfway up the stairs it came again bad enough for her to groan and bend forward. Concerned, Ben headed towards her. She waved him away saying, "It's alright, I'll be fine. Goodnight. I'll see you in the m..." Without finishing she headed upward because the last thing she wanted was Ben's company while she was being ill in the toilet.

After a short bout of sickness, she felt better, but she'd only been in bed about five minutes before the rolling gripping pain and nausea returned. In an attempt to relieve the symptoms she tried not to move, but despite trying to avoid being sick she ended up kneeling with her head over the toilet bowl. Oh how she hated that raw soreness in her throat, and the horrible spasm when your insides felt as though they wanted to be on the outside.

After the third bout, she went to grab more toilet paper when a hand appeared proffering a glass of water. "I hope you don't mind my intrusion, I did knock, but on hearing you obviously weren't well I thought you could do with this."

The man must be a saint. She couldn't imagine anyone, except perhaps Stephen, who would deliberately involve themselves in her sickness. She was reminded of Mrs P, their cleaner who had said to her and Jane, "You find a man me ducks who'll hold your head when you're sick and you'll know you've got a good'en."

"You're shivering. Have you a dressing gown – it'll keep you warm?" She managed the words, 'bedroom door' before another bout of retching hit her. Ben grabbed the glass from her hand, and a few seconds later her dressing gown was around her shoulders. All the while a light hand rubbed gently across her shoulders as if to relieve the tension from the sickness. At the end of the bout, he lent over her with toilet tissue and a glass of water with the instruction to "Sip it slowly".

How very kind of him, tears of gratitude pricked the back of her eyes, as she murmured, "Thank you. I'm sorry."

"No need to be sorry, unless it's for the waste of your dinner, which I suspect is the cause of your sickness."

"You aren't sick. Oh, you didn't have the pie." Her head felt light, her body wobbly, she pulled herself up. "The sickness and pains seem to have stopped."

Ben moved before her, pulled back the bedcovers and then tucked her in. Ridiculously she was tempted to ask him to get in and cuddle her warm! "I'll be downstairs. I opted for the sofa it didn't feel right being in Helen's bed, so if you need me, call. I'm a light sleeper, I'll leave your door open, so I'll hear you."

Her eyes felt heavy, she closed them, felt Ben kiss her forehead before he turned out the light and left. Perhaps he wasn't so awful, they'd had a pleasant evening, it was good of him to be with her when she was sick, maybe they could become friends.

It was dark, so dark. The fire was burning, yet she couldn't feel the heat, despite the roaring flame so close to her. She shivered, she had to get warm, yet she felt so weak and moving forward brought pain from the manacle of chains around her waist. There was a moaning on the wind, a cry in the night and suddenly she awoke in her dark bedroom, shivering as the net curtains waved in a chill wind. A spasm of pain hit her and she curled against it. Determined not to be sick again she tried to control that and the pain. Hand out she felt for her dressing gown on the bed, put it on and padded across the carpet to the toilet. At least this time she avoided being sick, but the several flushes of the toilet brought the knock, the call, at her bedroom door.

He was being kind, but it was embarrassing. She called from the bathroom, "I'll be out in a minute." When she did appear, he'd turned on a bedside light and was standing with bare chest and legs by her window looking out. His only covering a green towel pinned from his waist with Helen's ridiculously huge 'ban the bomb' badge.

"Sorry about this, but I needed my toga for the bed, and this was the best thing I could find to make me decent. I've closed the window it felt quite chilly in here."

Slowly and feeling very fragile she slipped back into bed, leaving on her dressing gown. "Thanks I do feel shivery and cold."

Ben sat beside her and took her hand, "You feel cold". He rubbed it gently bringing warmth. He did the same with the other one. Exhausted she closed her eyes. "I'd make you a hot drink, but I'm not sure whether you'd be able to keep that down, have you a hot water bottle I could fill?" At her slight shake of the head against the pillow he continued, "Maybe Helen, Rosemary?" She shook her head again. A warm hand rested against her forehead, then lightly touched her cheek, suddenly she felt like crying, her mouth trembled. "Are you in a lot of pain?"

"It comes in spasms."

In a thoughtful tone he said, "I assume it's not likely to be a miscarriage"

Cross he should even consider that her eyes flew open, her voice sharp. "No, it's not. I'm on the pill. And it's not period pains either."

"There's no need to bite my head off, I'm just trying to diagnose cause and effect. Would you like me to call a doctor?"

"What could he do? Would he know any better than you?"

Ben sighed. "If it's food poisoning then there isn't much anyone can do, just drink plenty of water, dry toast if you can manage it and keep as warm as possible. The symptoms could indicate something else, but he'd need to examine you for that. Do you think the pain is getting worse?"

Another spasm racked through her body, she groaned and curled away from him.

"Try and breath through it Jill, it's not easy but it helps relax the muscles." He rubbed her back, the touch and warmth were a comfort, even if it didn't assuage the pain."

Through it, and as it gradually subsided, she realised Ben was only trying to do his best. She uncurled and turned back toward him. "I'm sorry I got cross. Thank you for being here. The pain is about the same." Pushing back the bedclothes she touched her stomach through her nightdress. "It's sore here, and here, but when the pain comes it goes all over this area."

"Would you mind if I felt those places?" The embarrassment of being ill in front of him was one thing, but his touching her was another. A little sympathetic smile appeared. "In Victorian times doctors examined women through their underclothes because it wasn't considered decent to do otherwise. I could do that, and it would identify where the pain is actually coming from?"

"Go on then. You would have made a good doctor." As he sat on the bed beside her she caught a glimpse in his eyes of the depth of sorrow at the loss of the career he'd obviously loved. Unexpected empathy filled her heart.

His fingers gently kneaded her stomach, and he asked, "No pain here, here?" He glanced up at her face, and with a curious look he paused waiting for an answer.

Quickly she guided his hand, "It's here, and here. And I feel I've been kicked in the stomach just here." With a nod he returned to concentrate and pressing in the sore area she indicated she cried out.

"Sorry I didn't mean to hurt you, try to relax. Now does it hurt here?"

She bit her lip. "It hurts all over there."

Ben sat back. "The good news is that it isn't your appendix." He placed his hand over the sore area she'd indicated, "But this whole area is your intestines and bowel which from your reaction to my touch would seem inflamed, probably due to that pie."

Tired, closing her eyes and wishing to sleep, she murmured drowsily, "And your hand just there is like a hot water bottle, so lovely, warm and soothing." Her hands closed on top of his, "umm just keep it there."

"I don't think in the circumstances that would be wise."

"But you're so warm, I'm so cold, and it feels so nice."

"Maybe, but I'm afraid as nice as it is for you, it is becoming an embarrassment for me wrapped in only this skimpy towel." Without thinking her eyes flew open to see what he meant, and then smiled seeing his other hand carefully positioned to hide his predicament. At that she allowed Ben to slide his hand out from under hers. He stood and replaced the bed clothes over her. "There we'll both be safer now."

An amused smile flickered briefly before she sleepily confessed, "Your kisses are well off my Richter scale." The cheeky grin appeared, so she added, "But then I'm as frustrated as hell by Rich, who is all talk and little do."

Nonchalantly Ben perched at near the bottom of the bed and suggested, "Maybe he's gay."

Annoyed she pulled herself up to sitting position. "No, he isn't!"

With a wry grin Ben asked, "What makes you think that?"

"Well, he's all man, nothing mamby pamby about him, in fact now and then he's a little scary."

"And that makes him seem exciting. A good cover if your penchant is toward men rather than women."

Determined to stick up for Rich, she countered, "I'd say you have a warped sense of sex and love. Surely it's more acceptable for a man to speak of romance and aligning it to a delectable meal, its many courses to each be savoured to bring greater enjoyment and satisfaction, than for a man to grab a woman who doesn't like him and kiss her without any preamble.

Ben's eyes narrowed as he lent forward to retaliate. "And I rather think Jill that's a jibe at my behaviour, but when a man in love is constantly treated like the old bone the dog brought in, and another man is flaunted in his face, he doesn't act very rationally. However, when commonsense returns he knows he has to accept what he can't have and learn to live with it."

"Is that why, in the last few weeks, people have been saying that you've lost your ray of sunshine?"

"Have they, well don't kid yourself, it hasn't all been you. Sam's accident brought home again that I couldn't do what I love the most, and then I met Geoff at the hospital, that rubbed it in further. If that wasn't enough you turned out to be David Reinhardt's sister making you even more unobtainable, and I have a few other personal issues I won't bore you with."

Puzzled she spoke her mind. "Being David's sister wouldn't make any difference to us – well if there were an 'us'. David, as well as others, think you're wonderful and top runner for 'Employee of the Year' Award! After all, he sent us here to talk. And Jane is his ex-secretary so no snobbery there. I bet they are rubbing their hands in glee believing that as hostility between us has ceased something else might begin."

Ben frowned. "Your brother is a surprising man, but, is there any hope that something else might begin?"

In a tight voice she replied, "Saved by the pain, and a need to get to the toilet."

Ben pulled back the bedclothes and instructed as she made her way to the toilet, "Try using the breathing exercise for people in labour, it's a slow deep intake of breath counting 1, 2, 3 and let it out slowly, 1,2,3. Concentrating on that relaxes the womb, or in your case your bowel, and helps to expel what is causing the pain."

"Thanks I'll try it." Embarrassed she closed the door and hoped he'd go back downstairs.

Forty minutes later she emerged feeling the worst was over to find Ben asleep in her comfy chair, a spare towel as a blanket across his chest and cuddling her Benjy bear. Quietly she whispered to Benjy, "You traitor." Now what was she to do? Ben stirred and hugged Benjy tighter. The pair of them looked very endearing. In a motherly gesture she ruffled Ben's hair, "Come on Ben, you can't stay there all night."

Groggily he looked up at her, "I'll stay until you feel better."

"I do. You might as well get some sleep."

He gave a slight hum, and nodded off again. She sighed. Now what was she going to do? She couldn't leave him there, he'd get pneumonia with the room getting colder during the night. Asleep he wouldn't be any bother, it was only five steps to the bed, and she could put her cushions down the centre as a demarcation line!

Gently she coerced, "Come on Ben. Get up." Ben stirred and pulled himself out of the chair his eyes dazed with sleep, and like a boy sleep walking she led him to the bed still hugging her Benjy bear. With little direction he sat, then curled up on it while she murmured, "Ben Fletcher you were determined to get into my bed, but I never thought I'd be leading you by the hand and tucking you in." Ben hugging Benjy had such an expression of boyish contentment she wouldn't have been surprised if he'd put his thumb into his mouth! In the morning she would tease him something rotten about this, then realised Ben would be more likely teasing her at her willingness to invite him into her bed.

The cushions made a decent barrier, and exhausted she fell asleep.

Jill became aware of the sun pouring in through the curtains. Delightfully sleepy, deliciously cosy, she languished in contentment enjoying those first semi-conscious moments when all feels right with the world. Warmth pervaded her back and humming dreamily she moved her shoulders like a cat preening against the hard source of heat. Stretching her body down the bed she luxuriated in a sense of well-being before leaping from the bed to scream, "What do you think you're doing?"

Ben turned on his back and, hands behind his head, looked up at her. "Doing Jill? I'm not doing anything. I'm lying here enjoying the ambience, the view, and delight of sharing a bed with the one I dream so often about, and hoping I'll be treated as a nutty, full and fruity, wholemeal baked, icing on the top, three-tiered wedding cake, and not the dog's old bone."

Puzzled she stared at him until she realised he was parodying her example of Rich's romantic talk. Immediately she saw the funny side, gave a piggy like snort of laughter, picked up each cushion from the floor and threw them at him stating, "And these are the only things allowed to be erected in my bed, a barrier to protect against unwanted manifestations!"

Ben didn't attempt to catch, deflect or re-erect the cushion barrier, instead he commented, "Unwanted? I didn't get here by myself."

With a smirk she retaliated, "True, but last night a sleepy Ben cuddling my Benjy bear and sucking his thumb is different to the unwanted manifestation in my bed this morning!"

A big grin appeared, "You call your teddy bear after me, now there has to be something psychological in that."

"More like pathological to have felt compelled, after you looking after me, to ensure you didn't get pneumonia, and the only motivation for allowing you to sleep in my bed."

"But Jill I've been very restrained." She gave him a look of unbelief. "I did nothing, you threw the cushions off the bed during the night, and this morning you backed into me. I just didn't have the bottle when my red-bloodied, full bodied, matured cask needed to move away. But if it's any consolation stored in the dark it matures, and above room temperature it can prove a heady concoction to delight the most discerning of tastes. That description alone can turn any damsel weak at the knees!"

It was impossible not to laugh as she exhorted, "Stop it! You haven't got Rich's gift of the gab."

"No need for me to ask how the patient is this morning I think she is over the worst, but a bit of pampering will do no harm. How about you get back in bed, and I go and make a pot of tea and toast?"

"That's an offer I can't refuse." And with that she returned to the window side of the bed, pumped up the pillows and announced to his back as he re-arranged his towelling skirt, "This is the first time anyone has offered me breakfast in bed."

Ben didn't turn, but gave a self-deprecating laugh. "I bet it's the first time too that a man's slept in your bed without making love to you."

"I have never had a man in this bed that has made love to me." Astonished Ben whipped around to look at her, pricked his finger on the 'ban the bomb' badge pin, uttered an expletive and sucked on his wound. While she continued, "There's been plenty of pleasurable lust, and on occasion passion that didn't last, but making love, no."

His modest dressing completed he turned and with a sympathetic expression said gently, "I'm sorry to hear that Jill. You could go with two 'firsts' and make it a triple whammy."

Oh God what was Ben suggesting now? Eyebrows raised she gave him a questioning look.

"I'll get the breakfast, that's if I can find anything to make one with, then if you are willing I'll treat you to the genuine article. Don't look so puzzled. That would be a first for me too! And I hope that excites you, as it does me, and far better than imagining a vat of full bodied wine and a wholemeal, nutty fruit-cake!"

"Iced, three tiered and a wedding one, don't forget?"

Ben chuckled, "I'll discuss that bit with you later. In the meanwhile, now that I've got this dratted towelling skirt back on I'll leave you with a taster." He moved around the bed, lifted her chin, and gently nuzzled her mouth, and backed off the instant her arms came up to draw him closer. "Get off me woman, the menu is breakfast first."

"Oh really I've been told that kind of ploy often means a man is gay!" She preened and drew her tongue along her lips, "But the jury is still out on that." A shadow crossed Ben's face as he readjusted his towelling skirt. Was that because she was referring to Rich? In an attempt to look fragile and sweet she added, "However, if your bedside manner, medicine and operating techniques continue as favourably as previously experienced I shall look forward to your next visit."

He looked down on her, "Do you mean that?"

Her mouth twisted in a sexy little smile, "I rather think I do."

Ben's eyes filled with a triumphant glint, genuine joy which caused him to jump, punch the air and shout 'Yes' before giving her a sexy grin.

In a serious tone she countered, "I hope your excitement isn't premature, for I haven't agreed that I am willing for you to make genuine love to me." She saw the joy dull on Ben's face, and quickly continued, "But one thing leads to another and in the space of eight hours I went from disliking to liking you, the next eight hours from disinterest to interest, and now you aren't annoying me heaven knows what the next eight hours will change, so go, show me what kind of husband you'd make."

The cheeky smile that had reappeared at her words, froze. "Now look here woman, I've made no mention of marriage."

"Oh I thought it was…" she reiterated the words of the song, " 'love and marriage' go together like a 'horse and carriage' and you can't have one without the other.'" Ben's face was a picture and she doubled up with laughter, "Go and get my breakfast Mister, and think on these things."

He grinned back, doffed his invisible cap, said, "Yes Ma'am" and left the room.

It was impossible, incredible, her and Ben together, she hugged her knees. He 'wanted to make genuine love to her' just maybe, after all, he was Mr Right for she no longer hated him? He'd made her laugh, they bantered, had fun, and with his lack of clothing and finding himself waking up in her bed, he'd quite endeared himself by his restraint. She picked up Benjy sitting happily on top of the pile of cushions where Ben had placed him. "Perhaps you weren't such a traitor after all. Should I give up my self-inflicted abstinence, Benjy? The man certainly brings promise of pleasure." Benjy's head nodded wisely, she grinned, "Yes it would be silly to miss out on what could be such a treat." She snuggled down the bed her mind full of anticipation.

The door was nudged open revealing Ben carrying a tray bearing mugs of tea, a plate of toast, a dish of butter and pot of jam. He put it down on the bed between them, and announced as he slid into bed, "Not exactly the most exciting breakfast, but we can make up for that later. And whilst we drink and eat I'll tell you about my plan which I hope you'll like."

Liberally sugaring her tea, she stirred it while frowning at the thought of his plan and the very sparsely buttered piece of toast he handed her.

"If you were inexperienced I'd make the introduction to making love carefully and slowly, bringing you to the delights of passion and orgasm before making entry. But I suggest we first get over our frustrations with wild, passionate, quickly sated, satisfaction. Then we can move slowly into understanding how to pleasure each other, letting the pressure grow until we are ready to lift off as a rocket into the skies. Does that whet your appetite?"

"Um, there's a certain clinical approach in your plan, but I am sure I can get over that." A broad grin stretched itself across her mouth at her own naughty thoughts. "Can I have another piece of that toast before you scoff the lot" She mustered up a serious face, "My plan for today is to have a bath, wash my hair, and go to the shops before they shut at six, because as you know our cupboards are bare. Would you say we'll be back on earth by then?"

The cheeky grin appeared. "Let's see, I think we could make the shops by four-thirty, so hair wash and bath perhaps three-thirty. He looked at his watch, it's now nine o'clock so providing my timing suits you I imagine we could have been there and back quite a few times."

It was impossible not to chuckle at his expectancy. "I might just hold you to that assuming you can keep it up. Now, if you've finished your tea, we can put the tray on the floor." Ben leapt out to do as he was bid, then brought up his arms to flex his muscles, she giggled. "Yes, very impressive, honestly Ben you're like a big kid." He laughed and sat back on the bed. "And so much for your wearing that 'ban the bomb' badge because Mister your bomb is about to explode." Before he could comprehend her meaning she straddled his lap and watched the surprise, desire, pleasure wash through his eyes, he didn't remain passive for long and together in a frenzy they rode out the fulfilment of their need.

Much later, she found she had to compromise on the bath and hair wash, in order to go shopping. Ben's clothes were nicely dry and together they enjoyed the walk. It was wonderful to be with a man who genuinely cared for you, and in knowing the secrets of desire, the heights of passion and shared pleasure, even mundane shopping became fun.

Once back in the flat Ben was as practical as ever. "Jill, you run a bath, I'll put the potatoes in the oven. By the time I'm back up you should be out of the bath."

Jill giggled, "Really! And if you go down again in about an hour, it'll be the right time to cook the steak, prepare the salad, and open the wine."

Ben gave her a suggestive look, "I am, as always, madam, ready to be at your service."

"I'm pleased to hear it, and Ben, tonight, you can light the candles, and turn out the lights."

He kissed her long and deliciously, removing her clothes, trailing his fingers along her skin, sending tingling messages to those parts of her body already revving up for action. "Woman run your bath, I'll be back."

An hour later in a blissful state she giggled as she dressed for dinner. Wasn't Ben going to get a surprise? She moved down the stairs in a rustle that to her sounded loud over the gentle sound of classical music on the record player. The table was laid, the candles lit, she waited to make her entrance down the stairs when Ben appeared from the kitchen. He looked up as though to call her and stopped stunned. Even in the dim light from a side lamp and candlelight, she saw the glisten of tears forming in his eyes as he came and took her hand, "My lady, my beautiful lady! That dress is stunning, and I am so touched you are wearing it for me."

With her arms going around his neck she proclaimed, "Ben, you are one amazing man, I wanted to wear it for you. These last ten hours have been extraordinary, phenomenal and special. I feel we've been cut off from the world in our own love nest."

Ben gazed tenderly into her eyes. "And I can't believe that twenty-four hours my life has so changed. You have to agree this kind of togetherness more than compensates for differences of opinion and arguments. We will work it out. In the mean time, let's enjoy every minute of this weekend alone. I tell you, after what I've been through perhaps life is, at last, going to be good to me, but I'll not get into that tonight. Come, dinner's ready." He took her arms from his neck, lifted and kissed her hands, then led her in stately fashion to the table.

They didn't need to get drunk to be happy. They ate, drank, danced to music, and when they couldn't resist each other any more drew on their earlier pillow talk of sexual fantasies to make a night of memories secure in the belief this was a relationship that had potential for both of them.

CHAPTER 14

Sunday morning's awakening was very different from Saturday. Curled up together like spoons they awoke to pouring rain giving them no incentive to leave the bed, and they didn't want one. Ben cooked a full English breakfast, and set up a little side table in her room where, almost starry eyed from the giving and taking of pleasure, they fed each other playing silly childish games that only lovers do.

Filled with food, relaxing between passionate episodes she wanted to ask Ben about his past. "Ben, last night you said, 'perhaps life was going to be good for you from now on'. And I see no reason to think otherwise. Am I friend enough, to be trusted with whatever has been so bad in your life, because whatever happened in your past it is not going to affect our future?"

"Actually Jill I was just thinking it was time to tell you here in our cosy world, before tomorrow and work breaks in. Let's cuddle up in bed. It will make the telling easier."

Comfortable lying on their sides facing each other Jill put out her hand and touched the face she was coming to love, and gave him a tender and encouraging smile.

"I'll start at the beginning. You know about working for my Dad part-time to earn money for travel and med. school and the year out you were so interested in that I forgot you were interviewing me. Anyway at 19 when I started to train in medicine...oh I'd better backtrack. My Mum died when I was twelve, after two years of stomach pain which no-one diagnosed as more than an irritable bowel, it turned out to be cancer. I loved her Jill and she just faded away before my eyes, and I felt useless to do anything about it. Three days before she died I vowed to her when I was old enough I would become a doctor and listen to my patients and do all I could to help them. And she said, 'You do that my lovely boy, and I'll be watching from heaven and be proud of you.' But I didn't do that because I messed it up." The raw emotion in his eyes brought tears to hers. Quickly she shimmied into him to hug him. No wonder he'd been so worried about her stomach pain.

"Oh Ben, your Mum would be really proud of the fact that

despite what happened, you still are, 'her lovely boy', everyone at ITP talks so highly of you."

"Thank you for saying that." After a long kiss that nearly developed into more Ben chuckled, "Enough of this otherwise I'll never get to tell you about my life so far. Dad didn't cope with Mum's death he locked into himself, spent most of his time at work, and at home barely spoke to me other than necessity. Years later he told me he felt such guilt at not insisting the doctors do tests, and such shame in that he felt he'd let her die, that he couldn't face me, or anyone else. In those years I became a bookworm, especially on medical matters. I'd no siblings so I only had Edward my bear to tell my troubles to, wonderful things bears! No doubt your Benjy knows all your secrets as did, or dare I say, does my Edward!" He grinned at her and looked quite the little adorable boy he must have been.

"Once at med school I was in my element, the studying, the patients, the atmosphere, and even through often mundane routine I'd be researching stuff, visiting a lonely patient, trying to discover what was wrong when nothing was obvious, it became my passion." He laughed softly and cuddled her, "Now you are my passion, but I mustn't divert myself. I found the brain fascinating and determined when I'd finished my training I'd specialize in that.

"In my second year Dad, feeling the business was going well, and needing more than student part-timers to work for him took on a fifteen year old, black Jamaican lad as an apprentice. Leroy was a lovely chap, willing and friendly. He'd not much of a home life, his Dad drank and his Mum spent most of her time smoking and shouting out her frustration at his three siblings. Dad feeling sorry for Leroy began inviting him around and he helped pull Dad from his depression. That first year Leroy excelled, then gradually he became erratic by not turning up, getting simple things wrong and upsetting Dad with uncontrollable rages. In the end I had a word with him and saw he was seriously disturbed, and with a diagnostic mind, asked if he was taking drugs.

"To cut a long story short he'd gone from smoking a spliff with his friends, to LSD and was now using heroin. Not only was that messing up his mind, but he confessed he'd been stealing from Dad. He was petrified of his supplier because he constantly had to find money to get his fix and already owed him money. The expectancy was he did 'jobs' for payment in kind.

"I suggested he try and get help from the police or his doctor, but Leroy was too frightened to go in case of retribution on his family. Several days later, Dad contacted me saying Leroy hadn't been in to work and he was worried about him. As soon as I could I went to Leroy's tenement flat and could see his Mum was wary of having a white man at her door. But obviously upset she pulled me inside to tell me Leroy had been beaten up, but she was too afraid to get help. As a doctor, you see some horrible sights, but it's impersonal, with Leroy I cried with him. His face was such a mess he was unrecognizable, he'd severe bruising to his ribs and a broken arm. I insisted he go to hospital and called an ambulance. His Mum had the younger kids to look after so I went with him. Leroy was in hospital over a week. His Mum rang me to say he couldn't go home, men were hanging about waiting for him, and she was frightened if Leroy didn't pay up they'd take it out on another of her boys.

"Leroy owed a hundred pounds. I figured I could eat cheaply and drew the rest of my grant out of the bank to give to his Mum to pay off the debt. I then took Leroy home to my flat, five minutes from the hospital. For several weeks Leroy was so scared he wouldn't leave the place. He spent most of the day with my landlady who mothered and fed him. Many of my colleagues took uppers and downers just to keep on going with the heavy pressure of long hours and work load and because I was working in the Casualty Department drugs were easily available. It wasn't difficult to take home the medication which Leroy needed to help wean him off the hard stuff. Poor guy, I sat with him many hours through the painful and difficult process to get it just right. Dad believed people were watching the print works and said that he didn't think it was safe for Leroy to return, but he did contribute to our finances and my landlady got Leroy some part-time gardening where she cleaned.

"I wasn't home much, but found Leroy great company. We went to football matches, cinema, the local pub, it was like having a brother I never had. The more Leroy was weaned off the heroin the more interested he became in my books. It was obvious he had a bright mind, and I was just figuring out how best to educate that brain and get him a better life when all hell broke loose.

"Unbeknown to me the hospital authorities had had a suspicion for some months that hard drugs were being stolen and sold on the black market. So when, at the end of a shift, I pocketed what Leroy was going to need in the next week I found a hand on my shoulder and the police called."

"Surely when you explained the circumstances to them they understood?"

With a grimace, he acknowledged, "Unfortunately not! After several hours of questioning they put me in a police car and took me to the flat so I could introduce them to Leroy. It was obvious they thought Leroy was fictitious. And Leroy, fearful of the police from childhood, saw the car, thought they had come to get him and bolted out the back door as they came in the front."

"Oh no! How awful, your alibi had gone." She reached out to comfort him as she saw tears well up in his eyes.

"Jill it was worse than that, and it still hurts to think about it. Leroy not knowing where else to go returned home. It turned out his Mum had pocketed my money and the bully boys were still after Leroy. Eye witnesses said he entered the estate and a gang of younger boys surrounded him. He didn't seem that bothered, almost as if he were playing with them, until a car drew up, two men got out and headed towards them. The boys ran away leaving Leroy. I imagine he was terrified for the boys reported that he tried to make a run for it. No-one saw what happened next, but two days later his badly beaten body was found in a ditch five miles away. Both his legs had been shattered, not broken Jill, shatter..." Ben unable to go on began to weep, deep heart-wrenching sobs.

All she could do was cry with him while nestling him against her, rocking and stroking his back, wanting to bring love and comfort to what was so obviously deeply ingrained pain needing release. Who would do that to another human being? Was this what Chris and Rich did in teaching someone a lesson? She didn't want to think about it.

The grief inside Ben gradually subsided, he drew away and looked up at her. He said with a sob, "The post mortem found nearly every bone in his body had been broken. I can only hope he was quickly unconscious, and stayed that way. In that state he'd have been unable to get out of the ditch, where he subsequently died of his injuries."

Again her tears flowed at the unknown Jamaican boy's fate, her breasts wet with Ben's crying, she wanted to draw him back and hug him, but having opened up the rawness of it all he seemed to want to share the highs and lows of his relationship with Leroy. And she knew enough to know talking about someone you had loved and lost, helped the grieving process.

Pale and red-eyed after recalling heart-breaking memories he agreed with her suggestion of a cup of strong coffee, drank it gratefully, and said with a sad smile, "Thank you for listening. There's never been anyone I could really talk to about all that happened. I'm sorry, my tears must seem so stupid."

"Not at all. After what you've been through I am amazed you manage to always keep so cheerful." She snuggled against him, "Now drink up. I want to give you something to take your mind off it for a while."

Half an hour later, once more in the position for pillow talk those brilliant blue eyes looked across into hers as he asked, "Do you want to hear what happened next?" At her nod and gentle squeeze of his hand he continued, "I'm afraid that was only the beginning of the nightmare. It was two days after Leroy's death when they found his body and several more before they connected him with me. Up until then, with no Leroy the police thought I'd made up the story. They said my landlady, and her friend, were only backing me up because they liked me and wanted to get me out of trouble. Despite my Dad confirming my story, and later Leroy being found dead, the police still didn't believe me and at one point accused me of murdering him. This was not being innocent unless proved guilty."

Astonished she blurted out, "That's ridiculous! Why would the police do that?"

"I'd been caught red-handed stealing drugs! They suspected I'd been selling them on the black market. They reckoned Leroy was my contact, so I did away with him. Fortunately when the forensic people estimated Leroy's time of death I was still in police custody and they couldn't refute that alibi."

"You always think the police will be fair, that they'd take all facts into consideration. And they'd no proof of you selling them. I can see now why you rushed out of the flat that day when Richard said he'd call the police."

"I'm afraid when you've been branded a criminal anything said against you makes your actions immediately suspect. I was charged, but released on bail for the nine months before the trial. In that time I couldn't continue my training, so helped Dad out, who, understandably aged considerably with the stress. I tried to keep positive, but knew if convicted I'd never qualify to as a doctor. And this is where your brother comes in."

"David? What's he got to do with this?"

"David was the barrister engaged by the prosecution to prove I was guilty."

Even as she exclaimed, "Oh no!" something stirred in her memory. Frowning she recalled, "I can remember at a family Sunday lunch David ranted on to us about 'the law being an ass, and the injustice of a system when a good man, trying to help another not only loses his career, but gets sent to prison'." Wide-eyed she asked, "Was that you? Were you sent to prison?"

Sadly Ben looked into her eyes, "I'm afraid so."

"Oh the unfairness of it all. But now I know why, when David told you his name was Reinhardt, he gave you a potted history of his career. He'd recognised you, although I suppose you hadn't him because of that ridiculous wig barristers have to wear."

"Exactly! He said my face looked familiar that morning we met after the boat trip, but it took a while for him to remember where he'd seen me before. After the incident with Sam he told me how pleased he was I was working for ITP and he would do everything he could to further my career. For me what was worse than knowing who he was, was the realization you were his sister, so totally out of bounds for the likes of me." Ben raised his hand at seeing her about to protest, and went on, "Your brother is a very clever man, because, although I didn't recognize it at the time, he made a complete hash of the case from the NHS point of view. The jury was so divided they were out for several days. Finally, they decided for the NHS and I found myself with a two year prison sentence, and in the judge's words, 'I am using you as a precedent to set an example to others, to show that as a doctor, or professional in any field for that matter, it does not make you above the law'." David told me, that at that point, the judge glared at him, and it was as much as he could do not to throw down his wig on the bench and announce if that was British justice, God help us all.

"With good behaviour my sentence was reduced to eighteen months, and during that time I put my body through a vigorous training programme because there was always someone wanting to pick a fight. I did my best to befriend others and tried to come to terms with what life had dealt me."

"Oh Ben, I am so sorry. If only I'd have known about this before, have you told Helen, Rosemary, anyone?"

He shook his head, his reply defensive with an edge of bitterness, "I want people to love me, not pity me!"

"I don't think pity would have entered into it. More admiration that instead of being bitter and twisted, you still help people in need. In my eyes that makes you pretty amazing and I suspect

David is already thinking up ways to put your brain to a more satisfying use than the Print Department." She sat up with a start, "Hey, I've just had a thought. I wonder if David has considered asking Dad, he's into drug research, with your medical knowledge..."

Hope flashed in Ben's eyes, "Oh Jill, it was a good day when I saw that ad for ITP. Do you think I might have an informal chat with him and see what he says?"

"It's possible, but he doesn't usually have anything to do with hiring or firing, he leaves that to others."

"How big then is this research place?"

"Larger than I thought. You being in the medical field may have heard of Inhart Pharmaceuticals."

Ben looking astonished repeated, "Inharts!" His eyes closed, his face screwed up as if to cry. She frowned as he murmured, "Life really does seem stacked against me!" When he opened them to look into hers, the love he felt for her was reflected in them, but something akin to despair clouded that, and in a pained voice he stated, "I applied for a job there, that was when I thought honesty was the best policy." Puzzled she waited for him to go on. "When I told the truth about my gap in employment the man interviewing me asked if I thought they were stupid. He went on to tell me that no drug company would employ a man, even in research, who had a conviction for stealing drugs. And, with a two year sentence, the judge must have had good reason to believe I was involved with the black market. Untrue, but I could see his point."

Cross at the way Ben had been treated she blurted out, "My father, knowing the circumstances, wouldn't judge you like that. He's a man like David who weighs up a person's character, he values integrity and honesty."

"Look I don't want anyone at Inharts to get into trouble. I'm only telling you this because, although David accepts me, now I know who your father is, it's obvious he wouldn't want an ex-prisoner involved with his daughter." He gave derisive laugh, "He'd probably think I was after you to get his money."

Jill sighed, and with passion disagreed. "Ben you don't know my father! He is a stalwart for justice and believe me if David says you were made a scapegoat for others, he will believe him. I know he has a reputation of being fastidious in all he does, but let me tell you that includes parting with his money. Until recently I knew nothing of his wealth. David bought this house on what at the time he thought was our grandfather's inheritance, but it remained half derelict for five years before I pooled my share into that. No extra help from a rich daddy there, and we live as you would say like 'normal' people, with 'normal' work and salaries. I have two paying flat mates to balance the books at the end of the month. And from my understanding my Dad uses a great deal of his money to set up centres to supply cheap, or free drugs, to the poor and needy of the third world."

Ben's eyes filled with sexual yearning, his mouth a wry smile as he said, "I love you Jill Reinhardt when your eyes flash with anger, or fill with burning flames of desire. It makes me want to unleash the passionate, orgasmic, insatiable woman that you are, and I can't resist that?" His mouth met hers and everything else was forgotten in the pleasure of their mutual fulfilment.

Later, at Ben's insistence, and what she considered the height of decadence, they sat eating ice cream in bed. "You know Ben you have such a sad story, things can only get better from now on."

"I certainly hope so, but I've learnt not to bank on anything. I was only out of prison for a few weeks before my Dad had his heart attack. You see it didn't matter what I said, Dad still blamed himself for involving me with Leroy. His hope, if not in the medical profession, was that I'd find a worthwhile job. When I discovered being a convicted drug thief any employment seemed impossible, I think it was too much for him to cope with. You will remember I then worked for his business and how it failed in my hands. But what I didn't tell you at my interview was that two weeks before I met you at ITP Dad had another heart attack. I was with him, but without equipment or drugs, I did for him what I did for Sam, but it didn't work and he died."

The spoon of ice-cream stood poised between the dish and her mouth. Tears streamed down her face. "Oh Ben, I'm so sorry, I'd have thought you'd suffered enough?"

Ben frowned, "Obviously not! I've had to practice at concentrating on the good things in life, and in meeting you, the job at ITP, the boat trip and even your rejection gave me a new focus. It was wonderful how in helping Rosemary the way opened for me to continue seeing you. And coming here meant I didn't have so much time in an empty house without my Dad. Then, you practically threw me out, Sam's accident was too close for comfort having only weeks before failed to save my father. Next your brother turned out to be the barrister who officially put me in jail, and I met an old colleague at the hospital, so it was rather like four punches and I was out - cold!"

She wriggled her body against his. "Well, how about four kisses and you're back in."

"Good grief woman, what am I to do with you?" Her suggestive smile, her dish proffered to him to finish up her ice-cream so he could get on with the job was invitation enough to begin by taking the bowl from her.

"Thank you for trusting me. I'm sorry I was so awful to you. From my perspective I've watched you fit into, and play a role, and in fact any role that was needed. Everyone thinks you are Mr Wonderful, but I felt they weren't seeing the real Ben Fletcher. I now understand that to survive you've learnt to hide behind a cheeky smile, cocksure attitude, and trying to be all things to all people.

He nodded as he scrapped the dish. "It's the way I've had to be. This is the first time anyone has been there for me, and you have no idea how much you have helped me in two days. Everything about you is far better than I imagined. I've never been as happy as I am now. Even in the simple pleasure of shopping, laughing, dancing, making love it's been fun, exciting, adventurous, and I want more of you, and more of that."

"Oh Ben, I have enjoyed you as much as you have enjoyed me, and after this weekend I'd say there's a possibility it could work out for us. But we still have to find out if we can live amicably in a 'normal' environment and over a longer period. I need to tell you things about my life, nothing as tragic as yours, but I think we've had enough negativity for one day. So come on Ben Fletcher, you've finished that ice-cream, you've had some in flight refuelling, so wow, let's have an ignition, lift off and this time I want to boldly go where no man's been before, Mars, Venus, or any other galaxy you'd like to transport me to."

The flat door closing roused Jill from her sleep, she purred in contentment feeling Ben curled up at her back, his hand stirred from around one of her breasts. She opened her eyes to see that the afternoon had now turned into evening. She stretched slightly to look at the bedside clock and then nuzzled her bottom back into Ben enjoying his caressing.

"So what was the time?"

"Seven o'clock. I suppose we ought to rise and shine, have something to eat, and decide what we are going to do next."

A sexy voice growled in her ear. "I have already."

She giggled knowing what he meant. "I thought I was supposed to be the insatiable one?"

"I'm just keeping up with you."

"Better be quick then, because I'm hungry. And we'd better be quiet because either Rosemary or Helen has just returned." She giggled and then gave a little scream and while her mind was still rational she thought what a gorgeous hunk of lover he was.

Listening to his cheery whistle as he washed and dressed she smiled and wondered what her flat mates were going to say when they found out he'd been here all weekend. But what she wouldn't tell them was of the dozen and more times they'd made love, each time becoming more attuned to each other. Stephen had been gentle, and because he was her first partner she'd loved him and thought it had been good. But Ben had brought her to a deep abandonment and response. Was it because he genuinely loved her beyond all others? Sexual compatibility was one thing, but would they get on together in daily life? David and Jane's intimacy was the glue that seemed to get them over their marital hurdles. Of course Jane would insist it was because Jesus was in the centre of their marriage.

Engrossed in thought, her body in recovery, she almost jumped when Ben spoke. "Are you alright, I didn't hurt you, did I?" Opening her eyes she saw his concerned frown.

She shook her head and said dreamily, "No you sent me beyond the stars, beyond the planets, and I feel all peculiar, sort of light-headed, and haven't quite come back yet, and I don't want to."

He laughed, "Then stay there. I'll go and make you a cup of tea, and see what we can eat as we didn't get around to putting the chicken in the oven."

"Umm do that." The sheet floated over her to cover her. On opening the door Ben immediately said, "Oh hello Helen. Good weekend?" Whoops! Their liaison was uncovered.

Astute, Helen was quick to enquire, "What were you doing in Jill's bedroom?"

Ben drawing the door shut replied, "Jill's not been well, nasty upset tummy. I'm about to make her a cup of tea. You look rather pale. Was it a nightmare journey back from Southend?"

"You could say that, I've been sick four times."

"Oh nasty. Come on then, let's not stand here. I'll take that case downstairs, and you can tell me about it as I make us all a cup of tea."

Dear Ben, no doubt he'd be doing his doctor act on Helen to diagnose her sickness. Well time to get washed and dressed, she rather relished Helen and Rosemary's surprise at their announcement of oneness.

Ten minutes later, the bedroom door opened as she was brushing her hair at the mirror. "Ah there you are, I was wondering how long it took to make a cup of tea?" When Ben didn't reply she turned toward him. He was staring in front of him, his face ashen, his eyes dulled in obvious pain. Before she could say anything he'd dashed into her bathroom and was violently sick into the toilet.

"Oh God Ben, whatever is the matter?" She tore off a handful of toilet paper to give him, and filled the beaker on the washbasin with water. "Here sip this. Did you eat too much ice-cream?"

He shook his head, and over the top of his kneeling figure she saw tears were running down his cheeks. He bent over the toilet, as though about to be sick again, but then, as earlier she saw that his body was racked with, gut wrenching, heartbreaking sobs.

Love and dismay filled her. "Oh my darling man, whatever has brought this on?" She rubbed his shoulders in a similar manner as he had done to her two days before. Her hope to bring the comfort and the assurance he needed. "Come on, let's get away from here and let me cuddle you." In an effort to bring some lightness she said with amusement, "Nothing can be that bad, you've only been gone ten minutes."

Slowly he rose from his knees, his face so gaunt and pale that her anxiety grew, What in so short a time could have brought him to such devastation? She drew him to the comfy chair, "Sit down, tell me what has happened?"

He didn't sit, instead with eyes filled with misery he looked into her face, his voice gravelly and hesitant with emotion. "I'm sorry Jill, so sorry." And with that, he drew on her hand and led her out of the bedroom. Puzzled, her mind raced. Had the flat been burgled? It had to be more than a burnt saucepan or something damaged in carelessness. Had there been a bad accident for Ben's face spoke of tragedy?

It was a relief to see Helen sitting on the settee facing the stairs calmly sipping a drink. And in pointing to a cup of tea on the small table beside her, saying in an unperturbed manner, "Ben thought you'd want you tea down here, he's put two sugars in it." Rosemary sitting on the other settee looked up and sent them a sympathetic smile. Crossing the room she picked up her tea, sat next to Helen and became aware that Ben hadn't sat, but was standing behind Rosemary, his hand resting on the back of the settee, his expression one of impending doom. What was going on?

When no-one said anything she asked Helen who was looking drawn and pale, "I hear you were sick on the train, that's awful. I ate a pie on Friday and was ill, but at least I was at home." In the midst of her sentence she saw Rosemary put her hand over Ben's and give him a rueful little smile. Puzzled, she asked mindlessly, "Do you think it is something you ate? "

Helen grimaced, "Unfortunately it's not that simple." On looking around the room, she announced, "I'm pregnant."

"Oh Helen! Surely not! You're taking the pill?"

"I am. And I am pissed off about it. I'm going to sue the drug company for faulty pills."

"Well I hope they aren't Inhart's because that could be awkward."

Helen grunted, "Whoever they are, they are going to pay. I haven't got the money for an abortion." Was that why Ben was sick, and looking so distraught? Had Helen, knowing he had the skill, asked him to abort it.?

Ben glared at Helen, and, as though to confirm her thoughts, declared, "I told you Helen, no abortion."

In a vehement voice Helen challenged, "So what am I supposed to do? I don't want a baby. I can't have a baby here. My parents certainly wouldn't want me in their home. And how would I support it? If you feel that strongly perhaps you ought to marry me." With that she dissolved into tears.

For the first time since she'd known Ben he didn't jump into a role and play it. He looked shocked and strangely bewildered. She felt sorry for Helen's plight, but it was a bit much to ask any doctor, especially an unqualified one, to be an abortionist. She went on to assume that Helen had forgotten to take her contraceptive pill and Jill realised the worst, the father of Helen's child could be any one of the drugged or drunken hippies she'd met at a party. Tentatively she enquired, "Do you know who the father is, maybe he'll help you?"

Helen wiping her eyes said into her lap, "Oh I know who he is, he won't help, he's in love with someone else, and this news seems to have devastated him."

Jill sighed, "Well he can't be that much in love with his 'someone else' if he's been sleeping with you?"

Then Helen seeming in need to attack, turned again on Ben. Hands jammed in his trouser pockets, Ben, his face grim seemed to be standing behind Rosemary as if she, and the settee were a safety barrier against an expected onslaught. "I don't care what you think or say about abortion. To you it may be a baby, to me it's nothing more than a blob of jelly, no bigger than my finger nail. And as marriage it seems, isn't an option, what is worse, aborting the thing now, or ruining the rest of my life."

Angry Ben retaliated. "It's not a 'thing'. It takes a man and woman to make a baby, so both should have a say in what happens to it. It may be a blob of jelly to you, but believe me, it is a baby, and, if as you say, it's my baby, then I'm not going to have you murder it!"

Jill stared at Ben. What had he just said? She turned to Helen who was glaring at him. Had she heard it right? The words played back in her mind, 'if as you say it's my baby…' Helen was having Ben's baby? Now she felt sick!

Helen was already addressing Ben's doubts. "… you are the only man I slept with since Tania left so it has to be yours."

A deep, raw groan came from Ben, his hands gripped the back of the settee as though for support. When he broke the ensuing silence, his voice was quiet, calm and with an air of authority. An ability Jill guessed he'd learnt in medical training, but it took an iron will to action it. "Then Helen, I must take your word for it. You know my views on abortion so if you could have put someone else in the frame, you would have done. I still would have tried to dissuade you, but I certainly wouldn't be as adamant as I am now. This is my baby as much as it is yours, and I won't have you kill it." Despite his stand, Ben looked broken and wretched.

What Ben said was true. If only Helen had thought it through before telling Ben, the outcome would have been so different. Dismayed she looked across at Ben, he shook his head in disbelief. It did bring into question why if in love with her he'd still, in dating Helen, been intimate with her? As if in answer, his words echoed in her head. 'she gives more than she needs'. But Ben needn't have accepted it. Did he and Helen romp about like they had done? It had felt so special, far beyond a brilliant sexual encounter, friendship had begun to bud with the possibility of it blossoming into love. Tears prickled at the back of her eyes, she blinked them away.

Rosemary in a quiet voice decreed, "Ben, if you want to keep you baby, you'd better marry Helen."

Unexpected panic arose at the thought of losing Ben. It couldn't, no it couldn't happen, not to her, he could be Mr Right, and to lose him to another woman... It was now her turn to exercise her will to appear calm. With a frown she stated, "Helen wouldn't want to marry a man who doesn't love her."

Helen retorted, "Well, you've made it clear enough times that you aren't interested in him."

Jill looked at Ben who avoided her stare. This was hardly the time to announce that they had been having rip roaring sex all weekend, but surely he'd say something. The silence lengthened. Unable to contain herself she burst out, "I know all I've said about Ben, but this weekend we've talked at length and Ben and I, well..." She looked to Ben for support, his gaze was fixed to the carpet, Helen and Rosemary's gaze was fixed on her. She swallowed and cleared her throat. "I've got to know Ben, I've realise I've been wrong about him. And having enjoyed our time together, I, we, our intention is to build on that, see how things pan out, so marriage to Ben isn't an option."

Ben spoke in a pained voice, "I think Jill that's something Helen and I need to discuss."

Livid that now he had chosen to speak he wasn't declaring his love, or agreeing with her, she glared at him, and stated harshly, "But you've said you love me, so why would you marry Helen?" Ben put his hands in the air, "Because the life of a child, my child, is..."

"This is too emotive an issue. It's too soon for discussion." Rosemary's interruption took her by surprise, as did her taking charge. "Helen you need to rest." To back that up Rosemary arose from the settee, took Helen's hand and gently pulled her up. In leading Helen to her bedroom she past Ben and sent him a sad and sympathetic smile.

Jill couldn't deny Helen looked ill, and couldn't help thinking if she had a miscarriage it would solve the problem. The moment the bedroom door closed on them she hissed at Ben, "You and I need to talk, upstairs."

Ben nodded, and followed her. Her face tightened in seeing the unmade bed, the site of their unadulterated passion, their love nest. Their intimacy bubble had certainly burst with a bang. Ben sat on her dressing table stool with head in his hands. In a voice laden with sarcasm she parried, "Thanks for backing me up down there. What do you mean, you and Helen will discuss marriage?"

With a groan Ben answered through his hands, "What choice do I have? If I marry her my child lives. If I don't there is no guarantee I won't come around one evening and discover she's aborted it. With the security of a husband and a home I know she will go through with it."

"And me, what about me?"

"I love you." A sob caught in his throat, his eyes watered as he looked up at her, his words choked out. "I will always love you. But now it seems I will have to sacrifice my dreams for the sake of my child." He took a deep breath, let it out slowly as though to gain control over his emotions and addressed the floor saying, "I only slept with Helen once." He looked up as though to see if she believed him. His anguish of heart was clear to see. "It was the night you went out with your new hair cut to that party and made it clear you didn't want me turning up. Helen knew I was upset, she came on to me, really to take my mind off you, and I foolishly let her. We drank a fair bit and ended up in her bed, and I'm not saying I didn't enjoy it, but it had nothing of what we share together."

When she couldn't find anything to say, Ben's gaze returned to look at his feet and he continued. "Next morning, the Sunday, I was appalled at my behaviour for I'd let her get drunk and taken advantage of her generous nature. That was the morning you came downstairs with Richard. I assumed he'd spent the night in your bed, the place I wanted to be, and he was now invited to lunch. Your sarcasm on top of that was like a red rag to a bull in my heightened state of guilt and hopelessness."

The tears as he spoke had begun to trickle down his face. Several times he moved his arm to use the sleeve of his shirt to wipe them away. "Every time something good happens to me, something comes along to spoil it. This is me Jill, pathetic, crying, unlucky – who would have believed one assignation would have produced a baby. There's no telling if those pills were faulty, or if she forgot to take them. I don't know what the statistics are, their prevention rate is high, but even ninety-six percent proof would mean a risk of four out of every hundred."

"And what if I'm pregnant?" Ben looked startled. "Don't worry, I've been on the same pill, the same dosage for nearly a year and take it same time every day. Sometimes I don't get much of a period, if at all. But the question is who would you marry then? "

"How do I know? Will Helen want to marry me? Can a

woman live with the knowledge that her husband loves another woman, in fact pines after her?"

"I don't know. When my friend Gemma found she was pregnant she married an older man who wanted an attractive wife, and was happy to let others consider the baby his, as a kind of status symbol. His colleagues were astonished, one of his friends congratulating him said, 'Henry we didn't know you had it in you.' And Gemma telling me said grimly, 'Henry doesn't'. On top of which he's deadly boring, wants his own way, his career comes first, while she pines for lost friends, fun and freedom. What appeared the lesser evil has become a prison and she's definitely not happy."

For a while they pondered on their thoughts. What was the way through this? If she and Ben hadn't just spent a weekend making love, she would have probably felt sorry for Helen, seen her point about having an abortion, but been pleased Ben was considering marrying her. But after their intimacies, and Ben's revelations, it was impossible not to see this for the nightmare it was. She determined to be rational, there had to be another solution.

To Ben resting his head in his hands, his elbows on his knees she stated, "If I were pregnant I wouldn't threaten you with having an abortion, but then unlike Helen I believe I'd have both money and support from my family. Maybe if we offered Helen both money and support through the pregnancy she'd agree to having the baby, which could then be adopted."

Raising his head Ben countered, "But Jill, I want my child. Not just alive, I'd want to be included in his or her upbringing. I'd want to adopt the child."

"And to do that I am of the belief you would have to be married. So just supposing we got married. I'd have to look after yours and Helen's child for sixteen years of its life? That Ben is some commitment. Could I love the child as my own? Would I be fair to that child when we had ours? If Helen was willing, and you had a good job, I suppose it could be feasible for you to support her and the child, as well as having a wife and other children."

Ben's head once more slipped between his hands as he moaned, "I can barely take this in, let alone think about how to overcome it."

"You're a good man, but it does seem your smallest mistake turns into a major incident. Rosemary's right, the issue is too emotive to discuss right now, we, you, need time to think. Now

233

how about I get out the Morris Minor and take you to pick up your car from ITP? It will give you a chance to go home and think things through." In an attempt to lessen the tension she proffered, "And you never know what advice Edward the bear will come up with."

In response Ben raised his head, sent her a sad, but loving smile while his eyes shimmered with unshed tears. He stood, took a deep breath and stated, "My car is at the repairers. It's an old relic, it keeps over heating which smells like rubber burning, but they still haven't got to the bottom of it. I'll get the train home." He gave a despondent grunt, "I've just saved enough money to get something better, but well it looks ..."

Her hug stopped his words, her kiss cut off anything more he might say. They clung to each other not in passion, but in support and comfort. Jill stepped back, "Come on, I'll take you home."

In the car Ben was silent, obviously stunned by the turn of events. Several times she glanced across at him wondering how he would deal with this latest blow. Rationally she realised it was far easier for her to put the weekend down to a brief, brilliant encounter, for Ben it was different, he'd thought his dreams were coming true. Briefly she'd hoped hers might be too, but she wasn't going to get into self-pity.

Ben suddenly spoke as though thinking aloud, "I won't be skint forever. My Dad's left me the house. When his affairs are settled and probate sorted there will be equity in that. And from the sale of stocks and shares there will be enough to put in a new kitchen, central heating, do it up, not to the standard of your flat, but it will be a home. It's better than some having to start from scratch. And if I can keep the outgoings down with my wages as a manager I could keep a wife and child, although it might be a bit tight at first. Wembley isn't a bad area to bring up a child. Turn right here, it's up her on the left. They stopped outside a semi-detached house. "This wouldn't be the kind of house you're used to."

An almost suffocating sadness enveloped her; he was already separating himself from her. She took a deep breath and said, "Ben, your house looks very similar to the one Jane's parents live in. The Reinhardt's aren't snobs. I know it's difficult, but try to get a good night's sleep. If you feel able come around tomorrow evening we'll discuss it then, and talk to Helen. Distracted Ben barely managed to kiss her 'goodnight' before he was out the car into the house.

On the way home she considered the options. If Helen married Ben she would have a nice semi-detached house in a pleasant area to bring up their child or children. David liked Ben so she was sure he'd endeavour to get him something more suitable with a decent salary. Marriage to Ben, could she imagine it? Ben had already said he felt out of his depth knowing who she was and the money that would one day be hers. Would that have been a source of contention between them? But then what was the point dwelling on it, Ben was already considering marrying Helen. His dream of being a doctor had been shattered, but through that he'd met her. Now it seemed his second dream was about to disintegrate, but maybe rising out of the fragments he'd find a third dream which for now was beyond his imagination. Perhaps that was what life was about.

On her return she went downstairs for a drink. Rosemary joined her in the kitchen to say succinctly, "Helen's asleep. Hellish mess! How do you feel?"

Amazed Rosemary had commented and asked, she made a face and said, "To be honest I don't feel anything at the moment. I've just had an amazing weekend with Ben, I know he loves me, I thought we might have something going for us, but now..." As she reiterated her thoughts, Rosemary listened and nodded thoughtfully to comment before she left the kitchen, "He's a good man. He'll do the right thing."

CHAPTER 15

After a fitful night's sleep, her mind active with all that had happened over the weekend, Jill arose to face the day feeling drained and exhausted.

Fortunately, or unfortunately, depending on how she looked at it, David bounded down the stairs as she was going out the front door and offered her a lift to work. His jovial tone, a real cringe factor on any normal Monday morning was enough to evoke a scowl, but he got more than he bargained for when he asked with a wry smile, "And so, how did your weekend go?"

"Well if you are enquiring after the hostilities with Ben, we finally got over those, had rip roaring sex all weekend, Helen came home sick, announced she's pregnant, and Ben is the father of her child. Will that do you?"

David, the smile wiped from his face, stared at her. It was unusual for him to be struck dumb and the enormity of voicing the situation caused her to burst into tears. In his consternation, he drew her towards him, and hugging her invited, "Oh sis, don't cry, nothing is that bad, come on, you'd better come upstairs. You can't go to work in this state." He looked at his watch, "I can stay for about an hour, then I have to go." With that he boomed up ahead to call Jane, and putting an arm around her shoulders guided her upwards.

From the dining room Jane appeared, tousle haired in her nightdress and dressing-gown. Worried she asked, "Oh Jill, whatever's the matter?"

Unable to speak, David repeated what she'd just said as they led her to a seat in their lounge. Wide-eyed Jane shook her head in disbelief. Her bombshell dropped David suggested, "You talk to her, I'll go and make us a cup of tea."

Between blowing her nose and sobbing, she stammered, "I was just, just beginning to think Ben and I might have something going for us beyond the sexual attraction, when…" Her throat tightened and Jane hugged her. "I'm not surprised you are upset. David thinks Ben is a good man and so do I. He knew Ben was besotted with you, and I admit I thought it might work between you. How did you find out that Helen was pregnant with his child? What is Helen saying? More to the point what is Ben saying?"

The cup of tea arrived as she finished answering Jane's questions, and it was obvious David hadn't given Jane any details on Ben's background. Between them they filled her in, which brought Jill to enquire, "Do you think Dad might be persuaded in giving Ben a job, he's interested in research and his medical knowledge would be an asset?"

"That Jill, is something I too have been weighing up, but was first waiting to see if I could resolve your problem with Ben. My thinking that if there were a possibility of his being a future son-in-law Dad might be more amenable to considering him. Now I'll have to approach it from a different angle. I believe Ben is a man of integrity, I know he'll opt for marrying Helen, in which case it would be best if he doesn't continue to work at ITP." She nodded while realising that David knew of Ben's love for her, and he'd hoped it could come to marriage!

David looked unusually uncomfortable. "I'm so sorry, sis." She was reminded he only ever called her 'sis' if he felt upset or guilty! "I'm afraid I deliberately threw you and Ben together on Friday in the hope you'd see him in a different light. But I didn't expect, well, that the situation would be quite so fully resolved!" Nor could I have envisaged that life again would have dealt Ben such a blow. I can only confess, but for the grace of God, I might have found myself in such a predicament." He sighed, glanced at his watch and stood. "Now I must go. I doubt Ben will be at work today, but if he is I'll have a chat with him, he probably needs a friend. You stay and talk to Jane, and if you feel up to it come in later. Check your diary, cancel, or delegate." He patted her shoulder, moved to the door to pick up his abandoned briefcase and with an apologetic grimace at Jane said, "I should have listened to you Jane and left well alone. I feel really bad about this."

At David's remorse she wanted to reassure him. "It could have worked. If Helen hadn't been pregnant I would have been ecstatic this morning and thanking you for interfering."

Jane looking cross, grunted and suggested, "Before you go David, I think we ought to pray."

"Best make it short because I must go."

Before David had put his briefcase down, and with barely time to bow her head Jane launched into prayer. "Dear Father, You know our mistakes, the tangled web we can weave in our lives, but you use all things to bring us to an understanding of your love. I ask Father that Ben, Jill and Helen might be given your heavenly wisdom to know your will for their lives at this time, to do the right thing, and to find you, and your peace, through this. Amen"

David echoed the 'Amen' and picked up his briefcase.

She jumped up. "I think I'll come with you David, work will take my mind off this. It's been good talking it out with you both. And, as you prayed Jane, I made the decision, that if Ben wants to be with Helen then I will accept that, and no more self pity!"

David and Jane exchanged a glance before David boomed, "Great sis, let's go then. Although heaven knows what we are going to do about Sam's leaving 'do' because the ways things are going we shall be begging him to come back."

Once in work, Jenny on the switchboard informed her, as David had predicted, Ben had rung in sick, and that Rich had rung and was ringing back at two o'clock. If all had been going well with Ben this morning she'd have dumped Rich, but now… She might have decided to let Ben marry Helen, but it wasn't a forgone conclusion. Did she want the further complication of Rich? Yet he only came in and out of her life when he pleased, so why not do the same. And for the moment she'd make her excuses. Prompt as usual the phone rang at exactly two o'clock.

"Hi there, sweetheart. Glad you're in. Sorry I've not been in touch. I've missed you. Something cropped up. I had to be out of the country for a few days, but I've a room tonight at the Ritz. Come on over after work, no need to dress up we'll have a meal from room service. Then we can go through the files and discuss Saturday's dinner at the Westgates."

Trust him to expect her to be available, well she wasn't going. "Rich I…"

A sarcastic chuckle cut across her words and he continued, "You could walk, or it's only two stops on the bus. I know on your salary a taxi would be out of the question! See you later, oh and I'm in Room 117 to save you the embarrassment of asking at the desk."

The line went dead. The pig-headed swine, hadn't even given her a chance to refuse! Well later she'd ring Room 117 and tell the occupant she had other things to do than be available to come to his bidding when he decided to come to town. The last thing she wanted was to read his stupid files, put up with his sexual innuendos, or play any of his games.

But as the afternoon wore on it struck her to be out of the flat for the evening would give Helen and Ben time to talk without her being around. So at six-thirty she was knocking on the door of

Room 117, but ready to leave if she didn't agree, or like what Rich was up to.

The door opened, Rich gave her his sexy smile and invited her in. "You know doll, I'd forgotten how lovely you are. I'm so glad you could make it." He hugged her before bending to kiss her mouth. "Umm you taste good, makes me hungry to make love to you. I've been travelling. It's been impossible to get in touch." Had he noticed her reluctant response? "Let's have a drink, then you can order what you'd like to eat, in the meanwhile we'll get those boring files over and done with. First though I have something for you. Taking her hand in his he drew her into the bedroom of the two room suite, and pointed to the large four poster bed on which lay a large rather expensive looking black cardboard box. "It's a present – open it, open it."

His excitement made her smile, and curious she pulled the bow of wide gold ribbon. Inside amongst layers of tissue was a cardinal red dress made of shantung silk, its sleeveless boned bodice had a sweetheart neckline with slender skirt overlaid with rows of cut out, raw edged leaf-shaped flounces of lace. A large bow of the lace was placed under the bust, the dress was beautiful, but looked expensive. Immediately she felt guilty and cautioned, "Rich I can't accept this. It must have cost a fortune."

Excited Rich was already trying to help her off with her suit jacket. "Come on Jill, I want to see you in it, I think you are going to look fabulous. It's for Saturday, you can't go in your other dress, they've seen it before."

"Rich I've come over tonight to talk about this, I'm not sure I want to get involved further."

"Of course you do. Remember the idea is to enjoy life and have fun. Carole is looking forward to seeing you again. Oh, please put the dress on because I just know you are going to look stunning in it, the red against your dark hair. And look underneath the tissue there's a little bolero made of the leaf flounces to go around your shoulders just in case it feels a bit cold. Come on, put it on."

His excitement encouraged her to try it on. "But only if you leave the room."

He frowned, "Why? I've seen it all before, are we suddenly shy?"

"No, but the finished effect will be more stunning than if you see it going on bit by bit." He nodded in agreement and left the room. She breathed a sigh of relief. He might not be upset, but she'd have been embarrassed at his seeing the little love bruises she'd sustained over the weekend. The dress fitted like a glove, and like the other one the bodice was designed to be comfortable yet showing off her figure to the best advantage. The hem was just above the knee and ideal for her legs. Included in the box were gold-strapped sandals with three inch stiletto heels and in the complete outfit her reflection told her she looked stunning!

Rich's long low whistle revealed his opinion, and he rapidly crossed the lounge to run his fingers delicately over the edge of the neckline. His hand then slid into her hair, his mouth met hers. There was no comparison between the effect of Rich's kiss and Ben's, and in feeling so little desire for him she could only hope in the circumstances that Ben's love making hadn't ruined her for any other man.

Rich stepped back, frowned, and looked into her eyes. "Um I rather think your frustration has been sated. Perhaps you would care to tell me by whom?"

Cross she bit out, "No Rich I wouldn't. We aren't lovers, I have no commitment to you, and you none to me. We have enjoyed each others company, you do your thing, I do mine."

Outwardly, Rich didn't respond, but she felt the tension of his displeasure as he ordered, "Go and take the dress off. It cost the earth. A friend had it air-lifted from the States for me. I don't want it spoiled before Saturday." As she headed to the bedroom, he added, "Don't bother to get dressed, there are towelling robes in the bathroom off the bedroom."

Now would not be a good time to ask if he bought the dress from the States because Miss French Chic's shop had burned down. And she definitely wasn't going to sit about in a towelling robe all evening for she'd no stomach for an amorous interlude. Quickly she redressed in her office clothes and returned to see his sexy grin change to grim tightening of his mouth and his drawl develop a hard edge. "Hardly fashionable doll is it? Not the kind of clothes you wear to dinner in a hotel suite?"

Unperturbed, with a need for him to know he couldn't rule her, she challenged, "But more suitable than a towelling robe! And considering you only rang me this afternoon, with no opportunity to refuse your invitation, or go home to change, what do you expect?" She ignored his dour expression and added, "But hey, this is a business meeting, so to my mind an office suit is the most appropriate dress." Then plastering on a confident smile she suggested, "Now shall we call room service, because if that stack of files over there is for me to read I'd better start now otherwise I'll be too tired to concentrate?"

Appeased by her willingness to read his files he handed them to her. It took a while for the tension in the room to dissipate, the wine helped, and room service were quick to deliver them a delicious meal.

It seemed he'd gauged her mood for he talked of his expectations for Saturday night, but refrained from any romantic words, which gave her the chance to suggest they drop the lovesick fiancé act. "We can say you surprised me that evening, but I feel we should postpone any announcement until after my father has received his MBE."

Rich stretched out his hand to cover hers. "But Jill, my thinking is it would be an asset, for both of us, if this engagement became real."

'An asset' those words caused her to say heatedly, "Do you? Well, I'm afraid Rich to me engagement leads to marriage which represents love, respect, honour and certainly not becoming someone's acquisition to further their own ends."

He withdrew his hand, and in a voice as grim as his expression he asked, "So Jill, do tell me, am I treating you as an acquisition?"

Wound up by the events of the past twenty-four hours she spoke her mind. "That's how my friend's husband treats her. How are you different? Married he has someone attractive at his beck and call, to host his dinner parties; accompany him to business dinners; he uses her brain, then speaks as though it was his idea. The baby they have is not his, he knows it, but that doesn't stop him boasting of his prowess in the bedroom which according to his wife is well below par in all respects. So you tell me?"

His obvious annoyance at the first part of the comparison, turned to anger at the final phrase, his eyes glittering with such ferocity it made her aware of the challenge she'd issued, and her vulnerability.

With a humourless smile he stood, his hands balled as fists by his side, "Lady watch what you say for believe me you are playing with fire." A quiver of alarm arose as she watched him stroll to her side of the table and stand over her. "Any acquisition, or merger with me Jill, will not, I assure you, let me repeat, will not, be below par." Acutely conscious that his words contained more threat, than promise, she thought it best not to antagonize him further and didn't raise her head, but looked straight ahead.

He snapped, "You will look at me when I speak to you." Even

before she could respond his hand caught her elbow and pulled her to her feet to face him.

Her eyes clashed with the implacability of his. Her upper lip curled in sarcasm. "Rich you don't love me, or I you. Thus your words 'making love' should be changed for sexual intercourse between two consenting adults, and at this moment I don't wish to consent."

Fury, aggravation and something else that oddly looked like relief passed through Rich's eyes, before he bullied, "And this man you've been with, is it he who has been 'making love' to you?"

"Yes, because I know he loves me."

Rich's eyes narrowed, "So why are you here tonight, eating at my table, and consenting to wear the clothes I buy you?"

"It's a question Rich, I have been asking myself, several times during this evening. The only answer is that I promised the Westgates I would go to their dinner party, and I said the same to you. You said we needed a pre-meeting last week, when I didn't hear anything I assumed it was off, but as I said before, you gave me little choice of coming here tonight, but when I make a promise I keep it."

"Then you will come on Saturday, you will wear my ring, and you will make everyone believe you are in love with me. I've paid for the damn dress, and accessories with that expectation. After all if you do feel an acquisition it's not much of a step on from an escort, a role you are used to playing?"

At his spitefulness, she thrust back, "And you need to be aware Rich not to expect any further escort duties in the future. Don't accept invitations on my behalf with, or without you. Our engagement is about to be broken off, you can choose how and when you announce that."

Unexpectedly, the sexy smile and drawl returned. "Now sweetheart, don't be hasty. Keep your options open." He stepped forward and tried to kiss her, she wriggled out of his embrace. Coldly he announced, "I will expect more from you than that on Saturday." And then added pleasantly, "But you've only had a sample of the delights of the feast I am preparing for you when you agree to be mine."

Hadn't the man heard her refusal to being engaged? He must have seen the flash of exasperation in her eyes, but chose to give her a lethargic smile, his eyes brooded over her as he drawled "Now sweetheart it's time I put you in a taxi for home."

242

In the taxi on her way home she decided that after Saturday that was it. She didn't want any more of his kind of fun and excitement, and didn't intend to be sucked in deeper with this bizarre engagement. Was Rich gay as Ben had insinuated? Dear, dear Ben, she gave a deep heartfelt sigh. What she wanted more than anything right now was Ben. He was fun, his manner light-hearted, and he had the amazing capacity to make exciting, glorious, star blazing love. With a deep sigh she realised too that unless Helen miscarried the baby he was already lost to her.

Weary from the varying emotions of the day she was glad it was only ten-thirty. Once inside the front door she negotiated the inner hall door juggling the big black box under her arm with her handbag. In seeing a slither of light under her bedroom door she wondered if this morning she'd left her beside lamp on. But in opening the door, there, fast asleep on her bed, cuddling her Benjy bear was Ben, the man she wanted right here, right now! It may not be forever, but he genuinely loved her, she wanted him and he didn't belong to anyone else yet.

Quietly she kicked the black box under the bed, removed her clothes, gently moved across the bed to straddle him, and began to undo the buttons on his shirt. He stirred slightly. His belt was more difficult, she had to pull to tighten it in order to slip it off the hook. In that instant she was catapulted off him, flung down and pinned to the bed, with a knee in her groin, a vice like grip around her neck and another around her wrists. Time then seemed to stand still. Almost choking she watched Ben's eyes go from crazed to dazed. The shaking of his head came as he loosened his grip, but still holding her prisoner he demanded, "What the hell did you think you were doing? I could have killed you."

Cross she retaliated croakily, "Preparing you for the presentation of my body. I didn't expect to be attacked."

"That's a dangerous thing to do to a man who has learnt to fight off prison rape." His words conjured up such a picture of horror it brought tears to her eyes. "Oh my God Jill, I'm sorry. I've hurt you, let me kiss you better. Feather-light kisses showered her neck, her wrists, her groin, bringing a different kind of devastation in their wake. His face came up level with hers, he gently nuzzled her mouth and murmured, "And I didn't think you'd ever want me again."

Later creeping down into the kitchen to make them up a midnight supper she wondered why she was feeling clandestine in her own kitchen. Maybe Helen and Rosemary thinking Ben had headed for home hours ago had something to do with it?

On her return, Ben propped up against the pillows enquired, "Where were you tonight?"

Not wanting to spoil their time, she answered, "Monday is my night for meeting friends. I thought I'd give you time to talk with Helen."

"I came to talk to you both. David came round to see me and I came back with him."

Astonished she questioned, "David, visited you at home?"

"I'll admit when I saw him on the doorstep I was taken-aback, and rather nervous wondering whether he was coming as big brother or big boss! But he quickly assured me he'd come as friend, and thought the whole situation was terribly bad luck. He was keen to help in any way he could and told me he'd already taken up your suggestion of putting my brain to work and spoken to your father about a job at Inharts."

Amused she cuddled into him. "Crumbs, David must be impressed by you to act so fast."

His arm snuggled her closer. "Your father suggested I prepare and send him a detailed report of my medical studies and how I think my interests in research might benefit Inharts. Apparently from that, providing I have something to offer them, he would put me forward when a suitable vacancy occurs."

"Now that is truly amazing. David must have highly recommended you for Dad to be that agreeable."

"Ah, well, David was quick to point out that although your father might put my application forward, any employment would be up to the Department Head. I explained about my previous interview. David insisted I let him have the man's name to ensure he wouldn't be involved this time and explained that on your Dad's recommendation the interview would only be to assess my abilities and suitability for the position."

"And in that case knowing you are brilliant I'm sure you'll get a job and do well."

"I love you Jill Reinhardt, I just wish…" Ben gave a small sad smile and having eaten several chocolate biscuits took a long drink of his hot chocolate. "David was very supportive and said he knew I would make the right decision about Helen and the baby. He also suggested I wait until she is over the possibility of miscarriage before I marry her, but to ensure she knows my intentions I should start involving her now in decorating my house to her liking."

Jill sighed, "As much as I don't like the idea of you marrying

Helen, I'll admit to that being a good plan, but what about us?"

"I'll come to that. I've talked to Helen, she asked Rosemary to sit in for support. I didn't mind for she's very level headed. Helen was surprised that David had taken such an interest, but assumed that was because it would be awkward with me still being at ITP because of your involvement. I will need to tell her of my past, but I'll leave that until our future is clearer. But she almost beamed with delight at the thought of decorating my house and was agreeable to wait a couple of months before we made a real commitment? And in the meanwhile…well I'm here with you tonight, but I do feel I perhaps need to ask her if she minds. Oh this is all so strange."

Awkwardly Jill jumped in, "I feel being with Rich is like that. He wants me to continue with this pretence of my being engaged to him, and the Westgate dinner party is on this Saturday. I don't like it, but there's no real harm in it."

Ben sat up to retort, "Surely you're not still going to go out with him. He may be a Lord, but I don't like the sound of him."

""Ben. Ben. Listen to yourself. While you're decorating your house with Helen making it into a cosy nest I will at least have something to do to stop me drowning in my sorrows."

Sadness filled his blue eyes as he bent forward, kissed her, and asked, "Will you be drowning your sorrows? If I felt you were as madly in love with me as I am with you, I'd find a way to support Helen with the baby, and marry you. You know if I get a job at Inharts with the kind of money they pay, I could do that. She could live in the house, I'd have visiting rights to the child, in fact she could have the house for all I care."

"Oh Ben, I don't know, if only we'd had more time together. I say let's enjoy each other while we can. Helen will have time with you decorating the house, and in the circumstances I don't think she'll begrudge us a few nights together. And the baby, well we'll just have to wait and see how that pans out. In the meanwhile…" At her hand reaching for him Ben didn't need a second invitation.

The next three evenings Ben spent with Helen discussing finance, priorities and colour schemes for the house. And when Ben had asked, "Do you mind if I spend the night with Jill?" Helen had given a nonchalant shrug, "You're being good about the baby, it would be mean not to be good about you enjoying Jill's company, but you won't will you, once we're married?" Once Ben had reassured her on that point Helen happily continued planning the future with him. But to her it seemed surreal and there was an edge now to their 'love making' that each time could be the last. On Saturday she watched as Helen with much excitement went off to see Ben's house with a view to buying equipment and begin the decorating. Jill asked herself did she feel jealous? Ben might the nearest she'd come to Mr Right, but he still niggled her in the way he played different roles. Sexy, passionate, exciting in bed, and loving her, then equally interested, thoughtful and caring toward Helen, her pregnancy, her ideas, continually teasing her, making her feel wanted. What did he really feel? Had he buried his real emotions so as to make the best of life, whatever it threw at him? But he had been very disgruntled at hearing Rich had bought her another dress with accessories, and bluntly refused to see it. They'd rowed then about how she had to accept Helen, so why couldn't he accept Rich, but had ended up having such raw and impassioned sex it only proved to both of them how desperate they were.

On Saturday at precisely seven o'clock Victor rang the door bell and ready she slipped out to where Rich in the Rolls awaited her. Still uncomfortable about the whole scenario, this wasn't helped by Rich immediately placing her 'engagement' ring on her finger with great panache, and then spending the whole evening acting as the enamoured fiancé. If she hadn't recognized his manipulative tactics to ensure she couldn't hint at their engagement being broken in the near future she might have been fooled into thinking he cared about her. But she ensured that the guests present understood that their engagement was a secret, and that her father needed to get to know and approve of Rich before she could approach him about being engaged or married. The evening went so well several other invitations were extended. A party at Annabel's in two weeks time to celebrate the Westgate's son's twenty-first, and a dinner invitation from the other guests Doug and Claire Bessant which according to Rich on the way home had been a big coup. Excited, feeling his luck was definitely in he suggested she join him with Chris and Ange at the races the following Saturday. At her reticence, he encouraged her by saying, "Oh come on, it'll be fun, I'll give you some money to spend, and you might even get Rich! His amused eyes held hers, their depths holding the question was she willing to continue the charade of their engagement to these people he so wanted to impress.

Mellowed by the wine, and having enjoyed the evening she played him at his own game and teased, "The question is will I be happy if I get Rich?"

In true gangster drawl, with a devilish smile he retorted, "That depends, sweetheart, on what you term as 'happiness', but believe me I know how to dish up the pleasure." Did he? She doubted it for minutes later it was the usual quick goodnight kiss and he was gone.

The early October sunshine awoke her and stretching she thought of how last Sunday Ben had been sleeping beside her. No doubt Jane and David's invitation to join them and Rosemary for lunch was to take her mind off the situation. And dear Jane never missing an opportunity then suggested she go with them to church. Her reply was to laugh, "I don't think so! I'm hardly church material when I sleep with my pregnant, flatmate's boyfriend, and go out with a man who is probably a gangster pretending to be a Lord!"

To which Jane replied, "That's what church is, sinners who have found a Saviour and begun a new journey of life."

Monday afternoon she caught up with David as he strode across the hall to wait for the lift. "I just wanted to update you. Ben's organized for Fred to come in later to see the Print Department. He said if he travelled in with Ben each day it might work out. We know, but he doesn't, that Ben might not be here much…"

"Yes, yes Jill, what's that got to do with me, you're in charge of personnel?"

At David's abruptness she guessed he was still upset from yesterday when Jane had declared over lunch that even when she had children she wouldn't be the devoted type and would still want a life outside of motherhood. Rosemary being supportive suggested she could baby-sit any time, but at David's glare she'd become so nervous she'd knocked over her glass of wine. Jane had jumped up to get a cloth, while she entered into the fray by pointing out to David they were privileged to have such a willing and live-in babysitter, but it hadn't stopped him glowering at Jane for the rest of the meal.

Now, she gave him a wide-eyed look, and answered, "Yes David I know I am in charge of personnel, but I expected you'd want to know that Ben, having only sent in his report to Inharts on

Thursday, has heard from them asking him to go for an interview at 11.00 am on Friday which clashes with Sam's farewell buffet at noon."

"Oh hell!" David ran his hand through his thick black hair, "Why can't life be simple?"

"No doubt to try you brother dear, to see how well you are growing in love, grace, mercy and charity, in order you don't go to hell!"

"You're beginning to sound like Jane." Distractedly David waved his hand in the air, "Tell Ben to get the interview rescheduled, plead a prior engagement or something, he can't miss Sam's farewell. It might not be a farewell if we have to beg Sam to stay because Ben goes. Oh life can get so complicated! Could you persuade Ian to come back as manager?"

"I'll try, and I'll put an advert in the papers saying vacancies in Print Department and see the calibre of the people we get, we might strike lucky as we did with Ben."

The lift arrived they stepped in, and headed slowly upwards. David sighed and said tiredly. "I seem embroiled in difficulties so I'll leave you to worry and make decisions about the Print Department staff. I've the Brussels Exhibition coming up, Jane's latest hair brained scheme to start up a day nursery on the church premises, and there's Ben's predicament. Dad wasn't best pleased at my asking, or his having to get involved in employing staff, so I can only hope Ben doesn't let me down."

"It certainly wouldn't be his intention, but he does seem ill-fated one way and another."

They lurched to a halt at David's floor. At his worried expression, she questioned, "I thought you knew what to do under stress." David frowned, she grinned, "I quote Jane, I assume from the Bible 'Bring all things in thanksgiving and prayer before the Lord'."

David gave a deep and frustrated grunt, pulled back the lift gate as if it were the enemy and strode down the corridor without a backward glance. Closing the gate she pressed the button to ascend to the floor above and tried to imagine her brother praying. Did he demand and growl at God? Humility, pleading or begging didn't fit David's personality!

Fred turned out to be a delightful man. Tall as Sam was short, thin as Sam was fat, endowed with thick silvery white hair as Sam was grey and nearly bald, but they both had that same fatherly, kind, twinkle in their eyes. No doubt Fred would fit in with the

248

two young men he'd work with. Ben, delighted to see him hugged him like the old friend he was and she left them to talk. She'd only been back at her desk ten minutes when Sam rang and that conversation continued to unravel her arrangements for Friday, and put her in a quandary of what to do for the best. A knock on her office door caused her to grunt in frustration before calling out, "Come in."

Ben's head appeared. "Are you free?"

Delighted Ben should come to visit her office she chirped, "Business or pleasure?" And then realised as the door opened wider Fred was with him.

Ben gave her a look of innuendo, but said in a business tone, "We've come to talk to you about the possibility of re-organising the Print Department. I've told Fred I might be leaving and there is the possibility he could take over the Manager's job. The main problem is fitting in travel time with caring for Peggy, his disabled wife and really the maximum hours he could work each day would be five. I'd like to suggest that Joe is promoted to cover when Fred wasn't there."

Happily Jill smiled. "A good idea, but I think I may have a better one. Sam has just rung to say I quote, 'me Missus is doing me 'ead in, can I come back'?" Ben laughed. "But to appease Mrs B he wondered if we might consider employing him part-time, preferably mornings." She grinned, "My guess is he wants an excuse to eat here! In which case Fred, how about we split the job with you doing four hours every afternoon?"

Fred's eyes twinkled with delight. "I'll say, yes please! It would mean Peggy wouldn't have to get up so early, I'd have time to get her meals organized, and wouldn't leave her so long."

"That's settled then. So Ben you'd better get the job at Inharts because you are now out of the Print Manager's job here!"

Ben who'd been swinging happily on the back legs of the chair suddenly sat upright, and Fred looked dismayed.

A broad smile spread across her face as she declared, "Oh don't worry Ben, if Inharts don't come up trumps, ITP will. I've an idea how we can use that agile brain of yours, it might not match a salary at Inharts, but I'd definitely say it had prospects. Now I'd better ring Sam tell him the good news, then decide what to do about his leaving 'do' now he's not leaving."

Once that was done, she needed to update David.

Miriam smiled a welcome and stated, "You look pleased with yourself. Is it going well with that Lord of yours?"

"Yes thank you. Look I know David doesn't like interruptions, but I've had several unexpected things happen in the last hour and I need to update him."

In a lowered voice Miriam said confidentially, "Good things, I hope, for he's in a very grim mood today. Trouble at home I suspect. Maybe you can cheer him up."

Jill frowned doubting David would appreciate Miriam commenting even to her in that way, and moved across the room to knock of his door. At his rather gruff, "Come in," she began speaking as she entered. "I'm sorry to trouble you again, but I felt you needed to know Sam rang…" When she'd filled him in about Fred, she added, "Ben also told me he's changed his interview to Thursday, but maybe didn't need to because we can't have a leaving party, with no-one leaving! And there's also the problem of…"

David's eyebrows rose, "Good heaven's Jill, there's more?"

"Yes, but only if Ben doesn't get the job at Inhart's. In employing two part-time managers it means Ben is back on the shop floor. In the present circumstances he'll need to earn more money than that. However, I've a brilliant idea, now don't groan, brother dear, you'll like it. You've obviously more work than time to do it with the Brussels Exhibition coming up, so as you did with Jane, bring in extra staff, this time in the form of Ben. He'd make an excellent PA leaving Miriam to concentrate on the secretarial side. I gather Miriam didn't enjoy the Brussels experience last year, and her mother was very cantankerous so…"

David interrupted, "It's part of Miriam's job, but I've been considering asking you to join us."

"Me? To be honest David I couldn't work with Miriam, but if you took Ben I think I could manage that." She grinned happily at the thought of ten nights in a hotel sharing a bed with Ben.

David looked serious. "Let's hope he gets the Inhart job it would be best for him, and you, but I'll bear your suggestion in mind if it doesn't work out. And I need to say right now that if you and Ben come to Brussels I couldn't condone you sleeping together, it would have to be separate rooms."

She shrugged and said, "Fair enough" but she thought what the eye doesn't see… At that she moved on quickly to ask, "Now about Sam's 'not leaving' buffet lunch. Why don't we just use it to announce that Sam's staying on part-time, introduce Fred and use the opportunity to present the 'Employee of the Year' Award to Ben before he leaves? If he doesn't, then promotion would easily follow that."

A broad smile preceded David's exclamation, "Excellent Jill! Well thought out."

Pleased she went on, "So brother dear, Print Department problems solved along with contingency plans for Ben's future. The pregnancy and my intimacy with him, isn't a company issue, so for now you can forget that, and in solving family issues I'll confess I didn't think Jane organizing a church nursery was at all hair brained, because your kids, when you have them, will get looked after and she'd enjoy the admin side. And it might just be what is needed to encourage her to have a little Jane or David." At David's thoughtful expression, she hoped to have gained a victory for Jane. "Now, if you are going home you can give me a lift."

David picking up a file, arose from behind his desk. "Sorry Jill, I've still got figures to discuss with the Accounts Department." He headed out of his office door into the corridor then boomed, "I'll be back in an hour if you want a lift then."

"No its fine thanks, I'll take the bus." With that he was gone and she wandered back out into Miriam's office to comment, "Well I think I've improved his day."

Miriam, by the door, shut the filing cabinet drawer turned, her face sour, and her voice spiteful. "Well, you haven't improved mine. What's this about 'you can't work with me'? Let me tell you I couldn't work with you either! From what I hear you're a bit of a slut so believe me, I'd rather not be associated with you."

Shocked Jill stood rooted to the spot and stared at Miriam whose mouth curved in disdain. In a challenging stance in front of David's door she sneered, "You, a mere receptionist, jumped up into a plum job. It seems you are good at tailor-making jobs, what did you do, make one for yourself?" Hatred glittered in her eyes. "Who did you sleep with to get that? Then there's that Lord, and all your showing off. Ha! Well in lording it up one minute, you've now slipped up. Bit of a mistake getting yourself pregnant with that Fletcher boy's child, there's a come down for you! She gave a scornful laugh. "Even so, its still jobs for the boys eh? If you can't get him into the family business, you've planned that he should take over part of my job, so you can have a lovely family outing to Brussels. Strikes me nepotism is rife here."

Incensed, but determined to keep polite and cool she informed her, "If Miriam I was a slut, it wouldn't be nepotism I'd strike you with. And the reason I don't want to work with you is because you jump to conclusions, judge, criticize, and either see people

251

below you, or fawn up to those you consider useful to you. I don't know where you get your information, but it's slanderous and incorrect, so I'd advise you not to repeat it to anyone."

Miriam indicated with a jerk of her head to the room behind her, "Oh I got it from the horse's mouth. You can't deny what I just heard from in there."

Automatically Jill glanced over Miriam's shoulder, "Then Miriam you were eavesdropping and heard wrongly."

"It's not my fault you left the door open, and I heard you say to David about 'the pregnancy and your intimacy with Ben wasn't Company business'."

"Then if we wait nine months you will be proved wrong?"

At that Miriam was taken aback, but she retaliated with, "If that's the case, why would you and David help that Ben get into Inharts? And if that doesn't work promote him here?"

She sighed, but answered, "Miriam, Ben is far more intelligent than you, or me. There's no need to look cynical, it's the truth. I assure you friendship with Ben is not 'a come down' for he's a man of integrity, cares for people, and is widely liked. Could people say the same about you?" Miriam pursed her lips in annoyance. "That said, I expect an apology from you for the way you have spoken to me, and for the wrong assumptions you have made."

Miriam scowled and retorted, "Then Madam, you'll have to wait at nine months to get it. And if you go telling tales to that brother of yours, I'll make sure he has my side of the truth."

"And that is?"

"You came out here and said, "Well that's improved my day. I've drawn that brother of mine into my way of thinking to get what I wanted. And then, because I challenged you, you added, if you repeat this to him I'll make sure he gets rid of you'."

Jill smiled, "Oh really Miriam, do you think David would believe that?"

"He believed me last time."

"Did he? Well, David are you going to come out and give us your verdict?"

Miriam's hand flew to her throat as she spun around to look through the open doorway into David's office. Quickly she turned back to snarl, "Do you take me for a fool? I knew he'd left, I heard him go. I wouldn't risk my job for you, and you can tell him what you like, it'll be my word against yours. And you are a slut! And there is something going on between you and that Ben."

Jill kept her eyes on Miriam's face and gave her a rueful grimace, as behind Miriam a voice boomed, "If you aren't a fool, then you are an extremely bitter and unpleasant woman."

Miriam jumped, her eyes lost focus as she seemed to swoon and sway. Jill in a reflex action went to catch her, but she pulled round to snap, "Don't touch me. This is your fault. If you hadn't spoken to me in such a nasty tone, I wouldn't have said the things I did."

Open mouthed Jill looked at her.

In a grim voice David said, "Miriam I don't appreciate people who lie, and from what I've heard it is you who is being nasty."

Red-faced Miriam blurted out, "It was her, she led me to say those things. She doesn't like me. I was only getting my own back from how she'd treated me previously."

David's boom made them both jump. "Stop it Miriam. Don't try putting the blame elsewhere. Jill gave you a chance by asking for an apology. I have cautioned you twice about your attitude and behaviour to others. I put those down to overwork or stress. Today I see no excuse for your rudeness, or eavesdropping at my door or repeating what you thought you heard. Your employment at ITP has just ended. I will stay here until you have packed your things and personally escort you off the premises."

In disbelief, Miriam cried in dismay, "But you can't do that, you can't just sack me!"

David sighed heavily. "I can! You signed a contract, I have a copy in my files, and you should have one too, read it. Breach of confidentiality, unbecoming conduct, undermining of staff, character assignation, gossip are all listed as grounds for instant dismissal without money in lieu."

The enormity of David's words hit Miriam, she burst into tears, and they dispassionately listened as she burbled, "I only said those things because I felt Jill was getting at me, didn't like me and wanted to get rid of me. I just fought back, that's all. It was silly, I won't do it again."

"No Miriam you won't get the chance to do it again here. Jill go down to Reception give Duncan a ring and give him my apologies, I'm not going to make the finance meeting tonight. Then wait for me for once I have seen Miriam off the premises we'll go home."

While Jill waited she considered, did people at ITP regard her as a slut? Were people talking about her behind her back in a derogatory manner, similar to Miriam? It wasn't that unusual for

ITP to promote people into jobs most suited to their talents, even tailor-made them, she wasn't special. The big question though was how was David going to manage without Miriam? Who on the staff could she use to fill in the gap?

Fifteen minutes later David strode out of the lift with two boxes, lagging behind came a dishevelled and obviously distressed Miriam clasping her handbag and two carrier bags. "Jill, order Miriam a taxi home, at ITP's expense."

Jill picked up the phone and dialled. David drew Miriam to one side. "Right Miriam your salary up until today will be forwarded to you, as will the necessary paperwork. You may request a reference…"

Jill didn't hear the rest, but saw Miriam nodding in agreement. "David the taxi should be here in five minutes."

"Thank you Jill. I suggest Miriam you go to the Ladies and freshen up."

As Miriam disappeared she said, "Phew that was unexpected, and so vicious! Whatever got into the woman? I didn't realise you'd been listening to it all, I just caught a glimpse of you about halfway through."

David's hand brushed through his thick hair, "I thought we'd solved a few problems. Now I'm left with a major one."

"I've been thinking about that. Fred starts tomorrow. Sam can't wait to come back so Ben could step in right away. Inharts wouldn't expect him right away. Then, similar to Jane, Rosemary knows the details of the Exhibition from the publicity material, and it's time for her to have a promotion. Mike says she's really good at her job"

"Rosemary wouldn't want to work for me. Look how easily I intimidated her on Sunday?"

"I'm gratified you noticed, brother dear. Don't scowl at me. I've come to quite like Rosemary, and she likes Ben, so he'll encourage her, and make up for your deficit. Ask Jane, but I can guarantee she'll say something about it being good for your character building."

David grunted. "I can see the sense in using Rosemary, but would she be willing to put up with me?

"Well I sure if you go with that attitude it will help her to at least try it out."

"And it occurs to me Jill, we tried you out in creating this job, and you have more than proved your worth with your quick thinking and sharp brain. It was a good decision, so don't take anything Miriam said to heart."

Encouraged she smiled, "Thank you brother dear, I appreciate your confidence in me."

"Ah, I'll confess it was Jane who thought your potential should be drawn out, just as I know she will with Rosemary. And what we did for your job we can do for her, and Ben, which is take the elements of the work involved, and create the perfect job for each of them - excellent!"

Jill grinned as a taxi turned on to the drive. "Another opportunity then to use one of Jane's phrases, 'all things work together for good'. Come on let's get Miriam's stuff out, then we can go home – what a day!"

By Friday quite a few changes had taken place in ITP, although not all the staff knew of them until the lunch time buffet in the canteen.. Beer and wine helped everyone to lose their inhibitions so when David banged the spoon on the table there was much heckling as he announced, "Ladies and gentleman, as most of you know this buffet was to say 'goodbye' to faithful Sam, but instead he couldn't manage to say 'goodbye' to us." David smiled across at Doreen refurbishing the cold meats, "Nor it seems to Doreen's wonderful meals which we all so appreciate." Poor Doreen went red, looked embarrassed at the noisy agreement of those present. "So let's raise our glasses, and welcome him back into the ITP fold as part-time manager."

Sam rubbed his slightly shrunken fat belly and beamed around in delight. Mrs B who had accompanied him looked surprised and yet pleased at his obvious popularity. When the clapping and cheering died down Fred was introduced and he took the opportunity to say, "Sam and I only met on Wednesday, but we already feel like old mates, the machines are our babies, so we've got a lot in common and are looking forward to working together. I already feel at home here. Thank you."

David smiled at Fred, and continued, "This would be a good time to announce a couple of other changes taking place. Some of you already know Miriam has had to leave, so I have asked Rosemary, being well qualified in publicity matters to step into her place. And if she finds she can put up with me the job is open for her to accept on a permanent basis." Now it was Rosemary's turn to be embarrassed and blush, while Jane, who had persuaded David she should be there, linked her arm in friendship. "Some month's ago Jill suggested we should introduce an award for

'Employee of the Year.' The intention was to present this at the Christmas lunch, however, we've decided to bring it forward this year to acknowledge a man who I know you will appreciate and agree with me, has given outstanding performance in the short time he has been with us. The award this year goes to Ben Fletcher."

The applause, cheering, roaring and whistling was proof enough that Ben was a popular choice. He played to the audience, in being perky, and looking around with a cheeky grin as he stepped up to receive it. When the noise lessened David continued, "This award is given today for two reasons. First, as you all know Sam is here today because Ben saved his life." Unable to continue over another bout of loud appreciation, David paused and finally held up his hand for silence. "Thank you. The second is because Ben won't be with us at Christmas because yesterday he was offered, and has accepted, a research job in producing drugs to relieve brain deficiencies." There were several jokes shouted out, to which David smiled and continued, "However, Ben won't be taking up that post straight away, and in the next few weeks I've asked him to be my Personal Assistant to help with the Brussels Exhibition. So let's lift our glasses to Ben, Employee of the Year, and to every success in his new job."

At that, the cheers rang out and the congratulations flowed and it was wonderful to see how everyone was happy for Ben. But they didn't know how fate had dealt him some hard blows bringing him to a second best career and soon a second best wife. Ben would be a good father, his child wouldn't be second best, and maybe in time he'd find fulfilment allowing the real Ben Fletcher to emerge, but today anyone looking at him would believe him to have all the happiness in the world.

Tired from the week's dramas she was glad to return to the flat and just sit in front of the television with Rosemary, grateful Ben had collected Helen for the weekend before she'd arrived home.

On Saturday morning Victor arrived with Rich, Chris and Ange in the Rolls Royce. She was relieved to see that Chris sat in the front with Victor. Ange kept up conversation with her, Rich joined in now and then, but it seemed a long journey to Newbury Racecourse. Once Rich and Chris had established 'the girls' as Rich called them, in the bar overlooking the race course they left them with a 'wad' of money to use for betting, and wandered down to the track and the stabling areas. Now and then they spotted them amongst the punters, rushing around placing bets, talking to trainers and inveigling themselves with owners, causing her comment to Ange, "The way they strut about you'd think they owned the place, or at least had their own stables."

"I think they'd like to, but Chris says horses are like children, a responsibility."

"But you and Chris are married don't you think you'll have children one day?"

Ange gave her tinkly laugh. "Oh Jill, we're not married, I wear a wedding and engagement ring because Chris likes people to think he owns me, but he already has a wife and kids in Ireland. He bets, gambles and schemes, but he never sees them. I believe he sends them money from time to time to keep them quiet, but they don't live as he likes to."

The more she knew about Chris the less she wanted to be associate with him. Unable to resist the opportunity she said flatly, "Chris, he seems much tougher than Rich. I suppose Rich tries to live up to his older brother's style and he has a wife and kids tucked away somewhere too?"

Ange looked shocked and puffed even harder on her cigarette. "No way! Rich is... well, that's not his style. He enjoys the company of women, but married, children, I don't think so. Oh I'm sorry. I mean with you and him, he could be changing his... well, mind" With a troubled frown Ange went on, "To be honest Chris scares me sometimes, he doesn't like people getting close to Rich, so Rich always plays down his girlfriends, or friends. Chris though knows Victor is Rich's protector, so don't look anxious he wouldn't dare hurt you. And Chris has always been okay with me, he don't use his fists with women as some men do. Me Mam reckons Chris is a bit like a bull in a china shop, let lose he has no idea of the damage he can do. She says she wouldn't put anything past him." Jill grimaced at the thought of getting on the wrong side of Chris. Ange looked around, and said conspiratorially, "He tends to overdo things, doesn't know when enough is enough. Rich only has to say he's upset about something, and he's in there.

The words were out before she could stop them, "Would that include arson?" Horrified Ange paled, her hand went up to her throat. "Only I heard on the news a few weeks back that the shop where Rich bought my gown is no longer." Obviously frightened, Ange glanced covertly around then stammered, "Oh please, please don't say anymore. I didn't mean nothing, you know, 'bout Chris. Best you don't mention anything, or criticize anything 'bout him and what 'e does!" Below them a shot fired startling them. Then seeing the horses were off, she and Ange tuned into the excitement at seeing the outsider they'd back on a whim come in at one hundred to one! In the joy of winning she temporarily put aside her qualms.

Once they'd collected their winnings she resumed the conversation. "Waverley I assume isn't Chris' proper name, any more than Rich is a Mallory, or Lord Mallory?

Ange frowned, then shrugged, "I don't know, never thought about it. That's Chris' name, and I only know Rich as Mallory - he's got a bit of land in Scotland that gives him his title, but it ain't necessarily his surname, is it? I'd say again, best not to ask." Ange puffed on her cigarette, and took an interest in the goings on below them. Jill curious, and feeling this was a prime opportunity to find out more wanted to ask. "Where does his money come from, crooked deals, gambling, extortion?"

"Look Jill it's not my business, nor yours." With shaking hands Ange pulled out another cigarette from the packet and lit it from the stub of the previous one. Nervously she puffed on it, and in answering kept glancing towards the door. "Rich is the clever one. He's born gambler and determined to win whatever he's set his heart on. With the ability to card count, he can use that to his advantage and a few months ago came back from Monte Carlo with thousands of pounds, but he also upset some very dangerous people." Ange took several frantic puffs at her cigarette and muttered, "They're back. They'd skin me alive if they knew what I been saying. Now don't you say nothing."

There was only a moment to smile in agreement before Chris growled over her head, "So what's you two been nattering about? Bet doll you've spent all that all that 'dough' we left you."

Ange's hand shook. Jill diverted his attention, "In nattering about the nags we still have plenty of that 'dough' left. How about you?"

Briefly she caught the hostility in Chris' eyes, then with a lip curling gesture, in a drawl not unlike his brothers he said, "Take a look here, babe, we know how to do it." With that he produced a thick wad of notes from his pocket.

Jill opened her handbag, "Take a look her, man, we too know how to do it!" Chris' gave her a surly stare, but his eyes widened on seeing the bag of closely packed notes.

Rich's laugh reverberated around them. "So Chris you couldn't resist showing off, but this dame seems to have got the hang of it even better than you.   Just keep it coming in doll, the champers is on you tonight".

Hours later at a night club in the heart of London Chris was drunk, abusive and treating Ange like a prostitute. Why did she stay with the man? It was hard to disguise her disgust which Rich laughingly excused as 'a bit of fun'. The night club owner obviously didn't agree, because two henchman appeared, and despite Chris protests they physically removed him from the property. The three of them followed him out. Victor the mysterious rolled up at the kerb seconds later, and when they reached the flat around two o'clock it was she who said a brief 'goodnight' to Rich being fearful Chris' drunken shouting would echo down the empty street.

In the ensuing two weeks, Ben became embroiled in more domesticity with Helen, as well as spending weekends at the house. These days she felt she saw more of Ben at work than at home. On several occasions in visiting David she found Ben ensconced in his place. David, pleased with the way it was working out, was wondering why he hadn't employed a male assistant before, and they both were encouraged at how well Ben and Rosemary worked together. Rosemary was blossoming under Ben's tutelage, and so it seemed was Helen, for once over her morning sickness she was blooming in health and happiness, which meant Ben would soon be out of her life.

After the day at the races, she'd twice given Rich the brush off, which had him now rescheduling his appointments in order to spend time with her, and without a hidden agenda. One evening they enjoyed a Chinese meal, another went to the theatre, and then with nothing better to do she succumbed to going to the Westgates' daughter's 21st party at Annabels, again wearing the engagement ring, but this time with one of her own dresses. Last week they'd been to the Ritz mid-week for a meal and having her winnings from the races she purchased an expensive dress from Harrods for that, and they'd enjoyed a meal at the Bessants on Saturday, where again she posed as his fiancé.

Despite wanting to believe the best of Rich she noticed how continually he'd brush off difficult questions with a sexual innuendo or caress. His need to be engaged didn't include meeting her family. He always sent Victor to ring the bell while he waited in the car, and when he drove himself, he made a time for her to be at the door waiting. The excuses at the end of an evening ranged from tiredness, early appointments the next day, rushing off to unknown activities, and keeping Victor waiting. The fact that Victor waited patiently for hours outside the theatre, the night club, the restaurant, just in case he was needed somehow conveniently forgotten. She was just musing over these things as she pasted up David's Director profile for the monthly magazine when the telephone rang. Her figures sticky with glue she answered rather abruptly.

Rich's response was equally short and to the point. "Jill, Rich. I can't make that concert tonight. I'll be in touch when I get back." And before she could say, 'back from where' the pips went telling her that the call was from a phone box, and was at an end. She sighed. That put paid to the rest of this week and probably the weekend, perhaps time to visit the parents again, and hope her Mum didn't start asking about her love life, for with two men in the running it was still a non-starter.

CHAPTER 16

It had been three weeks since she'd heard from Rich, and although after each date she'd considered not seeing him again it now seemed he'd decided for her! With Ben working long hours and decorating at weekends she was seeing less and less of him. And David's continual lateness was even making Jane tetchy. But with Ben, David and Rosemary being continually together camaraderie was building bringing Rosemary confidence, although she was still reticent to go to Brussels. If she decided against it David would soon have a difficult decision to make as both she and Jane were vying to take her place!

Her first "Meet the Directors" article in the magazine produced much hilarity and embarrassed David, but he'd taken it in good humour, and insisted he help furnish her with similar photos and information for her next victim!

Overall life seemed to have fallen into a rut. Boyfriends weren't mentioned during her weekend at home, no doubt Jane had explained to her Mum the situation.

In the last week she and Jane had gravitated toward one another to discuss life's difficulties, and with Jane's clarity of thought she'd found an inner balm when pouring out her feelings for Ben, and realised how going out with Rich probably hadn't been the wisest thing she'd ever done.

Helen now over the shock of being pregnant seemed to accept it by being chirpy and chatty and one evening commented, "I still don't know how a one-off got me pregnant, I hadn't missed a pill. Did you know Ben offered me his house, and said he'd keep me, but I couldn't face living there on my own with a baby, I'm not ready for that kind of responsibility."

Those words had made her heart sink for they cancelled out any hope of her and Ben continuing to develop their relationship. Determined for Helen's sake not show her disappointment, she gave a small understanding smile which set Helen off to say enthusiastically, "However I'm surprised how much I'm enjoying planning and decorating. Ben may not love me, but he's a good guy, and is certainly trying to do his best by me. I'll be four months pregnant when he returns from Brussels in mid-December, he'll begin his new job at Inharts in the New Year so we've discussed a Christmas wedding." Upset she'd had to make an excuse then to go to the toilet to blow her nose and wipe her eyes - Christmas wasn't that far away.

Since Ben had hinted he would soon need to make a commitment to Helen, and last night added, "I don't know how I can end something that means so much to me, and the thought of not seeing you…" For the first time since their initial coming together they'd talked about their feelings with Ben concluding, "Let's enjoy what we have now, and believe as one door closes at Christmas another door will open for both of us. For me the Inhart job will be excellent, and the best I could hope for. Helen is a natural 'nest' builder. In maturing she will make a good wife and mother. From friendship I'm sure we can develop it into a love, although not with the passion and yearning I have to be with you. Despite Helen's pregnancy these last weeks have been the happiest of my life, but I am concerned that it seems I get everything, and you end up with nothing."

There was no doubt she had developed feelings for Ben, it would have been impossible not to, for as Helen said, he was good guy. If only she'd seen that earlier, but life was full of 'if only's'. Whether it was love or lust, whether it would have stood the test of time they'd never know, and after the wedding she'd probably never see him again. But in the mean time as he and Helen were spending the weekend at his house, they arranged he'd sleep over tonight instead of Friday.

Rosemary and Ben having just returned with David were getting a bite to eat in the kitchen, she'd just nipped up to her bedroom when the doorbell rang so, being the nearest she went to answer it. The wind howling down the street whistled in throwing a fistful of very late damp autumn leaves into the outer hall, from behind which, out of the darkness and chill November evening, came Rich. Unshaven and looking somewhat seedy he bowled in without any preamble trailing Victor behind him carrying a large suitcase asking, "Which way?"

At the unexpectedness of his visit she stepped back, closed the front door and instructed, "Straight down the hall, turn left." Why was she letting him in? Helen appeared around the corner causing Rich to halt abruptly and Victor to bump into him. Victor grunted and scowled, while Rich seemed flustered and on edge. Equally nervous Helen eyed Rich, Victor and the suitcase, and then looked questioningly at her. What could she do but give a wide-eyed shrug, move forward and watch Helen's expression flood with bewilderment as she introduced the two men who looked more like thugs than a Lord and his chauffeur.

Obviously keen to escape Helen murmured, "Oh yes, right, pleased to meet you. I only came up to see who was at the door." With that she turned and hurried off down the stairs. Jill could only hope Helen would now relay the message of her unwanted visitors, and what appeared to be their intention to stay. Using Helen's appearance to move in front of Victor and Rich she blocked the flat doorway to ask sharply, "What are you doing here, and what's with the suitcase?"

Rich having regained his composure drawled, "Sweetheart you've been inviting me in for weeks, so I have finally made it." He looked beyond her, "Is that your bedroom? Victor put the case in there." Without further ado Victor pushed past, dropped the suitcase just inside the door as Rich instructed, "Now you better get off. You know what you have to do."

Victor was already heading toward the front door as she protested, "Look here Rich this is…"

"I know sweetheart, all a bit sudden, but I've some urgent business in Amsterdam late tomorrow afternoon and, as I'd promised you a trip, it seemed, now was as good a time as ever". He picked up the case, flung it on her bed, opened it and took out a suit, "Where shall I hang this?"

Taken aback she opened the wardrobe door and pointed to the rail.

"You'll have to tell your office, you're sick, ha ha - sick of work!" He hurried on, "I shan't be working all of the time so we can do the tourist bit, we'll visit one of the diamond houses, you can feast your eyes on their amazing stones, and I'll see what I can afford." He'd grinned at her.

Wide-eyed she asked, "You want to buy me diamonds?"

"That's what you'd like isn't it? I'm afraid I had to let go of what I think of as your diamond ring, but there are plenty in Amsterdam. It's the place to get you an even better one." He stepped forward and with his thumb and forefinger caught the lobes of her ears, "And maybe diamonds for your ears too." Involuntarily she stepped back. Rich's eyes narrowed, but he kept his voice light. "I didn't think with such an offer you'd have any objections to my sharing your bed tonight?"

Irritated she bit out, "I haven't heard from you in three weeks. You come here out of the blue, want to share my bed, expect me to be pleased, and then expect me to change my plans for the weekend, so is it any wonder I feel peeved?"

"Oh fiery lady I've missed you! I'll make it up to you. It's not easy to be in touch when you are in foreign parts making a bob or two." Her mind whirled. Where had he been that he couldn't have had a wash and shave before arriving? One thing she did know was she didn't want his diamonds. And she wasn't sure she wanted to go to Amsterdam with him either. What would Ben make of this? They'd concluded he was gay, yet tonight he seemed keen to bed her because he was already stripping off his clothes. "It's great you've got this ensuite bathroom, so be a love and run me a bath. Once freshened up, we can settle down for the night because we must leave by 6.00 am. Don't look like that you'll enjoy this unexpected adventure." About to voice her qualms he continued as though to appease her, "Oh dear I hope I haven't come at a bad time, of course, how silly of me, you may have had other plans?"

Cross she folded her arms to state, "Actually Rich, I did. And I can't take even one day off work without prior warning because I have deadlines and responsibilities to fulfil."

Rich now in his underpants stepped forward to outline her mouth with his finger. "Shss sweetheart I'm sure if you spoke to that brother of yours he'd understand and organize for you to be free." His mouth took hers, his unshaven beard, scraping her face.

She pushed him off, "Leave it out Rich."

He attempted to look rueful. "Now is that the way to treat a man when he has thought up such a surprise for you? I'll make myself presentable while you make yourself free." Exasperated at his expecting her just to comply with his wishes, she said acidly, "Run yourself a bath Rich. You look as if you could do with one. I'll get you a cup of tea. And then I'll decide whether you stay or not, and whether I go to Amsterdam, or not." Rich grinned and headed to the bathroom.

When she came downstairs Ben looked up anxiously and mouthed, "Where is he?"

She beckoned him into the kitchen and shut the door. "I didn't know he was coming, and it seems he's staying."

Ben's eyes narrowed, "I thought he was gay?"

"Probably is, so don't go getting jealous. He has business in Amsterdam tomorrow, wants to take me with him and deck me in diamonds! He's insistent, but I'm playing it cool. I only have a couple of things scheduled for tomorrow, and I've still two weeks holiday to take this year and nowhere to go, so if you could do them for me I could easily take a day off."

Taken aback Ben questioned, "You want me to cover for you, while you swan off with Rich?"

She shrugged, "Well let's face it you are swanning off every weekend with Helen. What else have I to do?"

Tears formed in Ben's eyes as he stepped forward to hug her close. "I am jealous, and I know I shouldn't be. And I know it's irrational, but I fear that this man is not what he says he is, and you're going to get hurt. Helen said Rich looked more like a thug than the debonair and suave Lord she anticipated and something about him gave her the shivers! Is he coming down here, am I going to meet him?"

She drew back to look into his eyes. "I doubt it for it seems he wants us to have an early night as we are being picked up at 6.00 am tomorrow. I'll admit he wasn't looking his best having been travelling, but he's in the bath as we speak, that and a shave will make him far more presentable. He can be fun." The words caught in her throat as she admitted, "And not being alone here for the weekend will give me something else to occupy my mind." Ben moved to draw her close, she drew back, "Now as I've decided to go I'd better find my passport - can you help me out at work, or shall I ask Rosemary?"

"We've been living in a bit of a fool's paradise these last few weeks haven't we? I've tried not to think about when you're no longer in my life, and suspect you feel much the same." He bent his head, his lips brushing gently against hers, but within seconds the fire lit and in frantic desperation they didn't care who came in.

Rich's voice called from the bath when she entered the bedroom, "I didn't realise you would be so long?"

"Neither did I? But I had to reorganize my evening, my tomorrow's work schedule, and nothing is ever quite as simple as you'd hope. I've found my passport so that's a good start, and taken a suitcase out of the boiler room to pack. Your cup of tea is here.

The water churned in the bath, and a minute later Rich appeared with the towel around his waist and was rubbing his hair with the hand towel. "Now ain't this just nice and domesticated. That suitcase is too small, get a bigger one. I don't believe in travelling light. Put enough choices in to cover every contingency and weather for I don't know what we'll be doing with the exception of Saturday night. Put in that dark blue cocktail dress you wore a few weeks ago." He peered into her wardrobe, and ran his hands down the rail, "Put in this dress, that's a good skirt, what about a couple of different coloured twin-sets and have you got some chunky knit jumpers, always good if there's a cold snap. Trousers are always useful, take a couple of pairs then you've got choices."

"Rich we're only going for three days, not three weeks." He didn't answer but instead turned out to be an excellent packer as he inter-folded her clothes so they wouldn't crease.

"Now to relax you I'll give you a gentle massage and then I think we'll be ready to sleep."

Half an hour later she murmured into her pillow, "You should have been a masseur" as his fingers massaged and unwound the stiff nodules in her neck and shoulder muscles and his more fluid movements brought a sense of well being to her body. She turned to speak, and saw his eyes were quite blank, focused far-away as if on something, or someone else.

"Rich, are you alright?"

He flinched as though interrupted before a self-deprecatory smile slipped on to his face, "Sorry my mind slipped away." He took in her facial expression, "That's not very flattering is it, but I'm afraid something you'll have to get used to." Jill cringed inwardly. Used to? Was it feasible a man wasn't aroused by massaging a naked woman who he was supposedly interested in?

"I tend to get like this if I have a lot on my mind." He chuckled and sat down beside her to kiss her. But even that didn't last long because stroking her cheek he said ruefully, "I'm afraid I'm going to have to save you for later, we have a ferry to catch tomorrow and we must be up and out before the crack of dawn."

It was dark except for the bedside lamp. Rich was calling her name and proffering a cup of tea which meant he'd been downstairs to make it. The last thing she wanted to do was get out of a warm bed. The tea helped wake her and Rich getting dressed commented, "I met Ben when I went downstairs. He was sleeping on the settee. I'm not sure whether I disturbed him or he was getting up early."

Deliberately making her voice disinterested she said, "Oh did you, he's dates Helen?"

"He seemed very much at home. I felt he resented my presence."

Hardly surprising she thought in the circumstances, but she replied, "Probably because he's not used to being disturbed at such an early hour."

She climbed out of bed and went to the bathroom, but the moment she reappeared he asked, "So how long have he and Helen been going out? "

She pulled a thick jumper over her thinner one, to say as her head popped out, "A few months."

"Why is he sleeping on the settee and not with her?"

"Helen has a single bed. What is this Rich?" She gave a derisive laugh as she pulled on her trousers, "The third degree. Now where are my nice warm socks? I'll stuff a couple of pairs in the suitcase." Did Rich have wind of something between them? Still putting odds and ends in the suitcase she sought to divert his questioning. "If you felt any antagonism from Ben it was probably directed at me not you. He and I often don't see eye to eye."

"So what do you know about this Ben character?"

"Not a lot. He works at ITP same as Rosemary and I. Helen met him through Rosemary. She's pregnant and they're getting married in December, will that do?" She peeked a look at Rich as she zipped up her suitcase and caught his cool, but slightly nasty smile. Unless something drastically changed this weekend, she was definitely going to be unavailable in the future.

It felt very clandestine to be creeping out the front door into the cold, dark morning. The ever silent Victor appeared making her jump. He collected the suitcases Rich had bought out and headed behind him across the pavement to a navy blue Ford Escort parked across the road with its engine running. To her dismay Chris was in the driving seat, he gave her a surly nod, as she got in the back and ignored her question, "Why are we in this car and not the Rolls." The boot lid slammed, Chris accelerated away leaving Victor by the kerb.

Rich turned briefly from the front seat to answer. "The Rolls and Jag are far too ostentatious for a quiet weekend away." After several further attempts to strike up a conversation she closed her eyes and with the car motion nodded off to sleep, but when it stilled she opened her eyes to see they weren't at the ferry terminal, but outside a row of garages on what appeared to be a council housing estate in Greenway Close wherever that was. At asking the obvious question Rich's reply was curt, "We're changing cars."

Rich got out, unlocked one of the garage doors and backed out a red Ford similar to the one they were in. When she queried that Chris scowled, "You ask too many questions for your own good." But Rich helping her out intervened, "Early mornings don't suit

Chris any more than you." But what did suit her was Rich having transferred their luggage from one car to the other got in the driver's seat leaving Chris to back the other car into the garage. Their arrival at the ferry terminal in the last minutes before the boat sailed gave them a quick transit through passport control and on to the boat.

After a leisurely late breakfast, and a hand in hand stroll around the deck where the winter sun was reasonably warm for the time of year, she felt she'd made a good choice. "This is lovely Rich. Thank you for bringing me. It feels like being on holiday." She squeezed his arm, "I'm really glad I came." He smiled at her as she continued, "So tell me what the plans are for the weekend?"

Rich dropped a kiss on her nose, "Umm that's cold. We'd better go inside. Let's stroll around inside and get another warm drink and something to read."

Once off the boat, across the Belgian border into Holland the scenery was mostly flat countryside consisting of fields, dykes and dams. They stopped to fill up with petrol, enjoyed wandering around a village of small wooden houses, where waving in a brisk breeze washing was twisted between a double line and hung without using pegs. She was fascinated and couldn't believe that the wind wouldn't blow it away across the surrounding dykes. Further on they visited a cheese making factory, bought coffee, tried the local cheese and ate honey wafer biscuits. It was late afternoon and growing dark as they drove into the city of Amsterdam where waterways interlinked and water taxi's negotiated the canals. The hotel Rich choose was in the historic part of the city near to the museum district and the famous Leidse Square. At the desk the problem with the travel agent not having booked their room was almost instantly resolved when Rich announced he was Lord Mallory. And the very helpful manager was quick to show them to a beautiful, if somewhat old-fashioned room with high ceiling, four-poster bed, and huge ensuite bathroom. She smiled guessing that was one of Rich's ruses to ensure he got one of the best rooms in the hotel.

They had just time to unpack before Rich announced he must head for his business meeting, and not wanting to wander on her own in the dark, she went down to the hotel bar where other women sat at the small tables scattered around the area. But it wasn't until the third man approached her to ask her if her name was Anika, having already been asked by if she were Sofie or

Mina that she concluded the women were prostitutes waiting to be picked up! Was that a feature of this hotel, or all Amsterdam hotels? Embarrassed she quickly finished her drink. She was crossing the lobby to the lift when she heard Rich call and joining her he ordered, "Get your coat. We need to get a meal before my next meeting. It won't be a long one so you can come with me." Although there were restaurants around them Rich headed for the water taxi to take them to another part of town. It was a lovely way to travel, but the restaurant's only advantage was its convenience to the nightclub where Rich explained he'd an appointment. "Rich I'm not dressed to go night clubbing."

"Don't worry sweetheart no-one will notice, that dress is quite acceptable." That proved true for the place was dark, dingy and smelt of beer and smoke. Hopefully they wouldn't be here long. The music was loud, the singer not very tuneful. Her glass of wine, compliments of the house, tasted cheap and watered down, and she was about to speak of her dislike of the place when Rich was summoned and disappeared. Alone she felt distinctly uncomfortable especially when the exotic dancer started to divest herself of her clothes to the mostly male clientele's heckles. Where was Rich? She looked around, caught the attention of a middle-aged beer bellied man and was dismayed when he decided to join her. With distaste she curled her lip, peered down her nose, and in her most refined accent announced, "That's my husband's seat." His fat jowls wrinkled in a smile, he bent forward, clamped his large flabby hand over hers and said something she didn't understand. Intent on leering at her he had a sudden shock when Rich shot by, grabbed at his neck, and dragged him up by the front collar of his shirt. The man had to be seventeen stone, but the shock and the cold, hard glint in Rich's eye was enough for his expression to change to fright at which Rich gave him a hard shove. He stumbled backwards, hit a table, wobbled, knocked over a chair and landed on the carpet. Seated on the floor he made no attempt to get up, probably for fear Rich would hit him. Those around shook their heads and quickly returned their attention to the now almost naked woman on the stage. It appeared a brawl here was commonplace.

Rich grabbed his coat, and demanded, "Come on doll, let's get out of here," He marched out with her following like the call girl the man had obviously taken her for.

Angry she grabbed his arm, "First I'm in the hotel bar and I find it is a place where 'women' are picked up, then you leave me alone in that sleazy place, and now you're treating me like a call girl. Take me back to the hotel. And if that's the way you behave, the kind of place you frequent and the people you do business with, leave me out of it. I'll go sightseeing on my own tomorrow."

Rich's face and voice hardened, "As you wish." Nothing more was said until outside the hotel entrance where he dismissed her with "Goodnight," then turned on his heel and left her to walk in on her own. In order to calm down she spent a long time in a comforting hot bath, and then lay in the huge bed considering whether to feign sleep when Rich joined her.

She awoke to the smell of bacon, hot steaming croissants and other delicious aromas she didn't recognise. Rich, fully dressed was bending over a trolley table pouring a cup of coffee. Had he come to bed? The indentation in the pillow next to her indicated his head must have rested there. "Ah I see you are awake. Breakfast has arrived."

The food was hot and it tasted good. His response to her seemed minimal, making her unsure whether he was preoccupied, or still annoyed. With such little interest in her she was taken aback when he suddenly produced a wad of notes, put them on the table and suggested, "Take this, and treat yourself. See the city. Go for a day trip. I could be out all day." He bent to kiss her cheek. "It'll be special tonight, I promise." And before she could ask why, he'd gone.

She found a tour which started with a glass topped sightseeing boat on the main canal, a short walk and then on a coach to see places of interest within the city before heading out. She lunched with three other English people in a small café where they all agreed the speciality pancakes were delicious. They split up to do a tour of the market stalls and she watched fascinated at impressive moving parts of a decorative clock as it chimed the hour. That finished she knew she had a quarter of an hour before joining her group. In turning her heart lurched. The back view of the man walking away from her could have been Ben. First he'd haunted her because of dislike of him, now he haunted her because of her…did she love him? There was no point in dwelling on what couldn't be. Deliberately she turned her attention to a nearby stall. Barely focussing she looked at a pack of mixed cheese on tiled board, in the blue delft design, and purchased it for Jane and David. The remainder of the afternoon was spent in Delft seeing the china being hand painted, followed by a visit to a clog factory where the making of the clogs was demonstrated.

Rich, drink in hand, was in the lobby waiting for her. In a better mood she hoped by his greeting of wide smile, brief kiss and suggestion, "You go up and put on that pretty cocktail dress. I've an invitation to dinner at an upmarket floating restaurant which you'll appreciate."

The bath running, she took out her cocktail dress, grabbed her shoes from the wardrobe and as she did caught her elbow on the door. A sharp tingling pain shot down to her hand causing her to rub and wiggle her fingers. Aware Rich was waiting she hurriedly removed her ear-rings, but her still numb fingers dropped the butterfly clasp on the floor. She groaned, the carpet was dark, the light not bright. On her hands and knees she carefully rubbed her hand across the carpet and into the keyhole area of the dressing table. At the back she touched a shallow leather-covered box. Curious she took hold of it, crawled out backwards and found her lost clasp as it imbedded itself in her knee. Anxious to see what was inside the box, she quickly opened it and gasped! Inside, on black velvet, rested a magnificently sparkling large tear-drop diamond pendant, with smaller, but matching ear-rings, and in the centre of the display a beautiful diamond ring blazed in the light, which she guessed was of equal carats to the necklace! If these belonged to Rich why hadn't he put them in the hotel safe? How could he afford such extravagant jewellery?

As though guilty, she jumped as the bedroom door opened. Not surprising was Rich's demand to know what she was doing. She waited for his eyes to see the box in front of her. In a steely voice Rich questioned, "What have you been doing? How did you find these?" Before she could answer, he'd grabbed her arm twisting her toward him. And with cold, hard eyes he accused, "You've been searching the bedroom."

Afraid, but determined not to show it she retorted, "Oh don't be so ridiculous. The only thing I was searching for was the back of my ear-ring and I found that along with this box. It seemed strange so I picked it up and opened it."

His eyes narrowed in disbelief, his hands moved around her neck, his thumbs stroked her Adam's apple, as he murmured menacingly, "You know what they say, curiosity killed the cat." In that instant she thought he was going to strangle her, but laughing he let her go saying, "It sounds as if you're running a bath you'd better go and look after it."

Relieved to be free she dashed into the bathroom, she didn't want to contemplate what Rich would have done if he hadn't believed her. Alone in a foreign country she suddenly felt very vulnerable. Startled, she jumped as Rich spoke from the doorway, "I'm sorry sweetheart, I over-reacted. I'm tired." On a heavy sigh he explained, "I hid the box. It was to be a surprise. I know you were upset last night, and I couldn't be with you today, so I visited a diamond merchant because I didn't want to disappoint you. De Vries was expecting to meet you tonight, and wanted to see that ring on your finger, but unfortunately he's now unable to make it." Rich gave a cynical laugh. "But with a table booked at his favourite floating restaurant, we might as well use it."

Her mind leapt to the fire at Miss French Chic's, the Mallory family misfortunes and the death of his mother. Perhaps Ben's fear wasn't unfounded in that she could be in danger from acquaintance with him?

Had Rich notice her qualms for he chivvied, "Cheer up this is going to be that romantic evening I promised you."

In an attempt to be firm she stated, "Then Rich get out of the bathroom. Leave me to get ready. But remember I'm not engaged to you, forget the ring, your friend isn't coming so there's no-one who needs impressing."

He retorted, "Most women would jump at the chance to be engaged to me, especially offering them a ring like that."

Underlying the words she heard his aggravation and decided not to exacerbate it. With a little laugh she bantered, "Oh Rich, you really know how to propose and make a girl feel special."

His reply, "I could murder a drink. Enjoy your bath. Meet me in the bar."

Half an hour later she was unsure how many drinks he'd had, but looking very dapper in a beautifully tailored dress suit, he was waxing lyrical as arm in arm they strolled along the canal. The lamp lit walkways reflected in the water, stars twinkled in the clear black sky with its nearly full moon, and Rich's speech was his romantic best. When he produced the ring and insisted she wear it she squashed her misgivings.

On arrival at the very up-market floating restaurant Rich was very much a Lord in the way he commanded attention. He spoke of Jansen De Vries as a friend, and when the Manager seemed perplexed, he continued to insist the invitation was to use De Vries table at his expense. Rich, charm oozing from him gave him his card, followed by one from De Vries. Then lifting her left hand, her ring sparkling magnificently in the light Rich kissed her fingers, and reassured her, "I'm so sorry, darling, to embarrass you like this. Jansen will be so upset for he was so taken with you, and told me to treat you as the princess you so surely are. But I'm sure we'll have this quickly resolved. Do you think the lady might sit at De Vries table while we sort this out?" With that he challenged, "Now, if you need to check my validity…" He paused, raised his eyebrows and stared at the now mortified Manager who assured them, "No Sir, I'm sure everything is in perfect order, there's no necessity to do that."

Immediately they were shown to the best table on the boat with a magnificent view, but the wrangle in getting it, was far less embarrassing than Rich's ordering the best champagne, along with the most expensive wine and dishes on the menu. When she questioned his extravagance he waved his hand, "Sweetheart De Vries is a millionaire he can afford it, and you deserve it having been deserted all day. Your car running out of petrol was a wonderful quirk of fate. And you my dear have the potential to make me millions!" He chuckled, "You're just what I need, and the best thing that could have happened to me."

He probably expected her to laugh, but instead a sense of unease filled her, to get rid of this man was going to be difficult. To give the appearance of nonchalance she uttered, "Is that so?" And then she discharged an introductory shot. "You do know my Father definitely wouldn't approve of you. So any thoughts of marriage to me won't bring you millions from that quarter. And I don't intend in getting involved in anything that isn't strictly legal so I'm not sure where that leaves your expectations." The cold, blank way he stared at her reminded her of Chris. Apprehensive she felt a need to distant herself from him and dumping her napkin on the table she declared, "Now you'll have to excuse me, I must visit the Ladies."

Once there, and in need of fresh air, she opened the window and breathed deeply. About to shut it she paused, for the build and figure on the bridge looking out over the water reminded her of Ben. Tears pricked the back of her eyes. He obviously occupied more of her thoughts than she realised. Well, she was here and stuck with Rich so she'd just better drown her sorrows, because one way or another she'd have to get over Ben.

On her return Rich gave her a cool assessing look, she sent him an equally cool smile. They had each consumed two glasses of champagne and now she quickly finished a third and felt better for it. The diamond dazzled her in the candlelight as she put her hand over Rich's. "You know Rich this is romantic, the ambience within and the view of the canal without. We might as well enjoy it to the full, especially if your friend is paying." Their next course arrived on a huge plate the offering on it, tiny, but exquisite in taste. Each dish chosen in the seven course menu proved to be 'deliciously' special. Dreamily she commented, "This place is so romantic, I feel lulled by the music and the way the boat gently rocks.

Rich also mellowed now by the wine, lent across with a wry smile, "Sweetheart, are you a bit tipsy?"

"Do you know Rich I rather think I am?"

"Well, doll it's certainly improved your mood."

In the midst of eating the sweet course she began to feel very odd, her words beginning to slur making her giggle. "I feel in-eed of som-ad passion-onate love."

His response was his sexy smile, "Is that right sweetheart, well just eat up your sweet first."

In obedience she pouted her lips transfixed her eyes on his before transferring the cheesecake to her mouth sucking it slowly and seductively off the spoon then deliberately rolling her tongue across her lips before repeating the performance. Rich sighed heavily and commanded, "Just eat it."

The plates cleared Rich declared, "You look ready to pass out, and I think a quick, quiet exit is needed. So be ready to stand and go." He picked up her bag, caught her elbow, and hauled her to her feet. The boat seemed to sway alarmingly. She staggered against him to say loudly, "What's with the rocking boat?"

Rich whispered between his teeth, "Shut up, you're drunk!"

Belligerently she retorted, "No, I'm not, it's the boat, I can take my drink. Let's take the rest of this bottle back with us?" Carelessly she picked it from the bucket, dripping water around as she wafted it in the air. The waiter rushed across as Rich grabbed it from her. "I think I'd better get her home." From his pocket Rich dropped a generous pile of notes on the table which had the waiter being overly helpful, and assisting with their departure the Manager summoned a waiting taxi, thanking Rich for their custom for they had certainly spent an extortionate amount of De Vries money.

As he pivoted her off the boat with his arm around her she stumbled into him. If she couldn't have Ben, then Rich was handsome and was being very attentive. In the short taxi ride back to the hotel he chuckled as though pleased, and she clung lovingly to him. In a firm voice he ordered, "Pull yourself together, we're nearly there. The foyer of the hotel reminded her of the boat, it swayed and rocked, making her feel giddy. Rich dropped her into a seat by the lift and went to get the key, but she noted that the man on Reception glanced over at her. Probably didn't get many people as happy as she was, she called across, "Look we're engaged" and waved her ring at him. The man gave a cool smile. Rich's expression was one of annoyance, but his voice said lovingly, "Come sweetheart, let's get you in the lift."

As the doors closed, his grip tightened, "You silly bitch, what did you have to go and do that for." The harshness of his voice sobered her for a second or two, then she giggled, he was playing games, she rubbed herself up against him, and crooned, "I'm waiting for you."

The lift doors pinged open, and he trundled her down the corridor to their room, propping her up beside the door as he unlocked it. "Oh Rich, Rich" she flung her arms around him and heard his loud sigh as he lifted her off her feet to carry her into the room. Oh, how wonderful he was being so romantic and she was just so in the mood for some passion. He dropped her on the bed, and growled, "Undress yourself, get some sleep, I'm going out!" With that, he was gone, and she was alone.

What was the matter with him? Why hadn't he stayed? It was difficult to stand, a struggle to undress, then falling over on to the bed, leaving her clothes in a heap on the floor, she found her nightdress, got it over her head and fell almost immediately into an alcohol induced sleep.

CHAPTER 17

Was the knocking in her head, or outside it? Perhaps it was both. What time was it? Groggily she slid her hand across the bedside table and found the lamp. How did this thing work? She slid it towards her, and managed to switch it on. Why didn't Rich stop knocking, had he forgotten his key? From the bed she stumbled over her pile of clothes and headed to the door. Disorientated and head down she undid the lock.

Was she dreaming? Was this Ben, with a pot of coffee and cup, urging her to sit down on the dressing table stool? The cheeky face she knew so well looked deadly serious as he said with urgency, "There's no time to explain. Just believe me you are in danger. You have to get out of here." Seated, her elbow resting on the dressing table, her hand holding her head, she wearily lifted it to watch him pour the coffee before thrusting it before her. Her mind reeled. Ben here? What was going on? "I'll pack your things. Drink that, and then get dressed." Dazed she obeyed and saw him get her suitcase and emptying the wardrobe of her clothes. "Good grief woman do you always take so much when you go away for the weekend?" Her head didn't feel her own. Ben looked across at her. "You shouldn't have drunk so much."

Cross, she managed to retort, "I saw someone who looked like you, so I was drowning my sorrows, okay?" The effort made her moan and hold her head which didn't seem attached to her body. Gently Ben pulled her up into his arms. "I'm sorry for being cross, but I don't know how long we've got until Rich comes back and we have to be out of here by then. Take these painkillers and finish off that pot of coffee." He resumed collecting her clothes and laying them on the bed as he admitted, "You weren't seeing things. I saw you in the market, and on the bridge. I was keeping an eye on you while trying to organise our getaway. When David couldn't find out where you were staying I decided to come to find you for myself."

"David? I don't understand?"

In a grim voice he commented, "You will. Rich and Chris are making plans to abduct you."

Despite being confused she gave a sarcastic chortle before contradicting, "It looks to me Ben it's you who are doing that."

Not pausing, Ben scooped up the heap of evening clothes by the bed and shoved them into the centre of his pile. "Just believe me, Rich is going to have you kidnapped."

Her head shot up to reiterate, "Kidnapped?"

"Yes, so let's get out of here. Now where's your handbag? Have you got your passport?"

The realization hit her. She gulped down the hot black liquid. "Oh my God! Rich said I was going to make him millions, do you think he meant in ransom money?"

"It's my theory. Now hurry and get dressed, while I just put all this stuff into your bag and suitcase."

"Give me that jumper, those trousers that scarf." She dressed as Ben went into the bathroom to gather her toiletries. She pulled open several drawers, found her passport and stuffed that and other bits and pieces from the drawer into her bag." He emerged as she was putting on her walking shoes. "How are we going to get away?

"I came on the train, it's quicker than car. My idea was to hire one here, but all day I've been trying. Small companies don't allow cars across the border and the larger companies said they hadn't anything available for more than two days and wouldn't risk I'd get it back in time. I just couldn't wait any longer because Chris is here."

"Chris here? She stopped dressing, frowned and asked, "More to the point how do you know Chris?"

"Prison. Now have you seen any car keys? We'll have to use the car you came in."

Whether it was the drink or the shock she was beginning to feel sick. "Try Rich's suit pockets, he wore it here." She paused to drink more of the strong black coffee, it was clearing her head.

"No luck! He's probably got them with him. Don't worry I learnt many things in prison, one how to get into a car, and two how to hot wire it. Now I'll just push those pillows down the bed to make it look as if you are still asleep."

"How do you know about this kidnap business?"

"I'll tell you when we are well clear of here. I assume the car is in the car park. Now is that everything?"

Quickly she glanced around the room, and nodded, as he clipped the locks on the suitcase. "Didn't you think this amount of clothes was rather a lot to bring away for a weekend?"

She shrugged, "Not particularly. Rich said there was no reason to travel light." Ben put down the suitcase and turned out the lights as she heaved on her overcoat.

"It would be better if we slip out by the back stairs it's the fire exit and leads directly into the car park." Ben opened the door and indicated the long corridor was empty. Almost immediately the lift pinged at their floor. Could it be Rich and Chris? Ben obviously thought so because he hurried her back into the room, closed the door and put the lock down to stop the key working.

Scared she reached for Ben in the dark. Voices neared the door, she recognised Rich's as he put the key in the door. "The silly bitch should be well out of it by now, she drank enough." Rich cursed as the key wouldn't turn. "She's locked herself in."

Chris grunted, "Probably done it to spite you. Maybe she's caught on now that women aren't your thing." The handle rattled, and one of them obviously put their shoulder to the door, which fortunately was thick enough not to budge. Ben hugged her to him. Beyond the door they could hear Chris's mouth spilling forth the foulest of language and what he'd like to do to her when he got hold of her. Horrified, and frightened at falling into his hands, she would have collapsed if it hadn't been for Ben's support and whispered reassurances.

"Oh shut up Chris, that's not going to help is it? Let's think man? We don't want to cause a fuss because that will draw attention to us. We could delay our plan for 24 hours."

Jill didn't catch Chris' reply, but Rich said, "This could work better." Rich lowered his voice, she and Ben practically had their ears on the door to catch a drift of his words. "...hotel we've... tiff... locked out. ...home tonight...make her own way... I'll take...full roadrunner... deals in London." Rich chortled, "I can't be in two places at once! And whatever happens there's no connection to you or me."

Rich intended to leave Chris to abduct her, after what he'd just envisaged he'd do to her. She shivered against Ben, he rubbed her back in comfort. Rich chuckled nastily, "So...you... grab...into Belgium."

Chris replied, "I've found this nice little shack of a farmhouse out in the middle of ..." Rich shushed him. Jill strained to hear and then wished she hadn't as she caught the words, "...no-one will hear her screams!"

In hushed tones, but quite clear Rich warned, "Now bro, I want her alive, able to write and able to speak, so we can send dear Daddy tapes of his darling daughter pleading for her life." Chris gave a non-committal grunt.

Jill cuddled against Ben, his arms tightened around her, which was fortunate because there was sudden heavy thud indicating someone had hit their shoulder against the door. She screamed in fright, but Ben's shoulder muffled the sound, and Chris' loud expletives drowned it. It was obvious only a piece of wood inches thick separated them and she shook with fear. But that close meant they could hear Rich instructing, "Leave the basics of my stuff, take all hers so it looks she's packed up and left. Remove anything incriminating, there's the diamonds oh and my passport is by the bed. Once we have the money in the Swiss bank account, I'll get it transferred to Rio, and then we'll be set up for life." He laughed, "So Renee de Mer, I'll look forward to seeing you in a few weeks." His voice lowered, they strained to hear, she only caught 'Daddy' 'doesn't' and 'dispose', but the inference was shocking enough as was Chris' growled, "A pleasure."

Rich laughed. "I thought you'd say that! Now give me the car keys and get back to your lodgings." His voice went quieter, "We don't want to be seen together so I'll go down in the lift and state my case, you go out through the fire exit. You know bro she's …" Their voices drifted away as they moved down the corridor.

Rich was happy for Chris to dispose of her! What kind of monster was he? Tears ran down her face, in a cracked voice she whispered, "Oh Ben, if you hadn't arrived when…" Further words stuck in her throat.

Ben drew her back from the door to say, "I did. And I'm here. David told me that Jane once thought he'd been appointed her guardian angel, I'm beginning to think I've been appointed yours." At his attempt to lighten the moment she snuggled back into his chest, but it was brief for he drew back to advise, "Now we have to get to that car before Rich does. We need to follow Chris down those stairs." Ben switched the light back on and strode across the room speaking as he went. "Now I'm going to steal Lord Mallory's passport …oh, and money, from this bedside drawer. It'll be evidence of his using a forged one to get back into Britain."

"You could take his wretched diamonds, they're worth a fortune."

"No thanks. I'd guess they're stolen I don't want to be an accessory to that. Come on, I'll go first with your suitcase. Keep a little way behind me, but enough to see me. If anything goes wrong slip back to the room, or better still go to the lobby and get them to call the police. Try not to make a sound. Are you ready?"

She squeezed his hand and got a squeeze back. "That's my girl."

Quietly Ben opened the door and peered out. Once at the stair well he briefly slipped inside, then reappeared to beckon her. With only her handbag she ran up the corridor and followed him through the door. She quenched a scream of fright as the fire-door at the bottom of the stairwell slammed, and then realised it was Chris leaving the building. On the final flight down she caught up with Ben who asked. "Do you know where the car is in the car park?" She shook her head, but added, "It's a red Ford Escort, I think a 'B' reg."

He gave her a wry smile "Don't look so worried there aren't many English cars here, so red and 'B' shouldn't be too difficult to find. If Rich and I get into a fight, run as fast as you can into the hotel and call the police."

"Why don't we do that anyway?"

"If possible I'd rather not involve the police. Lets find the car." As Ben quietly opened the fire doors, and peered out into the darkness she could understand his reticence, but was it wise to try and escape them alone?

The deserted and poorly lit car park had a choice of about fifty cars, with just enough light to identify your car if you knew where it was! The fire doors were at one end of the building fairly near the car park's exit. Ben led her to the nearest row. "Wait in this dark spot with your case. I'll whip around, find the car and pick you up. If need be leave the case. Otherwise throw it in the back door and jump in after it. We don't want to be hanging about." Anxiously she watched as Ben ran between the cars. Where was it? Rich could be here at any minute. That thought made her stomach lurch in fear. Predictably she looked towards the side of the hotel. A figure came around the corner. It could be anyone. But a second later she knew it was Rich. Panic brought a keening in her throat. Desperate she glanced towards Ben. How could she warn him? But Ben must have spotted him for he'd disappeared. Instinctively she too ducked down despite Rich walking in the opposite direction to her. Crouched between two cars, holding her suitcase, her body shook with fear and a desperate need to cry. Supposing Rich came this way and saw her? This wasn't a time to be feeble. There was silence. How long would she have to stay here? Could she risk bobbing up to see what was happening? It seemed like minutes, she told herself it was probably only seconds. Footsteps were approaching. Was it Ben, or Rich? Her mind cried out, "Oh God, help me, make me invisible." She thought quickly, no car had started up it had to be Rich. Bent double she abandoned her suitcase and slid around to the front of the car just as Rich walked past the back. She froze and pushed herself against the car's front bumper. Could she, the car and the darkness become one? Rich's steps faltered. Had he seen something? Her heart beat so hard and fast in her chest she felt sure he'd hear it. Then as if God had indeed made her invisible Rich continued on his way.

Once the footsteps had faded away, she let go of the breath she'd been so tightly holding. Wobbly from fear her hand reached out to the bumper to steady herself. Mindlessly she read the car's number plate DMV123B. 1,2,3 breathe in, 1,2,3 breathe out, she must try to relax. Suddenly her brain engaged with her eyes, the number plate was English, the car was a Ford Escort. It wasn't red, it was navy blue - was this the car they'd driven to Greenway Close in? Ben said he'd seen Chris - had he driven here in it? A sense of relief flooded in because when Rich took the red car, they could take this one.

Bent double, she slipped back to join her suitcase, and felt her heart had stopped when beside it she saw a pair of legs, their owner tall, hooded and looking out over the cars. Terror like hot bile arose in her throat. Weakness caused her to wobble, her body bumped against the car. The figure turned, ducked down and held her. Ben whispered in her ear "It's alright. He's found the car eight up from here two rows across."

On the still cold night air they heard Rich thump the car several times. Curses intermingled with the words, "You stupid, stupid fool. These are the wrong keys, damn you!"

She and Ben looked at each other. Her terror turned to alarm, but no words came. Frantic, she pointed to the car they were squatting next to, and managed, "English!"

Ben didn't question or hesitate. He grabbed her case, and moved around the car. With hand movement he indicated she should get across to the next row of parked cars and hide in amongst them. He mouthed, "Now!" Once she was away, running bent double, she realised he hadn't followed. If she thought she'd been terrified before it had been nothing like this. Would Rich see her shadow passing down the middle of the cars? Would he shout or jump out at her? After passing six cars she felt too weak to go on and slid between the next two. Instinctively she prayed, Oh God, please, please help us. Then nearly yelped in fright when Ben doubled up, came up behind her. A second or two later a car engine started up, revved, and headlights lit up the exit aisle and the navy blue Escort left the car park.

Ben stood, and drawing her up, grinned, "If I didn't know better I'd say David and Jane are praying and we've just had a miracle. Chris it seems gave Rich the wrong keys, now all we have to do is take the red car and keep well behind Rich."

With great efficiency Ben whipped out a metal clothes hanger from his rucksack, and within seconds had opened the car door. She got in as he stowed her suitcase on the backseat and after a few agonising minutes wondering if Chris might discover his mistake and reappear, the engine jumped into life. It took a while to negotiate the myriad of small streets, but once on the main road towards the ferry port the nervous tension within began to dissipate.

With the road ahead clear and nothing much to distract him Ben gave her a rueful smile. "Are you okay? You're very quiet?"

"I feel numb with shock. And Chris, all he said, I can hardly believe it. I've had such a narrow escape."

"I think once we pass through into Belgium we ought to find ourselves a hotel for the night. The drive to the ferry is about two hours. Rich will have the same idea, but as he wants to get back quickly he'll be on the first ferry out in the morning. We'll make a leisurely return. It's too late now to ring David, but we can do that in the morning. He thought we ought to go to the police, but if I'd got it wrong he'd have been embarrassed, and Rich would have found out I'd squealed on them. And you now knowing the kind of men they are, you'll understand I didn't want unnecessarily to cross the man you know as Lord Mallory."

Jill shuddered. "Isn't that his name?"

Ben sighed, "It appears, only one of them." He reached across to squeeze her hand. "Now let's put this behind us for and enjoy the time we have. After all this is our first real date!"

Tiredly she smiled over at him. "I suppose it is. Unexpected and the first part not one I'd wish to repeat!"

The car was in darkness, she could barely see his face in the dashboard lights, but guessed at his expression as he responded, "In that case I'll do my best to make the second part very repeatable!"

"I'll keep you to that Mister. But can we make it the third part because if you aren't too tired, I would really like to know how you found out about Rich and this plot?"

Ben shot her a rueful look, "To me he isn't Rich, I'm afraid he is Peter Sanchez, my gay cell mate in prison." Her hand shot to her mouth, horrified her eyes widened. Rich was the man Ben had had to ward off several times during his incarceration. "Did he tell you he'd met me in the kitchen?"

"Yes. I thought with his interest he suspected something between about us. I was very negative about you."

"That was probably a good thing. You know how lightly I sleep. The stairs creaking alerted me to wake, I could hardly believe my eyes as Pete went by! But things started to click into place when I realised that Lord Mallory and Peter Sanchez could be the same person. I decided to get up to say 'hello' in the hope of finding out. I think Pete was so surprised to see me he didn't bluff it out. He told me he'd been on the run for several weeks, and two nights before had been caught in an ambush. Apparently he'd been gambling heavily and owed a mass of money. Chris always up for a fight muscled in, so he'd had opportunity to escape, and had slept rough for two nights in a caravan while Victor helped him make plans to restore his fortunes. It was then he laughed saying he wished he'd thought of coming here sooner, what a pleasant and useful bolt hole this was, the only problem was keeping randy Jill's knickers on."

"Did he really say that?"

"'Fraid so, but take it as a compliment because I've no complaints!"

She lent across to give him a playful thump.

Ben chuckled. "Later Jill, later, I'm driving! Now where was I? Oh yes Pete or Rich said he felt Amsterdam would prove a useful place to be, and he was taking you along as collateral." I didn't know what he meant, but nodded knowledgably. He went on to ask if I were still selling drugs? He said he could put some good deals my way. I dutifully thanked him, then he winked and said, "Fancy you being here, I'm surprised you aren't after Miss Reinhardt and her father's millions? I said that had been my original intention, but you'd taken an instant dislike to me, so I was going out with Helen. But I had inveigled myself with your family and would soon start at job at Inharts and had no idea where that might lead to. Sort of gave him the nod and wink as if I were up to something. The man is such a tosser. Even in prison he always wanted to have that one-upmanship. So as I hoped, that drew him out a bit and he tapped the side of his nose to say, 'Shame you missed out on the rich bird, but guess if you are infiltrating Inharts you've got a plan to make a bit'. He went on to tell me how you met. I grinned and said, 'Now come on Pete you can't tell me that you're intending to marry her?' His reply, 'Oh hell, no chance of that! But there are other ways to get a rich bird's father to part with his money. I've some leads and deals in Amsterdam, but I'm thinking if she's with me what better time to put my insurance policy into action, you know what I mean?' He tapped his nose again and picked up the mugs of tea he'd made. As he left he said, 'If you can move decent and regular amount of drugs out of Inharts and want somewhere to sell them contact The Vista Club manager, give him my name, he'll connect you to the right people and get you a good price.' I looked suitably pleased and interested, and he went off happily back up to you."

"How did you guess his insurance policy was to kidnap me?"

"Banged up in a cell for hours on end Pete used to dream about meeting a rich bird to set him up for life. Trouble was he couldn't face marrying a woman, so chatted around kidnapping her and ways to get the ransom money without anyone knowing his involvement. He would laugh and say 'Chris is fool enough to do it with me, let him be the front man. Whichever way it goes I'll set him up in Rio with money, and then make sure he can't return. No-one will suspect it's been anything to do with me I'll be rich, and be shot of a right pain in the butt. I never know what he'll do next.' And I got the impression Rich suspected him of involvement in some unfortunate family accidents."

"That's interesting because Rich told me that the Mallory family in particular seemed to be ill-fated and his Mum had an unexpected and odd death. So a double twist in the plot. I think if I was him I'd be looking for ways to get rid of Chris' too, he's a nasty piece of work."

"Exactly, and so is Rich in a different sort of way, and the reason I didn't want to go to the police. I've Helen to think about, as well as you, and after that conversation I just didn't know what to do for the best. In the end I went and banged on David's door. At first he was all for calling the police, getting them to bring in Interpol, but I'd only suspicion, no evidence. We went back and forth with thoughts and ideas. Jane went off to pray. David had Rosemary ringing the main Amsterdam hotels, but none had a reservation. I was worried in case he'd decided against Amsterdam and kidnapped you already. But, my thinking was if I was in Amsterdam I'd have more of a chance of finding you. David was all for joining me, but I didn't think that would help. I could just melt into the background and observe. I arrived late on

Friday evening, rang the list of hotels Rosemary had, and to my relief found where you were. After that I felt it best just to keep an eye on you, and observe Pete's movements.

"In an attempt to see what Pete was up to I decided to have a drink in the hotel lobby last night and saw you come in on your own. I nipped out in time to follow Pete to a gay club where he met several people he obviously knew. Most of the day I was keeping and an eye on Rich, but in trying to hire a car I nearly bumped into you at that market. When I saw Chris in a nearby bar this evening, and you had come in looking inebriated, I knew, if they were going to put their plan into action, now would be a good time. And Rich obviously knew Chris was there because he joined him after leaving you, so I felt I needed to get you out as soon as possible."

"And thank goodness you did. A few minutes later…"

Ben observed, "We've just crossed into Belgium obviously not much of a border. I'll head for the coast and find a hotel along the seafront. We have Rich's money, but obviously we'll have to be careful we don't have Rich's company!"

Despite it being November, they manage to find a sea front where brightly lit hotels were open for business. On the assumption that Rich would go to the nearest they drove away from the direction of the port, but they monitored the street and car park of a hotel before going in. The clerk took their money, didn't ask to see any identification probably because they were paying in cash, and Ben signed them in as Mr and Mrs Fletcher. At least with her suitcase they looked married, rather than his woman for the night. In nervous exhaustion Jill collapsed on the bed of the very mediocre hotel room.

"Dear Jill, you look as I feel. You may not believe this, but I was as scared as hell that I might find myself fighting Chris, Rich or both. I might have the edge on Rich, but Chris…" He gave a deep sigh of relief saying, "We're safe now, and frankly, even though I promised you a third part to this unusual date I need a bath and sleep – is that okay with you?"

"Isn't that what married couples do?" Ben ruffled her hair, she smiled up at him.

"If that was what we were I'd be the happiest man on earth. Now did you want to use the bathroom down the hall before me?" By the time he returned she was nearly asleep. His body cuddled into her back and happy in just being together they slept.

The early morning light filtered through the thin curtains, the small open window brought in that salty tang of sea air. Jill stirred, snuggled into Ben's warmth purring inwardly like a contented cat, and smiled dreamily at Ben's slow, gentle way of awakening both her body and brain. They'd been through a nightmare, it had passed, and their relief showed in the tender love making which brought them to a quiet, but fulfilling satisfaction.

But that was quickly diminished with the reality of their situation when Ben, pulling himself up on his elbow, looked down at her to state, "I suppose we'd better ring David and tell him you're safe."

"It's Sunday, they'll be going to church."

"I'll ring Helen she can pass the message on to say we'll be home this evening."

The mention of Helen reminded her it was only weeks before he'd be lost to her forever bringing her to question, "There's no hurry, is there? I just want to stay here with you." Despair, with tears, threatened, but not wanting to spoil this precious time she reached out to touch the man who could wipe everything from her mind, but her need of him. Ben's immediate response brought her to savour his every touch, every kiss, and it seemed he felt as she did. It was if they wanted to indelibly imprint themselves on each other. Had his willingness to sacrifice his life for her changed something inside her? The long closed door to her heart was now fully open and it took them both into a new depth beyond the passionate all consuming sexual pleasure. Her natural reaction as the waves of orgasm built was to close her eyes, but in their desire to share every moment they kept eye contact and the oneness became so beautiful, so wonderful, so all encompassing it felt she as if she were drowning in the blueness of his eyes and overwhelmed, tears of emotion poured down her face. In the aftermath without moving from her, Ben lapped them with his tongue bringing her to realise his tears were mingling with hers. They lay touching, kissing, snoozing, and each etching the other's face into their mind as the sun came up and the light grew brighter.

If only time could stand still, life didn't have to move on, and the maid wasn't knocking at the door calling in broken English, "time ten, please you leave."

Ben called in reply. "Merci beaucomp." He cuddled against her, kissed the tip of her nose and said with regret, "My darling, we have to go, and I need to ring David. We could walk on the beach and head for a lunch time ferry. I want you to know love making with you is always special, but these last few hours I've experienced a new depth of pleasure. A pleasure I don't suppose, without you, I will ever have again. I love you so much." He hugged her tightly, then wet eyed, drew back to say, "Our swan song, the best, the culmination of love, the celebration of a grand finale."

Her eyes feasted on his sad, but still cheeky smile, the bright blue eyes brimming with unshed tears and the inch cropped blond hair that never flattened which added to his charm. How could he have so annoyed her? Her hand smoothed down the plane of his cheek, her finger slid across those sensual lips. "Shush we still have a few weeks left, let's not think a 'finale' until we have to. There is no doubt you have touched my heart and released something which has been locked up inside me, but I can't think about a love because it cannot be, and to do so would only bring more pain. You have shown me that sex without engaging your heart is just an act with a consenting adult. Tears trickled down her face as she added, "And when you are gone to your new life with Helen, I'm not going to let my heart close down again." He hugged her, his hands comforting, stroking her back. When she'd calmed down she said more rationally, "You've have revealed and taught me that love comes in different ways, and if we determine to make the best of life we will find fulfilment in that. Ben Fletcher you are a wonderful man, and I feel privileged to have your love, but there is no use mourning for what we can't have, and know, like you I have to move on to what I can."

To her surprise Ben gave a cynical laugh. "Words are easy, the outworking more difficult. But I do have advice - don't look back on the past. No regrets, no 'what if's'. Start again as soon as possible. When you meet a good man, don't compare him to others just enjoy who he is, and give yourself wholeheartedly to that relationship. You will love him because you are a woman made to love and be loved. Love does come in different ways, but all is equally valid and valuable." Ben's kiss was long, loving and gentle, and as his hands caressed her body, that new tender passion began to build as did the more urgent knocking at the door.

"Mr, Mrs, I clean room. You leave please."

Ruefully they looked at each other, kissed one last time and slid apart.

Ben put a towel around his waist, delved into the pocket of his rucksack, drew out a handful of notes and opened the door slightly and thrust them at the maid. "I'm sorry give us 'dix' minutes." Her answer was a barrage of French, but she walked away.

Quickly they washed and dressed, deciding to go to the toilet on their way out rather than hold the room cleaning up any longer. In the hall the Manager accosted them, but most of what he said was beyond their comprehension, but another handful of notes seemed to appease the man, and they managed to get him to understand they'd like change for the telephone in the hall. There wasn't a reply from David's number, and Ben's conversation with Helen was brief, because of the constant pips indicating the telephone's need to be fed money.

The sun for November was relatively warm and the empty beach stretched for miles down towards the port. They stowed the bags in the car and hand in hand strolled briefly down the promenade and found a little café for coffee and croissant. The nervous tension, and probably the affects of all the alcohol she'd consumed was playing havoc with her stomach, but the food seemed to help settle it.

Back at the car having again hot wired the engine it was only a short drive to the port and they were quickly in the queue for the afternoon boat having had just the right number of francs left to pay for the crossing. Waved on they parked amongst the other vehicles cautiously looking out for a navy Ford Escort, despite believing it had gone on ahead. That done they felt somewhat relieved that the channel would separate them from Chris and realised Rich was probably back in London by now. Had Chris discovered yet that she wasn't in the room, and had he any means of contacting Rich to tell him?

They stood on the deck and watched the coast disappear. Briefly they discussed what the next step would be on reaching English soil. "Without involving me Jill you have to see it's only your word against Rich."

"But I know David, he will want to find a way to bring Rich to justice, even if not directly for his plans against me."

"In which case I think David is going to find he is again frustrated by the lack of justice, and that many known criminals don't get the punishment they deserve. I'm sure they will eventually catch Rich, but the safest thing for all of us is to move on and forget this incident. Now let's stroll around the deck and have a meal in the restaurant – this is a date with you, and my treat."

They really hadn't done much inconsequential talking in their relationship. From the Sunday lunches she knew he could be good company, and at times had made her laugh, but in those days she had determined to dislike him. Today was so different.

As the sun began to sink in the sky, the sea got rougher, and it didn't help her already queasy stomach. Ben insisted she wrap up warm and they stood outside so she could see the sea line, which helped. By the time the English coast was in sight breathing slowly and deeply wasn't enough and she spent the remaining half an hour with a sick bag saying crossly, "I hate being sick. I'll never eat meat pies or use a cross-channel ferry ever again!"

Finally they were in dock, in the car and waiting to get off. What a relief. All she wanted now was to get home, get in her own bath, in her own bed with Ben to cuddle her, but they still had a four hour drive ahead of them back to London.

The cars in front were edging forward. Ben did whatever he did with the wires, but the car wouldn't start. He got out and fiddled under the bonnet and tried again. Still it wouldn't budge. One of the attendants came over, "What's the matter governor? You got a flat battery?"

"Not sure. I'm sorry about this. Would you mind giving us a push start?" He poked his head in the passenger window, "Jill can you get in the driver's seat and jump start us?"

By the time she'd changed seats the cars behind them were managing to manoeuvre around them. She heard Ben talking with the attendant about how often this happened, and then she took the hand brake off as the men pushed. When they'd enough speed she slammed the car into second gear, accelerated as she took her foot off the clutch, the car jerked, and the engine spluttered into life. To keep up the momentum she drove on to dry land with Ben jogging behind. Ben waved and called his thanks to the attendant jumped into the passenger seat and instructed, "Keep going, once at the customs we'll swap places."

Sheer willpower after that jerk had kept her from being sick, but the moment they stopped at the customs barrier she jumped out and released the remaining contents of her stomach at the side of the road.

Ben rushed around to her aid. "Here have this hanky. I filled up this Coke bottle with water, take a drink."

A custom's official came out and didn't look too pleased. "We'll have to get that hosed down. You can't stay here. Just show me your passports and you can go through."

Ben reached into his rucksack and handed them to him and

gave his attention back to her as he returned to his booth. "I think Jill you need to sit down." He drew her back toward the passenger side of the car. "Hopefully the car will start, sit in it and drink this water, I'll get our passports and we'll be on our way."

Coming towards them were two custom officials. Ben turned to smile at them, but they didn't respond just looked rather grim. "Is this your car Sir?"

Surprised Ben admitted, "No I borrowed it from someone I know. Why is there a problem, officer?"

"You tell me? Because I see the lady is Jill Reinhardt, but if you are Lord Mallory you don't look like your picture." He waved the passport at Ben.

"Oh sorry I must have given you the wrong one." Ben dived into his rucksack and produced his passport and handed it to the officer. He looked at it, and passed it to his colleague, then asked, "Perhaps Sir you'd like to tell us why you are in possession of Lord Mallory's passport?"

Anxious Ben wouldn't get into trouble Jill rolled down the window to explain. "Lord Mallory took me to Amsterdam. We have his passport as proof he has re-entered England illegally this morning." The two officers looked at each other, at her, at Ben, and then the older officer who had been questioning them said, "Perhaps Miss Reinhardt you'd like to step outside the car."

"She's just been very sick I think she'd be better off sitting there."

The younger of the two asked belligerently, "Are you telling us what to do?"

Ben looked taken aback at his attitude, but smiled pleasantly, "Of course not. I was just explaining the situation."

The older man commented, "Why would you want to prove that Lord Mallory entered the country on another passport? I'd think we'd need to find out more about this. We'll find a seat for the young lady inside."

The younger officer approached as Ben took her elbow to help her out of the car. "Come this way. Leave the keys in the car." He called across to a port official, "George, arrange for security to put this car in the pound." Addressing Ben he went on, "You can collect it after we've had our chat." She and Ben glanced at each other. Now what? David always said 'honesty is the best policy' as lies became difficult to remember on questioning.

Jill decided to speak. "As we said, the car isn't ours. Lord Mallory and I drove to Amsterdam in it on Friday morning. In order to escape him and his brother we hot wired it so we could get away, and get home."

The young custom man's lips firmed into a severe line. "But by your own admission only moments ago you said you had his passport because you wanted to prove he'd entered the country this morning illegally. Now you are telling us you, and let's see Ben Fletcher here, are escaping from him. Doesn't make any sense to me?"

"No you don't understand it…"

He interrupted "No I don't understand, and the more I hear the more I wonder what you two are up to. Come, follow me please."

Feeling too nauseous to argue she let it go. Once she could sit down she could explain and it would all become clear to them. Ben turned to give her a rueful, yet loving smile. They reached the two storey grey building, entered the main door and proceeded down a long corridor. The customs man opened a door to a small lino floored room with a table and two chairs on either side of it. "If you could take a seat in here Miss Reinhardt someone will be with you shortly."

It was then she realised they were to be parted. She turned, Ben a few steps behind gave her a reassuring smile and advised, "Just tell them exactly what happened. It will sort itself out." But she saw his bright eyes clouded with apprehension. Hardly surprising when last time he'd had a brush with the law he'd suffered a great injustice. But honesty wouldn't be the problem here, more the danger to Ben's life if Lord Rich Mallory found out.

It was half an hour before a man and woman entered the room. By then feeling very fragile she'd folded her arms on the desk, rested her head on it and was drifting in and out of sleep when the door opened. She jumped and felt guilty so explained, "I was just resting my head, I was very sick on the ferry, and don't feel too good now." A stern, middle aged woman with hard grey eyes thrust a cup of tea in front of her. "Oh thank you, that is kind of you." The look she received in return caused her to wonder if the woman had thought she was being sarcastic.

The man, grey-haired and probably old enough to be her father introduced himself. "Miss Reinhardt I'm sorry we've kept you waiting. My name is Archer; this is Miss Trowbridge. We work for Her Majesty's Customs. I understand Mr Fletcher was carrying Lord Mallory's passport when two of my officers apprehended you, you spoke of escaping Lord Mallory. Would you explain that to us? Do you mind if I make notes?"

"No please do. Ben discovered three days ago that Lord Mallory intended to kidnap me. You see my father is a very rich man…"

To her surprise they listened without interruption. Light-headed she hadn't been altogether coherent, so wasn't surprised at their questions and was pleased at the opportunity to explain in detail. The man seemed eager to understand, while the woman's cold fish eyes seemed to stare into her very soul. Several times she made her repeat facts as if determined to catch her out on some small point. "So you are telling us that Lord Richard Mallory is Pete and he shared a cell with…?"

A knock on the door interrupted Miss Trowbridge's question a note was handed to her, she read it, raised her eyebrows and passed it to Mr Archer.

Miss Trowbridge continued, "Earlier you said your father is very wealthy, he owns Inhart Pharmaceuticals and this was the reason for this Rich, or Pete, wanting to kidnap you. Tell me what do you know of the drug trade?"

She frowned, "Not a lot. I worked with my father many summers ago in his Orders Department but other than that nothing. Why?"

"Let's get back to Mr Fletcher. Did you know he's been in prison for stealing drugs?"

"Yes, but I don't see what that has to do with a plot to kidnap me?"

"I would suggest that his story of a plot against you was a fabrication in order for him to smuggle drugs into this country."

Incensed at the unfairness of Miss Trowbridge's assumption, she said sharply, "No! Definitely not! Why would he want to do that? When he was convicted for stealing drugs it wasn't to sell, but to help a young drug addict he'd befriended, to get him off, not on drugs."

"That's maybe what he told you. But tell me why is the car you were driving, now in our pound, packed with drugs?"

"What? How is that possible?"

"That's what I'm asking you. It appears on examination the car has not only been hot wired, but the petrol tank is half the normal size, encased within the original tank is another packed with cocaine.

"Oh my God! You mean we bought drugs into the country? Thank goodness you found them. I told you that Rich was going to use the red Escort, no wonder he was so angry when he discovered he had the wrong keys, now we know why."

Mr Archer chipped in. "I think that's what you have been led to believe. I put it to you, that unbeknown to you Ben Fletcher set you up as a cover to bring in illegal drugs. You've told us, and we already know that he shared a cell with Peter Sanchez at Wormwood Scrubs. My feeling is they were cohorts in the planning of this."

"No, no, you've got it all wrong. You only have to speak to my brother, or my father who is about to employ Ben at Inharts. They believe Ben to be an honest man."

Miss Trowbridge with a glint in her eye spoke up again. "Ha. You aren't the first woman used as a decoy. He and your father could be involved in this together. After all, how much more money could your father make by selling illegal drugs under the cover of his company."

Tired and anxious about Ben, that comment was the final straw. Her voice raised in anger she retorted, "Oh that's absolutely ridiculous. My father is highly respected. He exports drugs to under-developed and under-privileged nations and is nominated for an MBE in the New Year's Honours List – but, well… that's privileged information. My brother is a barrister of law and knows Ben's conviction was to make an example of him to other doctors. It ruined Ben's career and he's never had any money except what he has earned – check his bank accounts."

Mr Archer stood. "Okay Miss Reinhardt, thank you. We will need to compare your story with that of Mr Fletcher and contact the others involved."

Worried she countered, "Just a minute don't go to Lord Mallory and ask him?"

"And why not, you are accusing him of planning to kidnap you, and like you, he has a right to defend himself." Miss Trowbridge's eyes challenged her.

"I have no evidence to back up that was his plan, I only heard what he said. But if he finds out Ben who shared a prison cell with him was involved and has spoilt his kidnapping plans, and taken his car full of drugs, well I don't want to think what his retribution might be. If you feel you have to make contact at this stage then say I overheard the conversation at the bedroom door, and I hot wired the car and drove it away. Rich isn't going to retaliate to my escaping him, but he's a dangerous character, and Ben has Helen and the baby to consider."

The woman asked sharply, "Helen and the baby? Who's that, his wife?"

"No, well not yet, they are getting married at Christmas."

"So you aren't his girlfriend?"

Jill sighed. How complicated it all sounded and she couldn't face more talk. "Another long story, but it isn't relevant here."

Miss Trowbridge frowned. "We'll decide what's relevant or not. Now we'd like you to come with us because we need you to be present when we search your suitcase."

With a shrug she countered, "That's fine by me." She stood, her head swam and she staggered slightly against the chair she'd just vacated.

"Are you alright Miss Reinhardt?" Mr Archer enquired.

"I was very sick on the ferry and feel quite shaky."

Kindly he took hold of her elbow as he stated, "It's not far to go, your suitcase is across the road in our customs shed."

They walked out of the room back along the corridor. Was Ben still being questioned? At least she was there to corroborate his story. "Will this take long because Ben and I really do want to be getting home we have about a four hour...? Oh, I don't suppose we can use that car now. It's Sunday it'll be difficult to hire one, and it's getting late." In her anxiety she screwed her hair around in her fingers.

"I'm afraid it's not up to me I'm just getting information, but you will be handed over to the police in due course."

"The police, why, what have we done wrong?"

Miss Trowbridge grunted as she came up beside them crossing the road, "How about bringing a car into the country packed with drugs? It's a major offence."

"But we didn't know it contained drugs."

Mr Archer opened the door to the long shed, "That will be up to the authorities to decide. Now here we are. Your suitcase is on the table ready for you."

"Well I've certainly got nothing to interest you." She unclipped the locks, pulled out her wash bag and tipped it into the plastic tray offered by Miss Trowbridge for her cold eyes to dissect. Next out was her nightdress, a couple of jumpers, and a huge roll of clothes that Ben had put together. With plenty of space she unravelled it in front of them. In the centre was a crushed cocktail dress, petticoat, tights, and pair of pants. Miss Trowbridge bent forward her nose raised as if they might smell, and with hands encased in plastic gloves she delicately picked up each item and moved it to make another pile. In picking up the sorry looking evening dress, she shook it. Something flashed, dropped and rolled onto the floor.

Jill looked down. At her feet was the diamond ring. Automatically she bent to pick it up and puzzled said, "My ring."

Miss Trowbridge must have spotted something else because she was now several feet away on her hands and knees while Mr Archer stated, "I've found what looks like a diamond ear-ring."

A moment later pulling herself up from the floor Miss Trowbridge exclaimed, "And I've found another. So Miss Reinhardt now what do you have to say for yourself?" Have you a receipt for these, or proof they belonged to you before you left the country?

As her eyes stared at the ring, all she could think of was how had these things ended up in her suitcase. Her mind struggled to remember where she'd taken them off. Rich had dumped her on the bed, her clothes she'd let fall as a heap on the floor. The ring she'd taken off and put it on the bedside cabinet. Vaguely she recalled her head on the pillow and the ear-rings hurting. She must have taken them both out, and put them on the cabinet too. But that didn't account for them being buried in her clothes.

The previously pleasant man now looked stern, his voice cold. "Miss Reinhardt we're waiting. Why are such obviously valuable diamonds wrapped up in your dress?"

"To be honest I was just trying to work that out for myself."

Miss Trowbridge snorted, "Oh come on, honesty it would seem isn't something you understand."

Insulted she retorted, "I beg your pardon. Lord Mallory gave me those ear-rings and diamond ring to wear on Saturday night. The restaurant where we ate and the desk clerk at the hotel saw me wearing them." Her mind reverted to the conversation with Ben. He'd certainly not put them there because he said the diamonds were probably stolen and if found they'd be accessories to that! Oh God! This was getting worse by the minute.

Mr Archer pointed out, "Then we shall need to get in touch with Lord Mallory to verify that the diamonds are his, and he gave them to you. But it would seem odd to me if they are yours to wrap them up in your evening dress."

It did look odd; it did look bad, so how did they get there. "Oh I bet I know what happened." Two pairs of eyes held hers. "I put them on the bedside cabinet. When Ben knocked on the door I reached for the bedside light and must have swept them off into the pile of clothes I'd left on the floor." Miss Trowbridge said nothing, but Jill noted her disapproving expression and saw the way her lip curled in disdain as she explained. "I remember almost tripping over my clothes to open the door so that's probably why Ben didn't see them when he picked up the pile and stuck it into the suitcase." Whether they believed her it was impossible to tell, but between them they continued to work through her things.

Mr Archer commented, "You took a lot of clothes away for a weekend?"

"Yes Rich said no need to travel light and practically packed the case for me. Of course in the light of his intention to kidnap me I now understand why."

Miss Trowbridge once again didn't make verbal comment but betrayed her thoughts by the raising of her eyebrows. With the contents of the case now on the bench, they carefully examined the sides and lining which fortunately didn't harbour any further nasty surprises. But then what could be more incriminating than that which they had already found? Mr Archer having carefully put the offending diamonds in a plastic bag now waved them at her. "So tell me Miss Reinhardt if Lord Mallory was intending to kidnap you why did he give you the diamonds?"

"I've been asking myself that too. I found the diamonds earlier that evening. At first he was annoyed and accused me of being nosy. Later he became romantic and said he wanted to marry me and insisted I wear part of the jewellery in the box, despite me saying it was very valuable and I didn't want to."

"And you didn't think to mention this to us before?"

Jill shrugged, "There was so much to tell I didn't think it had any bearing on the car and drugs. I think Rich wanted me to wear the ear-rings and ring to appear rich because we were eating in a restaurant where only the very rich go. The man we were to meet there couldn't come, but we ate their on our own."

"Can you remember his name?"

"Jansen, something like Detrees. I'm sorry Mr Archer, but could I please sit down, I'm feeling very fragile?"

"Well take you back across the road. I'll get you a cup of tea, and we'll see what the police would have us do about you."

As she walked across with Miss Trowbridge and Mr Archer flanking her she felt close to tears and asked, "Please can I see Ben?"

Mr Archer replied, "He's in police custody, he was transferred as soon as we found he had a prison record."

That was the final straw. Tears flowed. Anxiously she pleaded, "Oh you must believe me he's telling the truth. Ring my brother, he'll…" She didn't know what happened next except her hands went out before her, her nose barely missed hitting the tarmac, and the sudden slam against the hard surface expelled the breath from her body. Stunned she lay sprawled out in the wet road as Mr Archer above her exclaimed, "What the hell…" Her eyes briefly closed before he and Miss Trowbridge hauled her to her feet. Unable to breathe she doubled over, her legs were like sponge and she would have collapsed if they hadn't held her up.

Mr Archer instructed, "Let's get her inside in the warm." Between them they practically carried her into the office building as she continued gasping for air. When they lowered her on to a hard chair in the reception area, she stuck her head between her knees and struggled to fill her lungs.

A young male voice by the Reception desk asked, "What happened to her?" He gave an amused laugh, "It looks as though you two have been torturing her by the state she's in. Should I call an ambulance?"

Mr Archer evidently troubled barked out, "That's not funny. Where's the car?"

"Round the back. The police are anxious to talk to her, but I doubt in her state she's going to be of much use."

"Go and get it brought around the front." His hand touched her shoulder, "Now Miss Reinhardt that was a nasty fall, but you don't appear to be hurt, just dazed. Sergeant Owen here has come to take you to the Police Station." Between them they hauled her to the car with Miss Trowbridge looking very stern and official with a file of papers under her arm. Notes Jill guessed from her interview.

CHAPTER 18

By the time introductions were made, notes taken, and she settled on a chair in the foyer of the busy police station her body's numbness had turned to pain. Her right knee ached, her left foot throbbed and to put any weight on it was excruciating. And although her trousers were undamaged her left leg felt acutely sore. Gravel had imbedded itself in her soaking wet coat and into her hands which she'd put out to save herself in that instant she hit the road. She knew she looked a sight, her hair was obviously ruffled and matted but what did that matter compared to her concern for Ben. Was he here? Constantly she looked to and fro among the people coming and going in the hope of catching a glimpse of him.

From the perspective of the authorities she could see it did look bad, but, they must understand, and she must establish, that none of this had been Ben's doing. The Customs people interviewing her were one thing, but the police!

A pretty girl with golden-brown hair who looked about sixteen smiled at her from behind the desk, before turning to speak to the gaggle of policemen around her. Miss Trowbridge reappearing took her attention. Head in the air she walked by, gave her an acknowledging nod, then as an after thought stopped, turned and said with a disdainful smile, "It would appear Miss Reinhardt you have influential friends, always useful when in trouble. Goodnight."

The words might be reassuring, but there was little doubt of the underlying sarcasm in the woman's tone, or the total injustice of the remark. Inwardly she seethed, and scowled as a young female voice spoke at her elbow. "Hello, my name's Maria. Would you like a cup of tea and somewhere more comfortable to sit?"

The thoughtfulness of the young girl had her apologising. "I'm sorry Maria, I wasn't scowling at you, that woman…" Jill's gaze went to the door, and then with a shake of her head she continued, "I just feel ill, and want to go home to bed." Tears formed in her eyes.

A hand rubbed her arm, "Don't get upset. Come, I'll take you into the doc's room while you wait, there's a comfortable chair in there. I don't know why you weren't taken there right away you look a bit battered up to me."

That remark brought a rueful grimace. "Maria, I feel battered up, but am better for your kindness." Slowly, with her hopping and using Maria as a crutch, they made their way along the passage. Maria asked, "Is it alright for me to call you Jill?"

She nodded, and despite being breathless, she made the effort to ask, "Do you know if Ben Fletcher is here? I need to tell someone he's done nothing wrong."

"Let's get you settled first and I'll find out what I can. Here we are." Maria opened the door. "This room isn't exactly home from home, but there is that elderly person's chair you can sit in. First, let me take your coat. That's it. I expect too you'd like to wash your poor hands and face, I'll get a towel for you. Ten minutes later Maria had made her comfortable in the chair with a pillow positioned at her neck, her feet up on a pile of telephone directories and covered her over with a blanket. Once done she'd slipped out to get her a cup of tea. In no time at all she was back with tea and toast and while she drank and ate Maria perched on the edge of the old battered desk, swinging her legs as she chattered on about being a police probationer.

The door opened. Maria looked up, stopped talking and slid from the desk to stand almost to attention. With her back to the door, an elderly voice explained behind her, "This is Jill Reinhardt brought in earlier for drug trafficking and smuggling. Customs said at the time she was apprehended she was unwell. I believe she'd been sea sick. Later she fell heavily when they were transferring her from departments. We need you to look her over doc before resuming questioning."

The man she assumed was the doctor replied in a curt tone. "Has she been charged?"

"My understanding is she's being held for questioning. They only brought her in about an hour ago we called you as soon as we were… err alerted to her being unwell."

To her surprise Maria suddenly trilled, "It was me. I noticed what a dreadful state Jill was in. They left her sitting on a bench by the door. She looks a bit better now with a cup of tea and a slice of toast in her." Maria gave a wry grin as if in response to one sent to her, then stepped aside.

As the door shut, a man, Jill presumed was the doctor came forward with a chair, placed it beside her and sat down. Brown, golden flecked eyes that issued warmth and compassion came on a

299

level with hers, instantly bringing a reminder of the police surgeon who'd come to ITP. But no it couldn't be, for this man didn't have a beard. Her eyes took in the thick, brown hair and suntanned face with dark stubble. A small scar ran from his top lip to the left of his nose which made his little sympathetic smile somewhat quirky. "Hello there. Do you remember me, Paul Stemmings?" When he spoke the timbre of his voice reflected those golden lights from his eyes, soothing like oil upon her troubled mind. Dumbfounded she let him refresh her memory. "I met your brother and attended someone in his office, who rather like you had been in the wars. I'm hopefully here to make you feel better, and to assure you there'll be no more questioning tonight."

To be in his care, to know for a while this ordeal was over brought relief, but also embarrassment that at meeting him again it should be in this way. Strangely his face seemed to be growing smaller as though looking through binoculars from the large to small lens. His voice sounded equally distant as he said, "Now, don't faint on me. Meeting me again surely can't be that bad!" In removing the pillow and gently pushing her forward his close proximity brought a waft of fresh smelling aftershave or soap. Her eyes refocused on his tanned fingers encapsulating her wrist. "Stay like that until the dizziness wears off. In the meanwhile I'll look at your ankle." On her grunt of pain he looked up from where he was crouching and gave her a sympathetic look. "I'm sorry. It's so swollen it was difficult to remove your shoe." Carefully he examined the bones around her ankle. I think it's probably just a bad sprain, but you'll need an x-ray."

Without the softening and rounding of his beard Paul Stemming's face seemed longer and thinner. His features were heavy in comparison to the smooth, boyish face of Ben and like David he probably looked older than he was. The redeeming feature on such a plain face was those eyes. And she felt again that strange awareness she had thought he'd reciprocated on that first meeting. But seeing him now in his navy cords and hand-knitted jumper she guessed he was married, probably enjoying a pleasant Sunday evening at home with his wife and family before being called to attend to her.

"Now, is there anything else I need to know about?" Startled from her reverie she stared mindlessly at him, to which he gave a knowledgeable hum. Still tongue-tied, she lifted up her hands for his inspection and noticed Maria was studying him with hero worship in her eyes.

"Umm sore and badly scraped, and there's definitely grit in here. Maria would you like to make Jill comfortable again."

Swiftly he'd crossed the room and burrowed in the cupboard while Maria was quick to re-establish the pillow at her head, the telephone directories under her foot, and at Paul's bidding collected the water and painkillers for her to take. She murmured her thanks and got a sweet smile, but at Paul's praise Maria visibly blossomed. For amused he teased, "Well done. Are you sure it's a police woman you want to be and not a nurse?"

"Right Jill. Just relax. You might find it helpful to close your eyes." He was right the liquid he dabbed on the skid marks on her hands stung. A knock at the door broke the silence, she opened her eyes and Paul directed, without looking up, "Maria please see who that is?" His mouth twitched with his quirky smile as she almost skipped across the room to do his biding.

In an awe inspired voice Maria returned to say, "It's the Chief Superintendent, he's outside, he wants to speak to you."

With raised eyebrows Paul dropped the small tweezers he was using back in the dish and said comfortingly, "That's done. Maria please can you clear that up. I'll be back."

In the relative quiet it wasn't difficult to hear Paul getting exasperated, at whatever the Chief Superintendent was asking. "… she's clearly unwell... It's late… Look I respect you have… No I'm not sanctioning…"

Carefully she tried moving her ankle, and winced. The ever helpful Maria jumped forward to make her more comfortable and her chattering blocked the conversation continuing outside the door. Over that she strained to hear and caught the Chief's words "…are you suggesting we let her go home and call us in a few days time?"

Paul's retort wasn't hard to hear. "This woman isn't your common criminal. You'll find out more when she has rested, than now. I have an idea…"

Maria obviously realising she'd been trying to listen jumped in to reassure her. "Don't worry the doc knows what he's doing. I think it's amazing that he's met you before. In medical matters he has authority over the Chief Super so they won't subject you to further questioning unless he sanctions it. He's the best doctor in the world, I'm the number one member of his fan club, but then I'm biased because he…"

"Maria!" The sharpness of Paul's tone had her turning her head to look at him, and she caught the kindly, but, but quelling look sent to Maria.

However it didn't seem to deter her for she trilled on, "I was just telling Jill you'd fix everything for her."

Paul gave his quirky smile. "Were you indeed, well despite your faith in me I'm afraid I can't fix everything. But I have persuaded the Super that Jill, you need a hot bath, a good meal and a comfortable bed for the night which will make you feel a lot more like talking tomorrow."

Her mouth opened to ask about Ben, but Maria questioned, "You have? And he's allowing her to go home?"

"Well, not exactly..."

The expression forming on Maria's face told Jill she knew the answer before she asked, "And where is this refuge?" The word refuge echoed in Jill's mind, it sounded, uninviting, cold and miserable? Tears pricked her eyes, but she must stay strong for Ben.

"In the circumstances the fewer people who know the better."

Maria gave him a wide-eyed look. Paul frowned, and then said briskly "Right Maria, how about you put that cream on Jill's hands. Take that with you Jill and put it on again before you go to sleep. I'll go and make arrangements for your transfer."

He was out the door as she said tiredly, "Why can't I just go home?"

Maria made a rueful face. "If the people here still want to talk to you it's better you stay somewhere near. It would be a long way for you to go to London tonight. If I've judged right you'll love it where Paul's arranging for you to go." She wanted to ask further, but Maria who obviously loved her family started talking about them, chuckling over the antics of Barnie the dog, and dispirited she hadn't the energy to listen.

Reappearing Paul's first words were to ask with a sigh, "Maria are you still chattering away? You're probably boring Jill, and no doubt saying things to embarrass me?"

"I'm not! And I haven't, have I, Jill? Anyway what makes you think I'd talk about you doc? Jill's been enjoying my chattering, haven't you?"

Grateful for Maria's company she smiled and nodded. A rewarding smile from Paul flashed in Maria's direction, in turn she fluttered her eyelashes causing him to laugh and say with affection, "She's incorrigible, isn't she? She's had a crush on me since she was two." Obviously he'd dealt with it well, for Maria didn't seem perturbed by that revelation to a stranger, but then in his late-thirties he would be old enough to be her father.

"I won't bandage your ankle because I know you'll want a bath, and as Maria doesn't know whether its policing or nursing she's called to I expect she'd like to try out her first aid skills on you. Tomorrow you can go to the hospital and get an xray. Now the only thing left is a blood test."

Astonishment broke through her apathy to query, "A blood test?"

"There's a suspicion you've been involved with drugs."

"But I haven't. Basically we stole Rich's car and drove home, they are his drugs not ours. Do you know where Ben is? Is he here? I'm so worried. He came to rescue me. Yet I just know they'll accuse him for something he hasn't done. It's happened before you see…"

A finger on her mouth, and a quirky smile, stopped her mid-sentence. She stared at him the action so similar to that of when they last met. The golden eyes held hers. Again, something deep stirred within her. Quietly he insisted, "Relax, let's take one thing at a time!" He broke eye contact to move across the room speaking as he went, "All I can tell you is that Ben has been transferred to London, which probably means he's got some useful information for the Met."

Ben, London, the Met., drugs, smuggling, the Chief Super's involvement. Oh God what a mess. At least in London David would be on hand to help Ben. Her mind flew from one thing to another, so much so she barely noticed the syringe of blood drawn from her arm.

A disturbance in the corridor from someone obviously very drunk and belligerent had Paul look up as he removed the needle from her vein and pressed the cotton wool into her arm. "That sounds as though I have another customer. Now hold your arm there, I'll just complete this and then put a plaster on that. What good timing as we've just finished. Maria can you get Jill's coat. Your suitcase is already in the car waiting for you. Right let's put on this plaster and get you standing. Oh dear your coat's rather muddy and damp, but you'll need it on its cold out there." Once he'd helped her into it he asked Maria to pick up her shoe, and together they helped her to the door where a Sergeant waited to take over.

Quickly she turned to say "Thank you."

Paul's response was that quirky smile and "You're welcome" before he disappeared back inside the room. Life's coincidences were strange, he'd been very kind, and would she see him again? There was no reason to think she would.

Ten minutes later they were drawing up outside a picturesque small yellow and brown bricked cottage with wooden beams, a triangular slanted roof with one small latticed window upstairs, and one larger one downstairs. It reminded her of the gingerbread cottages seen in bakers windows. The oak door opened, light spilled out and there emerged a tall, well built, white-haired lady, in a green plaid skirt and green matching jumper.

"You'd never believe Beatty was seventy-five would you?" Maria commented as she opened the car door at the same moment as Beatty reached the gate in the white picket fence. With that Maria was out and around the car hugging Beatty as though she was her long lost grandma. The Sergeant came to her aid while Maria proclaimed happily, "This is Beatty, Beatty met Jill Reinhardt." Just as she liked the look of Beatty, she felt Beatty liked her for her welcome was accompanied by a broad smile, and between her and Maria they helped her inside. "Brr, it's cold out here. Bill's inside, I'm afraid he's a bit chesty at present so I told him to stay in the warm, but he's delighted he's going to have company. He gets bored just listening to me."

Beatty ushered her through a door and to the left of the stairs which went up opposite the front door. The large cosy room had a chintz covered settee and chairs and seated in the alcove by the fire was a frail looking man. Beatty instructed, "Just say 'hello' to Bill, then it's upstairs. There's plenty of hot water, have a good long bath, I'll bring you up a bite to eat once you're in bed." As she used the furniture to move forward to speak to Bill, Beatty continued, "Maria I assume you're staying so be a good girl and take Jill's suitcase upstairs and run her a bath."

The smell of stew wafted in the air, making her suddenly feel hungry. Bill was obviously older than his wife, but equally welcoming, but as he spoke he lapsed into coughing. Once the bout was over he looked over his half glasses, lent on the newspaper on his knees, and having observed her standing with one foot in the air, he picked up his stick and bantered with a smile, "Only got one of these, but I'm willing to share."

It would have been impossible not to have smiled at such an offer. But before she could thank him, Beatty who'd helped her off with her coat, was saying, "Jill's exhausted Bill, she needs peace and rest, if she feels better tomorrow you can chat to her all day."

"As you say me dear, and I shall look forward to that." Bill waved his stick, "You'll not need this yet then."

Beatty answered for her. "No I think the best way up the stairs will be for Jill to go on her bottom."

Maria was waiting at the top and having helped her to stand she drew her into the front bedroom with the pretty window. The room's sloping eaves, heavy wooden double bed and large wardrobe made it seem small, but cosy with the dark red carpet, light green candlewick bedspread, eiderdown and flowered curtains.

Beatty who'd followed her up instructed from the doorway, "The bathroom's opposite. Towels are on the rail, shampoo in the cupboard, soap in the tray across the bath. Our room is next to that and faces the back."

Overwhelmed by their kindness Jill swallowed hard and attempted to say, 'thank you' but instead a sob broke from her throat. Beatty hugged her, "There, there, love. You've had a bit of a time of it. Don't bottle it, let it go. Always best to cry it out." Drawn to the bed by Beatty she took the large handkerchief she handed her and mopped up the tears that gushed out rather like the unstoppable fountain in the flat's patio garden. The fright of last night, what could have been, Ben and the mess they were in, had finally uncapped the emotional faucet at the very core of her being. The build up of pressure over the years of squashed down hurt, pain and anguish rose to find release in Beatty's arms as she held, rocked and murmured repeatedly to her, "That's it, that's it, let it go, let it all go."

Time didn't exist, she was only aware of it when Maria knocked on the door and said quietly, "It's been an hour I thought you'd like a cup of tea."

Beatty drew back and gave her a little smile, "There, there, Jill you'll be better for having got rid of all that. When you want to talk about it, to rid all the ghosts, it won't be half as painful as you think, God loves you, and through this He'll work out His purposes."

Her mind raced. God? Beatty was talking about God! How many times had she called upon him in recent months, days, hours? Was this God's way of answering her calls for help?

"Now, drink your tea, have a nice bath, you'll feel a lot better in the morning. Maria will help you, won't you dear?"

Maria nodded, added more hot water to the cooling bath, helped her in and out of it and dried her hair with a hairdryer.

After that she made a splendid job of bandaging her ankle, cleaning, creaming and covering the side of her leg where she discovered she'd scrapped off the top layer of skin leaving it red and raw. Maria said, this kind of scrape was known as a 'strawberry'. Once that was completed Beatty brought them up a bowl each of delicious smelling and tasty stew, and suddenly weary she was almost asleep before Maria said 'goodnight' and turned out the light.

The bed was warm and comfortable. The smell of bacon began to permeate her nostrils, was Rosemary cooking breakfast? She stretched and groaned as a shaft of pain shot up her leg reminded her of her swollen ankle, sore leg and where she was. A series of pictures of the previous day's events scudded through her mind. Had Ben had a good night's sleep? Tears formed in her eyes remembering yesterday morning they'd been together and so happy. By now David must know the situation, but it was their word against much evidence to convict them of both drug trafficking and smuggling! Was it David Miss Trowbridge referred to as being influential? Was that the reason the police hadn't put her on a charge? Worried she thought of Ben, would everything be pinned on him? Already his motives had been misconstrued.

The sound of scratching drew her attention to the door. The next moment it burst open, a big hairy dog barked and landed with great delight on top of her. Large paws on her shoulders stopped her feeble efforts at trying to sit up; his head panted over her; his big tongue licked her face. He was adorable and laughing she could only cry out, "Get off me, dog, oooh stop it, get off me."

From the doorway Beatty called sharply, "Barnie!" Instantly the dog left her to stand meekly by Beatty, his tail wagging as he looked up at her. "I'm sorry I should have warned you he likes welcoming people and was cross yesterday when we wouldn't let him out…" Beatty talked as Jill's mind wandered to wonder who, where, when had she heard the name 'Barnie' before. Her attention was drawn back to Beatty asking, "I've another visitor who'd like to meet you, is that alright?"

Puzzled she nodded, watched Beatty turn aside, smile and step back to let her visitor in. Ridiculously seeing him she snatched up the bedclothes to cover her perfectly respectable white frilly nightgown. Would she ever be able to behave normally in his presence? Their first meeting she'd babbled like a demented child, their second she'd only just about managed to think coherently, now her mouth opened and shut as though struck dumb. This morning he was dressed more like a doctor in grey flannel trousers and tweedy jacket. His white shirt highlighted his dark facial tan which could only have been obtained from hotter climes, and after he'd shaved off his beard! The rather crooked, quirky smile took away the overall nondescript features of his face. Those observant brown eyes with their golden streaks seemed to express more of the attractive character of the man within, than that seen without. Casually he sat on the bed bringing his foot to rest on his knee and leaning forward he stretched out his hand as though wanting to shake hers. "Hello, I heard you were here."

In an automatic gesture she put her hand into his and watched the long, brown fingers enclose around hers. "It's good to meet you again Jill Reinhardt. Let me see..." he paused, considered and said, "It must be nearly two years ago." She lifted her head to meet his eyes as he continued, "As I recall it was Jane who had a head injury after a fall and your brother looked after her."

"David. And, yes, it was Jane. That was when I began to realise David had fallen for her. They got married in June last year."

The smile briefly appeared, "So one fall caused another! Love has strange ways of bringing people together. And from what I saw of David, I imagine that's an interesting match."

Jill couldn't help grinning. "They have their moments. We share the same house, I, in the basement flat, and they, on the first and second floor."

"That's better. It's good to see you smiling. I shall look forward to hearing more about this romance." Jill smiled and wondered if he was just being polite. "I suppose I'd better act the doctor and ask how your foot is this morning?"

"Swollen and painful. Maria did a good job of putting on the bandages last night."

"Yes, she's a very special young lady." Paul stood to suggest, "If you pull back the bedclothes I'll check it out."

As she obeyed, she commented, "I thought the other leg was sore, but didn't realise how badly I'd scraped it until in the bath. Maria looked after it, she put some of that cream for my hands on it, then bandaged it."

"I'd better take a look at that too." He talked as he worked, "Maria would make a good nurse she could even become a doctor if she put her mind to it. The police though are just opening up University opportunities for young recruits, the education will accelerate her career, but I'm not sure it's the best route for her. I think she's too soft hearted for the police force. But like all young people she wants to earn money, but I think she's being rather short-sighted." Bent over her ankle he gave a worried frown, making her wonder if that was concern over Maria's welfare or at the swelling of her ankle? "It's difficult with the swelling to tell if you've broken anything, you need an x-ray." He replaced the covers, sat back on the bed, pulled a bottle from his pocket and tipped a dozen pills out on the bedside cabinet and advised, "Take two of these painkillers, four hourly, when needed." On taking her hands he turned them to comment, "The bruising is coming out, but the scratches are healing. You are on the mend, but, if you wish you can stay in bed today, because I have advised 'no questioning today'. However I have to tell you that you are under a kind of house arrest."

Incredulous she sat bolt upright to question, "House arrest? But I've not been charged? My only crime, if that is what it is, was to escape from a kidnap plot." Tears of self-pity and frustration welled up in her eyes.

Paul lent over to place a comforting hand on hers. "All I know is you've been involved with some dangerous people and this is as much for your safety as anything else. You aren't accused of anything."

"But what of Ben? And David? They will need to know where I am?"

Paul sat back. "As to David I checked, he knows you are safe. Ben is in London and David has seen him."

"They've arrested him, haven't they? Why, when he came to rescue me? Surely David has told them what happened? Why doesn't anyone believe him? Why don't they believe me? I've got to talk to people today."

"Jill there's no point in getting worked up. The police have your story, it will tally I am sure with Ben's, and there are plenty of good people to sort this out. Now lie back and relax."

"I suppose it's all over the papers?"

"No, the police seem to want to keep it under wraps. I'm involved by seeing you last night and arranging this refuge for you, but even I have found it hard to glean even these smidgeons of information. There's a lot I'm not privy to, but from the general tension I'd say your situation is more complex that you think, otherwise known as 'opening up a can of worms'! This may be something of an enforced rest, but I think you'll enjoy the company, the good cooking, and maybe a bit of fresh country air. It'll help heal your body, mind and spirit. And I can hear Beatty coming to give you a good start, a real country breakfast in the luxury of your bed." Paul jumped up, organised her pillows, and as Beatty arrived to place the tray on her lap he said gallantly, "Your breakfast m'lady."

This time she had to blink rapidly to stop tears of gratitude overflowing. Beatty patted her shoulder, "Now, now, love, it's our pleasure to look after you, pamper you a bit, build you up to tackle both dog and man."

Paul, pretending to be affronted asked, "To whom are you referring? Barnie is the only dog around here, and I'm the only man. Jill doesn't need strength to tackle me, I didn't dash in here, pin her to the bed, and insist on licking her face."

That thought caused Jill to chuckle. And as he went out the door with a wave, saying "patients waiting" she picked up the knife and fork and considered what it might be like for him to pin her to the bed and do more than lick her face, and concluded the sex act without Ben had lost its appeal.

After enjoying her breakfast, she put the tray on the bed, and made a futile attempt to read the newspaper Beatty had left her. But her mind kept diverting to events and outcomes, Ben, their sexual compatibility and their conversation about determining to move on. Helen and the baby, and how Ben's rescue had been so right, yet gone so wrong. What now of his future? She sighed, and assured herself that David would sort it out.

Her mind refocused on Paul. He was of similar height to David, but medium build, in her eyes more attractive with his beard than without, but with brown, golden flecked eyes that drew her as a bee to honey, or just perhaps to the kindness and compassion reflected in them. Two years before she'd been sure he'd felt that odd jolt of, what was it, recognition, inner knowing that had passed between them? What an incredible set of circumstances, and coincidence that had brought them together again. And Beatty talking about God last night, it certainly made her wonder if he was after her attention."

In a need to go to the toilet she swung her feet over the side of the bed, and made ungainly progress to the bathroom. The balancing, the trying to hop on one leg, the jiggling her stomach, the shooting pain through her foot and soreness of her hands quickly culminated in nausea, then the release of a good breakfast. Here heart cried out to Ben. Where was he? How was he? She just wanted him? His comfort, his love. Crying she tore off the toilet paper to wipe her mouth, and pulled herself up, and putting her hands under the tap, drank water from them. If only she'd listened to Ben about Rich, none of this would have happened. Another bout of sickness kept her kneeling over the toilet bowl. Rich, she wouldn't have believed anyone could be so hard, heartless, cold and cruel if she hadn't heard it for herself. She just hoped the police would find a way to get him, then lock him up and throw away the key. She could only hope they wouldn't do that with Ben!

Weak and shivery she struggled back to the bed, cuddled back down under the covers and drifted back into sleep.

On awakening she felt better, but dressing was awkward. It would have to be trousers because she'd have to use her bottom going down the stairs. Bill appeared after she had slid, then bumped her way down half the stairs, and resting on his stick he looked up at her. "Ah there you are young lady, I thought I heard you. I came to offer you my arm. There's a nice…" He coughed hard. His whole body seemed to shake with the force, making her slide down the remaining steps at speed to support him. Over his coughing spell he said feebly, "The weak holding the weak eh, but we'll be strong together. Beatty's out, I'll make us a cuppa tea, and we can get to know each other."

Two hours later, seated at the large table in the centre of the equally large kitchen Bill had seemed delighted to drink several cups of tea and woo information from her about her family, friends and job. Now she questioned, "Last night Bill, Beatty mentioned God. I told you my brother David and his wife Jane are Christians, and recently I've found need to call on Him quite a few times. If he can hear prayers in your head, do you think he answers?

"Yes to both those questions, and it could be why He brought you…"

The back door opened and Beatty despite her age bounced in. "Oh good, you're up, I hope Bill hasn't been exhausting you with all his chatter." Beatty smiled at Bill, while Jill thought it was more likely her chatter had exhausted him!

"Now Beatty we've had a lovely morning and by the looks of you, you've enjoyed yourself too." The sudden cold draft from the door seemed to start his coughing inciting a severe look from Beatty. "Did you take that medicine Paul left?" Bill nodded, his thin frame shook with the effort of catching his breath. Beatty

310

turned to her, "He's better than he was. Last week Paul tried to make him go into hospital, but the stubborn old man wouldn't hear of it. Since then each morning and evening Paul's been round to check up on him."

Jill smiled, and ticked herself off for thinking Paul had come especially to see her!

"Beatty, don't talk about me as if I'm not here, I'll see a few more years before you need get into that habit."

"Then I'd better get lunch on the table otherwise you'll have something else to complain about."

It was obvious despite the banter that, even late in years, here was a real love match. And as if reading her mind Bill said, "Been married fifty-three years and never once have I ever complained about the time, or the content of one of her meals." He smiled mischievously, "Of course I've plenty else I could have complained about."

Waving a dismissive hand at him Beatty bandied, "Go on with you. Out of my way."

Jill chuckled and thought how she'd never heard her grandparents or parents behaving like this, and had often wondered what had drawn her tiny, delicate featured mother to her big, harsh, rather abrupt German father.

"Come on, we'll go together. I'll lean on my stick, and you lean on me."

"I'm not sure that's wise, we might both fall in a heap and I'd squash you."

Bill shook his head, his eyes held a naughty twinkle. "No, that's not the deal, you see you fall down first and I land on you. I rather think I'd like that." Jill laughed, Bill's body might be emancipated, but his mind wasn't.

"Bill you old rascal you! Don't listen to him. You stick to your stick. Jill can manage by hopping and using the furniture. Now out the pair of you from under my feet."

Once seated comfortably by the fire she asked, "So Bill tell me about how you and Beatty met?" There was no doubt he could spin a good tale. She giggled, laughed and gasped, as he described the ups and downs of his romancing his beloved Beatty. So how many children do you have?"

Bill preened, "Children, four, grandchildren ten and, so far, eleven great grandchildren, two more expected any day now."

"Goodness, you've quite a family."

"Not all here though. Some across the other side of the world, and we haven't seen them in years. We'd like to though, maybe one day we'll make the journey, or they will come for a visit." Bill's eyes lit up, "I've still got a couple of grandsons to marry off, if you're interested?"

Jill grinned at his eagerness, "Oh Bill, you're dreadful, but I confess if they're anything like you then bring them round and I'll give them the once over."

"What's this Jill, who are you going to give the once over?"

Bill's laugh turned to a brief racking cough before he managed a somewhat wheezy reply. "Ah Beatty, it seems my charms are still appreciated, this beautiful young lady says if my grandsons are like me she'd be interested in meeting them." His eyes twinkled with merriment.

Beatty curbed a smile, "Did she indeed, well we'll have to see about that!" Then, as though they were errant schoolchildren, commanded, "Right you two into the kitchen, and wash up for lunch." The wink Bill gave her as they obeyed made Jill chuckle.

After the lamb chop and delicious home grown vegetables seemingly cooked so effortlessly in the pressure cooker, Beatty served up a delicious apple crumble and custard. "I saw Jenny today, she is huge." Beatty turned to her to explain, "She's having twins, they've already got Sandra who is three, and Craig five, they are such a handful, and she gets very tired. I hope Bill, you are up to it because I felt so sorry for her that I said the children could come round today for a couple of hours after Craig finishes school. Paul said he'd collect them and take them for tea to give Jenny as much rest as possible, but he isn't always reliable with his work. Yesterday he was taking them to the swings when the police needed him, so Jenny didn't get a break.

So Paul was married and with a family! Now she understood why he'd never looked her up after they'd met. It was silly, but her mouth seemed to turn dry and the crumbs of the crumble stuck to the roof of her mouth. She fought to swallow, drank some water which swirled the crumble causing them to go down the wrong way.

Beatty jumped up as she coughed and choked to thump her back. Tears flowed down her cheeks not just because of the crumble, but in self pity. David had Jane, Chris had Patsy, Ben had Helen, Paul had Jenny. Rich wanted her kidnapped, and wasn't bothered if she was killed. "Here dear, have this hanky. I think you need a rest. Bill and I usually have a little nap after lunch, so why don't you go and have a lie down?"

She nodded, thankful to have an excuse to leave the room. What was the matter with her? In a brief moment at ITP in the middle of a trauma Paul had reached out to calm her - that was all. In normal circumstances she wouldn't have given him a second thought, but then and now hadn't been 'normal'! It was ridiculous, she'd no physical desire for him, so why did she feel she'd reached a life raft and found all the places taken?

Fully clothed she slipped under the eiderdown and allowed herself to wallow in tears until falling into exhausted asleep.

Children's voices awakened her. Should she join them? Maybe not! She looked around and saw beside the bed was a Bible. Curious she opened it and read, "Oh, what a wonderful God we have! How great are his wisdom and knowledge and riches! How impossible it is for us to understand his decisions and his methods!" Had it been God's decision to send Rich to bring her petrol that night? Ben to impregnate Helen, ruin their relationship, and maybe now Ben's life? If so His ways were impossible to understand. At a knock on the door she quickly put the Bible back.

Maria's pretty face poked around the door, "Hi, how are you?"

With a small smile she answered, "Hello, it's nice to see you, but I could be better in every respect."

Maria gave a bubbling chortle, "I think we could all say that! I think I'm going to like you. Do you want to join the family?"

Jill grinned, "Bill offered his grandsons earlier, what are you offering brothers, cousins?

At that Maria giggled. "Oh Jill very funny, but not what I meant! I came up because Gran thought with the children here you might feel awkward at coming down." Gran! Maria was one of their grand-daughters? And of course Barnie was her Gran's dog! Distracted she only caught the end of Maria's request to help them with the children.

Eager to assist and curious to meet Paul's children she joined the family in the kitchen. But as she helped them make gingerbread men she was disappointed because they were noisy and fractious. It was a relief when they joined Bill to watch 'Thunderbirds Are Go' on the television allowing her and Beatty a well deserved cup of tea.

The moment the biscuits were out of the oven the children reappeared to argue whose were the best. Tactfully she stated, "They all look wonderful. Well done, you've both worked hard. Sandra made the quality. Craig you made the quantity."

Paul's voice came from the doorway, "Very diplomatic." He gave a wry smile, "Do you like children?"

"I haven't had a lot of experience, but I have two nephews, older than those two".

"Is that a 'yes' or a 'no'."

Jill shrugged, "Well, my sister Paula in feeling our father was too harsh with us, has gone to the other extreme. They are loveable, but they drive you mad because they are so undisciplined. It's interestingly they adore David, he only has to say 'jump' and they 'jump'!"

The children screamed back in chasing poor Barnie who did his best to hide his enormous body under the table.

Beatty shouted over the din, "Children, children, children!" With her hand she reached in to first pull out Craig and then Sandra, saying fiercely, "That will do! No more screaming, or chasing poor Barnie, he isn't a horse to be ridden, nor does he like his tail pulled. Do you understand?" Sullen faces nodded, but once free they rushed back to watch television squabbling about who was going to sit on the pouffe.

With a sigh Beatty watched them go. "I'm too old for this, they wear me out. I'm glad you're here, your turn to tire them out."

With a grimace Paul replied, "That's the problem they never tire. I don't know how Jenny will manage when she has the twins?" Paul's attitude reminded Jill of Jim, Paula's ineffectual husband. Without thinking she advised, "Then, it's time you started disciplining and insisting on a bed time." Paul looked ready to defend himself so she cut across him. "Surely you, of all people, know about family planning? If you can't cope with two then…"

Beatty interrupted her flow. "Jill it's not like that!"

"Isn't it? Few men seem to understand that when they father children they have equal responsibility. It's not what Jenny is going to do, it's what you, Paul are going to do to help her look after four children." Paul sat forward, chin in hand to give her his full attention. "You may be out of the house most of the day, but when you are at home you need to opt into, not out of fatherhood." She pursued her lips as her mind dwelt on her father and Jim.

Unruffled Paul lent back, his head resting in his hands and stretching out his legs under the table he questioned, "So Jill, how do you propose I should go about this?" Beatty's sharp "Paul" had her glance at her, but Paul dismissed her interruption with a wave of his hand to comment, "I like people who know their own mind, and speak it." Warm golden brown eyes filled with amusement glinted at her along the table.

Appalled, realizing her rudeness, her hand flew to her mouth. "Oh my goodness, I am so sorry. I'd no right to say those things, especially considering your kindness to me."

As she spoke Beatty nodded, and a look of respect flowed into as he sat forward to acknowledge, "We weren't offended, were we Gran? I'm interested in your ideas on child discipline, please go on."

Her mind whirled, did he say Gran? She was staying with his Gran! Bill had said they'd a big family. With a concerted effort she drew her mind back to the question in hand. "Well basically I feel as parents there's a need to take responsibility to plan and prepare on how together you will educate and discipline your children. There's a need to provide a background of unconditional love, which gives children self worth, but not to an extent to make them precocious. Unlike you I haven't any children, but believe the earlier they know right from wrong helps in discipline and teaches responsibility. Jane said after a recent family incident that there should be an ABC of discipline, authority, boundaries and care, I rather liked that."

The doorbell ringing had Paul smiling broadly. He jumped up and responded, "Yes, I do too. I'll get the door Gran." Sandra and Craig rushed to collect their cooled gingerbread men. Paul returned, sat down, stretched his body and put his hands behind his head and and watched the proceedings with such a mischievous expression she didn't know what to make of it.

In the doorway appeared a harassed looking, thin and slightly balding man in his mid-forties. "Hi Gran. Thanks for having the kids I hope they've been okay?"

Beatty with an amused expression answered, "It's been interesting, the children have proved quite diverting. By the way this is Jill, she's staying with us for a few days." Beatty glanced at Paul and then gave her a small smile as she announced, "And Jill, this is my grand-daughter Jenny's husband, Hugh."

Hugh shook her hand as she coloured in acute embarrassment at her mistake. "Right yes, well, yes, nice to meet you." He glanced around the room, "Well, I must get these two terrors to the Wimpy bar, then home to bed, but whether they'll sleep..."

To her dismay Paul said with mirth, "Jill might have something to say about that."

A quizzical gaze from Hugh prevented her glaring at Paul. With a reassuring smile she offered, "My brother is good with kids. He reads our nephews a story, or a chapter a night of a book, their eyes often close as he reads, but if still awake when he's finished he tells them to think about what might happen next - they quickly fall asleep. They particularly like Worzel Gummidge, but the boys are older."

"Thanks err, are you staying long?"

Unable to answer she looked to Beatty. "A few days, maybe a week, or more, if she stays until Sunday she'll have the chance to meet Jenny."

The children with their coats were now vying for their father's attention. "Thanks Paul for all your help, I don't know what Jenny and I would do without you? You're so good with them."

Paul who'd crouched down to do up the buttons on Sandra's coat looked up, "Bless you for that, I was in need of a vote of confidence!"

Sandra gave him a hug. "I's luv you Uncle Paul" and kissed him.

He hugged her, "I love you to Sandra, now be a good girl for your Daddy." Craig not to be out done grabbed Paul's leg. Laughing Paul whisked him up and at his giggling whooshed him out the door after his father.

The kitchen emptied leaving her feeling awkward, and ashamed at her wrong conclusions. From the doorway Paul suggested, "It occurs to me Jill this would be a good time to take you to get that x-ray.

Politely she replied, "Thank you. I'll get my coat." But so absorbed in thought of how to apologise for her misjudgement of him she took a step towards him, and cried out as pain shot up her leg to reminded her of her injured foot. With an attempt to change feet, she wobbled, and made a grab for the kitchen dresser. Paul leapt forward to bridge the gap causing her body to slam into his hard frame. Warm amusement filled his eyes. Embarrassed she pulled back, looked down at her foot and said with feigned nonchalance, "How stupid of me, I forgot about my foot. Thanks." She straightened and expected him to let go, instead Paul's hand held her arm, and with quiet sincerity he said, "I believe I, and the woman with whom I share my life, will, plan and prepare for our children. And I agree it is absolutely essential for parents to provide a home with a healthy balance of love and discipline."

To Jill the underlying message was clear, he had a girlfriend, they hadn't discussed children, but the relationship was serious so she needn't harbour any romantic thoughts about him. Oh no, had he thought she'd deliberately fallen into his arms? Mortified, she managed a strangled, "Good, good" and disengaged herself. The movement brought a chuckle. "I think you'd be better holding on to me than falling over the furniture."

Beatty saved any further awkwardness by walking in and asking, "Are you two off somewhere?"

"Yep! To get Jill that x-ray." He lowered his voice, "And Gran, I'd say Gramps is definitely on the mend. Our guest here is giving him a new lease of life." Amazed, Jill blinked in surprise. Paul gave the hand resting on his arm a pat.

Beatty responded with a broad smile. "Sometimes those we seek to bless, become a blessing to us. Now get going and hopefully you'll not be too long."

In the ten minute journey to and from the hospital she discovered the slight twang of Paul's accent was because his parents lived in Australia and his tan was from a recent visit. He'd studied medicine at St Barts in London and did locum GP work. Paul, known at the local hospital, meant that after filling out the necessary forms she went straight in to have the x-rays taken. And being needed at the police station Paul took a quick look at the x-ray and didn't think any bones were broken, but left it that the hospital would contact her if the Registrar felt differently.

On the journey back she discovered he'd worked for a variety of police authorities because it relieved the boredom of being a GP! And he preferred locum work because it gave him the freedom to visit third world countries in need of a doctor 'until his money ran out'. In tallying up years she reckoned he was about 36. Obviously he didn't feel ready to settle down to that stable home environment needed to bring up children. She wanted to ask how his girlfriend coped with his nomadic spirit, but courage failed her to ask so personal a question on so short an acquaintance.

At the cottage Paul helped her to the door, opened it with his key, put his head around the sitting room door to announce, "Jill's back, can't stop, police business," and was gone almost before she had time to thank him.

CHAPTER 19

It was there. She reached out. It was unobtainable. There had to be a way to get it, and she'd find it. Her body bridging the crevice inched its way toward it. Every limb, every muscle felt stretched to breaking point. She touched, stretched, touched again, repeating this until finally it toppled, she caught it, but when she opened her hand whatever 'it' had been disintegrated into nothing. Ashes to ashes, dust to dust. In disappointment her body relaxed, it slipped, there was no foothold, no grass clump, no tree branch, only the black abyss, she was falling, falling...

She jolted awake! A cloud moved from across the moon bathing the room in translucent light. Fear churned her stomach, and pain from her injuries throbbed through her. Slowly she stirred her body into a sitting position and reached for the bedside light. In need of the painkillers she'd left in the kitchen she edged over the bed and put on her dressing gown. Beatty had said make yourself at home, did that extend to making a hot drink in the middle of the night?

The door creaked as she opened it, as quietly as possible she slipped through the gap and hobbled the few steps to the stairs before dropping on to her bottom. The moon from the lounge window lit the stairs, and helped her negotiate the furniture. At the kitchen door she could hear Barnie scratching, and fearful he'd bark, she spoke to him in a stage whisper, before slipping inside to pat the happy panting dog. Once she'd found the light switch she managed to persuade him to return to his bed, but he still kept a beady eye on her antics as she moved around the kitchen to make a drink. Only when she sat down did he close his eyes, but as she thoughtfully supped her drink she saw his ears prick up, his eyes open, his tail bang up and down in his bed, and before his expected visitor arrived he was by the door waiting for her.

Beatty, closing the door behind asked, "Not able to sleep?"

Jill nodded, "Nightmare! I'm sorry if I awoke you."

"Don't worry about it. I often get up in the middle of the night to pray, it's the best time." At that she couldn't think of a suitable reply so stared into her hot chocolate. "Would you like to tell me what you dreamt?" Wisely Beatty listened, nodded, then she asked, "Are you worrying about your boyfriend?"

"I am worrying for Ben, but he's not my boyfriend." She went on to explain how Ben had rescued her.

"Paul told me that he'd met you and your brother before. Paul's a bit like Ben, a good Samaritan and we're the innkeepers." Perplexed Jill frowned. Beatty smiled, "It's a Bible story. A Jewish man is beaten up and left for dead in a ditch. Two people pass by and ignore him, but the third a man from Samaria, a race outcast by the Jews, rescues him and pays his keep at a local inn until he is better."

"Oh sorry, yes I heard the story at school and see what you mean. And I want to say I really appreciate Paul rescuing me, and you for being my innkeepers." She sighed, "Although he may be regretting that after my behaviour today."

Beatty chuckled, "I rather think he enjoyed it. Bill told me that your brother and his wife are Christians. It occurs to me they are praying for you, and God is stirring your spirit to reach out to Him and His love, and the enemy is doing what he does best, maim, steal and destroy."

Jill grunted, "That figures, and fits the nightmare. And as for love, that's a disaster area!

"Would it help to tell me about it?"

Beatty's interest and concern spurred her on. Last night the tears had flowed, tonight it was words as she told her of Stephen, her string of men, to Ben, Helen and the finale of Rich's betrayal."

"It would seem to me Jill you want love, but in grabbing for it in the wrong way and place it does to turn to dust. I think God is revealing that to you, but if you allow Him to show you the right way, it will bring you peace and rest. Anyway time has gone on, it's nearly three o'clock, and we need to go back to bed."

Jill gasped, "I'm so sorry, but you are so easy to talk to."

Beatty patted her shoulder. "I'm pleased you felt you could. I feel if we can be open, speak of the dark, hurt and hidden things in our lives, in their exposure they lose the ability to harm us further, and that in itself brings healing." Jill nodded, for there was some truth in Beatty's philosophy. After talking to Jane, her 'big secret' no longer haunted her, and it had been easy to talk to Beatty of her past. "Now, remember it's God who loves you and it is He who listens just as I have done. He knows the plans he has for you, plans to prosper and not harm you and they will give you a hope and a future."

Dismally she replied, "What future? I'm in trouble and worse still, so is Ben."

"Jill we all make mistakes. Just tell the police all you know. God allows us free will to run our lives, but every now and then He intervenes to remind us of His existence. It may not have seemed to you God's had a hand in your life, but God's ways and wisdom aren't ours. I don't believe anything is coincidence."

Incredulous she burst forth, "Beatty, that's amazing, I picked up the Bible beside the bed and it opened at a verse just like that."

With a broad smile Beatty nodded, "That's my God!"

"Jane calls them God-incidences."

"She's right. And remember it's always darkest before the dawn. Things will brighten up for you, you'll see. And it will soon be dawn so we'd better get back to bed."

Normally she wasn't a very demonstrative person, but she just had to hug Beatty, "Oh thank you Beatty, I'll think on all you've said."

Minutes later she lay in bed and decided if Beatty was right, if God had His hand on her life then He'd probably do a much better job with it than she'd been doing, and with that thought drifted off into sleep.

Someone shook her shoulder. A voice was quietly calling her name! Half asleep she realised it was Paul and turned onto her back, instantly whimpering as her body reminded her of its aches and pains. The bed dipped.

She opened her eyes and Paul observed, "Pulled muscles can hurt, but they'll ease in a day or so. A cool slim hand picked up hers. "Your right hand looks badly bruised you probably tried to save yourself with it. The scratches are healing well though. Gran said you and she chatted last night, and you needed a couple of painkillers."

With a wince she tried to pull herself up.

Paul moved forward, "Here, let me help you." That freshness of his aftershave wafted past her nostrils, that nearness brought again that strange sensation of somehow 'knowing' him when she didn't, and embarrassed she closed her eyes against it.

"Are you feeling dizzy?"

Her eyes opened to see his frowned concern, and she acknowledged the truth that in sitting up she did now feel rather nauseous.

"You're probably hungry - it is lunch time. I'll run you a nice hot bath with plenty of Gran's Radox in it? She swears by the stuff for aches and pains. Soak for half an hour. You'll not spoil, or miss lunch, because it's only bread and cheese today!" His serious, bossy manner reminded her of David. She raised a painful salute and uttered, "Yes Doctor, anything you say Doctor!"

For a moment he looked blank, then the quirky smile appeared, "You may not feel A1, but you're bright enough. Now drink that tea while I start your bath. Then I'll come back and take off your bandages." She'd just taken a mouthful of tea as an exasperated "Oh drat" came from the bathroom, then the sound of flowing water drowned out any other words. A few seconds later Paul appeared in the doorway rubbing his hair with a towel, the front of his light blue shirt soaking wet. "I expected the water to come through the tap, instead it went to the shower head resting in the bath and up and over me."

Amused she commented, "Oh we've got those. Jane's got caught a couple of times because David forgot to put the lever down after a shower. You can't leave that wet shirt on, take it off and put it on the radiator, it'll soon dry."

"Good thinking." He dropped the wet towel by the bed and pulled to release his tie.

Beatty's voice called up "Paul, is that you running the bath?"

He called back, "Yes Gran. I suggested to Jill she have one before lunch, it'll help her aching muscles."

Footsteps coming up heralded Beatty's arrival just as Paul removed his shirt. "I've brought up a clean..... Paul what on earth do you think you are doing?"

"Taking my shirt off. Your wretched shower doused me."

"You'd better put on one of Bill's, I'm not having you roaming around the house half naked ."

"Gran! I am no more naked than if I were on a beach, in fact less so."

"This isn't Australia, or one of your African villages. And it seems very improper to me to be undressing in front of a lady."

Paul sent her a quirky smile. "Jill's not offended by my taking off my shirt in fact it was she who suggested it." He laughed, "Oh Gran, don't look like that, only because it was wet and would dry quicker on the radiator."

Uncomfortable, thinking Beatty, knowing her past, might think she was seducing Paul, she added for good measure, "Paul's right, if he were on the beach no-one would take a second look."

Paul chuckled, "Now Jill I didn't say that, but modesty prevents me from boasting."

Beatty snatched his shirt. "Oh God, give me strength! Go and look after that bath you naughty boy, it will be overflowing in a minute. I'll put this by the Aga it'll be dry after you've had lunch."

Paul left as Beatty enquired, "Now dear, how are you? Did you manage to sleep after our chat?"

"Yes, thank you and no more nightmares."

"Nightmares?" Paul appeared in the doorway buttoning up a check gardening shirt of Bill's which barely met across his chest.

Beatty tutted. "You know you could get struck off undressing and dressing in female patients' bedrooms?"

With a rueful grimace he expelled on a deep breath, "Yes Gran I know, but then I don't usually offer, or run baths for my 'female' patients." He gave his quirky smile, "Therefore it is unlikely that I'd get soaked by the shower that someone left in the bath ready to douse an unsuspecting doctor when he turned on the taps!!"

"Humph! Well Doctor, I suggest you attend to your patient, then come and eat your lunch for you've only got about half an hour before you have to be back at work." With that Beatty left muttering as she went down the stairs.

"Oh dear, is she really cross?"

"No, of course not, it's just her way." He chuckled, "Do you think she'd consider it an impropriety if I were to ask to see your ankles!"

Her laugh and answer were forestalled with a need to announce, "I'm going to be sick."

Paul gave her a puzzled look, but his expression soon turn to comprehension when wide-eyed she clapped her hand over her mouth. With quick thinking he whipped up the wet towel from the floor and advised, "Stick that over your mouth. Try and take deep breathes it might stop you retching. Right I can see we need to get you to the bathroom." Instantly he pulled back the bedclothes, hoisted her against him and with her one good leg they made rapid speed to the bathroom where she was violently sick into the toilet. By holding it in, her throat now burnt, her nose stung and tears flowed down her cheeks. What had made her so sick? She retched again, but nothing came up. She flushed the toilet and stood.

Behind her Paul asked, "Is it over?" She nodded miserably. "Don't cry, it was probably the painkillers upsetting you, I'll give you different ones. He gave her a brief hug and then as if realizing she might get the wrong idea, still supporting her he leant across, put the toilet lid down and instructed, "Sit on this. I'll take off those bandages then you can get straight in the bath."

It then occurred to her any testosterone filled male would be affected by her rather well endowed figure clad in only a cotton nightdress.

He crouched down to remove the two bandages. "I popped in to see how you were because I am being pestered by the police in their need to question you. And they insist I'm holding up their enquiries. I thought you could see them this afternoon, but you clearly aren't well enough for that. I'll explain, but can't stall them further, so will have to declare you fit for questioning tomorrow."

Anxious she asked, "Do I have to go to the Police Station?"

"I expect it can be arranged that they come here to the cottage. You aren't under arrest, just helping with their enquiries."

"Have you any news of Ben?"

"No. I'm constantly fobbed off. When I cornered the Chief Super an hour ago he said best not to talk because even walls have ears! You've certainly stirred up something. Now have your bath, I must get my lunch."

Paul had gone when she arrived downstairs, Beatty, up to her elbows in flour, was mixing pastry while Bill snored in his chair by the fire. With a nod Beatty indicated the plate of homemade bread, cheese and salad on the table. "Will you be able to manage that? Paul said you'd been sick."

"I hope so. It looks delicious. You weren't cross with him, were you?"

"It did seem unprofessional, but then Paul was being more friend than doctor. I'm very proud of him, but I wish he'd settled down to a proper job instead of going off to war torn, or famine ridden countries, to help out."

Curious, she hoped Beatty would say more, and watched her rolling out her mixture, turn it, fold it into three, roll it and do it all again. Her silence was rewarded for Beatty continued, "When Paul's parents, Alan our son and Vivienne, emigrated to Australia Paul was fifteen and stayed with us, so he feels more a son, than grandson." There was silence except for her munching on the delicious crunch bread. as Beatty concentrated on placing a circle of pastry on a plate. While adding the home-made pie filling of cold chicken and vegetables she expanded, "Paul's been back and forth to Australia ever since. It gave him a spirit of adventure and combined with a desire to help others he likes to be free to up and go where there's a need." It was fascinating seeing the pie come together, Beatty made it look so simple as she placed a lid of pastry on to one of her enormous pies. Thoughtfully Beatty commented, "This is the longest stretch I can remember him being home. Well, except for a recent four week visit to his parents in Australia. Maybe he feels he can settle now, it's been a long time."

"Perhaps his girlfriend has something to do with that?"

Beatty cutting off the excess pastry smiled, "Who knows? I'm just his Gran."

In seeing Beatty start a second roll of pastry she said with amusement, "Are you expecting an influx of refugees with all this baking?"

Beatty chuckled, "Just family. We usually try and have one evening a week with family members around once a week. Maria, Lillian and Bob with Mark, Paul's younger brother and his new wife Hazel are coming for dinner tonight, and I suspect too Paul will arrive if Maria has anything to do with it."

Into her mind came Maria's chatter on their first meeting. "So where does Maria fit into the family?"

"Lillian and Bob couldn't have children so they adopted her as a baby."

"Well, Maria's lovely, and there's no doubt she adores Paul."

"And he her."

"Perhaps he's been waiting for her to grow up, and why he's thinking of settling down?"

With a fork Beatty neatly sealed the edge of the pie and with her mind on her pastry began to speak of how God had led her to find this very successful recipe. Jill's mind drifted into considering the relationship between Paul and Maria because without a blood tie...

"Are you going to monopolise Jill all afternoon Beatty?" came a reedy male voice from the doorway,

"Oh Bill, I'm sorry I should have brought you a cup of tea. I'll make one now."

Poor Bill looked quite frail leaning against the doorpost. Jill smiled at him. "It's my fault I kept Beatty talking. I'll come in and talk to you, oh unless Beatty you would like some help, but my cooking isn't great!

Beatty chuckled, "They say the way to a man's heart is through his stomach, so if you like, while you are here I'll teach you. You go with Bill now we don't want him feeling left out."

The rest of the afternoon Bill chatted about his war time experiences, and before the family arrived she helped Beatty prepare the vegetables. It was obvious they were a close family by the way they hugged, laughed and bantered with each other, but better still they made her feel so much part of it. Paul as predicted had joined them, and after the delicious chicken pie and apricot sponge and custard, he washed up, while she sitting on a chair wiped and Maria put the dishes away. Everyone was keen to play cards, and Paul boasted, "I'm the family expert at playing Rummy, so stick with me." they'd loved her challenge.

Everyone had applauded her challenge, "Then Paul Stemmings this will be the battle of the champions for I'm pretty good myself, be ready to learn a trick or two!"

Lying in bed, waiting for sleep to come it occurred to her it was a long time since she'd laughed and had such fun with a group of people, and the Stemmings family were welcoming, yet not stifling. Guilt closely followed that thought, for while she'd been enjoying herself Ben could be languishing in a cell somewhere. Where was he, what was happening? Tomorrow she would demand information from the police, and do all in her power to ensure Rich was locked away forever after the way he'd so callously condoned her murder at Chris' hands!

The rock was hard, the crevice narrow, its granite edges going down into infinity. The rope wasn't taut enough, her hands burned with pulling herself along it, her back ached with the stretching, and as her body slipped and twisted, pain shot up her leg. She inched forward, her body bridging the gap, every limb and muscle stretched to breaking point. Nothing, short of death, would stop her gaining that prize. The rope loosened further, desperate she threw herself forward, and to her delight caught the prize in her hand, yet instantly she started to slip, the rocks were smooth, there was nothing to grasp, falling into the black abyss she screamed in terror "Nooooo"! Her voice echoed against the sheer sides of granite. A large hand reached down. She jerked and awoke to find Beatty, hair in rollers, bent over her, trying to tug off the tangled bedclothes. Bound barely able to move she said weakly, "I don't want to die."

And then felt very foolish as Beatty observed, "You won't! You've had a nightmare, rolled off the bed and wound the bedclothes around you like an Egyptian mummy. Don't move, let me untangle your foot." Shaken from the experience she lay still on the carpet, moving as Beatty directed. It wasn't long before Beatty helped her back to bed, and re-made it with her in it. Finally tucking her in she suggested they have a hot drink and by the time clinking cups heralded Beatty's reappearance she was sitting up, hugging her knees ready to apologise. "Oh thank you

Beatty, I'm sorry I cried out so loud and awoke you, but glad you heard and came to release me. I saw a hand grab me at the end of the nightmare, that was you, thank you."

Beatty gave a thoughtful nod "How about you tell me about it as you drink your chocolate?" When she finished Beatty nodded, "I believe God speaks through dreams, let me pray about it. Now best get some sleep you've a busy day tomorrow."

Despite the tiredness and comfort of a hot milky drink, tomorrow, like the darkness, loomed like the black abyss of her nightmare. Finally she switched on the bedside light and, seeing the Bible picked it up, opened it at random, and read, "He will vindicate you with the blazing light of justice shining down as from the noonday sun. Rest in the Lord, wait patiently for him to act. Don't be envious of evil men who prosper. Stop your anger! Turn off wrath. Don't fret and worry, it only leads to harm."

Astounded she read those words several times. Tears filled her eyes, how had God done that? This had to be God! He was telling her not to worry. And not to be angry or want revenge. He would act on her behalf. She began reading at the beginning of Psalm 37. It talked about trusting, committing and delighting in the Lord with the promise, "And He will give you the desires of your heart." Whispering into the empty room she asked, "Is it you God? Are you really speaking to me? It says here if I put my trust in you, you will give me the desires of my heart. Please, if I trust you, will you make sure that this time Ben receives justice? You see I owe him so much." She closed the Bible, then opened it again. Maybe God had something more to say? Displayed was the same page, she shut it. Under her breath she challenged, "Alright God, let's try this again. If it isn't Psalm 37 I'll know this is you. With a sort of toss she let it fall open. Her eyes arrested on an underlined passage which read, 'For God loved the world so much that He gave His only Son so that anyone who believes in Him shall not perish but have eternal life. There is no eternal doom awaiting those who trust Him to save them.'

Oh my God! That was the nightmare! That was the black abyss! Was it her sub-conscious reaching for God, no matter the cost? She searched and found Psalm 37 again and used it to talk to God. "John 3 says you sent Jesus into the world, to die, that I might live. Jane says we are all sinners, and Jesus came and died to take away our sin, and verse says so I might have eternal life. Okay I'll agree I've made a mess of my life. Jane says if we ask you forgive. So please forgive me. I want to do as this Psalm says, commit my life to you, and even if things don't work out as I hope, I'll know it's because you have other plans for me. Amen." But what of her heart's desire? She sighed, Ben, could have been Mr Right, but for Helen and the baby! God just hadn't meant it to be. Was there a Mr Right for her? "Please Jesus can you find him for me? Oh and for Ben please get him through this and give him the desires of his heart too. Thank you err Amen" She closed the Bible. It was now up to God, or Father, Lord, Jesus, Holy Spirit, one of them! She yawned, maybe she'd get used to calling God, Lord, one day, but right now that word made her think of Rich. Her eyes felt heavy, she switched off the light. David and Jane would be thrilled at her decision. In the end how simple it had been, and a relief to know her life was in God's hands. She felt such peace and wondered why she had waited so long, sleep encompassed her.

"Jill, dear, wake up. I've brought you breakfast".

Her eyes opened to see Beatty with a tray of cereals, toast and marmalade. She sat up and realised her body didn't feel quite so stiff and achy, perhaps God was healing that too. "Oh Beatty you really shouldn't spoil me like this."

"My you look perkier this morning. Barnie pattered in and headed in her direction. Beatty turned and grabbed him and admonished, "No jumping on the bed." Jill laughed, as Barnie, with his sad, endearing eyes, rest his head on the beside her. "Silly dog, he's really taken to you. Now eat up because the police will be here in an hour."

At the word 'police' her throat suddenly filled with hot acid bile. She whipped the tray to one side, clapped her hand across her mouth, leapt out of bed, and hopped her way to be sick down the toilet. Once over it, she washed her face and returned to the bedroom where Beatty waited with a worried expression. "Oh Beatty, when will this end? Every day there is a reminder of what happened and it just seems to sicken my stomach."

"Back into bed with you and see if you can manage to drink your tea, try a piece of toast it might settle you."

Jill obeyed and considered whether to share her new found faith, instead she decided to ask, "Do you often have people to stay?"

"Over the years we've had a friend from Paul's school, a chap he met in Australia and…" Beatty's happy expression faded as she added, "The beautiful, orphaned Beth. When she died we could scarce believe it. That was so hard, I'm not sure Paul ever got over it. Anyway it didn't stop Paul bringing people here, a girl from the streets of London, a depressed teenager who'd had his leg amputated, an abused wife and child and others. Some we've kept in touch with, others have gone their own way. I feel it's our opportunity to give something back for all the blessings our family receive from God."

Astonished she blurted out, "You're an amazing woman Beatty."

"No dear, I'm not doing anything I don't want to. I ask for wisdom and God helps and hears me, that's all. Now if you put the trousers on with that other jumper in your case I'll wash the things you've been wearing these past two days. At least with you we haven't had to send out an SOS to find clothes, but if you're short of anything the people in the Church can often come up with it."

"Oh no, no, I'm fine, in fact Beatty I must pay you, at least for my keep."

"We'll see dear, we'll see. Now eat your breakfast, then get yourself ready because I gather a Detective Chief Inspector will be here about 10.00 am."

Dressed and about to go downstairs she saw the unmarked car draw up outside and heard Beatty open the door to say, "Hello Phil."

Phil didn't acknowledge Beatty, but she could hear the awe in his voice as he introduced Detective Chief Inspector Gerald Maysfield with the additional information, "He's from the Met."

"How do you do Mrs Stemmings, it's very good of you to take in this lady and I believe it's been agreed you will sit in on the interview. Is there somewhere we can talk privately because I'd like to talk to you, first impressions and so on?"

The door to the lounge closed so she couldn't hear Beatty's reply, but didn't doubt it would be positive. Determined not to be intimidated and deciding they'd had long enough to discuss her she carefully negotiated the stairs. On entering the room two suited men were sitting on the settee talking to Bill, stood. About to say, 'Good morning gentlemen' as if she were entering a board meeting the tall, grey-haired and rather distinguished gentleman approached her with his hand outstretched. "DCI Gerald Maysfield, CID, you must be Jill Reinhardt. You may know Sergeant Phil Weatheral from the local police." Politely she put out her hand to each of them before Beatty ushered them into the kitchen to sit down around the table before she closed the door.

Before they could speak she jumped in to ask her own question. "Please can you tell me about Ben? He's a dear friend, he rescued me from being kidnapped and I would really like to know what's happening to him."

The Inspector, very much the gentleman, held out a chair. "Do be seated Miss Reinhardt. May I call you Jill?" She nodded in agreement. He sat down opposite her. "Well Jill you will be surprised to learn that your adventure has triggered the answer to a mystery and brought revelation into a series of crimes that go back a decade. Until this happened we had no idea that Lord Richard Mallory and Peter Sanchez were one and the same man. In fact no-one had even connected the likeness. In order to get the most out of this knowledge we are observing Lord Mallory's movements, and Interpol are keeping an eye out for his brother Chris. The problem is, in this case, no actual crime has been committed by either of them."

"But what of the car full of drugs and the jewellery?"

"It would seem that is your crime, not his!" If he hadn't smiled she would have been worried that they were the accused. "All we have is Lord Mallory's passport which is genuine and we'd like to gather further evidence on the source of the drugs, and the jewellery. Hopefully you can help us with that. You will also appreciate that Ben Fletcher has been in prison for stealing drugs, and we are still unsure whether he is playing a double bluff."

"Oh no, that's not possible. If you knew Ben you'd know he's entirely honest. He shouldn't have gone to prison because…"

DCI Maysfield interrupted, "In that case let's start with what you know of him, and then move on to how you met Lord Mallory."

When she'd told what she knew it became obvious she only had Ben's hearsay to back his kidnap claim. In her mind she pictured his face, could those bright, laughing eyes be a useful façade for what she previously had considered his chameleon like character? Although she didn't admit it she could see how Ben could have deliberately infiltrated her flat and life in order to be part of such a crime. In which case the incredible sexual frisson they experienced would have come as an added bonus for him!

DCI Maysfield having thanked her for her detailed account accepted Beatty's offer of a cup of tea and a piece of cake. In the pause as Beatty bustled about she felt to added, "I know it's Rich's word against mine about hearing through the bedroom door of his intention to kidnap me, and his collaborating, if necessary, in my murder, but the way I see it if Rich finds out about Ben's involvement it could then be to the detriment of Ben's life."

"And indeed Jill an opinion upheld by all of those involved." Relief washed through her, for even she'd begun to doubt Ben's validity! "We've suspected Sanchez's involvement in many crimes, but except for the two years he was in the Scrubs for GBH sharing a cell with Ben, he seems to have the ability to disappear into thin air. Now we are asking where was Lord Mallory during those two years? Until we can prove beyond reasonable doubt that Peter Sanchez and Lord Mallory are the same man, preferably without involving Ben Fletcher, then we need to keep you both in safe houses for fear of reprisals." Inspector Maysfield gave an amused smile, "And to put your mind at rest, Ben is being looked after, and is safe and well. You'll understand, I can say no more because Ben is the only one who can identify that Sanchez and Rich are the same person and may be our only option, but it may help if you tell us all you know about Lord Mallory."

Another hour passed and left the Chief Inspector looking thoughtful. Phil taking notes looked cynical, and at times seemed desperate to chip in, but had been stopped by the DCI holding up his hand. Now he took the opportunity to state brusquely, "So you are telling us that you had doubts about Sanchez, but when he comes to your flat looking rough, makes himself at home, announces you are off to Amsterdam, you agree to go with him, just like that?" Before she could answer, he went on to challenge, "Then he left you for the night, most of the next day and you still didn't suspect he was up to something? Not even when you found the jewels under the dressing table? I suspect his idea, and it seems to me, you were happy go along with it, that the ear-rings and magnificent diamond ring were to buy you off?"

In the face of Phil's attitude she felt remarkably composed and at peace. "I've already explained Rich asked me to act as though we were engaged, he said it helped his business. And yes, at times I did have a niggle about aspects of Rich's behaviour, but he was often fun and flamboyant, drew a thin line between fact and fiction, and being with him held a certain excitement and adventure. I admit I wondered about his business and told you I'd decided on not seeing him again, but when he turned up unexpectedly I'd nothing planned, so why not go to Amsterdam with him?"

Phil hummed, fiddled with his jacket, bit his finger nails, and continued, "These dinner parties, didn't you think it odd that he bought you beautiful clothes and asked you to wear expensive jewellery?"

She shrugged. "Not particularly, remember I thought he was a Lord. I didn't have clothes or jewellery that would fit his image and the people he met. I wasn't being dishonest, just accepting what I needed to live up to his lifestyle. I've just told you his very plausible story on his background and about Mallory Towers in High Wycombe. Rich kept files on people including myself, he knew more about my father than I did."

As though not believing her Phil demanded, "Who are these people he dealt with?"

She reeled off about half a dozen different names which Phil wrote down. Delving into her handbag she drew out a card. "This is Rich's business card with a Knightsbridge address. I once tried ringing the number, it was unobtainable. Rich explained it as a bill his accountant had forgotten to pay. With the exception of the house I didn't visit any of his supposed residences. I don't know the addresses, but could probably take you to Mallory Towers. On the files he kept and gave me he'd always removed anything he didn't want me to see."

By drinking his tea and enjoying a piece of Beatty's fruit cake she'd the feeling the DCI had allowed time for Phil to release his frustration. Now he entered in again to ask quietly, "Have you any idea of Rich's business ventures?"

For a while she relayed remembered conversations, but was acutely aware of Phil tapping his fingers on the table. Agitated he finally burst out, "That may be useful, but we need facts. I don't suppose you know the blue Escort's number plate, or that you might have any clues to identify the whereabouts of that row of garages?"

The DCI said more gently, "Put yourself back there, think about it."

She pictured the scene. "There were... seven garages in the row. The doors were different colours, they were faded and battered, and it looked like a council estate. Kids were shouting and playing football on a field, it could have been a school. In fact, as we drove away I remember the road was 'Greenway Close' about a thirty minute drive from the Port. And I do know the blue Escort registration because I was hiding by it when Rich was looking for the red one. It's DMV123B. And I've just thought of something else, Rich told Chris to use his French Passport and called him Rene de Mer."

Even that spurt of useful information didn't seem to have pleased Phil, but the DCI rubbed his hands with glee. "That's a great help. Understandably Chris Waverley has disappeared, but with that information we may find him. We are keeping this under wraps and haven't contacted Mallory. It maybe neither he, nor Waverley, know you came in with the drugs, but Waverley will have seen the diamonds are missing. I suspect with the kidnap plan hatched Sanchez and Waverley are in some kind of other mess we've yet to uncover, although Ben explained about the double bluff for Sanchez to get Waverley to Rio and out of his life. Waverley could be there already, but our intelligence hasn't spotted him."

Phil interjected, "You've just said you hadn't clothes or jewellery to fit Lord Mallory's lifestyle so where did he think the money would come from to pay a ransom if he kidnapped you?"

The Chief Inspector smiled, "Jill might not have money, but her father does. Now Jill, and if Mrs Stemmings you have no objection, we'd like you to stay here. If Sanchez doesn't know of the foiled kidnap attempt, we don't want to alert him that you are at home. You will be pleased to know the drug trafficking and smuggling issue is as if it hadn't happened! And in the hope of keeping Ben out of this he is absent from work having gone on a training course in connection with his new job at Inhart Pharmaceuticals."

Blustering with indignation Phil burst out, "Inhart Pharmaceuticals, how ridiculous is that! With his prison record no drug company would employ him?"

Jill looked wide-eyed at the Chief Inspector who smiled and turned to Phil to explain. "Professor Reinhardt, the owner of Inhart's is Jill's father. And the perfect cover for Ben because he told Mallory he had a job with them. Jill's father and her brother are highly thought of in business and legal circles and have assured us they have every confidence in Ben's honesty and their desire is to facilitate a speedy and satisfactory conclusion to what they see as a foiled kidnap attack against a member of their family."

Jill frowned, and asked, "Do you think Chris, believing I took the diamonds will try and recover them?"

"That's another reason why it's best you aren't seen. We have your house and workplace under surveillance. Our hope of course is to apprehend one of his men for information. Sanchez often seems one step ahead of us and we don't know how far his influence extends, but suspect, and I regret, it could be within the police force. Our aim is to gather enough incriminating evidence to put all his associates in jail, and this incident, and your information, is blowing his life wide open."

Beatty smiled, "Well we are enjoying Jill's company so she can stay as long as necessary."

The DCI stood, and politely they all followed suit.

A thought occurred to her, "What about my family, can I speak to them?"

Immediately the DCI answered with a smile. "Of course, as soon as we feel its safe I'll get your brother to ring you here." Then with great seriousness he stared into her eyes, "I just wish we could find concrete evidence that Sanchez and Mallory were the same man. Mallory isn't stupid, it won't take him long to suspect Ben squealed on his double identity, and his people act, they don't ask first!"

Fear gripped her and she prayed within, Oh God please don't let Ben be hurt, find another way to prove Rich has two lives. The Inspector thanked her, then Beatty, and moved toward the front door. A unexpected flash-back of picture of the day she and Rich spent in the pool, was enough for her to call excitedly, "Wait, hh my goodness I've got it!" They turned their eyes fixed on her. The words burst from her. "Rich has a long, fairly recent scar down his back, probably received since he was in prison. If Rich and Pete are the same man they will share the scar."

"And if we've only got Mallory how will that help?" Phil conjectured with a sneer.

With a smile she retorted, "Because if you could find who inflicted that knife wound and it was done to Sanchez…"

Inspector Maysfield cut in to say with enthusiasm, "I see where you are going… in fact…yes… even separately with the same scar…" He punched the air, "We've got him!" Phil's scornful expression froze as he processed DCI Maysfield's train of revelation.

Ecstatic that justice would be done, she stated, "So no need for anyone to know of Ben's involvement. And neither I, nor my family need be drawn into this."

The Inspector lifted his hand and cautioned, "Let's not rush ahead of ourselves here. There's ground work to do first. We can't arrest, or accuse Sanchez, for without Ben's evidence it's still only your word against his of this kidnap plot. Nor do we want to alert him that we are on to him for other crimes. I doubt he would organise reprisals against you, or your family, but we just want to be sure we've got our man before we relax our vigilance."

"It's not just that, well… my father is up for an MBE and I'd hate for me to be involved in something which would jeopardize his receiving it."

Detective Chief Inspector Maysfield gave a broad smile, "Don't worry it will be months before all this comes to trial, too late then for the Queen to change her mind."

Once the front door had closed she sunk into the nearest comfy chair and groaned, "How did I get so mixed up in this?"

Beatty on her way back to the kitchen assured her, "It'll sort itself out. Let's have some lunch."

Bill laughed, "Already on my way girl. I'm gasping for a cuppa. Now Jill what's all this about your dad receiving an MBE? My, I didn't know I was in such exalted company."

Tiredly she patted his arm, "You're not Bill. And don't tell a soul, it's supposed to be kept secret, I don't want to be sent to the Tower for treason! I'm just an ordinary girl, and live what I thought was an ordinary life until now."

CHAPTER 20

After lunch came the routine nap, but today she sat on the bed, picked up the Bible and started to read the book of John. Voices in the kitchen awakened her to the fact that life had restarted downstairs!

Paul leaning back against the kitchen dresser smiled as she appeared and then finished his sentence. "So let's just see how things come together. Hi Jill. Gran's been telling me it went well this morning. You must be relieved to hear Ben's not locked in a cell. Although I gather Uncle Phil could have behaved with greater empathy."

Beatty poured the tea as Jill countered, "Well to be fair there were times I could see his perspective, and it didn't always look good."

Paul frowned as he sat down. "From what I've gathered Ben isn't in danger of having his life ruined by the law, but by Mallory issuing reprisals because he guesses Ben has exposed his double identity, and was involved in scuppering his kidnapping plan."

Said like that fear for Ben caused her hand to shake as she took the cup from Beatty. "Do you think the police can protect him if his life is in danger? I couldn't bear it if anything happened to him."

"I don't know, but can understand the responsibility you feel. Whatever the outcome Ben must love you very much to have risked his life for you. Do you feel the same about him?"

"It isn't that simple I'm afraid. Tiredly she sighed, leant forward, rested her elbows on the table, her head in her hands and gave Paul in a nutshell a short history of Ben's love, Helen's pregnancy and their proposed marriage in December."

"Poor man, what a frightful position to be in. It's tough to face that alone. In difficult times my faith in the Lord has been my comfort and strength."

About to tell them she'd asked Jesus to come into her life Paul glanced at his watch and announced, "I must be going. I popped in because I wanted to know how it went this morning and was curious to know what was happening."

Beatty hands on the table, pulled herself up to state, "Well, Jill and I are going to take our minds off this with cooking."

Paul's eyes lit up, "Really! Can I come to tea?"

"Not tonight. It'll be good for you to have a night in with Maria. But you can both come tomorrow."

Boyishly he exclaimed, "Oh goody!" He hugged Beatty and kissed her cheek, then with a wave said, "Bye Jill, see you tomorrow," and was gone.

Immediately Beatty launched into recipes to which she only half listened, her mind taken up with what 'a night in with Maria' meant. Wasn't she rather young for Paul? But then Jane and David had eleven years between them. Both David and Paul had features which made them look older so maybe Paul was younger than thirty-six years, she'd calculated. Maria had to be between sixteen and eighteen, but even if Paul was only thirty-two and she eighteen it was a fourteen year gap. Beatty sounded as if she was actively encouraging it, and it would account for his comment on child rearing. Maria was set on a career, so far too early to discuss children. This was ridiculous, it was nothing to do with her, far more important was to listen to Beatty and learn some basic cookery skills.

Three hours later Beatty having involved her in a mass of recipe writing, preparing and cooking was taking cottage pie out of the oven. This basic mince recipe Beatty explained, with a variety of spices, could be used for many different dishes. Perhaps the 'good' to come out of this time was for her to become a decent cook in preparation for His chosen Mr Right. After all people often equated Christianity with homely skills.

Beatty and Bill were so lovely, and she enjoyed their constant bantering. Bill's mischievous sense of humour would have Beatty respond in amused crossness, but it was obvious she loved him. They were such a wonderful advertisement for a good marriage. Oh to have one like that, and as the three of them began a game of Scrabble, she said so!

Bill chuckled, "Takes a lot of hard work Jill, you women are such a mystery to us men. But Beatty and I have something special." He grinned complacently.

Immediately her mind went to a sustainable and brilliant sexual relationship, bringing an ache for Ben, but she determined to concentrate on Bill and begged, "Come on then, tell me."

"Beatty and I love the Lord, He is central to our lives and we'd consult him in all things. So I continually ask for His insight into how you women tick and how best to respond." He chortled, "Beatty of course asks the same about us men. And the Lord, or we'd say, the Holy Spirit who dwells in us brings us a unity, you've heard the expression, 'united we stand, divided we fall', well its true. Most importantly I'd say in any relationship, you must always think the best of each other, never to accuse or put the other down."

"I like that. It makes sense, and makes marriage sound a safe and secure place."

Beatty added, "But it takes commitment. We have had to work at it. Bill and I came together as individuals, its taken years to understand and enjoy our differences, and love isn't having our way, but seeing what is best for both of us. Love these days is often down-graded to lust. As Paul pointed out, Ben is a good example of loving. Without thought of the consequences to himself, or his life, he wanted you to be safe."

A wry smile claimed her mouth. "Err I rather think that lust played a part too."

In a rather sharp tone Bill contradicted, "From your perspective maybe, definitely not his."

"Oh Bill I'm not decrying what Ben did. I'll never know whether what we had would have worked because he can't be my Ben." Said aloud those words were like a stab in her heart, she blinked back the tears.

"Oh luv, now don't go upsetting yourself." Bill put out his hand to pat hers. " Our belief is if you let God have His way in your life He works on your behalf. That way you find peace and rest for your soul."

"Blow your nose." Beatty handed her a hanky.

In between nose blowing she stated, "I've already started reading the book of John in that Bible by the bed."

Beatty glanced at Bill before saying, "That's good dear we'll talk again when you've finished it." Her eyes went back to the Scrabble board, I think Bill it's your turn." And despite their age Bill and Beatty proved to be worthy opponents.

The following day looked dull and miserable, but her heart felt light and bright. Beatty arrived with the usual tray and Barnie sat by the bed cocking his head from side to side as if to ascertain how she was, then satisfied he lay down on the carpet as if to wait for her to get up. "That dog has really taken to you. Now dear here are your washed smalls, and I've pressed your trousers and blouse. I'll go and bring them up."

When Beatty reappeared she looked up from munching her cornflakes and started, "Oh Beatty you are so very k…" But the site of her overcoat in a cleaner's bag, which Beatty also carried, brought such reminders of Ben and her escape from Rich, that her stomach churned over and with that came sickness. In her haste to the bathroom she nearly fell over poor Barnie. Her weight went to her sore ankle, and if Beatty hadn't leapt to balance her she would probably have fallen and squashed him. The pain in her foot now seemed to add to the violence of sickness which fortunately was over quickly.

Beatty helped her back to bed. "I was going to suggest a short walk around the garden wearing Bill's large Wellington boots, but I think you need to rest that foot. Anyway it's a typical damp November day and the forecast is rain! I've friends around for a prayer meeting this morning, so stay in bed, or sit in the lounge. We'll cook this afternoon."

Jill snoozed, then hobbled to the window to see the miserable day just as three of Beatty's friends came up the path. How wonderful to have no need to get up so she snuggled down and read Psalm 27 which Bill had recommended. He'd said reading scripture aloud was like declaring and proclaiming her intentions. He was right the Lord God was her light and her salvation, she wanted to inquire at His temple and was waiting and believing she'd see His goodness released in her life. She thought of Bill and Beatty, and compared them with her grandparents. The Reinhardt grandparents had died in Germany while trying to help the Jews escape Hitler's regime. And she could only remember her mother's parents as elderly, frail and living in a rather up market old people's home near the Downs in Bristol. How different then the Stemmings' family was from her own. They seemed to thrive on one another and their friends. Their warm kitchen constantly provided delicious smells to pervade their house, and a dull afternoon was made bright by Bill and Beatty's banter and chatter where she was learning, not only cooking skills, but the fundamentals of Christianity which were built on God's desire of a relationship with those whom He had created. To be a child with their heavenly Father, a disciple with his master, a friend of God's Son Jesus, and a bride being prepared for a kingly bridegroom who again Jesus. The latter image particularly spoke to her romantic heart.

Both Paul and Maria arrived for dinner bringing more fun and laughter to the comfortable family atmosphere, and felt the words of Ps.27 which said the Lord would keep her safe, hide her and put her above her enemies were so right at this time, and she prayed

Ben would have the same blessing over his life.

They watched as Beatty hoisted out a huge dish of pancakes covered in a bubbling cheese sauce, put them on the table and declared, "Jill cooked these. Come on Jill you should serve them out."

In the enthusiasm of youth Maria clapped her hands. "Wow Jill. They look delicious I'm glad I invited myself for tea."

Self-conscious she looked down at her culinary creation while Paul took up the compliments, "Maria's right. I thought you said you couldn't cook?"

Behind her as Beatty brought out a further dish containing the vegetables, the heat from the oven made her feel rather dizzy, but she ignored it to comment. "Your Gran is an excellent teacher."

Hot, and having difficulty focusing, she determined to concentrate and carefully lifted out two pancakes on to each plate. By the third portion her hand shook as she passed the plate to Paul. Quietly, under Maria's chatter to Bill, Paul asked, "Are you all right?"

Not wanting to bring attention to herself she assured him, "Yes, yes, I'm fine." But it wasn't true. The inability to see properly was making her feel sick. Was it getting even hotter in here? She dished out Beatty's share aware Paul was watching her. Only her pancakes were in the dish, it felt a struggle to coordinate her brain with her hands. Beatty said sharply, "Paul." A chair scraped across the lino.

A cool wind fanned across her face. Gradually she became aware of lying on the carpet with a cushion under her head, and recognized Maria's voice, "I think she's coming out of it." In a supreme effort she opened her eyes to see Beatty's face looming over her. "Just stay still, you fainted, probably the heat." With no energy to do anything else she closed her eyes against the oddly heavy, yet dizzy, fragile feeling. From the kitchen came murmuring and plates chinking. Maria fanning from above her assured her, "Gran's putting the dinners back in the oven, so just relax. We can eat when you feel better."

At Paul's voice she turned her head to see him kneeling beside her. "I don't know Jill, it's bad enough getting a call out when I'm eating, but I don't expect the cook to fall out before I've started."

Tears filled her eyes. She closed them and murmured, "I'm sorry."

"Hey, don't go all weepy on me, I was only teasing. I'm just going to take your blood pressure." He wrapped the cuff around her arm, the tightness expanded then stopped and in the silence he watched, listened and noted the readings before unwrapping her arm and announcing, "Could be better, could be worse, but you're not a hospital case. How do you feel?

With a gulp she managed to whisper, "Sick and shaky."

He gave an understanding smile and sitting hugging his knees he faced her to ask, "Now tell me Miss Reinhardt do you often faint off like that, because I've only known you a few days and this is the second time you've nearly passed out on me?"

"Never."

Beatty appeared with a bowl saying, "Just in case" and then admonished with a smile, "If ever Jill you have the slightest inclination that you don't feel well, it's wise to sit down. If Paul hadn't caught you, you could have been injured, hitting the table, dropping hot food on yourself. Anyway doc, what's your verdict, will she live?"

"Oh I think we can safely say 'yes' to that, but if you feel faint again you should go and see your own doctor for a check up."

At her feet Bill came into view. Resting both hands on his stick he leant forward to observe, "You have had a bit of a time of it luv one way and another which with physical and mental turmoil, broken sleep and nightmares. Each day it seems a new stressful event turns your stomach inside out, it's hardly surprising your body isn't coping." Beatty who had moved to stand beside Bill shot Paul a questioning look which caused him to frown.

"Umm a difficult time indeed". He pulled out a bottle from the open case at his feet. Tomorrow Jill if you are willing to do me a mid-stream water sample I'll have it tested for you. Gran have you got any fizzy lemonade?" Beatty shook her head.

Maria piped up, "I've got a bottle of Coke Cola."

Immediately Paul admonished, "I thought I said you shouldn't drink that stuff because it rots teeth."

Unperturbed Maria laughed, "I drink it, not soak my teeth in it. But you know as well as I that it's wonderful for sick stomachs so be pleased I have it to offer."

Paul's response was a quirky grin with a sigh. "Go and get it then. But remember too much is definitely not good for you." He turned his attention back to her. "Now Jill, I'll just pack up my things, help you from the dining room carpet to the settee and hopefully after that normal service will be resumed." He gave an amused tut. "And it'll be me fainting off with hunger next if I don't soon get to eat those delicious pancakes."

An hour later the drink had worked, she'd managed one pancake and Paul made short work of his two, and her second one. All had consumed with relish Ben's inventive recipe of chocolate cornflake nests filled with ice-cream and covered in a toffee nut sauce, a recipe Beatty had added to her collection.

Relaxed over coffee Paul took up what she saw as his favourite posture - legs stretched out before him, his hands laced behind his head. "Now Miss Reinhart I don't want to be accused of taking advantage of your weakened state, but I had hoped for another game of Rummy."

Pertly she countered, "Dr Stemmings the only advantage you could have over me would be praying to continually get a good hand, which in my book would be known as cheating, otherwise I have every expectation of beating you again."

A long low chortle preceded Paul's amused retort. "That's the first time I've heard prayer identified as cheating."

Bill grunted, "You've met your match there my boy, and if I was a betting man I'd be backing Jill."

Later, having beaten Paul again she suggested to Bill that next time they played Bill have that bet. Paul not to be outdone said it was beginner's luck and Bill would be foolish to waste his money! Beatty with underlying amusement said crossly, "I'll have no betting in this house, and if you and Jill have nothing better to do than bicker, go and make the drinks while Bill and I watch the news."

While they sat waiting for the kettle to boil Paul suggested, "I was wondering, having been incarcerated here for four days, if you'd like to go to the cinema - it's about ten minutes drive?" He smiled, "Don't look so surprised, you aren't a prisoner here. The films aren't always very up to date, but they're showing Dr Zhivago and I'd like to see it, and thought you might too."

It would be churlish to refuse outright so she fielded the invitation with caution. "I'd like to, but you spoke the other day about your girlfriend, and I wouldn't want to come between you. Paul's brow puckered. Slightly irritated at his non-understanding she prompted, "The woman who will probably think like me when it comes to bringing up children."

That brought his understanding, and he gave a broad smile on commenting, "Oh that woman!" He shook his head, "Oh that won't be a problem." The kettle boiled and he moved towards it as Maria came skipping into the kitchen to tuck her arm into his.

"Have you asked Jill? Is she coming with us?"

Paul patting the hand on his arm turned to look questioningly at her for an answer. To have their relationship confirmed was still a surprise for Maria looked so young beside him, yet she could understand the attraction, she had an intrinsic, as well as outward beauty. "If you don't mind Maria, then I'd love to come."

"Good, that's settled then. It's very sad. Do you think you'll cry? I'll bring some hankies!" Before Jill could answer she skipped back out to announce their outing to Bill and Beatty.

In a very passable tenor voice Paul sang as he poured the water into the teapot, "How do you solve a problem like Maria? How do you catch a cloud and pin it down? How do you find a word that means Maria? A flibbertijibbet! A will-o'-the wisp! A clown!

She clapped as he picked up the tray, "Oh very good, doesn't it go on, and without a passable singing voice, she said, "Many a thing you know you'd like to tell her, many a thing she ought to understand, But how to you make her stay, and listen to all you say?"

Paul gave an amused grunt. "How right that is, perhaps we ought to go and see 'The Sound of Music' instead?" And laughing they entered the lounge where Beatty shushed them because they were listening to News at Ten.

The next morning, although she still felt sick drinking the leftover Coca Cola stopped her actually being sick. Perhaps now she was on the mend. Maybe the faint last night had somehow realigned her body back to normality. The reduction of swelling to her foot enabled her to wear a size 8 Wellington boot on one foot and a size 6 on the other and, with the aid of Bill's stick do a tour of the rather cold and wet garden. Annoyed Barnie barked continuously, shut inside for fear he get too excited and knock her over.

They ate their main meal at lunch time, after which she left Bill and Beatty for their nap, and lay on her bed to read John's account of Jesus meeting the Samaritan woman at the well, and of his telling her she'd had five husbands and to go and sin no more. That struck a cord, for in that context she'd had far more than five! The telephone rang in the hall, Beatty answering called up, "Jill, it's your brother."

In her excitement she nearly fell down the stairs. Beatty gave her a broad smile, returned to the sitting room and closed the door. "David, I'm so pleased to hear from you. Is everything okay there? What's happening with Ben?"

David response was a rather stiff laugh. "And I am glad to talk to you! The police said they felt it safe to give your number, but I'm not to ask, nor you answer any questions that could in any way give information, just in case Rich's influence extends to tapping telephone lines." The way he grunted Jill assumed he found that idea extremely far fetched. "As to, 'is everything okay here', the answer is, No! And frankly if we hadn't been so worried about you, we would have been extremely angry. I can't imagine what possessed you to take off with Rich without so much as a by your leave, and if it hadn't been for God's divine grace you would now be kidnapped, hidden somewhere in Europe, and I gather, could even be dead!"

Jill shivered at his bluntness, but in her anxiety she pushed past his aggravation, to ask, "Have you seen Ben, how is he? Where is he? I gather there are no charges?"

"I know you're anxious Jill, but please be careful. I have seen Ben, he is well. Not at work because he's been sent on a training course in connection with his new job. That, and other things, have given him a lot to consider about his future, which still depends on various factors, but, you're right, there won't be any charges. The management of his new company are covering everything and being very forward thinking, but its left me in one hell of a mess with Brussels looming up in less than two weeks. Not to mention being short staffed with you off sick. Jane has come in as a temporary measure to help Rosemary and is trying to cover your job. Helen has been in a constant flood of tears not helped by your escapades. And both she and Rosemary were extremely upset on Monday because the police turned over your flat leaving quite a mess, and for a brief time Helen found herself in police custody because she had some cannabis stashed away in her bedroom. So, you can understand, everything has been far from 'right' here! Plus the fact Mum is worried sick picturing you in some ghastly refuge, but fortunately Dad has remained calm, relieved that you weren't kidnapped, and doing all he can to assist in every other way – he's been terrific. So without giving anything important away how are you?"

She exhaled a long breath. "Right David, thank you for all that, I think I can make sense of it all. And tell Dad thank you too. Tell Mum I'm fine, I had a swollen ankle, but that's getting better, and I've been sick to my stomach with all this worry, but I'm living with a couple, they have a lovely family and home, and if it

343

weren't for the circumstances it would be more like a holiday than an imprisonment."

David grunted and said in a cold tone, "How good that is for you. Unfortunately you seem to have little concept of the worry, disruption, annoyance and upset your stupidity has caused to others! The only saving grace is the fact that in helping the police with their enquiries they seem to be covering ground previously uncharted."

Cross she bit back, "I'm not stupid! And I am sorry for all the trouble I've caused everyone. But how could I know what would kick off from going away with Rich? And you can't tell me you've never made a mistake in your life. Granted it may not have had as far reaching consequences as this, but how was I to know that an innocent weekend would turn out this way? And there has been some good come out of it, but I'll keep that until I'm home."

In a business like fashion he replied, "Right! And has anyone said when that might be?"

"No, I was rather hoping you might know something. I assume you are on my case?"

Again came that annoyed grunt. "I didn't exactly have any option considering the circumstances. But obviously once all the information came together it became clear it was the truth, so all round it's now a case of waiting to see how things develop. So far we have nothing to report here, and I will be pushing for your return after the weekend because I need you at work. And as it is I will now have to take Jane to Brussels for she now has more idea of the work involved in that, than you. Jane's here, she wants a 'brief' word with you."

Jill could imagine the look that flashed between them before Jane was saying, "Hi Jill, I gather you are alright. We've been so worried."

"God that brother of mine is a pain. No sympathy vote there. And if I was you I'd slap him for saying 'as it is I'll now have to take Jane to Brussels' as if you're going to disturb the well run order of his life."

The grimace was obvious in Jane's voice, "I did last time. But David didn't mean it that way. He's under a lot of pressure. We're ringing from the office on his private line. Don't worry about 'things' David and your dad have been amazing. And they do love you, despite the flack you've just received. Rosemary and I stayed up most of Monday night putting the flat back to rights, while David blew fire and fury over the police for the chaos they

344

left, and rescued Helen from their clutches. Poor Helen was already upset from the weekend because Ben was away, you know this course thing, but the police, and then David on her case, reduced her to a babbling wreck"

"Is she okay now? I'm so sorry Jane, do tell everyone. It was a series of events I couldn't have foreseen or forestalled."

"Don't worry, Helen understands that. Through this and because of the baby they've allowed her to be with Ben." A stab of jealousy hit her. Why couldn't they have arranged for her to be with him? Jane was continuing, "...it's hard to believe about Rich." Jane lowered her voice, "David's just gone to talk to Rosemary." She giggled, "If the place you are in is nice, stay away as long as possible, it's hell here! David's been working all hours with your problems, and with organizing Brussels, and you can imagine, he's been like a bear with a sore head. But you'll love this. David so upset Rosemary yesterday that she overcame her intimidation to say sharply, 'Rudeness and impatience doesn't behove you Mr Reinhardt' then carried on with her typing as if she hadn't spoken. I thought I'd imagined those few succinct words, but David stared at her, then glared at me, and when I smiled and nodded, he marched into his office and slammed the door! Rosemary didn't bat an eyelid and said nothing more. But I'd say it brought David up short, and he's gained a new respect for her, and life is less fraught here, and at home! He's coming back. I'll have to go in a minute."

"Good for Rosemary, tell her I said so! And I've lots to tell you. Remember that police surgeon, Paul Stemmings who looked after you, well believe it or not, he looked after me when they took me to the Police Station. I'd fallen heavily and hurt my ankle. Anyway, he recognized me, or our name. I didn't recognise him at first, he hasn't got his beard now, he organised this refuge for me. I wish I could tell you more details."

"I liked him. He had such lovely kind eyes."

"I feel much the same. And, you will love this, he and his family are Christians."

"Really! I did wonder when I met him. If I remember you felt unusually drawn towards him, what about now?"

"I have felt a friendship thing, nothing else, but to be honest I'm too busy worrying about Ben, and I rather think Ben will be a hard act to follow. I do have some news that you will be pleased about, but I'll wait until I'm back."

"Oh tell me now. Oh, okay David, yes, I know we have work

to do! The man's a slave driver, umm but I love him." Jill grinned just talking to Jane was a tonic she could just see her casting a loving look at David, and responding frown. "It's very strange to be back working here. David's not altogether pleased with the arrangement, but as I said to him, he's lucky to have me, and I'm quite looking forward to Brussels. By then let's hope this situation is resolved. Yes, okay David, he's saying I must go, we'll have a good chat when you're back. See you soon, take care, bye."

Despite David's rather heartless conversation, Jane made up for it, and she felt quite cheered, except for the police turning her flat over. Poor Helen, but at least she was with Ben through it. What were her Mum and Dad making of the tangled weave of her life? It was surprising to hear of her father lending his support to Ben, but then he had saved his daughter from kidnap, she shivered, and possible murder.

With a sense of fun she prepared a special presentation to Paul of a ribbon endowed filled specimen bottle. With a wry smile she presented it to him when he came to collect her for the cinema with the words, "Now don't say I've never given you anything."

Immediately with an equally dry voice he retorted, "And they do say it's the thought that counts!" With that he took hold of her arm and helped her down the path to where Maria was waiting in the car.

On the way she made them laugh as she filled them in on her conversation with David and Jane.

Predictably she did cry, especially at the end when Dr Zhivago suddenly spots Lara the lost love of his life, chases her through the streets only to have a heart attack and die before he could reach her. They were still wiping their eyes and discussing the sad bits when Paul arrived with the car to collect them. In an amused tone he commented, "I don't know, you women get so emotional, it's only a story!" Then added, "It was a long film, so straight home and to bed for you both."

Through her sniffles she laughed at Maria's cheeky reply of, "Yes Dad" and agreeing with her sentiment, retorted, "She's right, if not a Dad, you sound bossy like my brother." She giggled and told how Jane had been amused on the day Paul had attended her, because he'd so cleverly engineered David out of his own office, and commented that it wasn't often David met his match.

In following doctor's orders she lay in bed and considered that the film might only be as Paul said, 'a story', but life did have its twists and turns, and she knew what it was to lose, twice, the man she thought might be Mr. Right.

A trilling voice, which is recognised as Maria's, awoke her. Yawning she turned to find Barnie's head resting on the bed his sad eyes looking at her, and Maria's bright ones insisting, "Come on, wake up, here's your breakfast. It's Saturday, we're off shopping, time for you to step back into the real world."

Maria was right, a 'normal' activity was just what she needed, so she sat, took the tray and agreed, "I'd like that." While Maria talked about the film she began her breakfast. "Wasn't Paul a darling to buy us that box of chocolates?" She nodded as she was munching a mouthful of cornflakes, and smiled inwardly at Maria's adoration of Paul. Maria laughed, "Although having ate so many I did feel sick afterwards."

At the thought of sweet, sickly chocolates, Jill swallowed her mouthful to ask, "I don't suppose you have a bottle of Coke have you, because just mentioning those chocolates is making me feel sick?"

"Gosh is it. You know what Paul said about the stuff, but we can buy some at the..."

Hastily pushing the tray to one side, she moved to get out of bed. Maria acted as crutch to get her to the bathroom as quickly as possible. Why was her stomach still so easily upset? Surely not with chocolate, and it was a week since her fright with Rich? On her return Maria was waiting and concerned, suggesting she stay in bed, but she reassured her that after sitting quietly and sipping her tea, she would probably be fine. And half an hour later she was right, and determined to go out to buy some Cola or lemonade to avoid further sickness.

It was good to walk around the supermarket, and made her keen to get back into her life. Yet the outing, the thought of the flat, her bedroom and its memories began her mind's descent into depression causing Maria's immature babbling, Beatty's continual cookery teaching and Bill's droning on about their family, get on her nerves. Her urge was to murder Rich, hate Helen, and scream at anyone who thwarted her. So much for having Jesus in your life! But perhaps her life had been so bad Jesus hadn't been able to accept her? She didn't feel 'born again' more dead and buried in what she now knew to be classified by God as sin! Afraid she might be rude to the people who had done nothing but be kind to her she excused herself as quickly as possible after lunch.

Vexed she snatched up the Bible from the bedside table and challenged, "Hey Jesus, if you do speak through your Word, say

347

something to me?" The page opened at 2 Corinthians 4, and she started reading it aloud from verse 16 because it seemed relevant. "'These troubles and suffering of ours are, after all, quite small, and won't last very long'." She asked, "Jesus is that true?" Then continuing, "'Yet this short time of distress will result in God's richest blessing…'" Jill grunted, "Now God that's what I want to believe." She read on, 'So we do not look at what we can see right now, the troubles all around us, but we look forward to the joys of heaven… The troubles will soon be over.' Well God, that's your Word so I will take your promises and comfort, although it's easier said, than done!"

Her thoughts went back to her recurring nightmare. The rope across the chasm, the granite rocks on either side, the need to cross from one side to the other; stretching, falling, expectancy of dying, but there was something more. That hand, grasping hers. It had given her something – what was it? In her mind she re-ran the end of the dream. No wonder she hadn't noticed it, it was a small seed. She pondered that and picked up the Bible to flick through it. To her amazement the word 'seed' in Luke 8 seemed to jump out at her. What was this about? She read about seeds falling on hard paths represented hard hearts, and no growth. Falling in stony ground meant God's message heard, but no soil to root in. Then falling among thorns, listened to, but choked by worries of life. But seed that fell in good soil represented people who listened, clung to the truth and told others what they believed about God's word. That sounded like Jane and Beatty. Jane often talked about forgiveness. She closed the Bible and snuggled under the eiderdown. Forgiveness? God had already told her to forsake wrath and anger, so maybe that was what was missing, she needed to forgive people. Impossible, yet maybe if she asked God for help… "Right Jesus I ask you to help me forgive Rich for…" She concentrated on naming the things the man had done, and within minutes drifted into sleep.

The large hand that had caught her when falling was now holding her gently, and seemed like a parachute, allowing her to drift as a feather downward into the valley below. Below was a bubbling stream flowing over rocks between the two granite walls that enclosed her. The winds direction changed to allow her to drift along towards an ever widening blue sky, bringing a sense of coming out of darkness into light. The stream below widened, and was gathering momentum, she could hear rushing water, and as she came over the waterfall tumbling some considerable feet below into a pool, a warm light infused her, similar to the sun coming through glass on a winter's day. There was such peace in this enclosed, quiet world. She floated past the pond gradually loosing height as she followed the course of the deepening flowing river and the widening area of grassy bank on each side. Instinctively she knew her seed had fallen this way, carried on the same wind as her body, her prayer was it would fall on good soil, imbed and grow into all it was destined to be. Her body bounced slightly as it touched down on the green, verdant bank, her face became slicked with the wetness of dew. Her hand went to dry it and instantly she awoke.

Standing over her, his huge panting tongue inches from her nose was the big hairy body of Barnie! Laughing she demanded, "Get off me you wretched dog" and with that she playfully wrestled with him on the bed while he barked delightedly. The dream fresh in her mind, and the fun with Barnie had her almost bouncing downstairs.

Beatty sitting in the lounge commented, "You look better than earlier, doesn't she Bill?"

Bill nodded as she replied, "That's probably because I feel different. Barnie's just awoken me from a dream which I can only describe as being the next phase of that nightmare. I've gone beyond the 'dying bit' and found, 'new life'. I feel excited and happy."

"We can see that dear. I sensed this morning there was a battle going on inside you. And this proves prayer is a wonderful thing." Tears formed in Beatty's eyes, and Jill couldn't resist hugging her. "So do you want to tell us about it?"

"The other night I asked Jesus into my life, but today I felt I was struggling." She went on to tell them and finished, "I know He is the one who has made me feel lighter, freer, and it's because I have begun to forgive Rich, and others. I feel in a new place, with a new life, in fact eternal life."

Bill clearly affected by her words agreed, "God's forgiveness is a wonderful gift. Not just our being forgiven, but the ability for us to forgive those who have hurt us. It takes away anger, bitterness, brings peace and rest. Mind, it's not a one off thing, we have to live a life of forgiving for us to truly understand all that Jesus' death has provided."

Beatty nodded. "I knew God wanted to break through, but felt it had to be Him and you, so you would understand its all about a relationship with God, Jesus and Holy Spirit. I could only point you in the right direction. The Father longs to bless you and give you the desires of your heart."

"That's odd Beatty for God showed me those verses the first time I picked up that Bible by the bed."

Bill smiled as Beatty proclaimed, "That's my God. You talk to him, wait and He speaks, and the name of Jesus' is powerful when you call on Him. The Bible says 'all things work together for good for those in Christ Jesus', so He'll work everything out for you."

And Bill added, "And remember the Holy Spirit He will be a guide and comfort, talk to Him too. I did, He found me my Beatty and He's kept us as a match made in heaven."

Although Beatty smiled and nodded she seemed to be seeing something in her mind's eye.

"Oh Bill you are an old romantic. I've loved and lost twice I'm not sure that's possible."

"Everything is possible with the Lord, so don't let past experiences stop you being open to that."

Beatty coming out of her reverie said briskly, "Enough! It's time to put on the dinner. Jill come, give me a hand. Maria and Paul are coming again tonight because Maria wants to see the previously invincible Paul beaten for a third time at Rummy!"

Within a minute of Paul and Maria's arrival Bill was initiating the conversation to draw her to tell them of her new found relationship with Jesus. Maria bubbled excitedly, "I asked Jesus into my life when I was three, I was sitting on the toilet at the time, and since it's always been a place of revelation."

Paul with a quirky smile looked heavenward and muttered, "Incorrigible".

Jill laughed, "Maybe that's why the toilet in some circles is called, 'the throne room'."

Maria chuckled, "Oh I like it, and I like you. You shall be my friend forever." Jill caught the small smile between Bill and Beatty, and wondered what was behind the unreadable expression on Paul's face as he gazed upon Maria's animated one. Maria thrusting her arm through hers drew her towards the kitchen saying, "Come on Gran lets have the dinner, and then we can play Rummy."

Paul from behind commented, "What you mean 'incorrigible one' is you want to see Jill beat me again, to make it a hat trick."

Turning Maria agreed, "Of course, you've been too big for your boots for far too long."

Maria seeing Paul's fingers flexing with the threat of tickling giggled. "Protect me Jill for I'm on your side."

Beatty intervened, "That will do. Dinner is ready."

Much to Paul's chagrin and Maria's pleasure she beat him again, but he insisted with much bantering he'd get even one day.

For the first time since she'd stayed with Bill and Beatty she slept all night without tossing and turning in discomfort and awoke early enough to go down and get her own breakfast. As a precaution she'd bought several bottles of lemonade, so before she even felt nauseous she drank a glass. It was assumed she was going to Church with the family, just as she assumed Church would be a place of silent reverence, old fashioned hymns, set prayers, hard pews and an old man droning on about God. And she'd been wondering how necessary was it for a Christian to go to church?

But she was pleasantly surprised, for it reminded her of visiting Jane's church before she was going out with David. It was noisy and friendly before the service, the songs were upbeat, prayers came from the people, and although there were pews they had thick padded cushions! A young man stood at the front his words making the congregation laugh which meant it was a while before she realised he was preaching the sermon.

Afterwards she met the heavily pregnant Jenny with Craig and Sandra at her skirts. To her surprise they remembered her, and Hugh took charge the moment they began to squabble leaving Jenny to whisper, "We've been reading at bedtime, they've been falling asleep after half an hour so thank you for suggesting that."

It appeared all the Stemmings family went to church by the number introduced to her by Paul or Beatty. Bob and Lilian, Maria's parents joined them for a late, but delicious roast beef dinner with Yorkshire puddings. After which they went for a walk in the local park while Beatty and Bill had their customary nap. But only she, Paul and Maria returned to the cottage, where to give Beatty a break, she and Maria insisted they prepare the tea which they would eat after watching Songs of Praise on the TV. She couldn't help think 'how boring', but didn't voice her opinion. The evening news began just as they joined the others in the lounge. "Tonight's breaking news is of an explosion in Wembley, in which it is thought a man might have died. We have pictures just back from the scene."

To see the fourteen inch black and white television Jill moved nearer then sat, hugging her knees, on the carpet at Bill's feet. On the screen they could see firemen working to douse the smoke on a still smouldering car on the shared drive of two houses. Curtains at both houses were wafting in the cold night air showing the blast had blown out the windows. Jill spoke to the room at large, "That house and car are similar to Ben's. He's had trouble with his car and strikes me the sooner he gets rid of it the better."

The newscaster continued, "It is suspected that the owner of the car was caught in the blast. The occupants of one of the houses sharing the drive said there had been a loud bang, their house shook, and as their windows shattered their reaction was to dive under the dining room table as they'd done in the war when the bombs dropped. When they ventured out the fire engines were already on their way, and the car was burning fiercely between their two houses. Our reporter brought back this interview from the scene."

"I believe Mr Edgecombe you live across the street. Could you describe what you saw?"

An elderly man with a quivery voice answered, "Terrible it was. That car of his, been trouble ever since he had it. There was an almighty bang…" Overcome with emotion he paused then composing himself he continued, "I saw him out there with the bonnet up. I went to make a pot of tea, then heard the bang and felt the blast as my windows rattled. I looked out, but there weren't anything I could do, but call the fire brigade. I reckon it were the electrics, then the petrol took it, it went up like a torch. He was such a lovely, polite boy, I've known Ben since he were a littlen, lost his Dad earlier this year, he and his girlfriend were decorating, getting married…" The old man's voice broke, the recording stopped, and the broadcast returned to the newsroom where the presenter continued, "Police at the scene have now cordoned off the area and residents of the damaged houses have been evacuated until the air has cleared. Other news…"

Rigid in shock and disbelief Jill sat there. Ben, bright-eyed, cheeky, loveable Ben was dead! In self preservation she'd denied her love, but in death and its finality… The telephone rang as misery encompassed her, and a knot of hysteria built inside. Pictures of Ben and their time together paraded through her mind. How could God let that happen? But He hadn't, it was all her fault. If only she hadn't gone off with Rich, he'd be alive now. What about his baby? It would never know the man who'd accidentally given them life? How would Helen cope? An internal scream of agony built within her how could she live knowing because of her, adorable Ben, was dead. Head bent she subconsciously tightened her arms around her legs as though to do so would squeeze the very breath out of her body.

A hand grabbed at her jerking her to her feet. Wildly she looked around as Beatty turned off the TV, Maria was frowning at Paul who was gripping the top of her arms demanding "Jill look at me" and Bill whose feet she'd been sitting at said querulously, "What's going on? I was watching that."

With unfocussed eyes she obeyed Paul and heard him say in a. clear and concise voice, "Ben is not dead". He didn't know, he didn't understand, it was Ben. Gently he shook her, "I want you to hear me Jill, the news report is wrong, Ben is not dead?"

In a stupor she murmured in a questioning echo, "Not dead? But it said...?"

From behind her Beatty said abruptly, "Bill, Maria, to the kitchen, we'll pour the tea."

Unable to take it in she stared into Paul's eyes searching for truth. The flecks of gold seemed to grow and glow as he repeated, "Ben isn't dead. David as just rung, Ben is perfectly safe. It wasn't Ben, but it was Ben's car, outside his house. The neighbour probably saw the a young man planting the device and assumed it was Ben, but he didn't see the actual explosion." The words, the truth began to penetrate her numbed state, Ben wasn't dead. Paul sat her in the chair vacated by Bill, and crouched beside her. "Forgive us for not picking up on the news item, and me for catapulting you out of your shocked state. If you want cry, my shoulder is free, or we can go in the kitchen and get a nice hot, sweet cup of tea." 'Ben isn't dead' became an internal mantra as she tried to readjust from sorrow to relief. Tears rolled down her cheeks, Paul proffered a handkerchief, she wiped her eyes, blew her nose, as he waited, watching her. "Better now?" She nodded. "Right, let's get you a cup of tea."

Still numb she could only listen to the discussion and speculation at the tea table. An hour later policeman Phil arrived with an air of assumed authority to inform them that since the news report a seriously injured young man had been found under a hedge in a neighbour's garden. The police were assuming he was the perpetrator of the crime, rather than a passer-by blown there by the blast. The certainty was a device had been planted, probably to await Ben's return, but had exploded prematurely.

Rather pleased with his role of informant Phil continued magisterially to report that Miss Rosemary Dawes had reported that morning that a blonde-haired, young cockney woman, leaning on a broom and smoking outside a neighbour's house, had given her the impression she was their cleaner when she stopped her to ask questions about their household. Suspicious she'd alerted Mrs Reinhardt and together they'd watched the woman get into a car with her broom. They had taken the car's number plate, but when traced it was later found abandoned.

From the description Jill smiled, "That, Phil was Ange, Chris' girlfriend. She told me she had acting abilities, so obviously someone requested she put them into practice, probably to glean information on my whereabouts."

Phil stood, "I'd best be off then with that, so they can apprehend her as soon as possible. Oh, and I'm to tell you that DCI Maysfield recommends that you stay here until we can reassess the situation." On her nod of agreement he was out the door while they continued to discuss the latest events.

CHAPTER 21

So began her second week as part of the Stemmings extended family. The days fell into a similar pattern to the week before except she insisted on having breakfast in the kitchen, and as a precaution against sickness drank a glass of lemonade each morning before getting out of bed. Happy that Ben was still alive, she wanted to extend that sentiment to his being with Helen, and accept their enforced separation had just come sooner than envisaged. For two days she resisted the inner conviction she should write releasing him to Helen, and then spent many tearful hours putting together a letter, which she sent to David to pass on.

Each day she and David had spoken on the telephone he remained miffed at her non-return to work, but Jane was thoroughly enjoying being back at ITP saying, "I love your job. I'll happily take it on if you don't want to come back." On Thursday with David away, Jane rang. Her voice was serious as she reported, "Helen came back last night. She looks awful and not very coherent or informative. I gathered that despite the boarding up of Ben's house and the damage within, the police have issued a warrant to search it for drugs and insist she goes with them. She kept repeating, 'I can't do this without Ben.' Then in despair crying pitifully she added, 'It's all ruined, it's all ruined.'

"I tried to tell her the insurance company would cover it, and it would probably work in their favour, but words didn't comfort her, and she cried even harder when I said she and Ben would soon be together again. In the end I hugged and prayed with her, but I can see with all this, and Ben not being here, how alone she must feel. This afternoon she's going home for a couple of days. I suspect too she's worried about her parent's reaction to her 'having to get married because she's expecting a baby'. Poor girl, it's been one thing after another.

Before Jill could comment Jane continued, "Our house is still under surveillance. That police woman staying here does look a bit like you, but she hasn't stirred up any action. Rosemary is doing well in rising to the occasion both in work and at home. And David, of course, is still relying on your being back at work next Monday. Let's hope the police agree. Oh, I have to go, much love.

See you soon."

Jill smiled into the telephone for she'd had no opportunity to speak! Within a second of putting the receiver back in its cradle, it rang again so she answered it.

"Ah! Jill just the person! I've got a couple of days off and thought you might like to have a change of scenery. How about we go for a drive and have lunch at a nice place I know?"

Surprised by Paul's offer, she instantly responded, "I'd like that, but what about Maria, will she mind?"

There was a chuckle, "Ah, the incorrigible Maria. I rather think as she suggested it that she likes you."

"Then the feeling is mutual, she's a lovely girl Paul, you are lucky to have her love."

"Blessed I am. I'll pick you up in about an hour."

There seemed a speculative look in Beatty's eyes as she told her of Paul's invitation so felt she should add, "Paul said Maria suggest it."

"I'm pleased that she is so taken with you."

Puzzled she commented, "Paul said much the same. Doesn't she usually like the people who come here? What I've seen of her she seems such a friendly, open and happy girl?"

"Maria has her moments like every teenager, but where Paul is concerned she can be very protective."

"I'm not surprised he obviously means a lot to her, and vice versa."

Beatty gathered up the dirty crockery from the table. "Now dear if you are going out for lunch I think we'll have our dinner at lunch time, and have something light for tea. I know the place Paul has in mind, it's lovely and the food excellent, so you won't want much later."

Paul arrived in smart trousers, shirt, tie and jumper, but there wasn't anything pretentious about him. He drove a comfortable and reasonably spacious Hillman Minx; their discussion ranged from mundane likes and dislikes, topical news items and the inevitable weather which today displayed a clear, bright blue sky, and a relative warm sun through the windscreen of the car. The green tranquillity of the rolling hills and fields through the window matched the atmosphere within as they drove through Kent and its quaint and attractive villages. After an hour Paul announced, "Here we are, 'The Water Mill Hotel' where I can recommend the best duck in blackberry sauce that I have ever tasted."

"Umm now that sounds good I've a bit of penchant for duck."

Paul led the way across the cobbled courtyard through the narrow, low door, into a cosy bar area of wooden beams, filled bookcases, little nooks and crannies where comfortable chairs and low tables resided. A welcoming fire billowed up a wide red-bricked chimney from behind a wrought iron grate. The room wasn't dissimilar to the library at home, except that was of the Georgian era, and this looked more 17th century. Beyond she could see an equally attractive restaurant where thick cushioned, high-backed settles created booths to give a sense of privacy to the diners. "If you don't mind we'll eat first, we can have our coffee in the lounge." She smiled her assent, and followed Paul. After speaking to a waitress, she led them to a table for two which fitted comfortably in the bay window.

Paul remarked as he pulled out her chair, "It's better here in the summer, the gardens are usually a riot of colour. They put out comfortable chairs and tables so diners can eat and enjoy the churning water of the mill upstream. Look you can see it."

"This is a lovely place even on a winter's day. It was kind of you to invite me."

"My pleasure and I'll admit to being curious about David and Jane's romance and the events that led up to you waiting for my medical..."

The interruption of the waitress' turned their conversation to choices of white or red wine, their starter and main course. David and Jane's story had Paul laughing and she'd only just finished it when her smoked salmon terrine, and Paul's liver pate arrived. Paul's questions drew her to talk of Ben's arrival in her life, her dislike of him and why that changed. She told of how Ben had lost the career he loved, and the blow to their relationship.

It was fortuitous the main course arrived when it did for Paul's brown, gold flecked eyes were glistening over-brightly at Ben's misfortunes. And, his empathy, with her emotion bubbling so near the surface made it harder for her to suppress hers. To offset that she drained her second glass of wine, and noted Paul did the same. Their glasses refilled they turned their attention to the duck, with side dishes of freshly cooked vegetables. As predicted, it was delicious and they enjoyed it in comparative silence.

The main course dishes removed Paul gave his quirky smile and reminded her, "So we'd got to the bit where, before disaster struck, Ben, in loving you, and with his medical knowledge, brings a combination that begins to captivate your mind and body.

357

Isn't it strange how we spend hours practicing how to drive a car, read the Highway Code, use maps to navigate, yet seem to think that sexual compatibility needs no education or working on."

"Jane said David read books." She grinned at Paul's cynical expression, "Yes, well I suspect he'd had some experience too! But you're right, for few men have taken time to ask what turns me on, but Ben was always one step ahead, full of surprises and constantly checking my responses."

"Clever man. Yet it's that caring for the whole person which brings a oneness in the giving and receiving of pleasure and makes that union an almost spiritual experience." Paul chuckled, "How did we get on to that. Now would you like a sweet course, or shall we just have coffee?"

"For me just coffee, but the sweet menu looks tempting so don't let me stop you."

"Oh I think I've had sufficient, and I'm sure you would appreciate a comfy chair, in an undisturbed corner with a pot of coffee we can drink at our leisure."

Paul may not attract her sexually, but his attentiveness was in itself an attraction. He'd listened, questioned, commented, and she imagined when needed, he gave good and kind advice. The ideal doctor, yet she was coming to understand that it was the extra dimension of the Holy Spirit that brought this kind of wisdom and discernment.

It was only as they left their table she became aware of the hum of other diners around them. Paul steered her through the lounge, away from the main thoroughfare, to a quiet corner. And carefully selected for her a high backed, comfortable chair facing away from anyone who might pass by. He then pulled up another to sit at an angle to her, but in a position to see and ward off anyone approaching. He gave a quirky smile, "This is as private as I can make it, because, if you don't mind, I've many questions to ask, and know there is still a story to tell." With this thoughtfulness and interest she wasn't surprised Paul was Maria's hero!

The pot of coffee arrived quickly, along with a small basket of mints. Paul's polite thanks to the waitress was as if she'd done him a favour rather than a service. He poured it, handed her a cup, and with warm brown eyes filled with sympathy queried, "When Helen declared the child was Ben's you must have been devastated."

With a deep sigh, she drew in her lips and then admitted, "I don't know what I felt. Ben in thinking he'd no chance with me had only slept once with Helen, but it had made baby, which was rotten bad luck. I've spent hours thinking around the problem. Rosemary and I said we'd support Helen through pregnancy. Ben offered her financial support, but she said she couldn't contemplate bringing up a child on her own. Equally Ben is adamant his child isn't to be murdered or adopted." She shrugged, "What other choice is there, but that he marries her?"

Gently Paul probed, "But if you were in Helen's situation where marrying the father would cause unhappiness to another, what would you do?"

Jill gave a rueful grimace, "It would be different for me than Helen. Dad has always maintained we should stand on our own two feet, but I'm sure the family would support me. My father has proved that because it would seem he has put himself out to give Ben a much needed refuge. I'd prefer to remain single than know my husband loved another, or to be like my friend Gemma who married to get a father for her child and has become a slave to a man just for a legality." She looked down at her hands and confessed, "But I'll admit to hoping Helen might miscarry." The voicing of that, brought a deep twist of pain. Tears threatened, but she managed to say, "I, I wrote to Ben on Tuesday and w-wished him, Helen and the baby every h-happi…" The words stuck in her throat, tears overflowed and embarrassed she delved into her handbag for a handkerchief.

Paul sat forward to say quietly, "That was a brave thing to do, for it's obvious you care for him." Thoughtfully he added, "Perhaps enforced separation is harder to cope with than death. Don't deny the grief, and know you now have the Holy Spirit who is the Comforter, allow Him to help you look forward, rather than back, or to what might have been."

After dabbing her eyes, she blew her nose and agreed, "Ben said something similar. For him, life certainly hasn't been fair, and although I wasn't sure about Rich, it never occurred to me going out with him would come to this."

"So where does Rich fit into this?

As she launched into the story she recognized that Paul exuded that same enveloping peace she found with Jane. When she finished Paul appeared deep in thought, and looking at her watch she exclaimed, "I can't believe it's five o'clock. You should have been a psychiatrist you are such a wonderful listener – I must have been talking now for about four hours."

That quirky smile and his words reassured her. "Time Jill well spent. And I do have a couple more questions, you don't have to answer them."

"Have you got time?"

"I have, but I think first I'll order a pot of tea." That done Paul gave one of his quirky smiles and said, "From the things we've talked of I get the impression you've not been short of intimacy with men, but what started you on that road?"

Do you really want to know?" Paul's little nod and smile of compassion caused to her think that he knew so much about her already he might as well know the rest, which had her telling her darkest secrets without a qualm as she laid bare her soul.

At the end Paul changed his contemplative expression to say with sincerity, "I feel honoured you've felt you could talk so openly and honestly with me, I really appreciate it."

Pleased and surprised she countered, "And do you know what I appreciate about you? Paul, with a wry expression shook his head. She expounded, "It's the way you have listened to me without criticism, judgment or rejection. And probably why I have felt comfortable to speak to you of things I would rarely share with anyone. When I first met you I felt drawn to you, as if I knew you, but I see now it's the empathy and compassion of Jesus in you, and talking to you, well it's like talking to Jesus himself."

Paul's eyes glowed gold as they glistened with emotion. "I don't think Jill you realise what an amazing compliment that is." From his trouser pocket he pulled out his handkerchief, this time it was he who dabbed his eyes and blew his nose several times. In between, he stated, "Jesus is known as the wonderful counsellor. My desire is always to help others. You sensing that, well it's an answer to my prayers to have that aspect of His character revealed through me."

"Then I'm pleased I told you. And Maria is a very lucky girl to have your love. And I think it's time you did some talking. I want to know how you came to fall in love with her."

Paul gave an amused grunt and as his mind went to Maria his eyes filled with love. "Ah Maria! Now there is a tale."

"You said she'd been a fan of yours since two. But you must admit it's unusual for a man to wait for a child to grow up? Maria wants to go to university. She'll meet boys of her own age there. It's not really my business, and I don't mean to be rude, but haven't there been other women in your life of an age similar to you who'd be more suitable. Let's face it, you are probably old enough to be her father."

Even as she was speaking, Paul's eyes began filling with amusement, now he chuckled and lent forward to agree. "That's very true Jill, because you see I am old enough, and I am her father."

Astonished, Jill's mouth fell open. She threw her hands wide to exclaim, "You're what?"

Paul bantered, "Surely that's more feasible than me waiting for a two year old to grow up to marry her? Maria is seventeen, her mother was the same age as Maria is now. When she was born I was nineteen and in my first year at med. school. I'll add here that Maria is the spitting image of her mother, so you can see why I was attracted to her. She was a student nurse, which is why I think Maria is more called to nursing than policing."

Still reeling, but wanting to know she asked hesitantly, "So, so, where's Maria's mother now?"

Paul gave a rueful grimace, "Well perhaps it's my turn to start at the beginning. But as it is now seven o'clock and I could do with a drink, I'll get a beer, what would you like?"

She watched him go to the bar, while her mind worked overtime in considering Maria as his daughter. So her arithmetic had been right, Paul was thirty-six.

Once settled back in the chair, the drinks and snacks before them Paul gave a crooked grin before asking, "Are you sitting comfortably then I'll begin. It starts with a boy being away from home and the temptation of lots of girls living in the nurses' home and an easy target for a bit of romance, or to be blunt sexual pleasures. And because the girls were practically locked up like prisoners, the risk and the danger made it all the more exciting." He took a long drink of his beer.

"I'll add here my faith was very much Sunday School stuff and seemed irrelevant to life. I wasn't as it's called, 'born again' until later. So I did a bit of riotous living, drinking and wild parties where if a girl knew you were training to be a doctor they practically threw themselves at you. However there was one beautiful blue-eyed blonde who seemed shy of males, and yet so very sweet. I tried dating her, but my reputation put her off. Oh yes I had one, even at eighteen! With this face girls assumed I was older. You can see I could hardly condemn you for what I'd done myself? Concurrent with having a good time, I began worming my way into her affections by trying to be where she was."

Paul chuckled, "Not unlike your Ben! I constantly encouraged, and helped her, and being a good listener she began to trust me. Then her parents were killed in a car crash, and with no near relatives, it was to me she came. Distressed and almost out of her mind I brought her to Gran and Gramps, they gave her a refuge with lots of love and care, between us we arranged the funeral. Her stay started as a week, drifted into two months. Beth's studies got behind, in the end Gran and Gramps suggested she get a local job, stay with them and resume her nursing training later.

Jill put down her glass of wine. "Beth, Beatty mentioned that name when telling me of people who had stayed with them. She said how they'd loved her, and thought you'd never got over her."

"Dear Gran, I have, but I suppose I have run away from that kind of heartbreak since. Anyway I was totally besotted with Beth, as she with me. Gran and Gramps could see how it was between us and with no other family, it just seemed right to adopt Beth into ours by marrying. I was nineteen in that March and we married on Beth's seventeenth birthday in the May. There weren't contraceptive pills, I did take precautions, but she was pregnant in two months. Gran and Gramps said we could continue to live with them. It wasn't what we planned. I was a student and tried to transfer to a teaching hospital nearer, but that proved more difficult than we thought. Beth had a job as an auxiliary nurse in the local hospital, and she hoped to back to nursing training after the baby was born. With different shifts and living with Gran and Gramps we thought it could work out. Have you heard of pre-eclampsia?"

"Isn't that when pregnant women find their hands and feet swell up?"

"Yes but it's more than that, if it's very severe it can lead to kidney failure, liver problems, or even stroke. Pre-eclampsia is treatable once it's been diagnosed, eclampsia is rare. I was still very early on in my studies, not able to be with Beth as much as I'd have liked and didn't recognize it developing. Beth had morning sickness that continued throughout most of her pregnancy, and later she suffered from what appeared to be migraine headaches. In those days pregnant women didn't have the checks they do today, so it wasn't until her feet started to swell it occurred to me to take her blood pressure and it was well over the recommended limits. I rang the doctor, he immediately said she should be hospitalised and there they found protein in her urine. By now she was thirty-two weeks pregnant. The only cure is delivering the baby, but they wanted it to develop as long as possible before inducing the birth. They brought her blood pressure down, constantly monitored her, but at thirty-six weeks it suddenly rose and Beth had a fit which fortunately only lasted a minute or so. Immediately her vital signs were stable they delivered the baby by caesarean section. Being a medic I was let in to see Beth as soon as she came around, she was so thrilled with her little girl, we decided to call her Maria."

Deep sadness filled his eyes as he leant forward, picked up his beer and took a long mouthful. Guessing what was to come she instinctively moved forward to touch his arm, her expression one of sympathy.

"It's alright Jill, it was a long time ago. A few minutes later another fit seized Beth, the lack of oxygen to the brain caused severe brain damage and within days her bodily functions began to close down. I have never felt so inadequate in my entire life. There I was training to be a doctor and couldn't save my own wife. What it did was push me into learning harder and faster, and for the first two years of Maria's life I barely saw her, and in a way didn't want to see her, she reminded me too much of what I'd lost."

"Beatty said Bob and Lilian had adopted her."

"Yes, they found they couldn't have children of their own, so it seemed sensible for them to look after her, although once she was old enough they told her I was her real father. It wasn't until Maria's second birthday I really saw her for the first time. She was toddling about, chatting away and I crouched down to say 'hello'. To my surprise she put her arms around my neck and I swear she said, "love dad dad'. I tell you Jill my heart leapt in my chest, such a response of love welled up within me. It was as if Beth through Maria was saying, 'Love her, you are her Daddy, don't deny her of that, and I will live for you through her'. It was then I saw the resemblance, she won my heart that day, and I always say it was from then I became her hero. And although I am her official Dad, I'm probably more like the doting uncle. I'd entrusted Maria to Bob and Lilian's care I couldn't deny them and take her back so I threw myself into studying, and later it was easier to keep travelling abroad to help others rather than see what I was missing out on."

"That must have been a hard, but a choice that seems to have paid off. Maria is a lovely girl, and takes after you and the family in caring for others."

"Oh it hasn't all been plain sailing the teenage years have caused problems for us all, in who she decides to obey, and mixing it so we find ourselves at odds with her and each other. When I bought a house a couple of years ago she wanted to come to live with me, but I warned her I'd probably be harder on her than Lilian and Bob, and my job is fairly demanding so it might be lonely after the constant flow of foster children through their household. She thought it would be bliss to have some peace and quiet, so eventually I gave in, but really she flits between the two homes, and hopefully gets the best from both."

"Why didn't you marry again, and become a family yourself."

"Maria was happy with Bob and Lilian, and to be honest I've not encouraged relationships. I have colleagues and one or two women I'd call friends. When Beth and I married my faith was still wrapped in religion. But as I've enjoyed the challenge of difficult situations in third world countries and the fulfilment of seeing I could make a difference perhaps to hundreds of lives by providing medical care, I too began to see how privileged I was. I became a Christian by dedicating my life to the Lord on a visit home in 1961. From then on sexual relationships were out of the question. As you know to love and lose is a painful thing, and until I met someone who could be a potential Mrs Right, there was no point in pursuing anyone, especially with Maria to consider."

Jill bantered, "Are you pinching my analogy of Mr Right in looking for your Mrs Right?"

Paul sat forward, "No the funny thing is I've always said I doubt there could ever be another Mrs Right!" He stood and stretched, "I think as we've finished our drinks we better make a move otherwise the hotel will be asking if we want a bed for the night. I'll go and pay the bill."

She watched as Paul left the room, and considered, as she had done several times during the day, how different he was to her normal companions whose only interest in her was to initiate a sexual encounter. It was such a pleasure to be with a man who listened and made genuine responses. And by bringing her to a hotel hadn't taken the opportunity to drink heavily and use that as an excuse not to drive her home. Paul returned with their coats and helped her into hers. The desire to express what was in her heart burst out. "Paul, thank you for your organising my refuge at your Gran's, and have so appreciated today with you're taking time out. It was good to talk, it's brought me such peace. I'm so sorry I hogged the conversation with my troubles and…"

He drew her around to face him and rested his finger lightly across her lips. "Shush now, it's alright." His eyes smiled into hers, "No apology necessary. I think this time of trusting and sharing our lives has been a catharsis for both of us."

Immediately she countered, "I feel privileged that you felt you could share such personal issues with me." To that he gave a rather wry and sad grimace before he moved to put his hand at her back and direct her towards the door.

Tired from having talked so much their drive home was almost silent, but she sensed Paul had something on his mind for there was a tension about him she'd not noticed earlier. Perhaps he just didn't like dark, narrow roads, a reminder of Beth, and her parent's fatal car accident?

Back at the cottage, Beatty was at the door, before Paul could use his key. "I expected you home for tea, I was worried about you both."

"Oh Gran I'm sorry. Jill and I talked and talked, and it just didn't occur to me you'd be anxious."

Beatty having drawn them inside gave Paul a long look, and Jill noted Paul gave a slight shake of his head. Beatty said rather briskly, "Well you're here now and needs must. There are scones in the tin, make yourselves a drink, Bill and I have a TV programme to watch." With that she gave Paul a hard look leaving him to usher her through the room to the kitchen."

As he shut the kitchen door she stated, "I'm surprised at Beatty being so cross."

"Let's get the kettle on and find those scones."

"I'll just have a cup of tea. I'm rather prone to put on weight."

Paul's face became serious as they settled opposite each other their drinks on the table before them. "Jill I took you out today because I've enjoyed your company this past week, I wanted to know you better, and be a friend to you. No don't interrupt because I've something to tell you, but as we talked today it never seemed the right time to bring it up."

Worried, her forehead puckered at the grave expression on his face. A feeling of dread assailed so she asked quickly, "Oh no, not Ben, please not Ben?" Paul shook his head, before he could speak, she added, "Rich has vanished."

"Neither Jill, but what I have to say, I believe, does concern one of them."

"What then, tell me please?"

"There's no easy way to say this…" He looked so troubled her stomach churned nervously. "That urine sample, I had it tested, it revealed you're pregnant."

Wide-eyed, she exclaimed, "Pregnant, oh my God!" Her hand in an unconscious gesture covered her stomach. Now both she and Helen were having Ben's baby! Would that change things? In wonder she looked down at her stomach to state, "I'm going to have a baby."

"From your reaction, I assume you think its Ben's, but I can help with conception dates if that would help."

"No need. I told you Ben said Rich was gay and probably why he always avoided any more than a kiss or massage. Was that why you asked me today what I'd do if I was pregnant?" Paul nodded, and his relief was evident, for not only had he released his news, her reaction was positive and it wasn't Rich's baby! She smiled down at her unborn child and said protectively, "Even if it had been Rich's I would have loved it, but I know it's Ben's. Tears spilled over at the wonder of the new life within. With a rueful expression she looked up, "Oh dear Paul, so much for my lecture last week about couple's planning children. I know Helen needs Ben more than I do, but the good news is he won't now disappear from my life."

Paul's eyes filled with anxiety, "You mean you will share Ben with Helen, and you'd be, for want of a better term, his mistress?"

"Paul, that's not fair, what other choice have I got. I know he'll want to be as much part of this child as Helen's?"

With raised eyebrows Paul said dryly, "Granted. Ben has been adept at conceiving two children within weeks of each other, but unfortunately the law says he can't have two wives."

Puzzled she asked, "But how – how did that happen?" The sight of Paul's ironic expression made her rush on, "I never miss taking my contraceptive pill?"

"I thought about that as we drove back. And concluded if the baby was Ben's, conception probably took place the day following the night you were sick. My guess is that you take your pill at night which meant before ingestion took place you vomited its protection back up. Recently doctors have changed the pills strength due to the risk of blood clots. But that has lowered the cover time between pills and you should have been told it was important to take it at the same time every day."

"That is absolutely right! In fact Helen and I had our pills changed around the same time. And the weekend Ben slept with Helen they drank heavily and she spent the night being sick, which would account for her pregnancy. I'd better write to Ben again because my having his child changes everything. I can hardly believe it, I never thought I'd be elated at finding myself pregnant outside of marriage, but to have a little Ben, well rather like you having a little Beth."

A faint smile flittered across Paul's somewhat troubled face. "That's true. But there is Helen to consider."

"Well, we have the flat perhaps Ben could marry Helen and live with us. We could look after the children together – unconventional, but Jane commented recently that life as we know it was changing, and whose business would it be than ours?"

Paul gave a derisory grunt. "That's hardly fair on Helen for it would be as if she were living in Ben's mistress' house. And frankly Jill I would have thought better of you than that. You also need to take into account you have just become a Christian so that idea would be a complete 'no, no'!"

"But Ben would want to spend time as much time with my child as Helen's."

"True, but as far as any relationship with him goes, as a Christian you will have to content yourself with friendship."

"I'm not sure I can do friendship with Ben."

"You need time to think about this. Pray about it. Ben will have to know of course, but perhaps discuss it with family and friends first. Ask Jane and David, maybe as with Maria, they, or someone else in the family, could adopt or act as surrogate parents for you."

"I doubt I could give up a child I'd conceived and carried around for nine months. There is no reason why I couldn't keep him or her. Oh just imagine a little Ben? No I suppose you can't, you've never met him, but he has the cheekiest of smiles and bright blue eyes that light up in such a naughty glint..." She trailed off quite taken with the image she was creating.

The scraping of a chair on the lino made her refocus on Paul as he stood, "Yes well, I'll leave you to consider the future. Gran and Gramps have much wisdom if you want to talk to them about it." Briefly, his hand rested on her shoulder as he walked past her out of the kitchen. She could hear him talking quietly to Bill and Beatty while she pondered on all he'd said. When the front door closed, she arose, and as Bill and Beatty seemed engrossed in their TV programme she wished them 'goodnight' and went to bed.

Despite having so much to consider she slept well, drank her lemonade before she felt nauseous, and ate breakfast with Bill and

Beatty. They chatted about various things including her outing with Paul and then Bill excused himself to read the newspaper by the fire. The moment he'd gone she burst out, "Paul told me I'm pregnant, it's Ben's child."

Once she'd finished telling Beatty about her discussion with Paul she gave similar advice and on her way to answer the telephone she patted her shoulder adding, "I'm sure you'll make a great mother."

Her reply, "It doesn't seem as if I've got a lot of choice there, Beatty!"

A few minutes later Beatty returned. "That was Paul. Apparently the Met. now believe it's safe for you to return home and Paul said if you want to go today, and you can't go on the train with that big suitcase, he has the day off and he can take you after lunch."

"Oh that is so kind of him. And now I'll be able to talk to David and Jane sooner than I thought. Hopefully Ben too might get the okay to come home and we'll have a chance to talk together, and with Helen."

"It's certainly a complicated situation. And who knows dear what is going on with this Lord Mallory business? Each day Bill is scanning the newspaper to see if he, or Peter Sanchez are mentioned, but has found nothing. If there had been an arrest I'm sure we'd have heard about it. Still if the police think it is safe for you to return..." Beatty trailed off in thought.

"At least back in London I'll be kept informed and I'll let you know what happens. But I really want you know how much I appreciate all you've done for me. I am going to miss you, but it will be good to get home and back to normal."

CHAPTER 22

It had been hard to say goodbye to Beatty and Bill, and she wondered as Paul seemed to hustle her out of the door if he was keen for her to leave. He, like his grandparents offered friendship to the vulnerable. Now she was returning to her family, and despite the complication of her pregnancy without a man's support, she'd no worries about acceptance, or financial provision.

Classical music played on the radio as they drove along, and it seemed after yesterday's frenetic chatting, they didn't have anything to say. It didn't feel awkward, it felt good to have a man friend without sexual complications. And the more she became familiar with his long, plain and heavy features she began to appreciate the term, 'beauty is in the eye of the beholder'! It was strange too, that Paul, in the term of 'knowing, and being known' knew more about her life, than any man before him, and maybe, she of him, in his sharing of Beth, bringing that premonition two years ago into being!

The road ahead clear Paul turned to banter, "A penny for your thoughts, or are they so deep they're worth a pound?"

Cheekily she countered, "I'd say a pound, but then you probably wouldn't pay up?"

He wriggled in the seat and from his back pocket took out his wallet. "A pound you say?"

"Oh stop it you're being a terrible tease."

With eyes on the road, and wallet in his hand on the steering wheel he peeled out a pound note. "And you are a very beautiful and intelligent woman so any thoughts you have I'm sure are worth a great deal more than this." In between the two fingers of his left hand he thrust the note under her nose. "Take it, for I want to know what you were mulling over?"

The two fingers with the note kept up their tormenting until she said, "You need to keep your hands on the wheel, and eyes on the road, you should know better."

He gave her a quick grin, dropped the note in her lap and said, "I'm waiting."

If only she did have something intelligent to say. Perhaps she should share her thoughts. "Actually I was thinking about you."

Amused he agreed, "That's a good start."

She tutted and then laughed. "I was thinking how our conversation developed yesterday and how good it was to share some of those deep things with each other. And a novelty to have a delicious meal, with no recompense expected. Thank you for wanting to be a friend to me."

His eyes scanned the road, sent her a quirky grin before saying, "I'm glad to hear it, and I'd like to remain one if that's okay with you?"

"If you pay so well to hear such simple thoughts I'm sure that can be arranged!" Paul chuckled. "And armed with your Gran's recipes I could try my hand at a dinner party. I could invite David and Jane. You share the same faith and I think a friendship between you and David could prove interesting."

"Remember, it's your faith too! What makes you say that about a friendship with David?"

She chortled, "Let's just say you'd make him a good role model! And now, take the next turn left. Your knowledge of the back streets of London is excellent, for even on a wet, dark, Friday night we've missed all the bottlenecks. The house is that one with the garage on the ground floor. Oh, the front door's open. You can pull up on the hard-standing space." Light spilled out from the open doorway. Paul swung the car into the space as a man, wearing a balaclava, came rushing out, his body colliding into the bonnet. Jill exclaimed, "What on earth...?" Almost instantly the man recovered, gave them a shocked stare through the windscreen, and slipped sideways past the car to hare off down the road.

Immediately Paul was out of the car and chasing him down the road. She followed to see what was happening. Under a street lamp about thirty yards away she watched Paul rugby tackle the man to the ground. Admittedly, the man had looked, and had been behaving strangely, but she hoped he wasn't someone from the church who'd been seeking David's legal or financial advice, and his hurry, his need to get home! It was obvious Paul had winded him, and had him under control, so she'd better go and see what was going on.

She frowned as her heels clicked over the tiles in the outer hall, because the stairs and passage, usually lit by the hall table lamp, were in darkness. From out of the darkness Jane's strained and pained voice called, "Is that you Jill? Oh thank God." In the gloom, she spotted Jane sitting several stairs up hugging her arm. Jane broke into sobs, her words staccato. "Helen...Oh God...go see…her screams." A clutch of dread spiralled in Jill's stomach. "Couldn't help… he, he twisted my arm… crack…pain…feel faint. Oh God… don't let…Helen be dead."

A low female moaning from the far corner of the passage brought relief. Helen wasn't dead. The relief was brief for Jane said, "Rosemary! She attacked him, heard lamp smash, horrible gurgling… So other man…ran."

Through the panic tightening her throat Jill said, "Paul's got him." And resolute to get a grip ordered, "Go and ring 999." Bravely she added, "I'll see what's happened." Jane didn't move. Sharply she reiterated her instruction and simultaneously prayed inwardly, 'God give her, and me, strength'. In a voice stronger than she felt, as Jane moved she commanded, "Switch on the picture lights on the stairs."

Where was Paul? She squashed the unwanted vision of him lying in the road in a pool of blood and made her way along the passage. A large dark lump blocked her way, surrounded by shards of white pottery showing up against the dark red carpet. Rosemary must be beyond that. Her stomach lurched in fear as she resolutely stepped over the body. The four lamps over the pictures came on. Although the banisters deflected the light below, in the shadowy hall they still revealed a nightmarishly gory scene. It didn't take any imagination to see Rosemary had stabbed the broken, jagged bottom of the lamp, still attached to the flex, straight into the side of the man's neck and lower face. It looked as if he'd turned, buckled and left a trail of blood as he slid down the wall. Sick to the stomach she determined this was not the time to faint. By the boiler room door, Rosemary sat quietly keening on the floor, her knees hunched up to her face hidden by her curtain of hair, her fists balled into her eyes. In the darker doorway of the flat as though trying to escape, she could just see Helen's foot and the shape of her body. Oh God, help. She couldn't cope with this.

"I don't know what's going on here, but I've caught this one." She turned to see Paul pushing a man, his nose and forehead bleeding, his hands belted behind his back into the main hall. His eyes took in the carnage. "Good grief what has happened here?"

Pointing she said, "That man seems badly hurt. And Helen is…" She flicked the light switch just inside the flat corridor. The noise of a scream arose in her throat, her hand went to her mouth and her eyes closed against the scene. But she had seen it. Helen lying sprawled along the mid-green carpet, her face bloodied, her

371

body like a broken rag doll and something horribly dark soaking through her skirt around her thighs into the carpet. Horrified she staggered backwards into Rosemary who whimpered and buried her head even tighter into her knees. Not surprising, she'd liked to hide too.

In a stern and loud voice Paul commanded, "Jill, hold yourself together – go and ring 999." She looked over at him her where his captive now stood trousers around his ankles. Paul commented briskly, "I'm using his belt to tie around his ankles." From the top of the stairs Jane, announced weakly, "I've called 999."

Paul glanced up. "Good. Come down and talk to… is it Rosemary? Jill, fetch my case from the car." By the time she returned Paul had sat the man in his underpants at the bottom of the stairs in the corner facing the wall, Jane was crouched down by Rosemary her back to the revolting spectacle lying a few feet away and Paul had disappeared she assumed to Helen.

Although squeamish, she stepped over the man's legs to see how she could help and was relieved to hear bells and sirens in the distance. Thank God, for in that one glimpse at Helen, even to her unprofessional eye, she could see she was in a bad way.

At her appearance Paul instructed, "I'll have that here." She cringed as she stepped around Helen to put the case on the floor beside him. "I need towels and something to elevate Helen's legs." She thought quickly, the boiler room. Rosemary was blocking the door. Jane's quiet cajoling wasn't having any effect. Urgently she pulled her arm declaring, "Rosemary you have to move. Helen's haemorrhaging I need towels." To her relief Rosemary stood, her eyes fixed and blank. Jane hugged her and drew her slightly nearer the carnage to clear the way for the door to open.

Paul ordered from the corridor, "Get her upstairs out of the way." Jill thought, easier said than done with a gruesome body to negotiate. Quickly she dived into the boiler room, grabbed the black dress box she'd recently stored there and a pile of towels. At Helen's feet she asked, "Will she be alright? She looks terrible."

He didn't reply just instructed, "Squash one end of that box. Cover it in towels."

About to step on one end, a familiar voice boomed down the hall, "What the hell's going on here?" At that she turned, saw Jane cry out, "David," and Rosemary, no longer supported, sway alarmingly. Instantly she cried "Jane", but David was obviously near enough to snake out an arm around Rosemary's waist catching her before she collapsed on the body behind her, while muttering "Oh my God" at the gruesome sight before him. With that he lifted Rosemary over the body as if she weighed no more than a feather. And still supporting her, he stretched out the other hand to help Jane across. Rosemary moaned against him, so he drew her tighter into the refuge of his body. Jill fully expected her to push him away, instead she leant into him as he put his other arm around his shaking wife. At that moment, two ambulance men appeared in the hall, the first asking, "Which of these young ladies…?" Before David could answer, she directed, "Neither! Over here. This man doesn't look good, but my flat-mate looks worse. Paul, a doctor, is attending to her."

One ambulance man climbed over the body and examined it, as the other instructed David, "Take the young ladies upstairs out of the way and make a pot of tea. I'll call for another crew."

After that there was a whirlwind of activity. The police arrived in two cars and carted off the man with his trousers down having been amused at Paul's restraining methods. Paul response was a brief smile his mind engaged on 'vital signs', 'lines in' and 'blood transfusions' while preparing Helen for a speedy transfer to hospital.

Once Helen was on the way to the ambulance, Paul slipped upstairs verified Jane's arm needed medical attention and suggested she go with him. Badly shaken Jane tried to look brave at leaving David and it was a revelation to hear the gentle and tender way her brother assured his wife he'd follow soon. Then in typical David fashion he turned to bark, "Jill, go upstairs, stay with Rosemary and make that tea. I'll deal with this."

This wasn't a time for tea, but a time to help herself to a brandy from David's cupboard without asking first. She offered one to Rosemary, who was curled into a ball in the corner of the settee, and felt progress was made when she managed a nod in response. After a few comforting sips Jill moved to view the street below where a second ambulance had arrived just before the first left. Flashing lights and sirens had curious neighbours chatting to the policemen standing by their front door. It was another ten minutes before the injured thug left on a stretcher, his face swathed in bandages, and as the ambulance sped away another police car drew up spilling out DCI Maysfield and a woman officer.

A minute later that same uniformed lady knocked on the lounge door and asked with a small sympathetic smile. "Shall I put the kettle on?" She supposed it was the sensible thing to do and agreed. In the hall below DCI Maysfield was speaking to someone, but sick to the stomach she finally went upstairs to the bathroom to give way to it. There was no escape from the fact that this whole fiasco was due to her involvement with Rich, and although emotionally drained, it was Jane and Helen who'd taken the brunt of it, while she'd come out practically unscathed.

Slowly she descended the stairs. David, standing by the mantelpiece was distractedly running his hand through his hair as DCI Maysfield was talking. From the dining room the WPC emerged with a tray of tea and biscuits and seeing her on the stairs said quietly, "I hope you didn't mind me ferreting around in your kitchen and offering these."

Wearily she smiled and waved her into the lounge, she couldn't be bothered to explain they weren't hers. David spotting her behind the WPC boomed, "My God woman, you've got a lot to answer for?"

Taken aback the WPC stopped abruptly inside the doorway, the cups rattling. Nearly bumping into her she reassured her, "It's okay, carry on, it's not you he's talking to it's me. Now David, don't start! I've enough grief for one day. I couldn't foresee, or stop this happening." She turned to Gerald Maysfield, "Weren't you keeping an eye on the house? I thought you suspected something like this might happen?"

Obviously upset DCI Maysfield apologized, "We only took our men off at lunch time today believing it to be safe. I can't tell you how sorry I am. We came as soon as we got the call." We've already identified the men they are known associates of Peter Sanchez which brings a connection between him and Mallory. And you will be pleased to know we have temporarily stopped Lord Mallory leaving the country on the pretext of checking his German passport. His story is dual nationality because he had a German grandfather. I'll be in a better position to update you tomorr..."

Irate she snapped, "That man is such a con artist, he'd wriggle his way out of anything."

"He does seem a very cool customer with an answer for everything. I suspect Lord Mallory's confident, and somewhat amused manner, is that he's playing us for fools. But I don't think this time he's going to find it easy. Those who have infiltrated Sanchez's little Kingdom say he hasn't been seen for over two weeks because of some bust up with a rival gang…"

Jill cut in again, "That fits, it was probably the night he arrived here with Victor looking like a thug, but he obviously still has influence somewhere because it didn't stop his organising for Ben to be killed when he next used his car?"

The Inspector continued, "Ah Victor, yes he's vanished along with the Lordship trappings. The car and house were rented, not owned, but there's no law against that. For Sanchez to talk to Ben as he did he must have been caught off guard. Unfortunately, for Ben, Sanchez knows his mistake as much as we do. He also knows you wouldn't know how to hot wire a car, therefore the common denominator is Ben Fletcher. He's probably discovered he's in Ireland, and knowing he couldn't breach your father's secure research and training centre, had the bomb planted as a little surprise for Ben's return. It was unfortunate for his plans that the job was botched!"

DCI Maysfield having accepted a cup of tea, sat down. "I've no doubt too he's behind tonight's attempt to get the diamonds back. In being Lord Mallory he knew he'd have a alibi either being on a flight to Rio, or as has happened detained waiting passport clearance. It was regrettable that Mrs Reinhardt's engagement ring was assumed to be Sanchez's property."

David groaned, "She was told if she didn't hand it over, they'd cut her finger off." Jill gasped at such a grisly thought. His face was grim as he continued, "Jane said in opening the door they came in with such force she couldn't stop them. One man grabbed and dragged her from behind the door into the hall. The other said, "She's got the ring on." At that he tried wrenching at it and threatening her. It was then Helen emerged from the flat. The man Rosemary attacked recognized Helen because he said, "It's her, Ben's bird. I saw her up at the house. Hey, that'll be one up to us for taking out on her what that Ben should get. Dazed at the scene, it took Helen a moment to comprehend. She dashed to shut the flat door, and Jane said she could only watch in horror as he kicked it open. She struggled to be free, but injured and in pain there wasn't much she could do as Helen's screams rent the air, but it was worse when it went silent."

They went silent as they took in the picture David had painted. DCI Maysfield lent forward to put his cup on the coffee table. "I think we need to play Mallory/Sanchez at his own game. I don't know how Helen is…" Jill intervened, "She was in a bad way, but from what I gathered, Paul's rapid intervention was said would aid her recovery."

DCI Maysfield acknowledged, "Let's hope so. My thinking is if we tell him his mate has died, and that if Helen does the same, he'll take the can for murder, we'll uncover more facts."

From the settee Rosemary, who was still sitting with her knees up to her chest, looked up her face ashen, her eyes wide in terror. "I, I murdered him?"

Quickly DCI Maysfield assured her, "No Rosemary, as far as I know he's still alive."

Rosemary swallowed hard. "I, I hit him with the lamp. It barely hurt him. He came after me. I smashed the lamp against the wall, in the dark as he grabbed me. I shoved the sharp broken base at the white of his neck and face as hard as I could. I couldn't see what I'd done except he crumpled against the wall making horrible gurgling noises before sliding to the floor. Will I, will I, go to prison?"

"Not a chance." Gerald Maysfield smiled gently, "It was self-defence. And you are our key witness to the conversation between Mr Fletcher and Lord Mallory."

Jill looked askance at Rosemary. Rosemary looking relieved became unusually talkative, probably due to the brandy she'd drunk. "The night Rich stayed I went to get a glass of water and heard Ben saying, "What on earth are you doing here? A man replied, 'Could say the same to you me ole cell mate I hope you're not after the Reinhardt fortune too.' Shocked, I eavesdropped. Ben's conversation with Lord Mallory sounded very convincing. I think a great deal of Ben, so upset, I slipped back into my room. By the time I'd decided to speak to David, Ben was already here. David was agitated and barked at me, 'Jill's gone to Amsterdam with that Mallory fellow. Find out where they're staying. Ben suspects he's planning to kidnap her.' By the time I'd rung International Directory Enquiries, had a couple of dozen Amsterdam hotel telephone numbers and rung them, Ben had gone after Jill to spy out the land. Relieved Ben wasn't in cahoots with Rich I thought no more about what I'd overheard until the police questioned me."

Rosemary looked across at David. "I left the office early today to identify if the voice I heard two weeks ago was the same as the one of Lord Mallory recorded at Customs and Excise yesterday. "I left you a note David, and decided as it was then 3.30pm on a Friday and I'd worked hard this week I needed to come home to sleep. I heard Helen come in about an hour later. I thought she was spending two nights with her family. A short while later the doorbell rang, and the rest you know."

The DCI rubbed his hands, "We need to keep this between ourselves, we don't want to put Miss Dawes under any risk. You will be interested to know we've pulled in a doctor who we know is addicted to drugs and pays for his habit by being useful to gang members who need abortions; bullets dug out; knife wounds stitched. In that we had a spot of luck. For not only had he stitched up a knife wound on Sanchez nearly two years ago, but at the time heard the name of the rival gang member, who they suspected had ordered it. And providing we can give the doc a new identity, preferably abroad, he's willing to identify Sanchez in a line up."

David spoke up, "I am sure my father would help him."

"That's what I thought."

Puzzled Jill asked, "Why would Dad do that?"

Exasperated David boomed, "Jill you seem to have little, or no comprehension of the upset to all our lives your unexpected little trip to Amsterdam has made. Dad was beside himself with worry and guilt because he'd never considered his fortune might lead to the kidnap of his precious daughter. We kept it from Mum, but she was fretting because Dad was receiving calls at midnight, coming and going at all hours, uncommunicative and staying up here without her. Oh she knew something was up. However she found out all when Dad took Ben back with him, he stayed there for a couple of days, until Dad could organize for him…"

"Ben stayed at our house. Oh I was so worried about him, I bet Mum mothered him, and looked after him."

"Yes I'm sure she did while I fretted that something would happen to them as they shielded him. Still fortunately for you at least that went without incident, and he joined a group of laboratory technicians going across to Dad's training place in Ireland. And, at my busiest time I'm now two down in staff, Brussels looming in just over a week and wonder how Rosemary here, and Jane with a possible broken arm are going to be able to …"

"David?" He looked across at Rosemary who was giving him a long, hard stare. To her amazement David stopped speaking, picked up his cup of tea he'd not touched and drank it in almost one gulp.

The DCI broke the tense atmosphere announcing, "I must leave you. But hopefully we can get this sewn up in the next day or so."

Jill jumped up, "Before you go Inspector, what of Ben, if this works out surely he can come home, Helen will need him?"

The sight of DCI Maysfield's sad expression told her he was a kind man. "I understand your concern, but Helen knows it's not safe for him to return. And you will understand that at present I'm not at liberty to talk of the arrangements in place to protect him."

The telephone rang. David strode out to answer it as she showed the DCI and WPC out. Detective Maysfield shook her hand. "Thank you Jill, you and your family, have been an incredible help to us."

With a heartfelt sigh she could only say, "Thank goodness some good is coming out of all this." She shut the front door and looked along the hallway, how was she going to get into her flat tonight knowing what was on the carpet between her and it?

David came down the stairs, ran his hand through his hair and apologized. "Sorry Jill, bit tactless of me. It's been an emotional and difficult time for all of us. That was Jane on the telephone, her arm was dislocated, not broken, she's had it manipulated back into place, but she's very sore. Your friend Paul is with her. I'm off to pick them up. Whilst I'm away call the insurance company, find the emergency number, the policy is in the filing cabinet in my study, tell them the situation, tell them we need a specialist cleaning agency, tell them to get the job done tonight!"

Annoyed she bit out, "I'm not your secretary David." He ignored her and made to move out the front door. "Any news on Helen?"

David turned, his face grim, "Not too good. They are giving her blood transfusions, they can't stem the bleeding and will have to operate, and they're not sure how serious that might be."

Jill hardly dare ask, but had to, "And the baby?"

"She's lost it."

"Oh God, no!"

David ignoring her continued, "Jane said the major concern now was not losing her."

Before her eyes came the sight of Helen's battered face and her tangled body, she could only bemoan, "Oh poor Helen. It's all my fault."

"Yes indeed. But I must go, I don't want to keep Jane waiting."

With that, David was gone. How could she have known that going out with Rich would have such devastating affects on those around her. It also brought home how Chris as her kidnapper would have treated her! In a maelstrom of emotion, tears coursed down her cheeks and with nowhere to go, but upstairs, she was grateful for Rosemary's company where with few words they cried together.

It was obvious to Jill, when David, Jane and Paul returned, no introductions were necessary. David carrying Jane from the car up the stairs ushered Paul into the lounge. "Go on in. I'll get Jane settled, then we'll get on with that job you suggested." Jane in that moment mouthed with a nod at Paul's back, 'he's nice' before David whisked her upward towards her bed.

Red-eyed, Jill stuffed her handkerchief up her sleeve to politely stand and offer a cup of tea.

Concern filled Paul's eyes as he looked first at her and then Rosemary. "If you don't mind I'd rather sit down and talk to you both." Jill nodded and indicated for him to sit on the opposite settee to her and Rosemary. In his quiet way he told them of Helen's critical condition, but being young and fit she'd every reason to pull through.

Rosemary tentatively inquired, "And the man, I..."

"In intensive care, he's tough, he'll pull through. I've little sympathy for a man who beats up a defenceless woman for whom he has no grudge just to gain a few brownie points with his boss." He gave a heartfelt sigh, "That's the hardest part of being a Christian to forgive people like him, and as a doctor to work to save his life. Tell me Rosemary, what happened?"

Just as Rosemary finished, David appeared, his words directed at Paul. "Jane says she could manage a cup of tea, but doesn't want anything to eat, is that alright?"

"After being so sick I'd prefer she have something, even a piece of bread and butter, to settle her stomach and help the efficiency of the painkillers. Do you think you girls could do that while David and I sort out something downstairs?"

Relieved that the men were taking control Jill nodded and closely followed by Rosemary they headed for the kitchen to make a pot of tea and delve into Jane's emporium of food delights. At the sound of cardboard being torn she guessed the men were putting it over the messy carpet to give them entry back into the flat.

The tea brewed and realizing, with it being way past dinner time that the men might be hungry, she removed Jane's Victoria sandwich out of it's container, then thought to lay the table with ham, cheese, pickles and tomatoes along with a nice crusty fresh loaf in case they wanted more. Jane loved the crusty end of bread, so she sliced it off, buttered it, and took it up to her with a cup of tea.

Propped against pillows Jane gave a pained smile and seeing the cup of tea murmured, "Oh, Jill thank you."

"Paul said to try and eat. And I hope you don't mind we've raided your cupboard for food. Is it okay to eat the Vic sponge?"

Jane nodded and then said, "Um I like crunchy bread." Brightening she added, "And I like that man of yours too. I didn't recognize him without his beard."

"He's only a friend, but a very caring one." Jill sat on the bed holding the bread as Jane sipped her tea. "I'm so sorry about your arm. I know all this boils down to me, I wish I could have foreseen the trouble this would cause. But if it's any consolation I've been thinking a lot about God, and last week I asked Jesus into my life."

Despite her weakened state Jane's eyes filled with delight, her mouth opened wide in her excitement, before exclaiming, "Oh Jill, that's so wonderful. I want to hug you but I can't." The cup of tea wobbled ominously in her hand, her eyes glistened with unshed tears.

Jill leant forward to rescue the cup as David's voice boomed challengingly from the door, "I hope you aren't upsetting Jane."

As though guilty she leapt up from the bed as Jane retorted, "No David I'm not upset, I'm thrilled. Let Jill tell you."

She handed Jane the bread as David with a skeptical expression awaited her news. This time she gave more detail while Jane munching listened avidly, and David appeared unconvinced. Yet when she finished it was a great boost to hear him say, "An answer to prayer then Jane". Then he spoilt it by adding, "It's a pity we couldn't have received it without everyone being dragged into your traumas."

Crossly Jane snapped, "David, stop it!"

"Sorry! Of course I am pleased sis. I hope you realise it isn't just simply saying a prayer, it's a commitment of your life, a willingness to change."

She smiled and said pointedly, "Yes David, just like you are doing, obviously it takes time! And Helen losing the baby could certainly bring unexpected changes.."

David grunted at the first comment, and looked concerned at her second. He glanced at Jane who frowned at him. And in that unusual gentle voice he put his arm around her and said, "Look sis, we'll have this conversation another time. Jane needs to rest."

Jane did look pale, her smile weary, and David calling her sis again she felt sure was to offset his previous tone, her heart warmed toward him as he moved her out of the door.

On her return to the dining room Paul and Rosemary were speaking in quiet and subdued tones. In two weeks Rosemary seemed to have gained confidence, and she wondered if Paul might just be that special man to break into whatever it was that caused her to me shy of male contact. When David arrived, she retreated into the background, but didn't return to her shell. It was amazing to her, still feel queasy, that after what they'd been through the men seemed surprisingly hungry.

Paul talked about reactions in trauma. "It's your adrenalin that kicks in, gives you the ability to cope, but like the adage, 'a problem shared is a problem halved' talking about it after releases the horror and breaks its effect. And a good night's sleep helps your system absorb the healing it needs. Of course praying off the shock considerably lessens its effect."

Interested they each nodded wisely. David slipped out to check on Jane and returned to report she was asleep as Jill asked, "What about you Paul? I bet your adrenalin was pumping when you rushed off up the road. "

Paul gave his quirky smile. "I did the police 'attack and defend' training, but confess it didn't include the rather unorthodox method of tying up your prisoner with your trouser belt. In tackling him the guy was stunned by his hitting his nose on the road, and his head on pavement, but I then realised I'd no way of restraining him. In places like Africa you learn to adapt what you have, so I bound my trouser belt around his hands, and prayed my trousers wouldn't fall down as I marched him back here."

David chuckled. "Even with Jill's men friends in and out we aren't used to seeing them in the hall in their underpants trussed up like a chicken!"

Sarcastically she retorted, "Thanks for that David!"

Paul appearing not to have heard commented, "This is the third time I've been involved in a Reinhardt family trauma, is this something you find often happens?"

"I'd say only when you're around to rescue us." David chuckled.

"Well it would seem from the first one you have found a good wife in Jane, this sponge is so light, she's a good cook. And a very brave little lady. "

David drinking his tea put down his cup to agree. "And that

good wife also led me to seeking and finding the God she loves. And Jill's just told us out of all this she's become a Christian, so I suppose some good has come out of this."

"Yes, Jill told me about that because most of my family are Christians."

"Really, well no doubt, Jill staying with your Grandparents influenced her decision. Jill will make a good wife, but I can't recommend her cooking, but Rosemary I believe, on all accounts, cooks a good roast dinner, but I've never been privy to taste it."

Both she and Rosemary stared at him. Underneath she seethed, and she guessed Rosemary was doing much the same. Just wait until she could get even with him! A little thought, like a small voice inside said, 'Christians forgive, they don't get even!' And the quirky grin Paul sent her made her wonder if he knew exactly what she'd been thinking!

A short while later Paul needed to leave, and in removing her case from the boot kindly carried it to her bedroom, her door fortunately beyond the area where cardboard covered the carpet. Once over the area she didn't need to step on it again except to leave the flat. Embarrassed she remembered the state of the bedroom when she and Rich had left in the early morning nearly two weeks ago. However, when she walked into the room it was immaculate. It was then it came to her that Jane and Rosemary had tidied up after the police had searched the flat, and she'd yet to thank them for that.

Paul's enthusiasm about her room had her showing him the rest of the flat, and the kitchen initiated his saying, "This is a wonderful place to practice Gran's recipes. I hope I can still look forward to that dinner invite, it will be amusing when you prove to that brother of yours you are as capable as his Jane."

"Honestly, brothers can be the pits! Mind you Jane doesn't let him get away with things."

The quirky grin appeared, "That's a date then. And if you need any help I'll happily come and assist. Now I must go, I'll catch up with you tomorrow." His eyes scanned her face, "I know you've been having nightmares, I would leave you with a sleeping pill as I have done Rosemary and Jane, but I'd rather not with the baby…"

"Oh that's okay. I feel tired, in fact exhausted, but as I said to Jane and David earlier it's sad about Helen losing the baby, but it will change things for Ben and I, and I know it's horrible to be happy on the back of someone else's misfortune, but…"

Paul's finger placed across her mouth silenced her. His golden eyes seemed to plead with her as he said, "One thing at a time Jill. Don't start making plans, even in your mind. I'm not getting into it now, but if you've really made a commitment to the Lord you will need to consult Him. Things might not be quite as clear cut as you hope. Now let me pray for you." His hand rested on her shoulder, and looking into her eyes he said simply, "Father God, with Jesus our healer, we break off from Jill's life the shock and trauma of this past two weeks, and bind her to you Father for your love, care and rest to pervade every area of her life. Amen." He watched her and seemed satisfied when she smiled. The outcome of his prayer wasn't dissimilar to a dose of a cough mixture to a dry cough, a sense of warmth, relief and well-being filled her. "Don't bother seeing me out. Have a good night's sleep."

Instead of dreading being in her bed alone after so recently sharing it regularly with Ben she stretched out and fell instantly into a deep and restful sleep.

CHAPTER 23

Jane arrived the next morning as she, and a silent, pensive Rosemary were having breakfast. "Sorry to interrupt, just to update you. Paul rang David to tell him that the man in intensive care hasn't regained consciousness yet. Not from the blow, but the severing of an artery caused oxygen starvation to the brain. The good news is Helen is going to pull through. She's several cracked ribs, extensive bruising to the stomach, a broken arm and leg. Despite not wanting to be pregnant, I'm sure losing the baby will be a blow, but they had to do a hysterectomy, and well, no woman wants that at her age."

Rosemary who had looked tearful broke down with heart wrenching sobs. Bewildered at the intensity of her reaction Jill could only guess it to be a culmination of the varying emotions of the last days. Without doubt her sorrow, if only at Helen's news, would probably be far greater than Helen's! Concerned, Jane drew her into her bedroom, and it was two hours later before she re-emerged to say Rosemary had cried herself to sleep.

Jill expected David to appear wanting to know where Jane was, but guessed he was probably in the midst of demanding or organisating something, and hadn't noticed her absence.

Despite Paul's counsel, Helen's sad news was an incredible boost to her hope for a future with Ben. To alleviate a sense of guilt at being happy, she thought to offer Helen's parents Helen's bed to save them travelling daily from Southend to visit her. In her search for their telephone number she found in the dressing table drawer several photo albums, and sure Helen wouldn't mind her looking, she took them out. To her astonishment, they were of Ben from a baby through to adulthood. She wouldn't have thought of Helen as sentimental, but maybe having his baby made her want to picture how her baby might look. Tears rolled down her face, there wouldn't be a little Ben now to look like his handsome, fun and laughter filled Daddy, and it was all because of her.

And then it occurred to her, how ridiculously, there would be, because she was having his baby, and her baby could look just like this lovely little boy in the pictures. Love for Ben the adult welled up as her own pictures of him flashed across the screen of her mind. It wasn't difficult to imagine life with cheeky, naughty Ben who had such vitality for life. He'd love his son, or daughter, with a passion, he was indeed a passionate man, she grinned, they may have to curtail those activities with the baby coming.

With a need to occupy herself, she went shopping and came back to cook a chicken and make a sponge cake all the while envisioning Ben being around. And at his sadness of losing one baby he would be delighted in knowing he was having another with her. In the middle of carving the chicken, Paul rang to ask how everyone was. She gave him a brief resume, told him she was missing the Stemmings household, and the guilt of her happiness at Helen no longer needing Ben, and how she was sure he'd embrace her new found faith as well as his baby. He listened, then counselled, "Jill I understand how you feel, but don't anticipate anything." On questioning Paul seemed evasive, but said practically, "Remember God always has your best interests at heart, and it's good that you are doing something useful and practical."

Encouraged she finished putting her Victoria sponge together, and thought how Ben would enjoy her cakes. The result looked so like Jane's, and knowing David and Jane had gone out, she slipped upstairs and giggling swapped her cake for Jane's.

Finally Helen's Dad answered their telephone, he was abrupt, bordering rude in reply to her offer, saying, "No thank you. We thought Helen lived with decent people. First she tells us she's getting married, then having a baby, then she isn't, and now this." To her dismay, he began weeping and the line went dead.

Disconsolately she ambled up the stairs with the need to talk to Jane. David was speaking on the telephone. "Is that what they said? I don't know Paul what do you think? You can? How long? I'm amazed how quickly it's come together just shows the police can be…" He turned as she knocked on his open flat door, "Oh hi Jill, come in. Jane's in the kitchen brewing up a cuppa. I'd best go Paul. Yes okay, til then."

"What was all that about?"

"Well timed, Jill. Paul's just heard that that…"

"David I thought that you ate that Vic sponge yesterday?" Jane stood with the cake container under her good arm.

Gloomily she now wished she hadn't played her joke.

"We did, well half of it! I was just about to tell Jill that Maysfield told Paul that the man who stabbed Peter Sanchez has signed a written statement to that effect, and…" He broke off, "Oh sorry Jane, I'm not being very thoughtful am I? Look you go and sit down with Jill and I'll bring the tea tray, give me the cake, I'll put it on a plate."

As she and Jane sat at each end of the three seater settee furthest from the door Jane smiled, "Your brother tries, and sometimes is very trying! David appeared with the heavy tea tray and placed it on the table in front of them as she told of Helen's Dad's reaction to her call.

In their hall the telephone rang. David walked to the door, "I bet that's Maysfield, Paul said he was going to get in touch."

Jane looked puzzled at the whole cake on the plate, then asked, "Do you think Helen will want to come back here? It will be several months before she can return to work, not much fun sitting around the flat on her own all day."

David reappeared, "I've an extra cup. Maysfield said he'd be around in a few minutes to fill us in. "We ought to finish yesterday's cake first, but I couldn't find it so brought in this one, no doubt we'll manage to eat both."

Jane smiled, "David dear, in order not to exacerbate your weight problem, I only make one cake a week."

Crossly David touched his stomach, "I haven't got a weight problem, I just need to be careful. But I tell you we did eat half the cake yesterday, so you must have made another and forgotten."

With a deep sigh Jane said, "David my arm was dislocated, not my brain."

Jill ventured, "Does it look like one of yours, Jane?"

Immediately David assured her, "Of course it is. No-one can make a sponge as good as Jane."

It was getting harder to keep a straight face, but she managed to say, "Are you sure David, after all Jane's cooking may be excellent, but it's not exclusive." Jane shot her a speculative look. She passed David the knife and gave Jane a small smile.

David cut a fair size hunk from the whole, tasted it and said, "Definitely Jane's."

Jane shook her head, and took the plate on which she'd placed another slice. "That's impossible David, if as you say you ate half yesterday, cakes don't regenerate so this isn't mine, but umm it tastes good."

"Now you're being silly, who else would have baked a cake and put it in our Tupperware?"

Pleased Jill sat up straight and suggested, "Try me!"

"What, that'll be the day! You've never baked a cake in your entire life."

"Today is that day! And this is the second cake I've baked in my life. You can't take back your accolade of its being as good as Jane's. So I'll thank you, brother of mine, that next time I bring a friend home you don't rubbish my cooking skills, or anything else negative about me in front of them."

David's eyebrows rose at her vehemence, but he had the grace to say, "I'm sorry I meant it as a joke." His brow furrowed, "I seem to be doing a lot of apologizing lately."

Jane grinned. "You'll learn." Then turning she commented, "This is excellent Jill, I assume Paul's Gran's recipe? Oh and there's the doorbell, darling, for your sins you can answer it. In fact after yesterday I think we need to see who is at the door before we let them in."

David rose and heading out the door called back, "Don't worry, I'm on to it."

"Did he mean opening the door now, or that we see people before we open the door? "

Jane shrugged, "I don't know, but he's been busy all morning, which worked out well as I spent time with Rosemary. These last weeks she's been opening up, I just don't want this latest trauma to set her back."

DCI Maysfield preceded David into the room. Jane stood to shake his hand as he asked after her arm, apologized and admitted, "We really didn't expect Sanchez's men to try and retrieve those diamonds."

"Please, do sit down. It'll be fine in a couple of days, just feels bruised and sore when I move it."

"If it's any consolation Bob Gosworth was very apologetic for hurting you. Seeing Frank beat up a defenceless woman panicked him. And, he was quick to tell us the order had come from Sanchez to put a detonator on Ben's car, and collect his diamond ring. By the way the supposed expert who blew himself up is recovering, minus his right arm. And he, as well as Bob asked for a few other crimes to be taken into account. All in all I'd say a very successful round-up."

Jane frowned, "Hardly consolation to Helen for her terrible injuries."

"Quite so. In spite of what happened here, Sanchez or Mallory is more a con man, than a perpetrator of violent crime, but his brother is a different matter. He and Frank Griffiths are quite close, and we suspect together they have much to answer for. We also pulled in Ange Brightwell. Scared she admitted to being here last Sunday, but told us, 'I ain't committed no crime going there, Jill's my friend.' She was so shocked to hear about Helen she spilled some very productive beans about Chris' disappearance and why. But that needn't concern you all."

The DCI took a long drink of tea before continuing. "It's an understatement to say Ben's tip off that Sanchez and Mallory are the same man has been a breakthrough. I tell you it's been like finding the most important missing piece of a jigsaw puzzle."

Jane having poured the tea handed the DCI a cup. "Now, let me bring you up to date. On Thursday, having circulated Mallory's photo to ports and airports, we detained him in his attempt to fly to Rio using his German passport. It was explained due to an anomaly, his credentials had to be verified with the German authorities. He then pulled the Lord Mallory stunt and told us he'd dual nationality. We apologized assuring him he could travel on that passport, but would have to change the name on his tickets. He wasn't pleased, ranted and raved, and of course, he didn't have his Mallory passport, we did! However, this morning his passport checked out as genuine so we had to tell him he was free to travel."

Dismayed she burst out, "Oh no, you haven't let him go?"

DCI Maysfield smiled in assuring her, "Be patient, Jill. Oh my it was a very cocksure Mallory who came in to Kensington Police Station to collect his passport. He loved the apologies. Beautifully timed I arrived to say, 'Hey, you are just the right build and stature I need for an identification parade, it'll only take ten minutes.' He said he'd a flight to catch, and I laughed saying, 'Oh that's okay you help us, we'll help you, and you wouldn't want us to think you had anything to hide, would you?' He made several excuses which I covered so he couldn't do more than smile and agree, but I wonder then if he guessed we'd got something on him."

The DCI paused to drink his tea. "To pick him out of the six men in the line up we had the doctor who'd stitched his knife wound, and from Dartmoor Prison the rival gang member who'd inflicted it last year, both only knew him as Sanchez. Previously they'd drawn a picture of the wound as they remembered it. The bonus there was Gosworth, his evidence to be taken into account against the charges against him. I can't help smiling as I think how Mallory had put himself in the frame. We ran through the drill, all three identified Mallory as Sanchez. We then asked the men in the line up to turn around and take off their shirts. Mallory of course was the only one with a scar, but so similar to the drawings there could be no doubt. By then he guessed we'd rumbled him and although admitting to nothing, we arrested him on the spot for half a dozen outstanding crimes with this still to come. He insisted before questioning that his lawyer be present and I'm here now because we are awaiting his arrival."

Thrilled Jill clapped, "At last, you've got him. Now with him soon to be safe behind bars Ben can come home?"

DCI Maysfield gulped down the remainder of his tea and arose from the chair. "David I'll let you explain to Jill what's happening about that. I must get back. Thank you for the tea. I think we need to be mindful in the next week of other reprisals Mallory might have set up. Ben we know is his real target, but as we continue to gather information and arrest his associates the risk of any 'hit' being carried out will become less."

She and Jane watched as David and the Inspector moved from the room, the Inspector admonishing, "Whatever happens David the truth must never go further than your family."

Puzzled Jill poured another cup of tea, offered Jane one and asked, "What did DCI Maysfield mean by that last remark?"

Jane shrugged, "Perhaps to keep our involvement out of the press. It was bad enough, when reporting the blowing up of Ben's car they told of his drug offence and prison sentence, so those who hadn't known before, do now! I told you Helen was more upset when she returned from Ireland than before she went. I barely got a sensible word out of her. It makes me wonder if Helen came back early from her parents because they were upset that, not only was she expecting a baby, but the man she intended to marry had a prison record. In which case, that would account for her Dad's reaction to you, because if she'd stayed at home, she'd not have been beaten up."

They were contemplating that when David returned, sat on the sofa opposite and asked, "So Jill have you got the nub of all that's been going on?"

Still reeling from Helen's bad luck she snapped, "David, I may have been through a trauma, but I've not gone senile."

A grim smile touched his lips. "Good! Even Jane has only been privy to some of this, and best to be kept between ourselves. Three days after Ben's arrest for drug trafficking, the police had information to suspect Sanchez had put the word out to get Ben. Problem was no-one knew where Sanchez was because he'd done

one of his disappearing acts! However, now they knew of Mallory, although they'd no evidence to tie him to anything, they could watch his movements. The police were in a dilemma for if they released Ben, or put him in a prison cell his life would be in danger.

"On Dad's suggestion Ben went to stay with them for several days before onward transit to the Inhart's research and training laboratories in Ireland. His pending job there made it a good alibi for his sudden disappearance, its very private and secure facilities an ideal location. The police then arranged for his only dependent, Helen to join him. After the car bomb it was obvious Ben needed to be more permanently out of the reach of Sanchez. For Helen with a large family she had to decide whether to go into hiding or live abroad, both meant she'd have little or no contact with them maybe for several years. Faced with her options she decided not to go with Ben, thus marriage was pointless, but she did accept the generous offer of his house and regular money payments to cover all her expenses. Needless to say they were painful days for them both. I completed the legal paper work with Helen when she came back on Wednesday night. Next morning under the pretext of a search warrant she collected up everything Ben listed he wanted from his home. He particularly asked her to keep his family albums so his child would know what his Daddy looked like and he determined one day to return."

"I found them. The photos of the young Ben are absolutely adorable."

David continued, "Ben told Helen he hoped she'd find someone who would love her and the child because it was best she didn't wait for him. As a precaution he asked me to act as trustee for his child's welfare and manage the fund our Dad insisted we set up for Ben's child, because he felt as Ben had saved his child, he should help save his."

Jill's eyes filled with unshed tears. "I see what you mean about Dad being…" The doorbell rang.

Jane grinned, "Off you go David, with all this running up and down the stairs you'll be able to enjoy another slice of Jill's delicious sponge."

He met that remark with a satirical grimace and leaving the room divulged, "I expect that's Paul, he said he was going to pop in."

Jill frowned, "I spoke to Paul earlier he said nothing about popping in. Kent isn't exactly around the corner."

Jane shrugged, "Don't ask me. But be a dear Jill take this tray with the dirty crocks out to the kitchen for me."

On her return Paul was inquiring after Jane's sore arm. "Hi Paul, I didn't know you were coming. I've put the kettle on to make you a cup of tea, she nodded towards the plate, "Would you like a piece of my Victoria sponge which David has given the accolade of being as good as Jane's."

Amusement filled those golden-flecked eyes, "Excellent Jill. Yes, I would be delighted to sample something so obviously noteworthy."

Jill laughed, and noted David's look of discomfort. She cut a piece and handed the plate to Paul and then curled up in the opposite corner of the three seater settee to him. David seated himself on the settee set at a right angle so he could tell him the latest news. "I was just telling Jill and Jane how Dad and I have been working around the clock to get Ben's affairs in order so he could disappear, if necessary for forever."

Jill cut in happily, "But he won't have to now that Sanchez is arrested. The only danger will be if Rich doesn't get convicted and that isn't likely? Perhaps Ben and I can go to New Zealand or Australia for a year or so until it's safe to come back here to lead a normal life? "

The expression on the faces of the two men was enough for her to cry out, "No! What's happened? Tell me?"

David sat forward, "Ben has already left. I'm sorry Jill, Dad had it confirmed this morning."

In an effort to keep calm she challenged, "Left? When? Where? Why wasn't I told?"

"The 'when' apparently was yesterday afternoon. The 'where' we don't know because Ben if no-one knew he and they would be safer. And the 'why weren't you told was because he'd received your letter, and in emotional turmoil, afraid Helen would still terminate their child, upset about leaving them behind, he felt you'd already come to terms with the separation so he said, it would be best all round if he just, as he said, 'moved on'".

How could it be 'best if he'd just moved on'? Ben didn't know about their baby. The reality of having a baby on her own, it's growing up without him being there suddenly didn't seem quite so appealing. David was still speaking. "Ben's been a key player. The car explosion showed the police they couldn't guarantee protection for him or his property. With that they agreed that once they had others who could identify Sanchez and

Mallory as the same person. Ben would have a new name, supporting documentation and passport to begin a new life elsewhere. Yesterday that all came together and Ben decided he might as well go sooner rather than later."

Her voice quavered with emotion, "So he doesn't know his baby has died?"

"No. But maybe its better to have gone away with a hope of meeting his child one day, than hear what's just happened? And you must see the least encumbrances he had the easier it is for him to disappear. Would you really have wanted to give up your life and family for a man you barely knew, after all, unlike Helen, you weren't expecting his baby?"

The words burst from her. "But that's just where you're wrong! I am expecting Ben's baby, due, what did we reckon Paul, on or around 9th July?"

With a sad grimace Paul looked across at her and nodded.

Dismay etched itself on David and Jane's faces. Jane the first to recover responded with, "Oh Jill, I'm so sorry."

What was Jane sorry about? That Ben had gone, or she was expecting his baby? Irritated she bit out, "Oh please Jane, don't be sorry. Be pleased for me. After all it's all now I am to have left of Ben." A lump formed in her throat, she swallowed hard and went on in a strained voice, "And as you said David, one day he will have that hope of meeting his child, except I'll be his mother, not Helen." With a sob she went on, "What a surprise that will be for him."

Paul leant over, passed her his handkerchief and gently patted her arm as she blew her nose and wiped her eyes.

Ever practical David stated, "But it's not easy bringing up a child on your own, how will you manage? And even in this day and age there's a stigma." He sighed heavily, "What are Mum and Dad going to say?"

Cross she glared at him and stated, "I'd hope they'll get past any prejudices you feel they may have and be gracious enough to welcome their new grandchild when it arrives. And blow the thoughts of stigma because the way things are going by the time this child," she patted her stomach, "is grown up, I think there will be so many, so called 'bastards' in the world, no one will care any more." Both David and Jane cringed at her terminology causing her to say forcefully, "And, as Christians, I would expect you and others in the church to accept and give me moral support. And as for bringing up the child, it's not as if as a family we can't pull together and help each other. We're not exactly short of cash either, so I could employ a live in nanny, or perhaps free accommodation for baby minding duties."

With the familiar gesture of running his hand through hair David said apologetically, "Oh Jill please, I didn't mean any offence. Of course we will do everything we can to support you. I feel responsible because it was I who pushed you together, advised Ben about Helen, and with the latest developments what best to do in the circumstances. I helped him to get his affairs in…"

The doorbell ringing again Jane frowned, "Who can that be? Are we expecting anyone else that you've not thought to tell me about?"

"Oh yes, sorry Jane, it's the parents." Their parents' coming unannounced - that was a first! David wide-eyed looked across at her as if she'd spoken the words aloud. "Our parents, Jill. They were desperate to come and see the daughter they so love, have put themselves out for, and would have been desolate to have lost." With that he turned and bowled down the stairs to the front door.

That statement made her realise in all this she'd barely considered their involvement and worry. Ben's words echoed in her ears, "I rather think we've been living in a fool's paradise over these last few weeks." Wasn't that what she'd been doing in these last few hours? How could it have worked with Helen having his baby as well? Even now with changed circumstances they would have had little enough on which to build a relationship, to be estranged from her family in a foreign land wouldn't have been easy, and having a baby, bringing her parent's grandchild into the world, yet being unable to share that joy with them, all that would have been heartbreaking for them as well as her.

Tears filled her eyes as her petite, beautifully groomed, and usually sedate Mum rushed across the room to hug her saying, "Oh Jill, you're safe, you're home I just had to come to see for myself. What a terrible, terrible time you've had? We've been so worried about you."

Behind her taking large strides across the carpet came her father. To her astonishment his eyes looked suspiciously shiny, and as her Mum stepped to one side her normally undemonstrative father gave her a long bear hug and said gruffly, "I am so glad to see you."

Jane who'd gone to put on the kettle appeared and in her own inimitable way went to welcome and kiss them, saying, "Sorry I can't hug you, sore arm." Immediately they were all concern and her Father in unprecedented sentiment commented, "Dear Jane, always so welcoming and hospitable. And I see, as usual, you've baked a splendid sponge."

With a chuckle Jane replied, "Thank you kind sir, but in this instance I didn't know you were coming, and Jill baked the cake."

Astounded her Mum turned to ask, "Jill is that right? But it looks marvelous, I mean you never seemed interested in cooking and that was always reflected in the results."

Aware that Paul was standing waiting for an introduction she drew her parents' attention with a hand wave toward him. "Let me introduce Paul, it was he who looked after me, organised for me to stay with his family and his wonderful Gran who inspired and instructed me in cooking skills."

Immediately her father stepped forward to shake Paul's hand and, in a booming voice, similar to David's, said, "I am pleased to meet you. Thank you for all you have done for Jill. Please extend my thanks to your family. We were so lucky that you were there and able to help her when she needed it."

Paul gave a broad smile, "It's good to meet you Professor Reinhardt, but I'm not sure luck entered into it. I had met Jill previously and recognized her. I would put it down to an encounter orchestrated by the Lord."

"Oh you're a Christian, like David and Jane. I tell you I'm beginning to see there is something in this religion malarkey. Margaret and I are certainly intending to pursue a greater understanding of it in the days ahead. Please, consider yourself a friend of this family, and call me Franz. Now Jane where's that tea? I'm gasping after that long drive and want to taste that sponge."

In retrieving the remainder of Jane's cake from the flat for the unexpected tea party Jill invited Rosemary to join them. On her return she glanced into the lounge to see her father, Paul and David deep in conversation and it pleased her to know that Paul had been as welcomed into her family as she had been into his.

With Jane's kitchen too small for four people to work in, they took over part of the dining room table to cut bread, butter, and fill sandwiches, and with the hatch only between them she was still able to relay events so far to her Mum and Rosemary.

Her Mum smiled dreamily, "You know I really took to Ben. He was so appreciative of everything, and had such an endearing way with him, so bright and cheeky despite knowing his life was about to change dramatically. He said he'd picked himself up from enough knocks to know it was best not to look back, but go forward. I hope you don't mind, but he asked if he could sleep in your bedroom, he liked all your cuddly toys and said it reminded him of his room when he was a boy. He told me how much he liked you, but the misfortune with Helen expecting a baby had wrecked any relationship you might have had. I thought it was so sad because he was the kind of man I'd have liked for a son-in-law. Still your Dad did his best for him so he could start life again in a new country, and suggested he go back to study medicine and become a doctor. I think that idea kept him going especially when Helen was being difficult. How terrible though that man beat her up, poor girl, just because she was Ben's girlfriend. David says not only has she lost the baby, but can't have any more. One day Ben, poor boy, is going to come home and be so disappointed having held in his heart maybe for years the belief he will meet his child."

Jane looked across at her. Jill cleared her throat, "Actually Mum, he'll not be disappointed because there will be a child of his waiting to meet his Daddy." Her mother looked puzzled. She gave her a small, gentle smile and watched the comprehension dawn on her mother's face.

"You, you are carrying Ben's child?" Jill nodded. "You and he, you well, oh! But he's gone, we don't know where." Worried she pondered, "Perhaps we could find him. Oh dear! If only we'd known sooner."

A deep, mature boom queried from the dining room doorway, "Good heavens, you women, where's that tea? Oh sandwiches good. And Margaret, what should we have known about sooner?" Her Mum looked at her to answer her father.

"Well Dad I suppose now is as good a time as any to tell you, I'm expecting Ben's baby."

In the somewhat tense silence as her father looked at her in disbelief Rosemary quietly asked, "When did you find out?"

"Thursday evening. While away I kept being sick, fainted off one meal time, and put it down to all that had happened. Paul suggested he did a test, but it didn't occur to me I was six weeks pregnant. I always thought if I found myself pregnant without a husband I'd be distraught, but I'm not because I cared for Ben and because he'd risked his life for me I feel proud and privileged to have his baby."

When neither of her parents spoke, she folded her arms and

addressed the room. "I didn't know Helen had refused Ben. I saw no hurry to let Ben know. I feel awful about Helen, but after Friday night I thought with Ben no longer having responsibility for her, and as I was carrying his child, he'd now marry me." Wound up she knew the pitch of her voice was rising in her distress, "But it turns out Ben isn't free is he? He may not be in prison, but has lost his freedom to live here. And he can't work and have the life he once desired. He's gone, not knowing about his baby with Helen, or his baby with me. It's like a curse, that's what it is, a curse placed by others on his life. He does the right thing, and everything goes wrong around him. He helps someone on drugs: he loses a friend, his career and ends up in prison. He prevents my kidnap, his car is blown up, his house badly smoke damaged and boarded up. He does right by Helen she's beaten up, their baby murdered and her opportunity for a family of her own destroyed. Now he's off on his own in some god forsaken country to try and start life, without the knowledge he's free to marry me and I'm having his child." The enormity of it all brought a stunned silence and she fought the desire to scream and burst into tears.

Jane picked up the sandwiches. Rosemary took this as her cue to pick up the large tea tray and silently they slipped from the room. Defensively she asked her parents, "Even though Helen didn't want to go with Ben, what would you have advised me to do? Leave everything and everyone behind, or chose as Helen did to stay here and bring the baby up without its father?"

Her Mum looked up at her Father to speak, when he didn't she replied in a quiet and gentle voice. "My dear, whatever you had chosen to do, we both would have wanted you to be happy. Ben struck me as a caring and lovingly man and suspect if he'd known any of this he would have insisted on risking his life to be here now to support you both."

With gruff concern her father agreed. "Your mother is right. He is a good man. He wanted to do the right thing with Leroy, with Helen, with you, but each choice was wrong for him. All I can add is he earned my respect, he's had a raw deal from life and I have done all in my power to ease his way into the future. It was the least I could do." Emotion caught in her father's throat, "H-he saved you, my precious daughter, from the hands of a potential kidnapper." He paused and she forgot about the cold barrier her Father erected around himself because overcome with love, she threw herself into him as a child, thanking him and telling him of her love. Like David he was a big, broad man, more muscle than fat, his chest hard, yet at her response she felt him tremble, then as if something broke inside him he hugged her so fiercely she thought even as sturdily built as she was she might break.

Still holding her against him, he didn't boom, but spoke with that strange unaccustomed gentleness she'd recently noticed in David. "Money Jill is a curse, unless used wisely, and why we live comfortably, but don't appear to be rich. The more I reinvest into the business the more I make. Inharts is now a worldwide pharmaceutical company and my desire is to make the branches in rich lands support those in poorer ones. I sent Ben out with as much money as it was safe for him to carry, and instructed every Inharts branch across the world to give out the requested amount of money in cash when the recipient shows a signed letter by me and knows the pre-arranged code. He can have as little, or as much of my fortune, as he requires."

Jill pulled back, noted her Mum had disappeared, and looked up into the heavy features of her Father's face. Such similarities to David, yet the hair was receding and going grey. The raven eyes that were often sharp enough to pierce through a man's thoughts looked tenderly and lovingly upon her. She'd never seen her Dad in this light before. Had she changed, or had he? He gave a rueful smile at her prolonged study of him. "I've never really been a Dad to you, have I? Always busy, never time to stop, to listen, to encourage you. For me the curse is the ongoing, ever growing money with financial responsibilities which seemed to coincide with your birth."

The words money and birth jolted a thought that brought a ray of hope. "Dad when Ben goes to get that money, not only could that alert us to where he is, but surely we could leave a message to go with it to tell him about me and his baby?"

With a nod her father agreed, "That's a good thought, and can be done, but don't get your hopes up. You see Ben is a proud man. He was very reticent to receive the money I insisted he take with him. I suspect he'll use that carefully, while making his own way in the world, and doubt he'll come back for more."

Her Mum having come back in asked, "What about trying to trace him through contacts in the industry?

"First Margaret we don't know his new name, and second, too much digging might expose his whereabouts to the wrong people. If it's any consolation Ben's intention in a new country is to get back into medicine, he will be doing what he loves, and when your letter came it seemed to give him the release he needed, glad your heart was for his happiness."

Her Dad's arm went out to encompass her, the other to draw her mother too into the embrace. "One day Jill you'll meet Ben again because David is the trustee of his child's trust fund. But I'd say in the meanwhile, even though you are having his child, don't live your life waiting for his return. It might not be a comfort to you at this time, but I'd like you to know, and I guess I can speak on behalf of your mother too, we'll be proud to be grandparents of yours and Ben's child and provide for you both in any way we can."

Their acceptance and generosity over her situation released the emotion banked up within her. Tears poured down her face, her heart bursting with love at their response brought a torrent of thanks and appreciation for all they'd done. When that drained through she gave a tiny smile and looked between petite Mum and towering Dad to say, "I do have other news. While I was with Paul's family I felt God was revealing Himself to me, and I needed to respond by asking Jesus to come into my life. So like Jane and David, I've become a Christian."

As if unable to could cope with further revelations, her father stepped back, to demand, "I must have a cup of tea. I've been waiting for one ever since we got here."

With that, he marched out of the dining room, as her mother with a small knowing smile nodded at his back, "Don't mind him dear. He'll be alright." From her handbag she drew a white envelope. "Jill dear, we wanted to see you, and give you this as soon as possible. Ben left it for you. Don't worry about joining us, this might be a good time to read it."

Surprised, yet somehow knowing Ben wouldn't leave without some kind of goodbye she took the precious envelope and held it next to her heart. The scene of their parting at the customs post came to mind, his blue eyes, big, sad, encouraging her, yet she'd caught the fear in them. Had he known then it wasn't the police to fear, but the reprisals of Rich on his life? As her Mum entered and closed the lounge door, she slipped down the stairs. It was such a comfort to know they liked Ben and would love his baby. It seemed God gave, and God took away. But as her father had said Ben would one day return, and she'd have his baby to make up for the one lost. It brought an appreciation of being able to live in a familiar country, a beautiful home and a loving family. Ben had nothing except what he took with him, which she guessed, was mostly memories.

The sight of Benjy bear sitting in the midst of her bed, brought fresh tears and memories of what they had shared together. Hugging Benjy and Ben's letter to her chest, she cried over Benjy telling him of her grief and sorrow. Finally, tears abated she took a nail file and carefully slit open the envelope.

"Dearest and most beloved Jill,

Knowing and loving you, even for so short a time, has been the highlight of my life. I suspect you are sitting reading this with Benjy bear, hug him for me, and remember good things about me! Our bitter-sweet romance wasn't meant to last. It was too good to last, but too wonderful to forget. My only regret is we didn't have more time together, and our initial lack of understanding of each other has caused so much pain to others. Thank you for wishing me happiness, I will take that with me wherever I go.

Understandably, Helen didn't want to leave her country and family, but too doesn't want a baby without my support. David and your father have been amazing in making provision for her, and for me, yet I am still afraid she'll abort my baby if she doesn't have physical and mental support. The house damage maybe a good thing because for now she'll need to stay at the flat, and hopefully until the baby is born. If you and Rosemary could get alongside her, and help her to love my baby I'd really appreciate that. She's talking of giving it up for adoption. If she can't be dissuaded David has assured me he'll be there every step of the way.

My first thought when Helen so clearly didn't want to go with me was to ask you. Then I saw that to do that, would bring the same pressure to bear on you, as Helen and her family. You have wonderful parents and I saw to take their daughter away, out of contact, would, having rescued you from one kidnapper, make me another. After their generosity, love and care toward me, I couldn't do that to them, they don't deserve that kind of reward.

You know I always say never look back, but forward. With you I won't be able to forget the fun and passion we had. But I take the stance that I have had knocks, and pulled myself up, I can do it again. This time will be different. I am not trying to rebuild my old life. Without responsibilities I can build a new life. To be honest with you, but not to hurt Helen, I was pleased she didn't want to come with me. You know I was making the best of a difficult situation, but it's one thing to do so in familiar surroundings, quite another to have to build a whole new life with the burden and responsibility of a wife and baby, and it was something I was beginning to fear.

I don't know how long this enforced escape from my homeland will be, but I do know that with a new identity it brings the opportunity to do something I never dreamed possible – to complete my medical training and become that brain surgeon I aspired to be. I don't know where, or when, as yet, but I do know it will mean training for at least five to six years, although previous knowledge might help me to get through quicker. Once established as someone else, and the years having passed I will return, but for both of us Jill our lives and paths must change. Along with that belief, we will find fulfillment and happiness in what we do. I wish that for you, as you do for me. Our time was short, and in a few years it will seem as though it never happened, the name Ben Fletcher a distant dream of a romantic interlude of a man who loved you and lost, but through that gained a new start that would never have been possible without you, and your family. And for that I'll always love you, and thank them.

One day I will come to see my child, and hope I'll be able to make up for the missing years. That child may well have another man he or she calls father, but I have asked Helen and would ask you, to keep in touch with her and to talk to that child about me. I don't want my child to feel I didn't want, or abandoned them, but to know their life is constantly in my thoughts, as I imagine the boy or girl I created. Helen has photos of me and my family to show them.

The only way I can end this, is to say that as for me one door closes another opens. I would wish the same for you. Walk through, enjoy all it has for you, and know that in meeting you, you are still the best thing that ever happened to me, although it didn't turn out as I'd hoped.

My love, passion and happiness remain with you

Ben xxxx

CHAPTER 24

Jill glanced at the clock on Beatty's mantelpiece which was ticking away the last minutes of 1968, a year that had significantly changed life for her, and her family.

The last few weeks had passed in a blur, and except for some subtle changes in her body she could almost forget she was pregnant. David had insisted she, Rosemary and Jane should go with him to Brussels for his peace of mind, and their safety, at a time when the police were breaking the back of a crime wave which had lasted a decade. Together they'd shared the work, but there hadn't been time to get maudlin, although they had plenty of free time, which they filled with shopping, swimming, eating and just being together, and came home feeling refreshed for the change.

In the week before they left they each visited a battered, and very pale, Helen in hospital.

Her attempt at sympathy on the loss of her baby, and not being able to have others was met with "Oh well, that's life" which rather bore out Ben's worry of her not wanting the child. On hearing she was having Ben's baby Helen had sworn and added, "Rather you than me. I want to move on from all of this, you'd better have his photo albums."

When Rosemary visited, Helen told her she didn't want to return to the flat and jumped at Rosemary's suggestion of the tiny mews cottage where she lived before, which conveniently was still vacant. The very accommodating landlady had then agreed to keep it until Helen was well enough to move in.

And when Jane took her a cheque of a generous one-off lump sum payment David had decided to give her from the trust fund as compensation for her lost child, she commented she was beginning to think the guy who beat her up had done her a favour!

For Jill it was that which took the last vestiges of guilt away for all that had happened to Helen.

On their return from Brussels she'd found her father had been in cahoots with Paul, who was scheduled the fly out the next day to start visiting Inharts numerous branches across the world. The aim, to assess how they might better take from the rich and give to

401

the poor. Suspicious her Dad's employing Paul might also have a hidden aim of trying to locate Ben, she told Paul of Ben's letter and his relief at not having to start a new life with a wife and baby. And how she felt he deserved this opportunity to do his medical training and make a new life without any encumbrances. Paul admitted finding Ben had sparked the idea of an assessment of Inharts, but her Father had felt with his medical knowledge, experience of third world countries and the flexibility of his current job, their meeting had been providential.

In the three weeks before Christmas Paul had flown around America seeing the rich side of the industry, and after a break at Christmas and the New Year he was off for three months touring first Africa, then India, the Middle East and taking in Australia as an opportunity to visit his parents.

The man Rosemary attacked had come out of his coma, but not without damage to his brain. This meant he was unlikely to beat anyone up in the future, and with a sentence of GBH over his head and a previous conviction it was unlikely he'd have the opportunity to live much beyond a prison cell anyway. The court case was scheduled for July, Lord Mallory or Peter Sanchez hadn't been given bail, and almost weekly David heard of new evidence of his life of crime, even as an accessory to several murders which they suspected were committed by his brother Chris now living in Brazil.

Back at work her time was spent organising Christmas events. Everyone spoke of missing Ben, and the story was Inharts in Ireland had needed him sooner than planned.

Christmas at home had been different. Instead of her father shutting himself away in his study unable to cope with the family he'd engaged with everyone and appeared to be enjoying it. According to Jane, her parents had asked David about becoming Christians. His reply, 'It's easy. You just pray a simple prayer saying you believe Jesus is God's son; thank Him for dying on the cross for your sins; take the Biblical words, 'taste and see the Lord is good'; ask Jesus to come into your life in the power of the Holy Spirit and let Him do the rest.'' For two such an intelligent men Jane thought it hilarious, but then hadn't Jesus said all you needed was a childlike faith?

And the evidence was, the Holy Spirit was 'doing the rest'. Her father had turned into a gentle giant! When Paula's boys found a small step ladder, attempted to climb the Christmas tree to get a chocolate near the top, collapsed the whole thing to the ground smashing the fairy lights, scraping a thick branch against an antique rosewood table and smashed an expensive vase, he didn't do the usual rant, rave and roar in temper after such a heinous crime. To everyone's surprise he untangled the boys from branches, electric cable, tree dressings and fairy lights, told them next time they wanted a chocolate from the tree, or anything else they were to ask first, and then helped them to reinstate the tree to its former glory. From then on they were eager to please and learn from him, and happy to sit for several hour sessions to be taught the intricacies of chess until they could challenge him. And he seemed delighted at their interest in a game he so enjoyed.

On Christmas Eve instead of screaming like banshees because they were bored, they cuddled up to their Granddad on the settee and watched with unexpected, riveted attention the television broadcast from Apollo 8 as it orbited the moon. They even stopped asking questions when each of the three crew members read from the first book of Genesis about God creating the earth. It was then she thought of Ben, somewhere on planet earth. Had he been watching, sad and alone somewhere? In her mind, and by that same Holy Spirit that brooded over the earth, she sent him her and the baby's love. May he too find the love and peace of the Lord God as her family had done.

After Brussels she'd visited Beatty and Bill. They had been so welcoming and the reason why she was now standing in their lounge considering 1968 before the year passed into 1969.

The openness of her friendship with Paul was refreshing, and while in America, he'd written several times. And once back on Christmas Eve he'd rung and chatted to her each day.

Yesterday when she arrived, he and Maria had been waiting to greet her, there had been lunch and laughter, and an exchanging of not expensive, but thoughtful presents. She'd bought Paul what was proclaimed to be an indestructible suitcase for his travels, while he'd brought her a copy of the Amplified Bible she'd liked reading at Beatty's which was only available from the United States. The three of them went to see a film in the evening. On return to Beatty's they'd chatted so much in the end Beatty had said, "Time to throw you out, we need our sleep."

Today she'd helped Beatty bake, along with Maria and others and by 8.00 pm the kitchen table was groaning under the weight of so many delicious goodies which she wondered if they would all manage to eat. However she'd not taken account of the number of

Stemmings there were, and the appetites they had, and ten minutes ago they were reloading the table from the pantry stocks. She'd lost count of Paul's relatives and certainly couldn't remember their names as they spread through the house and garden.

Beatty's voice loud and clear came above the general din, "Okay everyone outside." It was dark and cold in the street, but no-one appeared to notice as people from all the houses in the road spilled out. There was a contemplative silence as the radio brought the twelve chimes of Big Ben echoing down the road. Even London's famous bell brought reminders of Ben. 1968 had been cataclysmic year for him and her. 1969 would be one of new beginnings. She patted her unborn child as the air was suddenly rent with penny whistles blowing, balloons popping, wooden spoons banging against saucepans, shouts of 'Happy New Year' with much laughter, hugging and kissing. The whole street began to link arms to sing together, 'Should old acquaintance be forgot...'" She'd never forget Ben, she had his baby to care for, and she would, one day have the pleasure of introducing his child to him.

The line split apart, and a gentle voice spoke into her ear, "Ah there you are?" She turned. The lamplight caught the gold flecks in Paul's eyes as he smiled at her. "I am going to prophecy that for you 1969 will be a wonderful year: new life, beginnings, expectations, and hopes for the future. So Jill, Happy New Year." With that he bent slightly his mouth melding with hers in a light kiss. Her heart and mouth responded to his warmth, his friendship and caused, she suspected, the kiss to extend perhaps a little longer than he'd intended! His forefinger touched across her lips, and with his quirky smile stated, "One thing at a time." Memories of their first meeting at ITP flooded in. Smiling he slipped her arm in his and drew her into his Gran's house where it was so crowded the only space was to sit on a stair near the top.

She giggled, "This makes me feel like a pair of kids having slipped from our beds to watch the party."

Paul laughed, "I can scarce remember."

Playfully she retorted, "Oh come on you aren't that old."

Ruefully he bantered, "I feel it sometimes. I've done much, but have little to show for it."

"You have Maria."

Thoughtfully he answered, "Yes, I do, she and my family are a great blessing to me." There was a pause and he went on, "Your father has indicated he'd like me, after I've made my reports in the next few months, to develop and oversee his plans into third world countries. It's been interesting to see his operation in the States, and with the kind of investment he can make there's much potential for him to provide both affordable drugs and employment for the poor and needy. I know he needs an advisor with medical expertise, and my experience could be invaluable, but I'm not sure I want to be living abroad again in the near future."

Several of Paul's family called up to them to say, 'goodbye' and it was a minute or two before Paul spoke again. "As you know the people renting my house wanted it for the year, so when I return in at the beginning of April I will have to consider the situation, and options, as they present themselves. David thought it would be good to discuss it with you."

At her puzzled expression, he added tentatively, "When you talked about having the baby you mentioned about having a live in babysitter. Well, I know its early days, but would you consider a resident, who could volunteer babysitting between their shifts?"

Was this just a convenient solution to his homelessness, and her need? Or had Paul thoughts of sharing her life, and the baby's? With a frown she queried, "Are you asking to rent Helen's room?"

He gave a quirky little smile, "That was my thought."

"I'm not sure how Rosemary would feel sharing the flat with a man."

"Oh, not for me, for Maria."

"Maria? Sorry you've lost me."

"Oh dear, I've missed a bit out in the asking. Yesterday Maria chatted to you of her career thoughts on nursing and desire to train at a London hospital. She's keen to do that, and I'd prefer her to live with people she knows, she likes you, and I'd pay her rent. On my return, David and Jane have offered me a bedroom in their flat, until I can assess my future options. It would be an ideal solution for me if Maria was living downstairs, and me up. And we'd both love to help out with the baby."

Slowly and thoughtfully she echoed, "David and Jane have offered you a bedroom - I see." In fact she could 'see' more than he thought. This had the mark of David's scheming and manipulative tactics! Surely Jane had seen through this, but she liked Paul, so was probably condoning it. And did she really mind?

Warm amusement filled those gold-flecked eyes, perhaps he could 'see' where her thoughts were heading. "What do you think, could it be," he paused, and said slowly, "right?"

Friendship with Paul and his family felt very right. She answered carefully. "I don't have any objection to Maria moving in. And I'd say there is a certain potential in the arrangement to which I'm not averse to exploring! I sense this could develop and become very 'right'!

"If, and assuming, I have a 'right' understanding, would it be possible to seal the deal with another of those kisses?"

She grinned, "I think that too, could be 'right' Dr Stemmings. But only if you realise to be 'right' too often can become habit forming."

"I'll risk it, if you will." At that his mouth met hers in a gentle, yet provocative kiss, his hand slid into the hair at her neck sending tiny shivers of delightful sensation down her spine. It wasn't unadulterated passion, more a comfortable friendship with an inner 'knowing' this was the man who could well be the one God had ordained to be her Mr Right!

**Turn over for a preview for the next instalment
of the lives of the Reinhardt family**

Book 3

Ruth Johnson

David

The chapter that follows
is unedited and subject to change.

Anticipated publication:
November 2009

LONDON, 1970

CHAPTER 1

David turned over, and was awake enough to ensure he didn't disturb Jane asleep beside him. Sleep seemed long to come, and impossible to remain in, during the hot, balmy night. At least now the open windows were providing them with a cool morning breeze. It was predicted the heat wave would continue, and in normal circumstances the temperature would be uncomfortable, but to Jane it quickly became intolerable.

Voices in the street below alerted him to look at the time. It was ten o'clock! Taken aback he slid from the bed and thanked God it was Saturday! In the street below Jill's laughter floated up, he looked out as she and Paul came into view. Between them each holding a hand, William was trying to toddle from the car back into the house. He gave a quiet chuckle, that little boy was going to be the image of his father, and as he often did, he wondered where and how Ben was faring in his new life.

David ran his hand through his tousled raven black hair and considered how his life had changed in the past four years. He'd gone from a quiet, bachelor existence, living alone in the only two decent rooms in the house, to converting it into two flats, meeting and marrying Jane, and being involved in his sister's life as she lived in the lower two floors, as they lived in the upper two!

The advent of Paul coming into Jill's life had been one of the best things that had happened to the Reinhardt family. Admittedly, he'd been furious at Jill's foolishness in putting herself in danger, but out of that had come many blessings. He looked back at the outline of his wife under the cotton sheet and smiled. Today, family and friends would be gathering for a party to celebrate William's first birthday next Wednesday, and Paul and Jill's first wedding anniversary last Wednesday.

David headed for the bathroom with a wry smile. Jill had held out against 'having to get married' believing they were entering an age when a child out of wedlock wouldn't be termed as a bastard, and that she had no need of a husband.

The family hadn't exactly put pressure on her, but it was obvious Paul's appearance in her life had been a godsend, and he'd quickly felt part of the Reinhardt family. Dad had him travelling abroad for the family business, he'd shared their flat and become his valued, and trusted friend. Paul's daughter Maria had lived with Jill, and in caring for them both, when at home, Paul was constantly in their company.

Under the shower David chuckled, Jill's saying 'yes' to Paul, had met with a resounding 'yes' by the family, and they'd rallied to organise a church blessing and reception after what, in the time available, could only be a registry office marriage. It was obvious it had been a right decision, they were so happy together. And Paul , in six months time, could find himself delivering his own child, for Jill had so quickly expelled William he'd arrived in the hall of the downstairs flat!

* * * * *

December 2008

Dear Reader,

Thank you for reading this second book, and hope you enjoyed the taster for the third. I'm always amazed at how the characters take on a life of their own and feel like real people as I get to know them.

Although this is a fictitious story, the triune God: Father, Son and Holy Spirit are real, and it is out of a close relationship with Him that I write. For thirty-five years I have had daily experienced the reality of a heavenly Father who wants to be part of our lives. He will speak, in a variety of ways to those who are willing to listen. Some of these ways are revealed in Jill's story.

In the difficulties, problems and traumas of life I have found and known God's peace and love. It is wonderful to have the assurance I am accepted, and loved by the very creator of the universe, the Father God, who has made me in His image, and thus I have His DNA within. I see that as a homing beacon, and if we respond as Jill did, and call out, 'Oh God, help' He will come. And from my experience when He does it isn't always as we imagine, the journey doesn't always go in the direction we would expect, but God knows us, loves us, and He has plans for each one of us to give us a hope and a future. So if you don't know Him, I invite you to read the next two pages.

RUTH JOHNSON

THREE GOOD REASONS TO TRUST IN JESUS

1. Because you have a past
You can't go back, but He can. The Bible says, 'Jesus Christ the same yesterday, and today, and for ever.' (Hebrews 13:8) He can walk into those places of sin and failure, wipe the slate clean and give you a new beginning.

2. Because you need a friend
Jesus knows the worst about you, yet He believes the best. Why? Because he sees you not as you are, but as you will be when He gets through with you. What a friend!

3. Because He holds the future
Who else are you going to trust? In His hands you are safe and secure – today, tomorrow, and for eternity. His Word says, "For I know the plans I have for you...plans for good and not for evil, to give you a future and a hope. In those days when you pray I will listen' (Jeremiah 29:11-13)

The Bible says, 'Taste and see that the Lord is good.' ask Him to help you understand, prove Himself to you. There are places to find more information mentioned opposite.

Or take a step further and begin a personal relationship with Jesus today by praying the simple prayer below. And once you have done it, allow Him to become real to you.

Dear Lord,

I am sorry for the things I have done wrong in my life. I ask your forgiveness and now turn from everything which I know is wrong. Thank you for dying on the cross for me to set me free from my sins. Please come into my life and fill me with your Holy Spirit and be with me forever. Thank you, Lord.

FOR MORE INFORMATION:
Access the website run by United Christian Broadcasters at
www.lookingforgod.com

Need prayer: UCB prayer line is manned from 9.00am – 10.30pm
Monday to Friday on 0845 456 7729

UCB *Word for the Day* – daily stories of ordinary folk touched by an
extraordinary God. It has Bible references for each day and when
followed means you get to read the whole Bible in a year.   Telephone: 0845 60 40 401 to get your copy.

IF YOU HAVE PRAYED THE PRAYER:
To fully receive all the blessings God wants to bestow upon you, I'd
advise you do the following:

1. Get yourself a Bible - New International Version

2. Ring UCB for *Word for the Day* to be sent to you.

3. Ask the Lord to become real to you and even if you don't   understand what you read follow the plan for each day asking God's Holy
Spirit to open it up to you. It took three weeks at about 15 minutes a
day before it began to make sense to me.

4. Try out the churches in your area. Find one that you feel   comfortable in, then join it and get to know the people in it.

5. Please email me: Ruth.Johnson@theartsdesireseries.com as I
would love to know that this booked has helped you, and I shall be
thrilled to hear if you've found the Lord through it..

If you would like to make contact with a local Christian, or would
like further help from someone living locally to you please write
giving your full name, address, telephone number and email — include your age group, to:

   3 reasons, FREEPOST, WC2947, South Croydon, CR2 8UZ

Jane's sheltered existence is disturbed by the caresses of a stranger in a darkened room. Haunted by the incident she determines to experience life. Her encounters and challenges bring fun and fear as she searches for the reality of love. But love is gently hovering awaiting release and its unexpected arrival encompasses all her heart's desires...

LOOK OUT FOR INFORMATION ON THESE FORTHCOMING TITLES AT:
www.heartsdesireseries.com

DAVID

David likens his marriage to riding a rollercoaster blindfold, their shared love the track that holds, keeps and guides them. It's in going from the greatest exhilaration to the darkest despair that he draws on love's strength and finds it casts out fear, brings restoration and expands his vision to re-evaluate his heart's desires....

ROSEMARY

Rosemary has found love and contentment, but anguish squeezes her heart as history seems to be repeating itself. Hurts and fears taunt her as she struggles to decide if a marriage of convenience is too high a price to pay for the joy of motherhood. The tenacity of love draws her to confront her heart's desires....

JANICE

Janice, battered and homeless finds an unexpected refuge. Her arrival causes shock and dismay, her attitudes and behaviour lock those involved into a battle to hold onto love. Even as she holds them to ransom, she experiences an unforeseen love growing within her, making her rethink her heart's desires....

MATT

Matt's past haunts him across continents, in spite of unexpected friendship, love, provision and fulfillment in his chosen career. His caring heart brings a chance encounter and brings rewards he hadn't envisaged, unveiling that love that has no bounds as he is set free to know his heart's desires....